PHYLLO CANE

AND THE
MAGICAL MENAGERIE
~ 2 ~

SHARN W. HUTTON

Copyright © Sharn Hutton 2022
All rights reserved.
Star City Press
Paperback ISBN 978-1-8383487-1-7

No part of this book may be reproduced in any form or by any electronic or mechanical means, including information storage and retrieval systems, without written permission from the author, except for the use of brief quotations in a book review.
This book is a work of fiction. Names, characters, businesses, organisations, places, events and incidents either are the product of the author's imagination or are used fictitiously. Any resemblance to actual persons, living or dead, events or locales is entirely coincidental.

For more information visit sharnhutton.com.
Book design Sharn Hutton.
Map design © Sharn Hutton 2022.
Cover design © Sharn Hutton 2025
First edition July 2022.
Cover redesign June 2025
10 9 8 7 6 5 4 3 2

For those who strive to make the world a better place.

PHYLLO CANE
AND THE
MAGICAL MENAGERIE

OFF SEASON PITCH

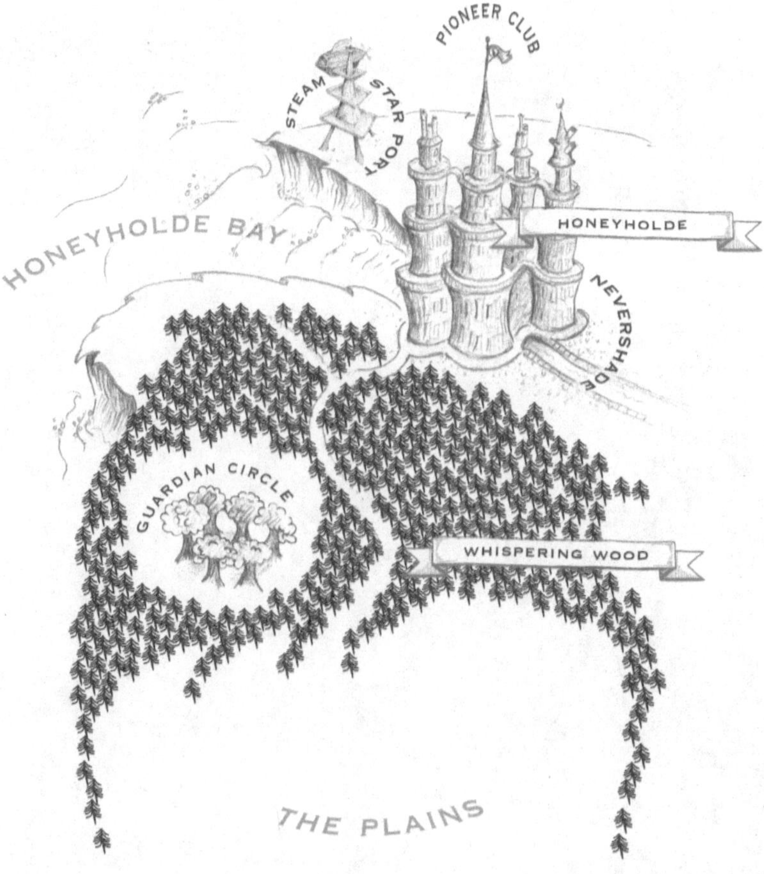

1

Pushing It

Beyond its canvas walls, reality spun and changed, but the Circus of Wonder big top held steady. The air inside was thick with magic. The power of the Machine pulled them *on*.

Phyllo's tunic rippled against his skin, static sliding over him to gather in his scalp, until every hair stood out on end in a puff. The howl of wind slowly faded and the final crackles of electricity popped and fizzed in the rafters.

They had arrived.

The party spirit among the cast, paused by their journey, now returned. The Circus of Wonder had just won its first Gilded Pennant in over a decade, an award which recognised the supreme talents of *The Fabulous Volante* – the flyers with whom Phyllo had been an apprentice. It was their first step in lifting the Circus of Wonder back to the heights it used to thrive at, to saving the fading magic and giving them their pick of the routes for the coming season, but Phyllo didn't feel like partying.

He'd been part of the act that had won it for them and

learned more in his time with the trapeze act than he could ever have imagined. Without him they could not have done it, he knew that. Even so, it had been so much of a struggle that he also knew with certainty that flying was not his destiny. He was still just an apprentice running the circuit, looking for a place to fit in.

Phyllo's stomach ached. The initial joy at their victory had faded to reveal a horrible truth; his place in the Circus of Wonder was still not secure. He continued to be a disaster waiting to happen.

If he got thrown out for having no magical talent, his family would leave the Circus of Wonder in an instant to stay by his side and he could not allow that. He couldn't expose them to the dangers that lay *in-between*, to the lawless vagabonds that existed without a circus to call home. He had to find his talent and keep them all safe, he just had to.

In a frenzy of motion, the cast came to life. They happily wove between each other, like bees over honeycomb, pausing to hug or shake hands here or plant a congratulatory slap on the back there. For everyone else, life was sweet. They flocked to their cabins and made ready to push them out of the big top to form the horseshoe-shaped neighbourhood they all called home.

Engineers hauled the canvas walls up to the rafters, the rope and hoists roaring together to reveal their new location, the Plains. Phyllo looked out into the night.

Their pitch was a broad open space with plenty of room for the circus cabins to spread out. In the middle distance a woodland stretched out its dark fingers toward them and beyond that the towers of Honeyholde reached into the sky, where lights twinkled in distant windows. The night sky was clear and speckled with stars.

Phyllo's father, Marvel, was waiting beside their cabin when he and his brother approached and together they pushed it outside. Roly pressed his back against the wooden exterior while Phyllo leaned in to shove the cabin with his hands. Phyllo looked down to the bandages that wrapped one of Roly's hands, fingertips to wrist.

"Is the pain bad?" Phyllo asked.

Roly shrugged, "Just putting put my back into it."

He was deflecting the question and Phyllo decided not to pursue it. Roly's hand had been horribly injured in their struggle against the demon Jester. Their success had freed their friend Emmett from its curse, but it had been Roly who'd paid the price. Phyllo couldn't help but feel responsible. It had been his idea to confront the Jester. He'd risked all their lives, and when they'd succeeded it was Phyllo who'd got all the glory. Roly had just gotten hurt.

Around them other cabins rolled out of the big top to form a wide circle and the Ringmaster paced its perimeter, clutching the business end of a measuring tape. "Let's set her up double wide, Skinner. Give us plenty of room to work."

The chief engineer, Skinner, jogged out with the far end of the tape and marked the ground with bright squirts of paint.

When he'd passed by, the Cane family pushed their cabin back to the mark, their father dancing about at the front, waving them forward or holding them back with the flat of his palm, but Phyllo knew it didn't need to be accurate this time. They weren't joining up to neighbouring cabins. This was their over-wintering pitch. Safely nestled beyond the Whispering Wood, there were no customers to tempt so no bandits of the In-between to fear. They were setting up with plenty of space to allow for maintenance. The extra distance felt freeing.

Phyllo stretched his arms above his head and rolled out the cricks in his neck. His part in *The Fabulous Volante's* performance might have been small, but the whole experience had been exhausting. Learning their magic had taken enormous effort and although he'd managed to maintain it for his small part, it had been demanding and unnatural.

He knew he wasn't alone. By this point in the year all the cast were tired. Arrival at the Plains signalled a holiday before preparation for the next season began. Ordinarily this was the time for carefree days spent exploring or lounging on the nearby beach while the weather held, but Phyllo couldn't imagine relaxing. Not when he didn't know what was coming next.

Around them the other cabins rolled into position and the Ringmaster made a second circuit, flicking out his cane ahead of each step and arching it ostentatiously around himself as he prowled on. He stopped outside his own cabin, ten yards or so away. "Heads of cabins, expand at will," he announced and a second wave of activity began.

The Cane family gathered at the front of their cabin, the Confectionary. Phyllo and Roly to one side of their father and Phyllo's little sister, Dodo, to the other. Marvel held her hand and drew the brass cabin key from his breast pocket.

"Been quite a season, hasn't it eh?" He looked around them all, smiling. "You've all done wonderfully well. Phyllo, it goes without saying I'm incredibly proud of how you've stepped up. At the beginning of last year we could never have guessed that by now you'd be working the circuit, your first apprenticeship already complete." He nodded to Phyllo, blinking rapidly, then looked down to Dodo.

"And you, my little sherbet, have turned into the most

incredible popcorn popper I have ever encountered." Dodo giggled and Marvel pulled out a large striped handkerchief to noisily blow his nose. He gave her an affectionate pat on the head and cleared his throat.

"And, Roly. I'm so impressed by the progress you've made. Your toffees are a treat and those peppermint truffles —" Phyllo's father looked up to the stars and let out a whistle "—Barnum's britches, they were good."

Roly beamed, but then looked down to the ground. "I did have help," he said, "It wasn't all me."

Marvel laid a hand on his shoulder and waited for Roly to look up. "A good leader is key, Roly." He held his eye and Roly straightened up. Marvel held out the cabin key to him. "Open her up."

Roly looked right and left. Heads of talent were opening up their cabins around the horseshoe.

"It'll be up to you now, Roly," Marvel said and placed the brass key into Roly's unbandaged hand.

Roly's eyes widened with surprise and then flicked up to meet Phyllo's. The boys were twins and at twelve years old they were both much too young to be head of talent, but these past couple of months had brought significant changes. Their previously accepted future of running the Confectionary together some day had been dashed. Now that Phyllo had been forced onto the circuit, the Confectionary's future *was* up to Roly.

He turned to face the lock and rolled the key around in the palm of his hand, trying to manoeuvre it up to his fingertips, his other hand much too unwieldy, wrapped in its bandage, to help. He fumbled and it fell to be lost in the grass.

"I'll get it," said Phyllo and he dropped to his hands and knees to search, thinking Roly would never be able to feel for it. He found its hard shape in the darkness and jumped up to unlock the flap revealing the expansion lever. It was recessed in a box that Phyllo judged much too small for bandaged hands to manipulate, so he released that too. Somewhere deep inside gears engaged.

Motion began with a *whump*.

The Confectionary shuddered then spread out sideways, roof panel sliding over roof panel, the rear section stretching farther than the front, reshaping the cabin like a wedge of cake with the nose bitten off. Inside counters slid out from beneath shelving and rotated into position. Locating pins thumped and clunked into place, finding home quite audibly from the outside. The left-hand wall was the final piece to slot into place and when it ground its way down into position, Roly pushed past Phyllo and in through the narrow door.

Phyllo stumbled from being shoved out of the way. "Oi! What's your problem?" he complained.

Behind him Marvel sighed. "I gave the key to Roly, Phyllo. He wanted to do it."

"I know. I know you did. I was helping. He dropped it, didn't he? I didn't want him to struggle. I didn't want anyone to think he couldn't do it, that we couldn't even get into our own cabin."

"Phyllo, it was his moment."

Phyllo looked up to where the Ringmaster had been standing, but it seemed, for the moment, Lazarus Barker had better things to do than watch the Cane family struggle. He had gone. Marvel followed the direction of Phyllo's gaze and seemed to understand.

"You know sometimes, trying as we are to improve ourselves, it is other people's journeys that are more important," Marvel said.

Phyllo ground one foot into the earth. "Some of us have more to improve."

2

NO PLACE LIKE HOME

WAKING in the Confectionary felt as natural and normal as if he'd never left. In honour of his return Dodo had returned to her old bunk above their father, so Phyllo could draw the curtain across his own familiar nook and fall into a sleep worthy of a hibernating honey bear.

His first conscious breath of the new day sang with the aroma of baking. Cinnamon apple muffins, unless he was very much mistaken. A classic Confectionary treat that marked the start of the off-season. Happiness crept through him. To be back in the Confectionary was brilliant. The Volante family had taken him in and taught him what they could, but the Birdcage had never had the warmth of home.

He stretched then sat up, peeled back the bunk drape and put his feet on the floor. No perilous clamber down from the heights of his Birdcage cot for him that day – this alone was a great start.

On the other side of the thin wall his father pottered about in the kitchen. The tinkle of kettle on hob and cup on plate told Phyllo where Marvel was in his morning routine.

Phyllo pulled on his dressing gown and walked out through the arch just as Marvel was heaping hot muffins onto a cooling rack. Tea was brewing in the pot, just as Phyllo had known it would be.

"Morning, Dad."

"Phyllo, just in time. Pull up a stool, eh?"

Marvel poured them both a cup and snatched a couple of hot muffins onto a plate, which he slid between them. He blew on his fingers and settled down on a stool, gazing at Phyllo fondly.

"So good to see you at breakfast," he said, "I've missed you, son."

"I've missed you too, Dad. I'd rather be here than the Birdcage, any day of the week." It was true, the Confectionary's proportions seemed much smaller to him now after living in the lofty heights of the Birdcage, but space wasn't everything. He was glad not to have to worry about going up on the trapeze anymore. It was a relief to be back with the small clutch of people who accepted him for who he was.

"I've made a present for Signor Volante." His father tapped at a red and white box on the counter. "A selection of family favourites. Raspberry whips, winter truffles, some of Roly's peanut toffees, chocolate mice and some of those rosemary bonbons that Signor Volante liked that time. I'm not sure they'll be up to your mother's standard, but he should enjoy them all the same."

Phyllo eyed the box unenthusiastically. He'd just escaped from the Birdcage. He didn't want to go back.

Marvel gave him an admonishing look. "I'm sure he won't hold you captive. It's the least we can do. The Volantes got us out of a hole. We ought to say thank you."

Phyllo had to reluctantly agree. Without Signor Volante's

help there was a good chance he'd have been posted out to a different circus entirely for his first apprenticeship. At least he'd been able to stay close to home. It was going to be a challenge to find another act willing to take him on so close at hand, but a year's worth of apprenticeships would be required. A year to find his magical aptitude and save his family from being ejected from the troupe.

The joy of being at home was so easily replaced by anxiety. He still had to prove himself worthy.

~

By the time Dodo and Roly appeared in the kitchen for breakfast, Marvel had wiped every surface down to a sparkling shine and Phyllo was dressed, ready to take their father's gift to the Birdcage.

Dodo skipped straight out into the shop, pulling with her the low stool that would bring her up to the height of the corn popper. She stopped short; her blue eyes staring. Buttery yellow puffs were already tumbling from the hopper to gather in the glass box beneath.

"It's already popping," she said in her small voice.

"I was up early, so I thought I'd do it, like the old days," Phyllo said from the doorway. At least there were some things he knew how to do.

"Yes, no need to worry this morning, Dodo. Phyllo's done it." Marvel gave her a pat on the shoulder.

"Of course he has," Roly grumbled. He slumped onto a stool at the counter, "Why wouldn't he?"

"And that's the last of it now," said Marvel, "The new sacks will keep well enough until the start of next season. You can help give the popper a good clean down later, eh?"

Dodo didn't look nearly as enthusiastic about cleaning the machine as she had about running it. Phyllo watched her drag the step back to where she'd found it and then climb rather heavily up to her own stool for breakfast.

He'd just been trying to slip back into the old routine. He'd been trying to be helpful. Dodo didn't have to look quite so miffed about it.

Phyllo scooped up Signor Volante's gift. "Right, well I'll just run this round to the Birdcage then, shall I?"

Roly grunted and Phyllo was quite glad to get outside.

It was odd to see the horseshoe path quite so broad. With cabins pushed out to twice the normal distance, the path lacked its usual mysteriously magical atmosphere. Wide gaps between cabins expanded their huddled community to feel more like an unfamiliar village.

The sun glowed weakly in the misty morning sky. It had not yet had a chance to warm the late summer air and Phyllo pulled his jacket tighter around him. Only Skinner and Bain, of the engineers, were to be seen out of doors, standing at the corner of the Confectionary, examining the mechanism which under normal circumstances attached it to its neighbour.

Phyllo hurried past, but felt their eyes boring into his back.

"What'll he do now, do you think?" Phyllo heard one of them mutter, "Can't see him blagging it twice."

"Whatever it is, he'll likely make a right bags of it," the other replied unkindly. Both men snorted.

Phyllo pretended that he hadn't heard them and hurried on. He'd always found Skinner and his lumpy friend Bain hostile at best. In Phyllo's opinion they'd enjoyed the bossy lockdown rules instigated by the Ringmaster a little too much and had been way too keen to dish out punishments.

Out here on the Plains they were too far out of the way for passing scallywags of the In-between to bother them though. Phyllo had hoped that the same would apply to Skinner and Bain.

He picked up his pace to head past the Magical Menagerie and on to the Birdcage.

The Menagerie's doors were open wide. This cabin, usually part of backstage during performances, was the mirror image of cabins on the other side of the gate, namely the Ticket Booth, the Archive and the Ringmaster's quarters all rolled into one. It was by far the largest cabin of all.

Phyllo supposed that even *the Machine* was only capable of so much manipulation of space and that the animals all had to go somewhere when the rest of the cabins folded to travel. They certainly weren't out in the ring with the rest of the troupe.

A kind of earthy moistness met Phyllo's nostrils as he drew up level and he couldn't help but peer into its semi-darkness.

Like the Ringmaster's cabin, the ceiling rose to double height with a great circular window on the far wall, but that was where the similarity ended. Where the Ringmaster's cabin was clean and smart with an entire wall devoted to the polished gubbins of *the Machine*, the Menagerie had animal pens to either side, with yet more up on a mezzanine. Bedding materials spilled out of barred gates and their occupants shuffled in the shadows, munching and snuffling.

Bast Venor, the Circus of Wonder's animal tamer, backed out of a pen dragging what appeared to be an extremely heavy chest. With every backward step she tugged with a great arch of her back to scrape the box along the ground just a few more inches. She clicked her tongue in rapid bursts.

From this angle she had rather the look of a lion about her. Her hair was full and thick, separating into tight black curls at its tips. Her tamer's whip was held in place behind her back by a wide leather belt. Fat tongues of red fabric danced at the whip tip, a loose ten inches or so swishing back and forth with every strain at the box.

Something was rumbling.

"All that fine curiosity is going to waste stood there," she called out.

When Phyllo didn't respond, she let go of the chest handle and turned to face him. Golden feline eyes stood out vividly from the darkness of her skin. She was even more cat-like from the front. The hair around her face, plaited close to the scalp, extended the profile of her face to reach back to the impressive mane of hair. "It's heavy?" she said nodding questioningly to the box in Phyllo's hand.

Phyllo shook his head, a little wrong-footed. "Oh no, it's just sweets."

Venor flicked her eyes to her own weighty trunk and back.

Phyllo turned to look over to Skinner and Bain and when he saw they were watching, pulled himself up to his full height and said loudly, "I'd be happy to help you, Tamer Venor. I'm sure I can manage that chest."

When he heard them laughing, an increasing need to be seen as capable propelled Phyllo into the Menagerie, where he put down his own box and went around to grasp the chest's other handle.

The rumbling he'd heard before rolled up a notch. Venor clicked her tongue in another series of bursts.

Phyllo looked around for the source of the noise, but couldn't see it. "What is that, actually?" he asked. He'd never ventured inside the Menagerie before and didn't really know what was in there.

She heaved against the weight of the chest. "Lift at your end. A few feet more." She made the clicking noise again. The skin on the back of Phyllo's neck prickled.

"That noise," he persisted, "What is it?"

"I am begging, like a baby to its mother. For me it is my tongue and teeth, but they make it in their crop." She made the noise again to demonstrate then stamped at the floor: four unevenly spaced stomps followed by scraping the sole of her boot around her in an arc. Phyllo stared at her and she did it again.

From the pen to Phyllo's right a tufty ginger trunk reached through the bars to sniff at Phyllo's box of sweets where he'd left it on a barrel, just out of reach. It sneezed.

"Leave it," said Venor plainly and the trunk curled away.

The rumbling came again and this time gained in depth to pulse in a growl. Phyllo snapped to look over his shoulder. It was definitely the direction of the sound and the open pen behind him ran deep under the mezzanine to melt away into darkness. It was impossible to see clearly to the back, but something was definitely moving.

"Begging, did you say?" Phyllo's heart picked up its pace.

"She has refused to come out of her pen all season. Well, no more. She wants to sit in there on her hoard? Now she'll have to come out here to sit on her hoard." Venor flicked back the catch on the chest and hauled open the lid. The chest wasn't full by any means, but the base was covered with gold. Coins mostly, but here and there lay statuettes of deities Phyllo didn't recognise, and chunky goblets studded with jewels.

"Crackers," breathed Phyllo, "No wonder it's so heavy."

"Not nearly heavy enough."

The gate of the pen to the right rattled and a wide furry face pressed up against it from behind. A butterphant, but not the small and obliging kind Phyllo had experienced at Fortune Falls. This specimen was the full-sized version. Its beady eyes looked down at Phyllo from twice his own height. It butted the gate to bounce it on its hinges.

"Leave," Venor said again. The animal harrumphed.

A busy chattering began in a coop with fine mesh to its front on the other side of the Menagerie. Miniature thin-legged monkeys in colourful waistcoats clambered up and down a framework of bamboo. Two in particular clung to the wire and screeched. It set Phyllo's teeth on edge.

Venor fed them peanuts through the wire. "Go gently, little ones," she said. The monkeys snatched at the nuts and screeched some more.

The butterphant's gate creaked and its trunk stretched out through the bars.

The rumbling roar came louder and closer and a new heat radiated onto Phyllo's back, as if he'd suddenly found himself out in the mid-summer sun. Venor clicked her tongue and Phyllo saw that she was gazing now at something high above his head.

"Be still," she said quietly then stamped her feet in that odd little dance.

A rumble rattled through Phyllo's ribs and hot breath tousled his hair. The beast from the pen was directly behind him. Venor side-stepped away to Phyllo's left, away from the chest. She clicked her call and Phyllo felt the hot breath leave his neck. The urge to run surged through him.

"Edge away from the hoard, away to your right," Venor said in a low voice, "Softly, while she's looking at me."

Phyllo couldn't help but let his eyes slide around to find the creature and what he found was a curiously terrifying mixture of things. As tall as the butterphants, its head resembled a spiny lizard. Its jaw was solid and broad and hung slightly open to reveal jagged rows of long spiked teeth. Its hide was scaled, or was it feathered? The texture was hard for Phyllo to define beyond being sandy and matt. The surface rippled in and out of focus. At once it was both peculiar and spine-chilling. It was also unmistakeably a dragon.

Phyllo let out a squeaky gasp.

A rumble came from the dragon's throat and rose to a roar as it stretched its mouth wide. Venor did not flinch, but Phyllo thought his knees might melt with fear.

He stumbled away sideways into the barrel, sending the box of sweets tumbling to the ground where it burst open and scattered its contents. The butterphant trumpeted with joy and lunged, but the spilled sweets were still out of reach. It snorted and shoved at the gate which groaned, then cracked and finally exploded in a shower of splintered wood.

"Chocolate mice," Phyllo breathed as first one then two butterphants trumpeted their way out of the pen. They buffeted Phyllo back toward the dragon and Tamer Venor flashed her eyes at him, aghast.

The dragon snapped around, a foreleg catching the chest to shove it over and spill treasure across the floor. It roared, arching its back, and curled side to side, swishing an enormous tail. It swept a jet of flame low to the ground, then the clawed elbows of its wings slashed through the air above Phyllo's head. He shrieked, ducked and scrabbled away in the only direction left – into the butterphant pen and just in time.

The largest butterphant reared up, pedalling stocky

forelegs and trumpeting, indignant at the possible theft of its chocolate mice. The dragon, who was more concerned for its gold, stretched out its wings and spat flames that licked the ceiling. Animals in cages erupted into a cacophony of squawks and shrieks and howls, the little monkeys screeching loudest of all.

Phyllo clamped his hands over his ears. On the other side of the cabin Tamer Venor was dipping stiffly at the waist and waving her arms in what Phyllo had to assume was an impression of a baby dragon. If she was making that clicking noise, Phyllo couldn't hear it above the din.

The dragon extended its colossal wings then pushed down against the air. Once. Twice. There wasn't room to fly inside the cabin, but its clawed feet left the ground and grabbed for the bars that closed off pens, scrambling, lumbering. Too big for the space, too heavy for the gates to hold, they snapped and crumbled in its grip.

The butterphants trumpeted furiously, flapping their own kite-like ears in an attempt to leave the ground too. A clutch of tiger-striped ponies and a tumble of monkeys rushed from their now destroyed cages and into the melee, a particularly brazen one pausing to search through the hay at the butterphant's feet. It screeched excitedly at uncovering a toffee then bolted for the main cabin door, his comrades bowling after him.

The dragon leapt from one side of the cabin to the other, wings beating down to dislodge sacks and barrels that had been neatly stacked. Shelving snapped. Water butts turned over. The ears of the butterphants swished back and forth determinedly, but Phyllo could see they would never make it off the ground.

More damaged cages burst open. Kitten-faced owls and

pink parakeets, shaggy bears and scuttling jewelled crabs dashed from their confinement. They shimmied down support posts or flew in tight circles. Cawing and screeching. Bellowing and barking.

A crack rent the air and cut through the raging roar of it all.

Tamer Venor stood in the centre of the cabin, arms and legs spread wide. She clutched the whip in her right hand and swirled it about her with a flick. The red tongues spiralled and cracked. Creatures froze in place.

"*Waqef,*" she yelled and cracked the whip again. The dragon roared from the heights of the mezzanine, but the butterphants trampled immediately back into their pen, effectively pinning Phyllo to the wall with their furry enormity.

A lick of flame scorched the ground where they had been standing seconds before.

In the doorway Panya, the Tamer's assistant, appeared clutching an armful of supplies. She stared around at the mayhem open-mouthed.

"*Waqef,*" yelled Tamer Venor with another crack of her whip. Panya dropped the packages and spread out her own arms. "*Waqef,*" she shouted too, although not with quite the same authority.

The jewelled crabs stopped in their side-stepping snake for the exit and sidled instead for a corner. Panya took a small step into the Menagerie, arms still open wide. "*Waqef,*" she said again in a smaller voice.

Behind her the Ringmaster blustered into view, striding across the horseshoe toward them. The one person Phyllo'd been most anxious to impress would now bear witness to his latest disaster. He'd come to investigate, no doubt drawn by the racket and the random animals tearing out of the Menagerie doors.

Lazarus Barker strode to Panya's side in the doorway, his cane clutched by the shaft. "Where is your master?" he demanded, scouring the cabin. His eyes jumped to the snarling dragon on the mezzanine.

"*Thamineh Monzel*," commanded Venor, cracking the whip high in the air.

A growl rumbled from its throat, but before it had finished, she cracked the whip again.

From his hiding place in the butterphant pen Phyllo heard the great weight of it drop to the ground.

"Good girl," Venor soothed and a few moments later Phyllo heard the sound of the pen gate latching.

Escaped animals still inside the Menagerie froze in place, water dripped from the mezzanine and a metal bucket rocked back and forth to a tinny stop.

The Ringmaster dropped the tip of his cane to the ground and leaned ostentatiously on its head. "Having trouble?" he said, voice bland.

Panya scurried to pick up her packages and into the next pen along from the butterphants. Around Phyllo's age, she still had lots to learn, but was smart enough to get out of the Ringmaster's way. Her wide eyes met Phyllo's through the gaping slats in the wall.

"A temporary glitch in our harmonious ecosystem," said Tamer Venor smoothly, coming into view. She banged the chest over and scooped the spilled coins back inside, snapping the lid closed as the Ringmaster drew level.

"You have to wonder if it's still worth the investment." He tapped at the trunk with his cane and looked about at the destruction.

"She pines," said Tamer Venor.

The Ringmaster tutted. "She needs to get over it. Skinner is helping me with a project, but I'll send him in when we're finished." His eyes skated over the ruined gates. "There'll be a bit less in that chest when all this is fixed. We need to consider our options, Venor."

Tamer Venor gathered herself and arched pinched fingers away from her mouth with a respectful bow of her head. "With all pleasure," she said and the Ringmaster turned away to walk back to the door.

"I'm in the middle of something now, Venor. We'll talk later—" he paused in the doorway "—But you and I, Phyllo Cane, will talk now."

Phyllo's heart sank.

3

SCHLEPPER'S RUN

"Quite incredible how quickly it is possible to fall from grace. Only yesterday you were the hero of the moment and yet today here you are, back to being the centre of disaster." Lazarus Barker shook his head incredulously. Phyllo was thankful that the Ringmaster was looking imperiously into the distance and not piercing him with those pin-sharp eyes.

"I was just trying to help," said Phyllo, who thought that it really wasn't fair.

"Indeed."

"It wasn't even my idea. I was just passing—"

"Such casual impactfulness. Barnum help us should you ever mean it."

Phyllo bristled.

"What were you even doing? Actually, never mind. Released from your responsibilities for just one morning and already you're wreaking havoc. Freedom clearly doesn't suit you. What you need is a job and I've just the thing." He nodded the head of his cane to the distance and Phyllo followed his gaze.

Distantly, Honeyholde reached its spired chimneys into the sky, ribbons of smoke curling into the morning mist. A thick forest skirted and obscured the majority of its buildings from view, the trees only petering out ten miles or so south, where the flat fields of the Plains began.

A single vehicle travelled the unmade road out of the Whispering Wood toward them.

"I was doing a job for my dad," Phyllo countered, "He wants me to help him." He hoped that was true, he really wanted stay with his family for a bit longer.

"We've already established that Confectionary is not your destiny. What Marvel wants is no longer relevant, I'm afraid. What *I* want however, is much more your concern and what *I* want is for you to assist our new act in settling in—" he paused to give Phyllo a toothy smile "—At least for now."

Phyllo returned his gaze to the approaching vehicle. The closer it came the better he could make out its form. A lozenge-shaped camper van towing a trailer twice its own size, which jiggled in and out of potholes and rocked alarmingly. When the road faded out to soft grass it slowed to a crawl and circled their cabins, finally drawing to a halt when the driver spied the Ringmaster striding across the grass toward him, waving his cane. Phyllo trailed curiously behind.

He had thought that the van was painted brown but, now that he could see it better, realised it was entirely covered with rust. All kinds of additions had been welded on to the sides and roof. Hooks for a hammock that hung rather stiffly, hand rails to the roof and racks which supported tightly roped suitcases and solid crates.

The driver's door clunked then slid up to the roof, instead of out to the side on a hinge as Phyllo'd expected.

The driver's entire seat swivelled to face the side and a wheel slid out from beneath to stretch to the ground on a hinged spring. It rolled forward, pulling with it the seat and two much larger wheels. Together they created a compact three-wheeler which neatly slid from the van to hold its driver at eye level.

"Schlepper, glad you could join us," said the Ringmaster, grasping the man's hand and shaking it heartily.

Schlepper paused to smile genially, the tips of his thin white moustache curling upward. "I am happy to be here," he said. He was dressed in a combination of practical looking khaki and leathers that wouldn't have been out on place on a pilot, right down to his head-hugging leather hat. He pulled brassy goggles away from his eyes and snapped them back to his forehead.

From the waist down his body was obscured by a tartan woollen blanket and Phyllo wondered if the three-wheeler's purpose was actually that of a wheelchair.

"My engineers have been looking at our couplings to see what can be done. This your unit?" The Ringmaster strode around to the trailer and Schlepper's three-wheeler trundled easily alongside under its own propulsion.

Schlepper patted the trailer affectionately. "She is a little rough around the edges, but it's what's on the inside that counts," he said. He spoke quite slowly and deliberately, rolling his r's and ending his words sometimes with a rise in pitch. There was the faintest hint of an accent that Phyllo could not pinpoint. "Near side is forward facing. She's quite compact as you can see."

The Ringmaster eyed the equally rusty trailer dubiously. "Perhaps a full encasement would be best, to match it in with the other cabins."

"So long as the front is free and clear we shouldn't have any difficulty. She has her own awning when I open her up."

The Ringmaster nodded congenially. "I must say, I'm very much looking forward to seeing it in action." He tucked his cane under his arm and moved forward as if meaning to press the seductively large red button on the side.

Schlepper put up his own hand to block him. "Transit can be tricky. Checks must be made."

The Ringmaster diverted his hand to smooth his extravagant beard instead. "Later then. Ah, here are my engineers."

Skinner and Bain lumbered across the grass toward them. A few yards behind a small gang of escaped monkeys scrabbled haphazardly in pursuit, Phyllo recognising the toffee thief at their head. When the two men came to a stop by the trailer, the thief nimbly climbed Bain's trouser leg and extended a thin arm into his pocket. Panya was rounding up ponies by the Birdcage. The monkey's minutes of freedom were numbered.

"Skinner, this is the unit I was telling you about," said the Ringmaster, "It's fairly small so I think we can reconfigure minimally to slot it into the horseshoe. Just before the Confectionary seems optimal, then it's one more stop before the Grand Entrance."

"Right you are, Ringmaster," said Skinner. Bain grunted. His monkey mugger extracted a key from his pocket and passed it down to an accomplice waiting on the ground, then a rubber band, a boiled sweet and a toy soldier. Phyllo snorted and the Ringmaster threw him a sharp look.

"Stretching the horseshoe is easy enough. I can take the coupling from the next cabin along, but I'll need a new pair. Getting it under the roof when we travel will be a different story. She might have to stack up on another." Bain scratched at his big potato-shaped head, "Not sure how we'd lift it," he mused.

"I might have something that'll do it," Schlepper said, "It's in my workshop. I'll have to collect it."

"Capital," said the Ringmaster, "I wonder, Schlepper, if you're heading back, if you might do me a favour? I've a package waiting at the Club. I'd be greatly obliged if you'd collect it for me? From the Brigadier?"

"No problem," said Schlepper.

"Phyllo, run along with Mr Schlepper and make yourself useful. I assume you could use an extra pair of hands?"

"Oh, certainly." Schlepper unhooked the trailer and gave Phyllo a nod. He returned to the driver's door and the van seemed to almost suck his three-wheeler back inside, wheels disappearing smoothly under the seat as it slid into place.

Phyllo bristled. "Actually, I'm meant to be helping my dad," he said and then remembered that the gift he'd been delivering was now likely trampled. Over by the Menagerie, Tamer Venor wove left and right, wielding an enormous net on a pole, while pink parakeets swooped around her head. Phyllo swallowed and looked at Schlepper.

"I'll open the other side," Schlepper said and reached for a button. The door slid into motion and Phyllo climbed gratefully in.

The passenger seat was much more ordinary than the driver's; although darkly leather and buttoned, it would have felt more at home by a fireside than in a van. Phyllo settled in and they were off, Schlepper driving the van back the way he'd come, back toward the trees and ultimately Honeyholde.

The dashboard was jam-packed with instruments. A switch close to Phyllo's knee allowed the operator to choose between 'Most Likely' and 'Absolutely Not' whilst a whole raft of buttons in reach of Schlepper had a strip of masking tape stuck over them on which was written the single word '*No*'.

An illuminated screen with a sweeping hand, like a fast-moving clock, pinged with every pass of a dot that pulsed brightly green.

Schlepper hummed to himself.

"So where are we going, exactly?" asked Phyllo.

"My workshop," he smiled languidly, "is in the Nevershade. We'll be there in no time." Schlepper tapped a dial with an unmoving needle and tutted. "Well, twenty minutes in any case." He gave every impression of a man who would not be hurried, and the careful slowness with which he spoke made Phyllo want to finish his sentences.

The Nevershade. Phyllo knew of it, but had never been. It was an industrial district and Honeyholde had so much more to offer the curious mind. He'd regularly dropped by Steam Star Port to ogle the dirigibles docked on towers, and the cliffs on the south side of the river mouth had seen many happy hours of exploration. Honeyholde itself sprawled on multiple layers, neighbourhoods increasing in opulence as they rose up from the ground.

He caught glimpses of the golden stone towers through the trees as the road wove through the wood, but Schlepper's route took them down slopes into shadowy darkness as they got closer. When they finally reached it, their parking spot hid under a corrugated iron shelter at lower ground level.

Beneath it the van was immersed in an extra layer of gloom and when they got out, all the tiny hairs on Phyllo's body pricked up on end. It felt like emerging into a cellar despite them officially still being outside. Schlepper's workshop was just a few paces away, a wall of metal shuttering sealing its frontage. He deployed his key in a heavy gauge panel to one side and the solid clunks of bolts receding rolled around its perimeter, allowing them to roll it up.

The workshop was huge. The considerable wall space was covered in shelves packed with gadgets and bits and bobs: disconnected dials, coils of wire and tubs of switches. Tall sections were devoted to sheets of copper and steel, some misshapen with chucks cut away. There were overflowing tubs of nuts and bolts, welding equipment and hundreds of tools, the likes of which Phyllo had never seen before. Phyllo drifted toward a wood-clad wall where tools were suspended by well-placed nails, each with a carefully drawn black line around them to mark their place. It was an incredible selection of everything Phyllo could ever have thought of to keep in a workshop, organised down to the last pin.

The thing that stood out the most, however, was the vast emptiness in the middle of the room. The wide concrete floor was spotted with puddles of oil and scraped in evidence of something hugely heavy having been moved across it. Phyllo couldn't help but wonder what it was that was missing.

Schlepper made for a well-used wooden desk, littered with rolled-up papers, pens and the scraps of old projects. He rooted through a drawer then pulled out a palm-sized box with a couple of buttons.

"Now then," he said, waving the box at a particularly robust looking set of shelves, "On here somewhere, I think."

A motor burred to life and the shelves rolled smoothly down. Not to crash into the floor, but to roll away backward when they got to the bottom, a new shelf appearing at the top. It reminded Phyllo of the shop shelves in the Confectionary.

"Fetch that trolley, would you? We'll need a bit of help to move them."

While Phyllo fetched it Schlepper located what he was looking for – four weighty concertina springs with flat rubber feet on one end and a motor on the other, coloured wires springing haphazardly from connection panels.

"Jack springs," he said by way of explanation, "The trailer's very light, comparatively speaking, because of the dimensional shift."

"I see," said Phyllo, who didn't, but didn't want Schlepper to find him lacking so early in their relationship.

Schlepper nodded. "You take the feet end and we'll get them on the trolley," he said and together they wiggled the jack springs off the shelving, onto the trolley and then into the van.

The back of the van was another revelation. If he'd thought that the dashboard was packed with gadgets it was as nothing compared the number of things crammed in the space at the back. Phyllo looked about it incredulously. A bed with a nightstand and lamp, a sideboard with a gramophone on top, a sink, a two-ring cooker with a small oven beneath, a set of drawers, a wardrobe and a small table with two chairs all sat perfectly comfortably inside the camper. There was even a good deal of floor space.

Phyllo frowned at it.

"If we're going to the Club I'd better get changed," said Schlepper. He rolled into the van and closed the door.

The Club. Phyllo wondered what it was like. He looked down at his own outfit and realised belatedly that it was a bit odd.

He'd got used to the flyer's blues and their silky comfort and had put them on automatically, as he had his sash because without it his tunic was just too flappy and annoying. That morning he'd put on his old boots, as the soft shoes of the flyers didn't seem quite the right thing. He'd also put on his Confectioner's coat, just because he could. Its violet and lemon structured stripes stood out garishly against the baby blue satin.

He was just considering this mish-mash when Schlepper re-emerged.

Phyllo had expected perhaps a tie or a jacket, but the man wore neither. Instead, he'd lost the three-wheeler and replaced it with legs, but they were quite unlike any legs Phyllo had ever seen before.

Phyllo blinked at him.

Schlepper's outfit could not have been further from a smart suit either. Now, along with the goggles, snug leather pilot's hat and coat, he wore wide khaki shorts with too many pockets, which would have stopped just shy of his knees, if he'd had any. In their place shining brass concertinas extend to his sturdy boots. He strode, rather bouncily, past Phyllo and into an alleyway.

"This way. Hollow Spire Hall is a bit of a climb, I'm afraid." He still spoke slowly but moved extraordinarily fast. Phyllo jogged to keep up.

"Your legs," Phyllo managed, "What—"

Schlepper cut him off. "Perambulator Mark IV. I've made a few adjustments. The Mark III had a longer stride, but were rather unstable," he looked back at Phyllo, "And I kept banging my head on doorways. Oh sorry, I'll slow down a bit."

Phyllo caught him up. "You made them?" he asked.

"Oh yes." Schlepper's white moustache curled upward again. "Now watch your step here."

Their path led between damp dark buildings and a canal, the surface of which was mossy with algae. Starved of light, the cobbles beneath their feet were slippery and black. Buildings towered on all sides and Phyllo looked up to see the undersides of bridges that criss-crossed the canal paths high above. Sunlight illuminated paler stone walls higher still, as the buildings tapered gradually away.

They turned into a stairwell that wound up in a corkscrew and proceeded to climb. With every revolution a new doorway revealed itself and through it Phyllo saw an increasingly familiar and improving view of Honeyholde.

The first was a pathway busy with traders unloading canal boats, then a congested market street with the first direct puddles of sunshine. On the next level the lanes broadened and the people were cleaner and moved about rather less purposefully. Phyllo was starting to struggle for breath, but Schlepper bounded unerringly ahead on his Perambulator Mark IVs without breaking a sweat.

"One more turn," he called over his shoulder and Phyllo was delighted to follow him out of the dark stairwell a few moments later and into the light.

It felt much warmer here. The creamy stones of this level's buildings were already soaking up the heat of the sun. Ahead a broad promenade led in gentle curves around buildings which were embellished with carvings and elegant canopies. Manicured trees flourished in flowerbeds and the sky stretched out above them, clear and blue.

It was a far cry from the Nevershade.

Phyllo found himself drawn irresistibly to the balustrade and looked out across the city to Steam Star Port. A handful of dirigibles were moored at the docking towers. Huge dark galleons, slung with nets and steering flaps like the fins of a fish floated alongside pleasure cruisers, brightly coloured and swagged with gold.

Schlepper stopped to gaze out at them too. "The thrill of a new voyage," he said.

"Have you flown in one?" asked Phyllo, desperate to do so himself.

Schlepper considered him for a moment and then pointed out to the docking towers. "*The Nelly Bly*. She used to be mine."

"Really? Which one?"

"The gundalow with brass fins."

Phyllo spotted it. It wasn't the biggest, but it looked loaded with gadgetry, even from this distance. "Wow."

"The first breath of vapour is the best." Schlepper sighed rather wistfully, "But the trouble with air ships is their lack of floor space. That and gravity." He gave Phyllo a wink. "Thirsty?"

4
THE PIONEER CLUB

PHYLLO SLURPED on his lemonade and examined the room where he waited for Schlepper. The Pioneer Club lounge had immensely tall windows that looked out to the west, where the river stretched out into open sea and the ocean-faring vessels of traders and travellers lined up at the docks. The sea shimmered and Phyllo imagined what it would be like to leave land behind, to be surrounded only by water or even by air, as Schlepper once had on *The Nelly Bly*.

The *whine*-then-*tap* that Phyllo recognised as the sound of Schlepper's legs echoed in the hallway. Conversation rumbled low and Phyllo leaned forward in his seat for a better view out of the door. From just out of sight came an oddly familiar man's voice that Phyllo couldn't quite place, "Good luck. Try to keep me informed."

"Of course," Schlepper said in his slow way.

A hem of a black cloak flicked in and out of Phyllo's line of sight, shortly followed by the click shut of the external door and Schlepper's bouncy arrival in the lounge.

"Phyllo." Schlepper's eyes flicked to the window and

back. "The Brigadier has the Ringmaster's item awaiting us in the Arctic Gallery. Would you come with me?"

Phyllo followed him across the entrance hall to another room. A long boardroom table sat centrally, giving away the room's most likely use, but numerous glass display cabinets lined the walls also giving it the air of a museum. Phyllo followed Schlepper to the far end, where a broad man in a military jacket waited rather stiffly.

"Schlepper, good to see you, old man. And who's this young fella?" He flicked his head to Phyllo, grey bushy moustache jiggling.

"This is Phyllo, my assistant for the day," said Schlepper genially.

"Brigadier Alfred Valentine Grosvenor at your service, sir," he barked and extended a hand which Phyllo felt compelled to shake.

"First visit to the Club? Course it is." He patted Phyllo on the shoulder then gripped it rather firmly to steer him over to a wall of photographs.

"Stonewall and Bounder, our founders. Ran the first expeditions to the North Pole. Stonewall shot that polar bear." He pointed at the huge white stuffed bear that stood at least eight feet tall on its hind legs beside the grand stone fireplace. It was frozen mid-swipe of its black-clawed forepaw.

"You mean that's real?" Phyllo hadn't thought it was possible for bears to be quite so enormous, nor that anyone would want keep a dead one.

"1,500 pounds if you like. Took a 4-bore to bring it down. Shot as big as your eyeball," bellowed the Brigadier.

Phyllo frowned.

Other taxidermy trophies peered down from the wood-panelled walls too. The stuffed head of a tiger, whose jaws were so huge Phyllo felt sure it could have swallowed him whole in life, stared out glassily from its mount high above the mantel. Beneath it the Pioneer Club emblem was displayed on a plaque: a man in fur-trimmed exploration gear planting a flag. The motto 'Discovery by ocean, land and sky' ran boldly around the outside edge.

The Brigadier must have noticed the squeamish edge to Phyllo's smile and added, "Specimens from every corner of the globe. It's important to record the discoveries. The appetite for it's insatiable. Your man Barker knows it. Why, he wants this." He knocked on the glass display box sat on the table.

Two feet long and one wide, it encased another taxidermy subject the like of which Phyllo had never seen before, dead or alive.

The creature inside lay on its stomach, reaching forward clawed hands. Its head, arms and torso were human-like in appearance, although much smaller even than a baby. Its face was horribly ugly and square-jawed with a mop of dark hair on the top of its head. At its waist the dark wrinkled skin gave way to silvery scales that were the beginning of the tail of a fish. Phyllo gawped at it.

"The Equatorial Mermaid," said the Brigadier reverentially. "First of its kind captured on the most northern tip of Papua New Guinea. A beauty, isn't she?"

Phyllo grimaced and the Brigadier roared with laughter.

"She'll put a smile on any accountant's face, don't you worry about that."

Phyllo thought that Albertus Crinkle was unlikely to be charmed by it either.

"Is it heavy?" asked Schlepper, taking the Brigadier's attention.

"Weight's in the case. The thing itself is mostly sawdust. The lad might even manage it on his own."

"Perhaps that might be asking too much. Phyllo, take that end and we'll slide it off the table," Schlepper said and Phyllo found that it really wasn't very heavy at all. The worst thing about it was looking into that hideous frozen face. Phyllo diverted his eyes to examine the floor and they made crab-like progress out of the room.

The Artic Gallery's plush carpet gave way to the patterned stone tile of the entrance hallway, but now Phyllo noticed that a good number of the tiles had names engraved upon them.

Brigadier A. V. Grosvenor

"The Brigadier's got his name on the floor," said Phyllo tapping the tile with his toe.

Schlepper look at it and nodded. "Some members are celebrated with a tile in their honour. Usually after completing a great expedition or such. They become part of the fabric of the building. The Brigadier was a big noise when the Egyptian treasures gallery was set up, I think." He changed his grip to hold the case behind his back so that they both could walk forward. "Be sure to tell me if I'm going too fast," he said.

Phyllo wished that he was at the front so he wouldn't have to look at the mermaid. He returned his gaze purposefully to the floor, reading names as they passed and just before they reached the door found another name that he recognised. *Malum Oswald, Lord Protector Corvus.*

On their way back to the workshop Phyllo's mind churned.

"Why on earth would the Ringmaster want something like this?" he said as they slid the mermaid's case into the back of the van. "I mean, it's just revolting. And that polar bear, well I know it was huge and must have been scary, but did they really need to shoot it?"

"And stuff it," said Schlepper, completing Phyllo's thought. "I like to think that my approach is a cut above."

"Your approach?"

"There is a thirst for knowledge, an appetite for the unusual, I dare say macabre. Taxidermy of this sort taps into the growing interest of the general public into what lies beyond our own shores." Schlepper smiled in his slow manner. "Hop in."

They pulled out of the Nevershade and made for the Whispering Wood. Schlepper tapped at that gauge on his dash and smiled a small smile when the needle jumped to point directly up.

"Our world is a broad and complex place. Habitats and weather systems vary enormously, as does the life that flourishes within it. *The Pioneer Club* is a group of likeminded individuals, all seeking out new wonders. They bring samples back so that they can be recorded and we might learn from them."

Phyllo harrumphed. It didn't seem to him that finding a new species so that you could shoot it was a good idea at all.

"Next time we go I'll give you a tour. The Club has many fascinating galleries: plant and insect life, artefacts of lost civilisations, ceremonial paraphernalia from other cultures. Photographs from the expeditions are extraordinary."

Phyllo had to admit, that did sound more interesting. He thought being an explorer would be brilliant. If Schlepper had once owned *The Nelly Bly* maybe he'd been one once too.

It made sense for him to be a member of the Club, but the Ringmaster…

"Is the Ringmaster actually a member?" Phyllo asked.

"An associate membership. He's a professional traveller so it's perfectly appropriate. Some members are there for the network more than the knowledge."

"And Malum Oswald?"

Phyllo had encountered Malum Oswald for the first time in Star City when he'd seen him sniff at the Ringmaster's piffling attempt at a bribe for protection.

Schlepper paused before giving his answer. "The Crows have talons everywhere."

5

BEASTLY CHANGES

LAZARUS BARKER RAGED on the other side of the door and Phyllo couldn't help but feel just a little bit pleased that, for once, it wasn't directed at him.

"You persuaded my father to purchase the beast only for the other to abscond. I can't see any point in keeping it. It's madness, Venor. Even putting the recent destruction to one side, it's taking up valuable space. Space that could be inhabited by an act that pays its way."

"She would be the most wondrous beast if—"

"If she wasn't pining. I know, but an animal that cannot work—"

Phyllo sidled in through the door, following his father and Signor Volante. The voices were dulled by the vast wall of pipes and valves that made up *the Machine* just inside the cabin door, as tiny cogs whirred in its inner depths and dampened the sound.

Phyllo hadn't intended to come early. In truth, he didn't want to spend any more time in the Ringmaster's company than was absolutely necessary. It seemed Venor's appointment had overrun with this telling-off. Phyllo felt sick on her behalf.

"Over here," murmured Signor Volante, beckoning them over to the map table at the back of the room. He was far more at home in the Ringmaster's cabin than Phyllo had ever felt. More at home than his father too, who perched stiffly on the very edge of his seat while Phyllo bumbled around behind, trying to look casual and failing.

Historically, his visits to the Ringmaster hadn't gone well. Today Signor Volante was to report on Phyllo's apprenticeship with his act, *The Fabulous Volante*, the Circus of Wonder's artists of the flying trapeze. After that, they would no doubt discuss what was to become of him next season. Phyllo worried it could mean being sent out of the troupe and away from his family. It was a fate he was happy to delay.

For the moment it was Tamer Venor and Panya in the hot seats though and Phyllo felt horrible for them. The incident in the Magical Menagerie had not exactly been his fault, but he couldn't help thinking that had he not been involved, things might have turned out better.

Miss Fitz, the Octowriter, jabbed tentacles to the keys of her sit-up-and-beg-typewriter as they spoke, rattling out the meeting minutes.

"If she had her mate and a fitting hoard, she would be a spectacle worthy of ten times the gold she guards now, a hundred times," Venor implored, "Don't you remember? Think how she soared before—" Her words stumbled to a halt.

The Ringmaster bristled. "Before my family was murdered, you mean to say?"

The room held its breath. Venor nodded. "I was going to say *when your father was Ringmaster*, but yes, regrettably that is also true." It was a subject nobody ever mentioned. She paused for a moment in reverence. "I cannot say why Mohareb left us. It is exceptional for a Sand Dragon to abandon their master and their mate. I pray every day for his safe return."

"I know, Venor. I've heard it all before," said Barker testily. He leaned over his desk to stare her down. "How long do you expect us to wait?"

She looked away. "You are right. Too much time has passed to continue to hope. He must be lost to this world. Only death can tear a dragon from its master. It is the only explanation." She sighed deeply, then continued in a smaller voice. "Finding another would not be easy, but without it Thamineh will not recover."

"Then find it." The Ringmaster thumped his desk, looked up and caught sight of Phyllo at the back of the room. Phyllo snapped his eyes away and, for the second time in as many days, found himself examining something that was only meant to be a distraction, but turned out to be rather interesting.

It was a large pencil drawing that curled at its edges on the table; a plan of the cabins of the Circus of Wonder with carefully noted dimensions. Next to the *Confectionary* the artist had slotted in an extra cabin labelled only 'Schlepper' and a roughly sketched addition had been made to the *Odditorium*, almost doubling its size.

"I regret, I have not found time for a search," said Venor, "The Sand Dragon is rare. Incredibly rare. You cannot pick up an egg in a market and besides, we'd need a fully grown male. One hasn't been seen in a decade or more. That is why what we have is so special. Before long there will be none to be found anywhere in the world." Venor's voice was as smooth as silk, almost a purr.

Lazarus Barker sat back in his chair and tipped his head to survey her down his nose. "This is the off-season. Your time is now."

"The other animals cannot be abandoned. They need knowledgeable care. Who would tend them? Panya could do it, but catching a dragon needs more than one pair of hands."

Venor and the Ringmaster stared defiantly into each other's eyes and, for a long silent minute, no-one spoke.

The Ringmaster stood. "Aldo."

Signor Volante jumped to his feet.

"Our meeting today is to discuss how Phyllo's apprenticeship with *The Fabulous Volante* concluded. What say you?"

Phyllo's attention snapped back up from the plan. Signor Volante stepped out from behind the table. "I think he did very well." Signor Volante stood solidly to meet the Ringmaster's eye.

The Ringmaster nodded sedately and waved his hand over, indicating that he should continue. Signor Volante shuffled, somewhat uncharacteristically, and flicked his eyes to Phyllo.

"Is very difficult. The Volante family have performed in the flying tradition for generations. Two months, it is *nothing*." He embellished the statement with a toss of his hand. "He tried. He believed. He helped us to win the Gilded Pennant."

Phyllo's heart was in his mouth. Signor Volante's words could make or break him. So far, they were sounding OK. He gave Phyllo a proud kind of frown.

"We had some problems, San Giuseppe, it was no easy. I no think it is unfair if I say it did not come naturally." He looked to Phyllo quite kindly. "Nothing wrong with the effort, but the talent... Meh."

Phyllo puffed out a breath. He was a little surprised, but he had to admire the succinctness of it. He'd been going over what he might say in his head for days. He'd been trying to think of the best way to say that he never wanted to go up on a trapeze bar *ever* again.

The Ringmaster did not look perturbed by this news. In fact Phyllo thought that strangely, he looked rather happy.

"Then we will not be bringing your journey around *the circuit* to a premature conclusion, Phyllo. Still, it is an ill wind that brings nobody any good. Venor? You have your helper."

The Ringmaster sat back down in his chair looking extraordinarily pleased with himself. He took up a pen and ostentatiously crossed out a line on the document laid on his desk.

Phyllo and his father looked at each other.

"Excuse me?" Marvel said uncertainly, "I'm not sure I quite follow."

"Phyllo is not a flyer. Aldo has confirmed it. A brave effort. A commendable first apprenticeship, but without Phyllo's magical talent found, the circuit must continue."

"But it's the off-season," said Phyllo, "There won't be any shows. I thought—"

"You thought you might mess about for a couple of months and cause havoc wherever you went."

"Well, no, not exactly that."

"You thought that your destiny was secure?"

"Well, no—"

"You thought that I'd forgotten our arrangement then, perhaps?"

Phyllo looked back at him, lost for anything to say.

Lazarus Barker twirled the tip of his moustache around one finger thoughtfully. "Miss Fitz."

The Octowriter's tentacles pulsed in unison then came to rest, tips poised afresh over its keys.

"Finish our minutes with a note to Albertus." The Ringmaster looked thoughtfully to the ceiling for a moment, composing his words in his head.

"In our continuing efforts to streamline the economies of the Circus of Wonder it is deemed essential for all parties to operate in a contributory manor," he said imperiously, "To this end, our Tamer, Bast Venor, will secure the addition of a male Sand Dragon to the Menagerie and complete the pairing with our *very* expensively procured female, whose performance in shows has been woefully lacking and not worthy of a place in our proud troupe." He flicked a small smile to Venor who stared back at him, her golden eyes devouring his every move.

"The additional labour required for the search will be provided by one Phyllo Cane, who seeks his next apprenticeship position in any event. Multiple problems are solved. Venor has her help and Phyllo Cane; his next apprenticeship. He will train with the Magical Menagerie."

Venor smoothed down the fabric of her utilitarian jodhpurs. "I already have an apprentice, Ringmaster. Panya has been with me for many years. Two would be an excess—"

"Quite right," the Ringmaster interrupted. He stood up. "This is but a temporary arrangement. An opportunity, if you will, for our homeless waif to put down some roots. Consider it a charity, Venor."

She stood up to face him, at least a foot shorter, but not at all deficient in presence. She was dressed in natural browns and greens and looked like a warrior. A snug tan leather waistcoat and utility belt holding her whip, pinned a long green tunic to her athletic frame. She stood squarely, hands on hips, her boot-clad feet set widely beneath her.

The Ringmaster glared, as if waiting for her to pounce.

Venor lifted her chin to speak. "My apprentice joined the Circus of Wonder at my side many years ago. Panya came from the streets of Luxor as my ward and my aide. She has grown with the troupe and made roots of her own. One apprentice is all that I need." She touched clenched fingers to her chest and made a small respectful bow, but there was an edge of defiance in it.

Lazarus Baker twirled at his beard and stared her down. "Phyllo Cane will apprentice with the Magical Menagerie until a male Sand Dragon is found or other more economical conclusion." He waved his hand dismissively. "When the job is done just one apprentice can remain, after all, we are trying to *save* money. I'll leave that choice up to you."

Panya turned in her seat to stare at Phyllo, her dark eyes wide and fearful. Phyllo gawked. He didn't want to do her out of her apprenticeship, he didn't want this any more than she did, but if this was what the Ringmaster wanted, he couldn't see a way around it. Experience told him that whatever the Lazarus Barker wanted, Lazarus Barker got.

He pulled his own expression into a thin-lipped grimace of apology. Panya scowled.

6

SHOPPING

Phyllo eyed the spiked ball dubiously.

It swung on a wrist-thick chain from an equally solid-looking club. The great hulk of a shopkeeper patted it affectionately.

"The Peacemaker," he said thickly through a nose which had been squashed almost entirely flat to his face, "A personal favourite. Makes 'em run away, or gives 'em a headache. Either way, you get a bit o' peace." He rumbled at his own joke and passed it to Phyllo, whose knees buckled immediately under the weight.

Schlepper's moustache tips twitched. "Do you have anything less *taxing*?" he asked coolly, "He won't do very well if he's pinned to the ground." The words rolled from Schlepper's tongue as if he were trying to voice them as clearly as possible.

The troll of a man gazed down at Phyllo stupidly. He looked for all the world like he couldn't understand why anyone wouldn't want a Peacemaker. "Well, if you *like*," he grumbled.

Next, he produced a fat stick with a knobbly metal scoop on one end.

"And what's the method here?" asked Schlepper, seemingly giving it the benefit of the doubt.

"Well, you hold it like this, see, and you get a big rock in this end, here, and you *fling* the rock." He demonstrated the swing. "*Fling it*. Load. *Fling it*. See?" He swung the stick dangerously back and forth.

Phyllo, who'd only just got to his feet, ducked out of the way. He couldn't believe he was being demonstrated troll weaponry. What a day.

Albertus Crinkle had been rather surprised by the turn of events too. When Phyllo and Marvel had delivered the Ringmaster's minutes to the Archive, Albertus had gone rather stiff reading the part about Phyllo's next apprenticeship.

"I'm going to die, aren't I?" Phyllo had wailed, "It's going to be Prunella Devlin all over again. Do you think that he's actually trying to kill me? Do you think that's what he wants?"

"Now, now, Phyllo," Albertus had soothed, "The Ringmaster only ever has our welfare at heart. I'm sure he's made this decision with the best of intentions, best of intentions, yes."

"Has he? Has he though?" Phyllo wasn't convinced.

The shopkeeper loaded his rock-flinger with a cannonball from beneath the counter and flung it to demonstrate. It punctured a hole in the wall. Schlepper shook his head.

"What about this?" The shopkeeper clunked a weighty slingshot down in front of them with a pouch so large Phyllo could have sat in it. "Rocks. Gravel. Shingle. You could get all sorts in there."

Schlepper leaned on the counter and spoke slowly,

directly into the shopkeeper's face, "Do you have anything that does not involve rocks?"

Phyllo sighed. It wasn't going well and Albertus had convinced him that preparation was key.

"People work in menageries without coming to a sticky end all the time. All the time, Phyllo," Albertus had said, "I'm bound to have a book on the subject." He'd got up to peruse the shelves. "Being a Tamer is a talent like any other. If they all met untimely deaths, well there wouldn't *be* any, would there?" He looked between Phyllo and his father, nodding.

"Absolutely," Marvel had added, but a bit too slowly.

Phyllo shook his head at them, feeling sick. "I think we already know that I'm not a natural. Venor only asked me to help shift a box. Look what happened."

"*Tamer* Venor," Albertus corrected. "Now that you're her apprentice you should show her the proper respect.

"Tamer Venor. Right," Phyllo whined.

"Ah, here we are." Albertus had pulled a fat book from the shelf. "Menagerie Management by Digory Crisp." He opened the cover and ran a finger down the contents page. "Kennelling and quarantine, Indestructible pen construction, Species integration…"

"Anything in there about not getting toasted?" Phyllo asked rather acidly.

Albertus turned the page. "The Proper Use of Chain Mail, Elvish Steel and Dragon Hide. What about that? Take the book, Phyllo," Albertus insisted, "See what you can learn. I'm not in the Menagerie day to day, but I can tell you it's been receiving less and less of the gate. I'm not at all surprised that the butterphants got so excited by the prospect of a few chocolate mice. Who knows when they last had any?

As for the animals with more expensive taste, well, I should say times are very lean indeed."

Phyllo mulled that over. Tamer Venor had hinted that there wasn't enough in the dragon's hoard. If they weren't getting much of the gate there never would be. It seemed the Menagerie did need help.

"What we are after," said Schlepper even more slowly, "is something *defensive*. These items are all rather *proactive*."

The shopkeeper squinted at him then produced a twelve-inch machete with what Phyllo interpreted as a knowing nod.

"That's still quite *off*ensive," said Schlepper, "It's protection that we're looking for rather than murder weapons."

The shopkeeper huffed and swept the blade away. "You should have said. Have a look over here."

He clumped across the shop to a rack of bulky clothing and pulled out a very large jumpsuit which he held up against Phyllo. The fabric shimmered darkly in overlapping gunmetal-grey scales.

"Romanian Long Wing. Not the prettiest, but they're fat, you know." He held his hands out wider than his own quite considerable girth. "Makes them the economical choice. Try it on. Get it over your clothes. Yeah, that's it."

The jumpsuit was enormous. It bagged out at Phyllo's wrists and dragged along the floor beneath his feet.

"Just roll it up. Yeah, that's it. Don't want to cut anything off, that way it'll grow with you. Couldn't anyway, unless you've got some diamond shears?"

Phyllo shook his head.

"Nah, don't s'pose you do."

The fabric was stiffly thick and heavy. A collar rose inflexibly behind Phyllo's head and tapered down to his chin at the front so that at least he could see around it. The shopkeeper pulled the buckled straps that ran around his chest taut. The crotch sagged to his knees.

"What's that smell?" asked Phyllo as a pungent whiff of rotten egg completely engulfed him. It seemed to be coming from inside the suit.

"Sulphur," said the shopkeeper, "'Cause it's fresh, see? At its most fire retardant while it's stinking."

Phyllo looked at his ridiculous reflection in the shop's dirty mirror, holding his breath. Fire retardant was good.

"I'll take it," he said.

Phyllo hugged the packaged suit to his chest and hurried to keep up with Schlepper, who lolloped springily ahead. "This will just take a minute and we can be on our way," he called back.

As this errand was the reason Schlepper had wanted to come into the Nevershade in the first place, Phyllo was happy to tag along. After all, it had given him an invaluable opportunity to shop for potentially life-saving equipment.

They crossed the murky water of the canal by a slippery bridge, then turned down an alleyway, lost to gloom. Hair stood up on the back of Phyllo's neck and prickled him into a shiver. The Nevershade was oppressively damp and cold and dark. It felt like being lost down a well.

Up ahead he heard the echoing jingle of a shop bell and was surprised to see the Brigadier emerge in a puddle of light from a doorway, the gold brocade on his military jacket sparkling all the more for its drab backdrop. He turned and hurried away in the opposite direction. When Phyllo and

Schlepper reached the doorway themselves, it turned out to be exactly where Schlepper was heading.

An oversized pestle and mortar hung above the entrance, and writing on the window identified this to be *Pepperwort's Apothecary*. Schlepper pushed open the door and the bell tinkled again.

The shop was small but every inch had been put to good use. The walls were furnished with dark wooden shelving that was divided into sections by small ornate arches. Some were filled with huddles of bottles, their contents on display: dried herbs and seed pods, colourful powders, and weirdly formed roots. Others held hefty earthenware jugs with taps at the bottom for draining out liquids. In places there were foot-high heavy doors, secured with padlocks and a parade of cauldrons lined up on the floor, filled to high cones with colourful spices.

The air was thick with heady smoke. Phyllo scanned about for its source.

At the counter he found the Apothecary himself. He was as thin and knobbly as a stick insect and moved with the same angular judder. He was sweeping a smouldering bundle of leaves along the length of his countertop as if clearing away dust, his face deeply etched with a criss-crossing web of wrinkles.

This much activity seemed to exhaust him as he returned to his perching stool behind the counter with much puffing and sighing, and made an enormous production of climbing the single step to collapse on its seat. His complexion was as darkly grey as the ash which he showered over the counter and stood out in great contrast from the long white cotton tunic he wore with a sage silken waistcoat. He wedged the smoking herbs into a tin box and jammed the lid shut.

"Good morning," said Schlepper, and headed straight for a display of copper items. The Apothecary shifted on his seat, beginning the struggle to lever himself back to standing. His watery brown eyes were shrunk to pinpricks behind bottle-bottom glasses and they darted from Schlepper to Phyllo and examined them both from top to toe. They were the liveliest thing about him.

"I am wearing them myself," he said rather creakily, waving one wrist about that jingled with copper bracelets. "Keeping me young. Curse of the old, arthritis. Is it your joints, sir? Best copper from the Cornish coast, mined by piskies, of all creatures. It is the proximity to the sea that gives it its vigour." He slid stiffly off the stool.

"Don't bother yourself, Pepperwort," said Schlepper genially, "I can manage." He unhooked a couple of bracelets from the display.

"Is it your hips? My hips are a plague upon me. Two for you? The thicker band, I see. Most practical. I have the best pouch for you, lined with Mugwort. It is most agreeable to the senses." Pepperwort reached out his bony hands to take Schlepper's items.

Schlepper laughed gently, "No need. I might like some tea though." He relinquished the bracelets and went to examine the range.

Pepperwort had a great array of containers on his counter alongside a set of well used brass scales. From solid boxes to gauzy bags, he looked eager to fill any of them with his stock and, despite Schlepper's protestations, selected a pouch of buttery satin and put the bracelets inside.

Numerous copper bands adorned his own arms, along with plaited leather and something that looked horridly to Phyllo like matted hair. If any of these items were giving medicinal benefits, Phyllo dreaded to think what state Pepperwort would have been in without them.

A similar plaited bracelet also appeared on a display rack next to the scales and Pepperwort noticed Phyllo looking at it. "Amulets are interesting to you, sir? Do you know their powers?" His sharp eyes scoured Phyllo up and down. "Something for luck?"

He plucked one of the plaited bracelets from the rack and pointed out the small glass bead threaded within it. There was something green inside. "Four-leaf clover?"

Phyllo shuffled with the awkward weight of his package before finally conceding to put it down. Once his arms were free, he leaned in for a better look. As Pepperwort had said, a four-leaf clover was forever frozen inside the glass.

"No. Not luck," said Pepperwort suddenly, "Strength. That is what you are in need of. Will you be returning to Pepperwort's, sir? Just this morning I have taken delivery of an exceptionally rare bear claw consignment. By all accounts a most ferocious beast whose strength still lingers in the keratin. By this time next week, I could construct for you a magnificent necklace."

He patted a rough wooden box on his counter. It was a blond packing crate, entirely plain save for an emblem which had been scorched onto its surface: A circle with a man inside holding a flag.

"Or a ring?" Pepperwort scooped a clenched fist through the air rather feebly, imitating the swipe of the creature itself.

"No plans to come back at the moment," said Phyllo.

"Shame." He made a gesture somewhere between nodding and shaking his head, "Perhaps luck is more like it after all. A rabbit's foot then? And something herbal for strength, yes." He tottered off to clonk through jars and

Phyllo considered the collection of furry feet jumbled in a box. He really could do with some luck.

~

Back at the van, Schlepper settled himself down at the small table in the back, pulled his three-wheeler in close at hand and began to dismantle a section over the wheel. He unrolled a toolkit and motioned for Phyllo to get in and make himself comfortable.

The curiously enlarged internal dimensions felt all the more peculiar from the inside.

"The pneumatics leak," Schlepper said and emptied Pepperwort's silky pouch onto the table. "I discovered in an earlier experiment these copper bracelets to be the perfect size—" he slid one into the mess of tubes and cog-crowded gubbins, screwed it down and reassembled the coverings "—to reseal the gaiter."

He picked up the other. "And a spare," he smiled, "And a pouch that I didn't really want, but that's Pepperwort." He sniffed at it and wrinkled his nose comically.

Phyllo giggled.

"Actually, it's not unpleasant. I could tuck it under my pillow. And what do you have?" he enquired, craning his neck.

Phyllo tipped his own Mugwort pouch out onto the table. "A bit of luck to go with the protection," he said, "Look, the rabbit's foot has come with a certificate."

Schlepper picked up the small slip of parchment and read it aloud.

"Congratulations! You are now the fortuitous owner of a genuine Ms Pennyfeather rabbit foot." He looked up to

Phyllo and gave him a wink. "For your guaranteed and continued improvement of fortune, this hind left foot was gathered at full moon by the cross-eyed witch, Ms Pennyfeather herself."

Phyllo raised his eyebrows, "Goodness."

"For greatest effect, be sure to keep it about the left side of your person and look forward to receiving the very best of luck in all your endeavours."

Phyllo picked up the rabbit's foot and put it immediately into his left trouser pocket.

He also had a small glass jar of something labelled *Ginkgo Root* which Pepperwort had said was renowned for strength. To Phyllo it just looked like a couple of inches of knobbly wood.

"What do you think I'm supposed to do with this?" he said, holding up the jar to examine its contents more closely, "Eat it or just hold on to it?"

"Committing yourself to the improvement is likely the most important thing," Schlepper said and Phyllo considered that. What was it he was committing to here?

If he was going to deal with the huge animals of the Menagerie, he'd definitely be in need of a bit more strength. Just actually surviving was his top priority, but beneath the bubbling surface of panic he was feeling, he knew that there were other problems.

He *had* to find his magical talent and it wasn't just about him. He had to do it to keep his family safe, to stop them heroically following him out into the *In-between* when he inevitably got chucked out. He was committed to that, for sure. This particular apprenticeship, however, posed another thorny challenge. Competition.

He didn't know Panya particular well. She was just

another child in the troupe whose path he'd never really crossed. Just a little brooding kid who he'd recently discovered was a rescue Tamer Venor had snatched from a life on the streets. She'd lived and worked with Venor for years. His chances of polishing up to be better than her were ridiculously minute, and if he did by some miracle manage it, how guilty would he feel?

It was a lose/lose situation.

He wanted to find his magical talent, but more than that now, he felt determined that he would not be found lacking. Not by the Ringmaster. Not by anybody. He didn't want anyone to think that he wasn't good enough.

Training with the flyers he'd managed to pick up enough to get him through. He could do it again. He had to do it again and he'd show anyone that cared to watch.

7
THE UNSUITABLE SUIT

PHYLLO'S RETURN to the Confectionary was all too fleeting. His hopeful dream of an off-season at leisure, already dashed by the Ringmaster, was cut even shorter by his father's long-standing belief that there was *no time like the present*. That and the stink seeping evilly from the dragon hide suit.

Even Roly didn't care to stop him. He rolled his eyes whenever anyone mentioned the apprenticeships and shooed Phyllo away if he dared to offer him any kind of help.

Phyllo tried not to feel hurt by this enthusiasm for him to leave, but wouldn't let them hurry him out so fast that he didn't have time to suit up first.

The very opposite of the sequin suit he'd squeezed into for his appearances on the trapeze, the dragon-hide jumpsuit ballooned around him and filled the gap between his legs with heavy folds that forced him to swing his legs out in wide awkward arcs.

He wobbled around the horseshoe, inflated and clumsy.

Other members of the cast beetled about in the afternoon sun, examining their cabins unhurriedly, considering the condition and making mental lists of the jobs to be done. Frú Hafiz swept at her awning with a broom, dislodging spiders and knocking out dust. The small silver knife on a chain that hung from her waist dazzled with a glint. She paused in her work to give him a nod and a fleeting glimmer of solidarity.

Phyllo stomped on. Such an ordinary day for everyone else. The fabric of his jumpsuit, so adept at keeping out fire, was also keeping all body heat *in*. It was bulky and hot, and his tunic stuck to his back in a slick of sweat.

He lingered at the Menagerie door. He worried that, as much as his suit would protect him from unexpected jets of dragon flame, it would also seriously slow him down if he had to run away.

The moist earthy smell he'd experienced on his last visit swelled in the warmth of the day and mingled unpleasantly with the stink that puffed from the neck of his suit.

He cleared his throat. "Hello?"

Animal feet clomped and shuffled. A butterphant sneezed.

"Anybody here?" Phyllo hesitated at the threshold and strained to see into the gloom.

"We are many," said the voice of Tamer Venor. She strode out of the shadows, golden feline eyes slanted in a smile. "More than in any other cabin I suspect. Please." She bowed her head briefly and swept one arm, welcoming him inside.

Phyllo shuffled forward onto the straw-strewn floor. He was relieved to see that the gate to the dragon's pen was closed. He craned his neck to look inside. The floor melted into shadow with no sign of it.

Tamer Venor scooped a bucket of food pellets up from the ground and then trotted up a metal staircase to the galleried upper level.

She seemed invigorated, far more purposeful than when Phyllo had last seen her. In the Ringmaster's cabin she'd been on the defensive, almost hostile, but now she hummed with energy.

"Staff quarters are up here."

Phyllo lumbered after her, struggling to climb the steps in his suit. When he gained the top step, sweating, he saw that it was a mirror of the mezzanine to the other side. Four animal pens with sturdy gates, only these had been given over to human habitation.

"Stores. We keep this locked at all times." She pointed to the door directly in front of them then to the pen beside it. "You. Panya." She pointed to the next and then finally the furthest, "and me."

"Quite open, isn't it," said Phyllo. He was thinking about the large amount of nothing between him and the dragon he knew to be skulking in one of the lower-level pens.

"You are safe. It would be a foolish thief who broke into the Menagerie."

Phyllo hadn't really been thinking about thieves, but as she'd mentioned it, he couldn't help but wonder, "So why lock the stores?"

Tamer Venor smiled broadly, "Food is the one thing that is never safe." She extended a hand down to the butterphant pen. "Manana would eat day and night if he had the chance and it would be the apprentice that paid the price for it with their pitchfork and barrow."

Phyllo imagined that a butterphant produced more than enough poo at the best of times. "Surely they are in their pens though," he said.

"It is true, but you saw for yourself that the animals of the Menagerie are not always quite where we would like them to be. Their pens would not hold them if they truly wished to leave. It is a bargain of trust. A symbiosis of trainer and beast. Food can be our greatest tool but a most dangerous motivation if it is too easily accessed. So always locked. Ah, Panya."

Panya chose this moment to appear on the mezzanine. She looked hatefully at Phyllo and then quickly away.

"You two know each other already, I suspect."

"We've seen each other around," Phyllo confirmed but he had to admit, he didn't really know her at all.

Panya bustled past them and into her own pen.

Phyllo watched her through the gaps in the slats. She appeared a little younger than he was but he found her actual age rather hard to pin down. She wore men's baggy overalls, rolled up at the ankle and cuff and pulled in at the waist by a wide leather belt to which she'd attached a variety of small tools. At the wide belt, however, the similarity to her mentor ended.

Where Bast Venor stood tall and feline, Panya was short and squat. Where Venor's feline features swept back into an almost regal mane of hair, Panya was rounded and scruffy, springs of hair exploding from her two thin plaits.

He'd rarely seen her beyond the confines of the Menagerie but when he had, she'd always looked hard-faced and serious and quickly melted away into the shadows.

"Panya was about to check the ponies' hooves. Why don't you help?" said Tamer Venor, "Leave your bag."

Panya hurried out of her pen clutching a slim tool, swept past them wordlessly and scurried back downstairs.

"Right, OK then," said Phyllo, determined to be confident. Ponies seemed OK. They were quite small if he remembered rightly. He dropped his bag just inside the pen gate and lumbered after Panya. By the time he'd shambled down the stairs and caught her up she was already in the pen, had one pony hoof clasped upside down between her thighs and was deftly picking out stones.

Phyllo bowled in after her and the ponies, who'd been standing about quite contentedly before, streamed away and bumped together to form a jittery pack at the back of the pen. The animal Panya was working on snatched its foot free and skittered away to join them. She glared briefly at Phyllo, all dark eyes and crinkled nose, then turned her back on him. She nodded her head deeply, heaved a great sigh and side-stepped over to the herd to stand very close to the same animal she'd been working on before.

Phyllo clanged the gate closed and Tamer Venor came to lean on the other side. Her expression was neutral, but Phyllo could feel the air of unspoken observation and a tangle of nerves grew in his stomach.

He had to show Tamer Venor he was capable. The tiger-stripe ponies weren't even as tall as he was. Cornering one was totally doable. He spread his arms out wide and took a step toward them.

The herd jittered and bounced against each other.

"I'll help you get one," he said confidently.

Panya glared at him and shook her head, then turned her back on him to huff another breath of air into the pony's mane.

"No really, I'm here to help," Phyllo insisted. Panya wouldn't be able to keep him at arm's length forever. He could see she'd had the place to herself in the past, but now there was no getting away from it, she'd have to share. They were both apprentices now.

Phyllo thought that he might as well start as he meant to go on and get straight in there. He was here to learn the magic, and all that huffing and puffing Panya was doing wasn't going to get them anywhere. He took a long step forward and the scales of his suit rubbed together in a rasp. The closest pony kicked out a back leg viciously.

Panya shuffled about with the herd, seemingly determined not to look at him. She ran one hand along the pony's back and then down its leg to grasp the fetlock.

It was sweltering in the suit. A bead of sweat rolled into Phyllo's eye, blurring his vision, but he didn't need to see Tamer Venor to know that she was watching. The kicky pony was still jiggling about, stamping its feet. If Phyllo could just get that one separated from the herd, he thought that the others would probably calm down. Panya didn't seem to be doing much about it. This was his moment to take charge.

He stepped forward again. "Ha," he said confidently. He was sure he'd seen someone do that with horses.

The nearest jumpy pony whinnied and reared up onto its hind legs, its forelegs whirling out in front. Now it was most definitely taller than Phyllo and the true solidness of its stout body came sharply into focus. Those legs might have been short, but they were muscular and strong.

Panya twisted around, but the pony's forelegs were whirling again, too far from Phyllo to reach him, but close enough to Panya to knock her sideways off her feet.

She hit the ground hard.

Other ponies in the herd reared and whinnied too.

Phyllo gawped at Panya, who had curled into a ball to avoid the trampling hooves, her hands tight over her head.

Horror froze him in place. They'd seemed like such gentle creatures, but now Panya was on the ground with the herd stampeding around her. He wanted to help, but at the same time just didn't know what to do.

Then Tamer Venor was in the middle of them and pulling Panya up from the ground. She grabbed Phyllo by his immobile arm and pulled at him too, dragging them both out of the gate.

It had all happened so fast. One moment, Phyllo had been sure that he knew what he was doing and the next, Venor had had to rescue them both. Shock lodged in his throat like a stone.

Venor sat Panya down on a barrel to examine her shoulder. "Can you move your arm?" she asked, feeling along the bones. Panya lifted it a little then winced.

"A-are you OK?" Phyllo stuttered. He couldn't quite believe how quickly his bravery had turned to disaster.

Panya glared at him.

"You have much to learn," Tamer Venor said evenly.

"I-I just wanted to show you that I wasn't scared. That I can do it."

"I do not wish to chase that from you, Phyllo. Fear does not prevent death, only life." She laid one hand on his shoulder. "But you must have knowledge to inform your actions. Only a fool dives in unknowing and unprotected."

Phyllo straightened his heavy jumpsuit, trying to draw Tamer Venor's attention to his preparations. Her eyes ran over him.

"Our animals are wondrous and various. Each has their own quirks and needs and magic. To imagine that one approach fits all would be a mistake and this borrowed coat will not keep you warm."

Phyllo squinted at her.

"Its true owner," she waved her hand up and down the jumpsuit, "Do you think it would be in the pony pen, grooming their hooves? No. The true owner of this coat would only have one reason to be in that pen. For its dinner."

Phyllo swallowed hard.

"Every move you made; every rasp of the scales sent a warning to our pony friends that a dangerous predator was amongst them, but of course, they would have smelled you first." She wrinkled her nose. "Come, Panya." She helped her to her feet, "Rest a while on your bunk and I will fetch balm for your bruises. I do not believe anything is broken."

They came past Phyllo and climbed the stairs, Panya holding herself stiffly and avoiding Phyllo's eyes.

Tamer Venor gave him a consoling nod. "Trust is the key to the Tamer's exchange and for that, you must be found trustworthy."

8
THE WHISPERERS

WHEN MORNING CAME it was the smell of coffee that Phyllo became aware of first. He rolled over in bed, lulled into consciousness by the rhythms of quiet conversation that drifted to him in the still air. The bed was unfamiliarly lumpy. He stretched out the ache in his back and peeled open one eye.

For one blissful moment, he'd completely forgotten where he'd gone to sleep and had expected to awake in the familiar comforts of the Confectionary, snuggled up in his bunk. Now he remembered. He was sleeping in a pen.

Phyllo huffed out a sigh.

As pens went, he supposed that it was quite a large one, probably just as big as the Confectionary's entire living space, and made all the more spacious by the lack of furniture. It nestled up in the iron ridged arch of the ceiling which, at this level, felt like being in a pigsty.

Boxes of animal act paraphernalia were stacked against one side, opposite his bed. If you could call it a bed. Really it was just a long lumpy pillow laid over what Phyllo suspected were packing crates and topped with an itchy blanket.

He'd tossed and turned for hours. Initially it was the prickly, hot discomfort of the Menagerie that had needled him, but then, whenever exhaustion had dragged him within touching distance of sleep, he'd been sucked back into awareness by stomping or snuffling or some other unidentifiable animal noise.

In particular, a low sort of purr had rumbled intermittently through the entire cabin. Phyllo had suspected that it was coming from the pen directly across from his own, at ground level. The pen that he knew contained a dragon.

It had been very hard to relax.

But, somewhere in the dead of night he *had* fallen asleep and now opened his eyes to rediscover the animal stall he was to call home for at least the next two months.

He unhooked his clothes from the board of pegs on the wall that was to serve as his wardrobe, got dressed and padded sheepishly along the mezzanine walkway to the pen between Panya's and Tamer Venor's.

It served as a common room of sorts, where they'd settled in the evening to eat odd food Phyllo hadn't really liked and for Panya to studiously ignore him. Mismatched rugs layered together to cover the floor and large robust pillows heaped to make seating. Books were stacked on untidy shelves and framed drawings and paintings of all kinds of animals jostled for place on the walls. Now Tamer Venor and Panya stood examining something on the table at the rear with their backs to him.

"Morning," said Phyllo quietly.

Tamer Venor turned and her eyes fell immediately to what he was wearing.

Phyllo looked down at himself. Heavy boots, silky flyers blues and his confectioner's jacket in its stripe of violet and lemon. He shrugged, slightly self-consciously.

"You look good enough to eat, which may not be to your advantage," she smiled, "but I like it better than the other suit. You are welcome, Phyllo. Please." She ushered him into their shared space and poured him a glass of bitter coffee. "How did you sleep?"

"Oh, OK," he lied, not wanting to complain.

"It is as Thoth has willed it," said Venor with a smile. Then she said to Panya, "Let us see what we have, although I think there isn't much. Mohareb was connected to me so I had no need, but to find another it will not be the case. We will need much more."

She opened the latch on a polished wooden box that stood alone on the table. It was about a foot tall with two even-sized doors, like a tiny, ornately carved wardrobe. When she opened them together, they folded out once, twice, three times, revealing a series of small drawers that curved to stand in a crescent. In the centre a mirror, whose silvered backing was dappled with age, glowed ethereally in a silver filigree frame. Animals of all kinds were depicted in the frame. Phyllo could pick out butterphants and ligers at the bottom gazing serenely out from open fields whilst birds and dragons soared amongst clouds at the top.

To either side a hundred tiny drawers or more were stacked in ordered columns.

"Hmm. What do we have?" Tamer Venor opened a drawer to one side. The face of it had a flying dragon inlaid in the dark wood.

She drew out two pewter candlestick holders, each with a Chinese dragon curled around it. Panya reached up to take them from her, added two butter yellow candles and set them either side of the mirror. Next a gauzy pouch, secured with ribbon at the neck. Inside four or five metallic feathers caught the light dully. Tamer Venor laid them between the candles. Lastly, she produced a photograph.

The familiar round of cabins and welcoming arch of the Circus of Wonder served as its backdrop. A much younger Tamer Venor in flying leathers sat arms folded and proud on the raised knee of a golden dragon. Phyllo had never seen anything like it before. It was at least twice the size of the formidable animal Phyllo had met in the Menagerie a few days previously, and where the dragon he'd seen was comparatively slender in its proportions, this beast was broad, with a full ruff of shining feather-like scales at its neck and an iridescent glow to its pelt that shone like fire.

"My Mohareb," she breathed and placed the photo reverentially to rest against the mirror.

There was nothing else.

She sighed then said, "This is my altar, Phyllo. Every Beast Whisperer has one and so shall you. It is the means by which we will locate the dragon then be transported to its location. Most inconveniently, I regret each altar can take only one. This means you will need to build and activate your own to come with me. It is no small task, but you will not need one as comprehensive as my own. To create such a thing would take much more time than we have." She drew Phyllo's attention to the images of animals on the face of each drawer, every one different.

"Each drawer holds the artefacts that helped me to align with a particular creature, all alignments strengthening the altar's magical power over all. Some are more difficult to achieve than others, as you might guess, and, although we seek to capture a dragon, to ask you to align with such a beast so early would be most unduly challenging."

Phyllo gazed mutely at the altar, glad that her expectations of him were much lower.

"So, if not the dragon we seek, then what?" She allowed Phyllo a small smile. "You must achieve at least one connection to activate your altar and travel alongside me. Every Whisperer is able to align with one creature more readily than any other. This animal is your *familiar*, a spirit that comes more naturally than the rest. With a true familiar the link can be empathetic, telepathic even. You must find yours."

"So how?" Tamer Venor gave him a questioning look, "For now, you will look out for wildlife and try to notice animals that notice you. See what draws your attention and make a collection of natural items that pique your interest. This is where you begin."

"OK," said Phyllo. That seemed doable.

"Mindset is key. Your senses must become razor-sharp so you can experience them from the consciousness of any other creature, put yourself in their minds, do you see? You must tune in." She pinched her fingers together. "There is much for you to learn."

Phyllo didn't doubt it.

"You cannot assist me until you are able to form a link with an animal and are able to understand its thoughts and intentions intuitively." She considered him. "I wonder, have you ever had a pet?"

"Well, we have Glumberry," he offered.

"The *Rotundum Loquibis*. Yes, he is a most interesting specimen. More useful to our purpose however would be a creature unable to voice its feelings so eloquently."

Phyllo didn't suppose much intuition was needed when Glumberry was quite capable of talking. He shook his head.

Tamer Venor shrugged. "And so, we both have work to do, it seems. I must find a way to locate our dragon and you, my friend, must travel the road to building an altar of your own. Come." She strode out of the stall and along to Phyllo's, where she rooted around amongst the boxes, haphazardly knocking containers over and pulling out their contents. Her random messiness made Phyllo twitch.

She drew out a tin that looked like it ought to hold biscuits, but turned out to contain one final vial of *'Doctor Mandrill's Monkey Wormer'*.

"Here." She removed the tube of wormer, banged out the dust inside the tin and gave it to him, then produced a large floppy notebook and gave that to him too. "And this. Your Shadow Book."

Phyllo flicked through the pages, hoping for some insight, but found that they were disappointingly blank.

"We are a team and each must play a different role. Panya already has much experience. For now, she will tend to the animals and I will supervise so that when we must leave, she will have the confidence to work alone. For my part, I must build our gateway if we are to locate a bull and you, Phyllo, you will help Panya with unskilled tasks as her workload is great. Mucking out, fetching water and such, but not today. Today I want you to go to the Whispering Wood and *feel*."

Phyllo frowned at her.

She nodded at him. "The male of the species is referred to as a bull, the female as a cow."

Phyllo blinked uncertainly. "It was really more the *feeling* part," he said.

"Ah yes," she smiled at his confusion, "Every sense must

be honed. In your practice you will focus on one at a time. Today you will notice how what you *see* affects how you feel. The magic of Beast Whispering is rooted in this connection." She punctuated her words with enthusiastic hand gestures that reminded Phyllo of Signor Volante, but her rolling 'r's didn't belong in Italian. They placed her heritage in Arabia.

Phyllo nodded without comprehension.

Tamer Venor straightened her back and looked over his shoulder, into her own thoughts. "You must learn to fully experience the moment. Yes. Most importantly, today, you must *see*. Go into the wood and see, really *see*." Her eyes snapped back to him. "What is the weather? How does that affect how things look? Examine the trees for patterns. Be still and observe. What life can you see?" She pinched her fingers together again and squinted at him. "What colour is the earth? What shape are the clouds? What plant life? What does that tell you? Witness. Take notes. *Feel*. How does it make you feel?"

Phyllo fidgeted with the book. "I've been in the woods lots of times," he said, "I could probably just make some notes here."

"No. This will be seen by the Phyllo of today." She clapped him on the shoulder. "When you think you have seen it all, change your view, climb or lie down and look again. What has changed? What difference does it make?"

"And make notes," said Phyllo, waggling the book.

"Exactly." Tamer Venor smiled benignly down at him.

Like the dragon, she was a curious mixture of things that Phyllo couldn't quite get comfortable with. On one hand, she was exceedingly welcoming and humble, so much so that Phyllo often felt as if she was putting his comfort ahead of everything else.

She bowed to him regularly, almost as if she believed him to be the most important person in the room. Phyllo suspected that her intention was to make him feel at home. Instead, it kept him perpetually on edge, wondering when he might see the other side of what he felt sure was a double-edged sword. The side he'd glimpsed in the Ringmaster's cabin.

She was the master of the Menagerie. She had magic beyond his grasp and everything about the way she held herself elevated her far beyond his lowly position in the troupe. Combine that with those golden feline eyes and lion's mane of hair and she could easily have passed for some kind of Egyptian Goddess.

Phyllo worried that at any moment, the benevolent façade might shatter.

He nodded obediently. "All right. I'm sure I can manage that."

"The alignment begins with an incantation. I'll write it down, but you must memorise it. Find a place where you can relax your body and your mind. Repeat the incantation and open your heart to learn. Breathe." Venor herself took in a great deep breath that inflated her to stand even more proudly than before. She gave the long blink of a cat and looked down at Phyllo serenely.

She tapped on the monkey wormer tin. "You will build an altar of your own. Keep your items of interest in here. This is where you begin."

It didn't seem like a very auspicious start. Phyllo looked past Tamer Venor out onto the edge of the mezzanine. "Will I be going with Panya?" he asked uneasily, "It's just that she doesn't really seem to like me."

Tamer Venor tossed her head back and laughed. "Panya

doesn't like anybody, so don't imagine yourself special," she said and then added as an afterthought, "Unless you have four legs. She'd like you well enough then."

Phyllo hadn't expected a warm welcome, but the chance of a truce would have been nice.

Tamer Venor puffed out a sigh. "Panya came from the streets. I found her sleeping in a broken drain with a family of hyrax. They'd shown her where to find food and shelter and it was more kindness than she'd ever received from any human. I was without doubt that she had the Whispering gift. A toddling child who'd stayed alive by learning from rodents. She was an irregular, even by charmed standards and took some persuading to come away. In the end it was Mohareb that did it."

"The dragon you used to have?"

"Then he was still just a calf, but when Panya saw how we communicated with each other, she knew we were the same, in a way. She recognised Mohareb as my familiar, just as she had experienced the hyrax as her own."

Tamer Venor's eyes glazed in a sparkling shine. "We are as family," she said.

9
THE WHISPERING WOOD

WITH THE TIN and book tucked under his arm, Phyllo made off across the open grass. It was rather a relief to get out of the Menagerie. Swelteringly hot and smelly, he'd felt increasingly uncomfortable all morning, not least for his unwelcome encroachment upon Panya's home turf.

The Whispering Wood crowded to the north, the spires of Honeyholde distantly peeking out above its canopy. The closer he got, the larger the forest loomed until eventually it blocked out all else. He tried to see it with new eyes.

Trees. A heck of a lot of trees. Just like every other time he'd been there.

He opened his notebook. On the very first page Tamer Venor had written down the incantation he was to learn. He cleared his throat and read:

By ray and beam,
By dell and mound,
By sip and stink,
By sight and sound,
Let east meet west,

Let all be seen
Of creatures known and in-between.
Lady of the Elder bow
Reveal to me, thy servant, now.

Phyllo looked tentatively up from the book, but nothing appeared to have changed. He sighed and stomped on, his boots slashing dark lines into the long grass.

Beams of morning sunlight peeped through occasional gaps in the cloud and bounced from the treetops. The leaves were beginning to turn. Brilliant green giving way to lime and yellow, to gold and vermillion. The trees still wore their summer clothes for now and he watched the lick of a breeze brush through branches, one tree to the next. Was that the sort of thing he was supposed to notice? He paused to jot down a note on the rough paper of his scrapbook.

Wind from the east ruffled leaves, but they have not fallen yet.

He tucked the pencil behind his ear and wondered how long it would take for autumn to slip into winter and for the trunks and spikey branches to be revealed. Was that usually November? December? It was an event that happened every year without fail, but he'd never really taken the time to notice it, not properly.

Who did?

Well, apparently now he would and, determined to see everything, Phyllo concentrated hard on his surroundings. A trampled earth path led in amongst the trees, and walking under the leaf canopy he saw that the quality of the light was different. The same day, the same sun, but now the daylight was filtered into patches. Some leaves were lit like brilliant stained glass while others hung dowdy and greying in the shadows. He made another note.

Bright impressive colours appear in the sunlight. Sometimes the light shines through, not just on.

He knew that their colours had not changed in reality, just the way he was seeing them, just the way that they were being presented. An airy feeling of hope filled his chest. He felt sure this was good. It seemed like just the sort of thing he ought to be noticing.

In this part of the wood the tree trunks were as broad around their middle as he was, their silvery bark smooth for the most part, but with horizontal lines that wove through it like the lumpy threads in linen. Phyllo ran his fingers over it. It was like a natural fabric and Phyllo saw it suddenly as wrapping that protected the tree beneath. Another layer of clothing.

You'll still be dressed, even when the leaves have fallen, he said to himself and made another note.

He wandered on, looking at everything as hard as he could. The stone speckled earth he walked on. The tiny leaves of bushes that trembled all over at the slightest disturbance. He let his fingers brush against them and noticed the springy stems that let the leaves jiggle. On he walked, the canopy above his head getting thicker, the density of the forest increasing around him.

A sudden movement caught his eye.

He'd been watching the effect of a gust of wind, but this movement was other, unconnected and away to one side.

He stopped and stared into the undergrowth. The bushes in the movement's general vicinity wavered, as if drawing to a halt, the swell of energy melting away. Phyllo stood statue still, watching and waiting, but nothing else moved.

If he was honest, he'd been hoping for an animal. After all, he had to find his familiar somehow and that was the part of this mission that seemed the hardest of all, if not impossible. To have discovered it so early would have been nothing short of miraculous.

He sniffed and returned his attention to plant life and noted that now the species of tree were becoming mixed. There was a new kind in a triangular form, their long thin branches drooping down to graze the floor. Leaves shaped like tulips perched in lime green cups along their length. Fat beetles with shining ruby-red shells scuttled between them, scooping out aphids. He watched their thin angular legs and round clumpy feet transport them along the branch, but they paid no attention to Phyllo at all. *Not beetles then*, he thought to himself.

Leaves shuddered in his peripheral vision. A twig snapped.

Phyllo craned around to look. Was there actually something over there? Here the undergrowth was so dense that animals could easily be scuttling about unseen. He waited and it felt as though the Whispering Wood was waiting too.

"Ridiculous," he mumbled and stomped on.

The gaps between trees broadened into a clearing and Phyllo suddenly recognised a spot that he and Roly had visited many times in the past. Huge gnarly trees loomed like giants around the clear scoop of a dell. Their makeshift swing from last year still dangled from a branch that reached out over the best and deepest drop.

It wasn't that he'd forgotten it was there exactly, just that his mind had been somewhere else. Now a buzz of delight ran through him. This place had been the scene of many joyful afternoons, where he and his brother, and occasionally Dodo, had built camps, raced around with sticks for swords and grazed knees. Being there alone felt odd.

He walked the circumference and examined the trees, trying to see them anew.

The trees were colossal and old. Even he, Roly and Dodo all holding hands together had not been able to encircle any one of them. Roots bulged from the ground at their bases, knobbly fingers reaching into the earth, their cracked knuckles brimming with moss. He examined the bark of a favourite for patterns. Vertical lines swept up in ragged grooves. They flowed like a stream around rocks, swirling around stumps and mysterious bare patches, perhaps where a branch had come off. One part looked rather like a mouth and then above it he saw a nose. Phyllo stepped back to see it better. Yes, now that he really looked there were eyes too and fine leafy sprouts that could easily be eyebrows.

He delighted at the discovery. A face in the tree! He sat down on a root at its base, a much-used perch smoothed by time into a comfortable round, and looked out over the dell.

Beyond the leaf-litter and rust-coloured earth, he saw the carefree off-seasons of his past. He and Roly swashbuckling across the dell. The innumerable camps, branchy wigwams and collapsing lean-tos. Their adventurers' home from home. The dell that was always the last place all around to be touched by rain, protected as it was by the interwoven canopy above.

A breeze rippled through the leaf canopy, but it did not touch Phyllo. The huge old tree funnelled it away and protected him in its familiar snug embrace. He pulled out his Shadow Book and made some more notes. Was this the sort of thing Tamer Venor had meant? Things that only he could see?

He wasn't sure how long he sat there playing memories in his mind's eye, but came back to himself with fingers jammed into the dirt and a pang of longing in his chest. Subconsciously he'd expected to return with Roly again this year. Long irresponsible hours now replaced with the pressure of the next apprenticeship. Things had changed. He was no longer free to just be. The Ringmaster had insisted once more that he *become*.

He huffed out a sigh. All he'd become was lost in memories. He shook his head and decided that a go on the swing might help clear the fug.

The swing itself was a foot long piece of fallen branch, strung by a rope from the highest point Roly had dared to climb to the year before.

Standing in the hollow, he found he could reach it at full stretch, when only last year they'd needed an extra piece of branch to capture it. He walked it up the slope to the launch point, tucked the makeshift seat behind his knees and reversed as far as the rope would allow. He took a deep breath and, heart rising in a flutter, lifted his feet to let the rope take his weight.

The swing creaked ominously but held and he swung away, first dipping low over the ground and then out over the cut-out of the hollow and climbing. He laughed at the rush of it. Then he was on the return swing and spinning. He lifted his legs and leaned back to stop himself from colliding with the bank. Low over the ground he swished, then back again for another pass.

In comparison to the terror of the trapeze it was joyful.

Eventually, the motion back and forth slowed to a stop and he just hung there a while, hugging the rope. It was certainly a change in viewpoint, just like Tamer Venor had asked, but the change he felt was less about what he could see than it was about how different he'd become.

Last year the swing had given him a thrill of fear, his phobia of heights being tweaked just enough to make him squeal, but not so badly as to reduce him to jelly. He and Roly had laughed and shrieked. Now it seemed so much tamer and smaller. In reality, this place was just the same, it was he who had changed. Phyllo wasn't sure if that was good or bad, but it stuck in his throat enough to make him wish he'd remembered to bring a drink.

How much time was enough time to spend there?

He scanned around for animals and resolved to stay still until he'd seen at least one.

He scoured through the bushes, although most looked even more solid from above, and up into the treetops. Birds went about their business distantly and a couple of squirrels were in and out of a hole in the trunk. None came close enough for Phyllo to stare meaningfully into their eyes, as he imagined he ought to, and before long the knobbly seat of the swing was jabbing much too uncomfortably into his backside. He called it a day.

Phyllo was almost at the forest edge when he realised that he'd not put anything into the tin. He set about hunting for items of interest and found a twig that reminded him of the forked branch he and Roly had used last year to capture the swing, only in miniature. This seemed to reflect his experience in the wood. Then a fat yellow catkin he thought remarkable for still being in perfect condition, and a fluffy white feather, which was just quite nice. He stashed them in the tin and carried it back with a little more reverence.

Beyond the cocoon of the Whispering Wood the air seemed thinner and sounds drifted to him from the Circus of Wonder encampment. The slow rhythm of a hammer gave him a beat to walk by and soon he was back in the huddle of cabins and walking toward a figure he recognised to be Schlepper.

Schlepper had just emerged from the Ringmaster's quarters and was bouncing along on the Perambulator Mark IVs toward his own. A fat golden dog trotted behind him.

Phyllo hadn't known he owned a dog and sped up to reach them. As he got closer, he saw that the dog had an unexpected kind of metallic sheen to it and that it walked on legs curiously similar to Schlepper's – concertina springs that jiggled it jauntily along. When Phyllo saw that its body was boxy with thin handles on the top, he realised that, despite the appealing canine build of its mechanical face and a wagging tail, it wasn't a dog at all.

"Good morning, Phyllo," said Schlepper, pausing to allow him to catch up.

"Hi," said Phyllo crouching down to pat the 'dog' on its shiny head. The articulated tail wagged a little faster. "Who's this?"

"Meet Stanley, my odd-job companion and self-propelled toolbox."

Phyllo chucked. "He's brilliant. Did you make him too?"

"I did." Schlepper nodded humbly. "We have been helping the Ringmaster. I have a certain knack when it comes to machinery and the Ringmaster is a busy man. *The Machine* is complex and maintenance is required. It's an ongoing job."

"Oh, I see." Phyllo's eyes slid to the Ringmaster's cabin.

"On his way to Honeyholde," said Schlepper, following Phyllo's eyes, "Another meeting at the Club. Can't seem to get enough of the place, Phyllo. Excited to tell the Brigadier about his latest venture, in any case. The acquisition of a male Sand Dragon, no less, and I understand you are on *Team Capture?*" Schlepper raised his eyebrows questioningly.

Phyllo nodded.

"Oh, bad luck."

Phyllo snorted in surprise and Schlepper grinned impishly.

"If I were the Ringmaster, I might not be so quick to broadcast it, however. As I understand it, the Sand Dragon is an endangered species and there's nothing the hunters of the Club relish more than the capture of an endangered species. He's courting competition."

"I suppose he is," agreed Phyllo. That was the last thing they needed.

"Starting your search in the Whispering Wood?" Schlepper looked back the way Phyllo had come.

"That would be handy, wouldn't it?" said Phyllo, "No. That was just me starting my apprenticeship."

"I see."

"Getting back to nature."

"How was it?"

Phyllo thought for a moment. "Unexpected."

10

THE PANYA PERSPECTIVE

Phyllo perched on the edge of his bed and laid the tin collection out on his table.

A fork-shaped stick, a catkin and a feather. Not much of a haul. Then he remembered the lucky rabbit's foot and dug that from his pocket to put that with them too.

Panya was ferreting about in her own stall next door and Phyllo thought that if he could actually get her to talk to him, she might be able to offer some advice. He called to her through a gap in the slats.

"Panya? Do you have an altar, for your familiar I mean?"

She stilled to turn and find his eyes in the haphazardly gapped wall. She folded her arms, jutted out her chin and raised her eyebrows to ask him, '*Why?*' It wasn't friendly, but at least she was engaging.

"I just wondered what sort of things you had on it? I mean, I picked up some bits and bobs today, but it doesn't really feel all that good." He pulled what he hoped was an endearing smile.

She pursed her lips.

"Would you have a look?" he ventured, "Please?"

She took a deep, sulky breath, but then scurried around to his side of the wall. Panya only ever seemed to move at one speed. Always busy. Always purposeful. Always in a hurry. She stopped at a distance two or three arm lengths away, her dark eyes as mistrustful as ever and gestured for permission to touch Phyllo's things.

"Be my guest," he said and backed down onto his bed to get out of the way.

Panya picked up the empty tin, turned it upside down and set it at the back of the table, against the wall. She then took up the lid, examined the inside and buffed up a portion of it with the end of her sleeve. She stood it on the upturned tin to lean against the wall and shrugged.

Phyllo could see that together they had created a kind of altar and that the inside of the lid had a dull shine to it in the spot she'd polished. "Oh, I see. Is that my mirror? Do you think that I could shine it up to be better?"

Panya did not answer, but scurried over to the boxes on the far side of the room, where she located a couple of plain candles and came back to stand one either side of the tin. One immediately fell over and she gave it a little dismissive waft with her hand, indicating that that was Phyllo's problem.

"Candles, yes, I see. I can do something with that, I expect."

Panya didn't bother to acknowledge him and Phyllo shuffled on the bed, not quite able to arrange his limbs comfortably.

She picked up Phyllo's stick and turned it in her fingers for examination.

"Ah yes. That reminded me of a bigger one I had, another time," said Phyllo, feeling slightly foolish.

She nodded almost imperceptibly and put it on the upturned tin plinth.

"That there is a perfect catkin," said Phyllo introducing the next item, "and that feather…" He stopped himself from saying *is nice and fluffy*. Panya's expression was much too serious for that. The rabbit's foot seemed like safer ground. "And that's a lucky rabbit foot. A genuine left hind one, the certificate said."

Panya's usually dark face paled and her eyebrows crept up toward her scalp. Her expression rolled from surprise to shock, then horror and finally disgust. She clamped her teeth so tightly together it seemed that even if she had been willing speak, she'd never have been able to get out the words.

It didn't look good, but Phyllo swallowed hard and persevered. "Um. It said it was harvested at full moon by a—"

Panya's eyes snapped to him and the prickles of a big mistake stabbed at Phyllo's neck. She kicked angrily at the little table, sending his collection flying, then threw both hands up as if protecting herself from his very presence, spun on her heel and clanged away down the metal stairs, leaving Phyllo gaping.

OK, that hadn't gone quite how he'd hoped, but at least she'd shown him how to set things out.

He gathered up his collection and examined the tin. Its octagonal shape made for quite an attractive platform really and, as the bottom face had no printing on it, its monkey-worming heritage wasn't quite so obvious upside down. He replaced it on the table then buffed at the inside of the lid with the cuff of his jacket. Pretty quickly he'd managed to get the whole thing up to a cloudy sheen that reflected his face with misty magnifying distortion. Phyllo thought that if he spent a little time on it he could probably make it quite good.

The sound of footsteps coming back up the stairs signalled the inevitable approach of Tamer Venor. No doubt she'd want to know how he'd upset Panya this time and, in all honesty, Phyllo didn't know what he was going to tell her, other than it being something to do with the rabbit's foot.

She nodded appreciatively at his altar efforts when he'd finished explaining.

"The natural world is commonly abused, Phyllo," Tamer Venor said kindly, "Only now that you are learning the way of the Whisperer will you comprehend the full scale of it.

"It is true, many preparations, herbs and potions have meaningful helpful effects. It is also true that many do not. Unscrupulous traders, focusing on the coin in their pocket, have hunted wondrous species to destruction, harvesting body parts that actually have no medical nor magical properties at all. Superstitions and outdated beliefs perpetuated for profit.

"The majestic unicorn and rhinoceros hunted almost to extinction for their horns, which are no better in actuality than hoof clippings. The great white shark hunted and terminally maimed for a fin that offers no healing properties whatsoever – its scarcity propelling it into even greater demand. It has become a symbol of wealth to afford such abominations and it is a tragedy."

Phyllo hadn't seen the rabbit's foot in this way at all when he'd purchased it. "Th-There was a certificate," he stammered, "I got the impression it was official. You know, like they did it all the time."

Tamer Venor frowned. "They *do* do it all the time, Phyllo, but that does not make it right. A Beast Whisperer is at one with nature, not stealing from it, not taking the limbs of small animals to make powerless amulets."

"I didn't!"

"Or supporting those who make money from doing so."

Phyllo flailed around for reason. "But isn't it a sort of a rodent?" he said desperately, hoping for a vermin angle. He realised too late how ill-advised that was.

"No, it is not," admonished Tamer Venor, the tone of her voice hardening, "And if it were, do you think that would make Panya any less furious, given the creature who saved her life on the streets? The Cape Hyrax, Phyllo, known to some as the Rock Rabbit. Any life traded for a useless luck token is wasted. You must ask yourself how lucky it was for the rabbit."

Phyllo shrank away from her. "I, er, yes, I see."

"If you carry pointless lopped off bits of animal in your pocket, you'll never be worthy of trust."

Tamer Venor bristled and Phyllo felt thoroughly chastised. How could he not have seen how inappropriate it was?

"It is our way to work with nature. Not to destroy, but only to enhance. All creatures make an impact on their surroundings. Aim to make yours a positive one."

"I'm an idiot," Phyllo mumbled but Tamer Venor laid a hand on his shoulder. "The only thing that is humiliating is helplessness," she said, "and in opening yourself up to learn you begin to redress the debt. Look forward, Phyllo. All we have is now."

He resolved to do better.

"I see you have made inroads in the creation of your altar at least. Reuse. Repurpose. Recycle. Already you have the right spirit. Don't look so dispirited. A person who makes no mistakes learns nothing, hmm?"

Beyond the mezzanine balcony an odd noise came from one of the lower pens.

"Panya is cleaning out the capuchins," said Tamer Venor, "Why don't you go down to observe."

Phyllo immediately got to his feet, but she held him back. "Your enthusiasm continues to be admirable, but go gently. I would suggest taking a bit less initiative today."

Giggling came up from the ground floor pen. Panya? He didn't think she knew *how* to laugh.

"A contented mind is a hidden treasure," said Tamer Venor, reading Phyllo's expression, "Lost with the animals is her paradise found. Go," she waved him on, "Now might be a good moment to show her you are willing to learn."

He waited outside the pen this time, instead of bowling in uninvited. Beyond the chicken-wired gate, Panya swept clean a platform that lodged amongst a small huddle of trees. Trees? Phyllo stepped back to compare this pen to its neighbouring stall.

Initially the ceiling height was the same, but somehow beyond the distance where Phyllo knew their upstairs stalls to end, the roof space opened up to allow for a number of trees. He knew for a fact that the cabin wall should be much closer and the roof much lower. It looked both normal and completely wrong.

It turned out that Panya wasn't laughing. Instead, she made a kind of soft *chucking* sound and a small, entirely white-headed capuchin in a gold brocade waistcoat swung smoothly down from a branch to patter onto the platform. It made the same *chucking* noise. Panya put down the brush and opened her hand to reveal a grape which the monkey took, then sat down to peel. Others gambolled around her on the floor, picking through the litter she'd swept off the platform.

"Cute," said Phyllo, which got her attention but when Panya saw him, her expression immediately fell.

"Can I come in?" he asked, "I promise I won't do anything mad."

She glared at him for a moment then sighed and pointed to a broom by the gate as she turned away. Phyllo grabbed it and sidled in. The capuchins on the ground rippled away from him into cover, but one brave one with tufted brown ears and a purple waistcoat edged back to pick at his shoelaces. It didn't take the little monkey long to find out they were inedible and, upon this discovery, to sit back on his haunches and screech.

Phyllo's hair stood on end. They might have been small, but they had sharp little teeth and, Phyllo'd noticed, an unpleasant tendency to overreact. He held his breath and looked to Panya, just mastering the urge to shoo it away.

She stared impassively back, as if weighing up whether to help him or not. She did not move, but made her soft *chucking* sound again and nodded meaningfully.

Phyllo knew it was unhelpful, but the virtually teenage boy within was not happy at all about this power she wielded over him. She was much smaller than he was, and taking instruction from Panya felt like being bossed around by his little sister. A desperate desire to prove himself snaked about in defiance at being told what to do.

He had to get to grips with it. Trying to assert himself in the pony pen had been disastrous, he could see that now.

Panya made the noise again, then turned away. She wasn't going to help him if he didn't try soon.

"Chuck, chuck, chuck." Phyllo tried the sound himself,

the shape of it wrong in his mouth. It got the attention of several of the monkeys on the floor.

Panya tucked her chin into her chest and made the sound again – it was lower than Phyllo had managed. He tried again and this time the monkeys started closing in. He wasn't especially keen on that, but Panya was. She smirked, not bothering to hide it before looking away. The one with a white face dropped to the floor then climbed her trouser leg and dipped a skinny hand into her pocket. It came away with a nugget of dried fruit.

"Cheeky," breathed Phyllo.

Panya reached into a pouch around her neck and gave Phyllo a handful of the dried fruit too.

"Aw thanks."

She rolled her eyes, then took some from the pouch to place very obviously in her own pockets. Already another capuchin on the floor was standing on its hind legs, tapping at her pockets from the outside. They knew where she'd put it, Panya had deliberately shown them.

The tufty-eared monkey by Phyllo's foot tugged at his laces again and without really meaning to, he jerked his foot away. Tufty screeched and jumped back. Panya sighed heavily then began to move with deliberately small slow steps toward a second platform, *chucking* as she went. She pointed to the mess on the ground and Phyllo got the idea that he should sweep it up. He looked down at Tufty, who still watched him beadily, sharp little teeth protruding over his thin bottom lip.

"OK, little guy," Phyllo said quietly, "The fruit is going in my pockets, see? I'm going to sweep the floor. Nice and slow."

He deposited the fruit and took a step forward. Tufty jumped back.

"It's OK. No problem. Chuck, chuck, chuck." He looked up to see Panya watching him.

"A frightened monkey is an aggressive monkey, am I right?"

She flicked her head in what Phyllo took to be confirmation. The capuchin now dangling off her boiler suit fished a piece of apple from her pocket and stuffed it straight into its mouth.

"But a monkey that thinks it's getting one over on you is a very happy monkey indeed," Phyllo concluded and popped a piece of the fruit into his own mouth with a grin.

Panya's hard little face softened. She was finding him amusing despite herself, Phyllo thought. At last, he was winning her over. Then she produced an empty tube of Dr Mandrill's Monkey Wormer from her chest pocket and held it out to show him.

Why was she showing him that? Then suddenly he could taste something other than apple.

Panya bit at her lip, but it was too late to spit it out.

"Ugh."

She definitely laughed then.

A weird gritty slime stuck to the roof of his mouth. He grimaced and tried to get it out with a finger once Panya had turned away. It was disgusting.

He started sweeping to take his mind off it, making the soft *chucking* noise again, and then tried not to freak out when one of the capuchins started climbing his leg. Sharp little monkey claws stabbed through his trousers and scraped at his skin as it hoisted itself up to hang on the back of his jacket.

While Panya worked on, seemingly unaffected regardless of how many monkeys dangled from her thick overalls, Phyllo squeaked and winced with every new scrabbling simian. He was fast realising that the silky blues were completely impractical, their comfy softness offering zero protection. Suddenly Panya's mannish overalls held a much greater appeal.

The monkey with tufty ears skittered away to return with a walnut which he gave to Panya. She made a new lower noise which Phyllo took for gratitude. He tried it himself. Then the same monkey came to Phyllo with a gift for him too. A single heavy key.

"What's this?" said Phyllo, surprised.

Panya squinted at it.

Tufty the monkey *chucked*.

"What did he say?" Phyllo asked, but Panya shrugged. He guessed there was only so much shared language.

Phyllo could feel a memory fighting its way to the surface. A monkey and a key. Then he'd got it.

"He pinched it from Bain," said Phyllo, "I saw him do it that first day we were here. You know that day there was, er, a bit of a breakout."

Panya rolled her eyes.

11
BEEN THERE, DUNG THAT

THEIR EVENING MEAL was a kind of spicy bean stew that Phyllo gobbled down despite its unfamiliar flavours. He'd hoped to collapse onto his bed to digest it, after what had been an exhausting day, but it became clear pretty quickly that this was not to be. Dinner was just a break in the never-ending roster of chores.

The larger animals especially needed to have a little extra care in the evening and Phyllo was dragged in to help with the inevitable wheelbarrow hauling. Poo. There was a heck of a lot of poo to deal with in the Menagerie and the biggest producers needed additional maintenance if they weren't to be overwhelmed.

Phyllo closed his eyes to let the furry trunk of Manana pat at his face and sniff him over. The butterphant puffed air into his ear and skimmed along his collar, tickling his neck.

"Here, Manana." Phyllo offered up a peanut still in its shell.

Manana sneezed at it in a manner which Phyllo took be contempt.

"Yeah well, that's all there is, so suck it up."

Manana plucked the nut from his palm and tossed it into his mouth.

Phyllo gave him a pat and moved farther into the Butterphant pen, forking up dung and transferring it to his wheelbarrow. Manana shuffled around to keep him within trunk-sniffing distance. Tamer Venor had been right about the necessity for keeping food locked up. If the butterphants could, they'd have eaten all day long. Manana sucked at Phyllo's hair with the tip of his trunk.

"Nope, pretty sure there aren't any chocolate mice in there either," he said ducking away. The male butterphant in particular liked to give Phyllo the once over. Phyllo suspected it was unable to forget his one-time ability to supply its favourite treat.

Phyllo scooped up another warm pat of poo and dropped it into the barrow, and a splatter escaped to land on his jacket.

"Brilliant," he breathed and Manana exhaled peanut shell bits into his face. Too tired and too slow to duck, he felt them bounce off his forehead. "Also brilliant," he said.

The barrow was about as full as he could get it and still have enough strength to roll it along, so he backed out of the pen, pushed it outside and around to the rear of their cabin. The dung heap had already been established another fifty yards or so away. He tipped his contribution out at its edge.

Phyllo paused to pick at the muck on his jacket and managed to dislodge some shell, but only smeared the brown splat. "Crackers," he said with a huff, and noting the additional dung on his boots, wheeled the barrow around to trudge back into the Menagerie. This was not the image of success he'd been hoping to achieve.

Back inside Panya was no longer in the butterphant pen and he realised she must have moved on to their final job; the dragon's den. He'd been instructed to interact with the dragon as much as possible, whenever there was someone else there to supervise, so if Panya was in there, he had to go in.

He paused at the gate feeling conflicted. He really *wanted* to work with the dragon, was excited to even. He wanted to win this apprenticeship. He wanted to show everyone he was worthy, but for Barnum's sake, it was a dragon. A genuine, enormous, ferocious, spike-toothed, fire-breathing dragon.

He tried to breathe away the hammering in his chest, then strained at the spring-loaded pin and manoeuvred it back. It took his full body weight to heft the gate open and manhandle the barrow inside. Panya clattered about in the darkness beneath the mezzanine, shadows flickering from an unseen light to lick along the ground and peter out to nothing in the illuminated outer pen.

Phyllo sidled along the wall. His eyes were trained on the void, scouring for signs of the dragon itself. He wished he could wear the dragon hide suit, but also couldn't help wondering how kindly the dragon would take to him sporting a relative's skin. On balance, he had to concede, he was likely better off without it. Phyllo craned to see further into the darkness. The dragon's proximity dried his throat and he swallowed hard.

At least he had Panya. She might not have been his first pick for a bodyguard, but she knew the animals well enough to be allowed inside alone. Speed – that was the key to this particular cleaning job. He turned to shovel at the mess of blackened straw and dung.

Phyllo's brief was to be Panya's shadow and help where

he could, when he wasn't working on finding his familiar. As the newest member of the team, it was inevitable that his tasks would be menial, he got that, but shovelling poo was becoming his trademark activity. He puffed out yet another sigh, which was also becoming a bit of a habit, he knew. The sound of it triggered eye-rolling in Panya, which was extra annoying, but why would anyone expect him to like it? Phyllo was trying to prove himself capable of magical talent, not stink up the place. He dug up the old bedding and hefted it into his barrow.

From behind he heard the sounds of Panya dragging stuff about and worked his way across the outer yard of the pen to where a heap of bones stood out, striped and white in the gloom: evidence of Thamineh's last meal. He grappled them one at a time into the barrow, glad that he hadn't had to go into the inner sanctum to find them. That was one good thing about the dragon, it would kick the larger items of waste out into the pen for its human maids to clear away.

An uncomfortable wave of pins and needles rolled over Phyllo's skin and a creeping itch scrabbled at his neck. It was the sensation he'd come to associate with the dragon watching him and with it came an intense impression of not being welcome.

Panya dragged more things from the den depths and Phyllo hurried to move across the outer area, keeping his eyes down, scooping and rolling his barrow along. He wanted her to hurry up so that they could get out of there. He reached the far wall and carried on in his circular sweep to work his way back to the gate. It was then that he noticed.

Crouched and still, Thamineh had come out from the depths and stolen forward to the very edge of the shadows. She scrutinized Phyllo through half closed eyes.

Her nostrils were dilated and twitched as she took in every inch of him, from his suddenly gaping mouth down to the dung-filled barrow. She was not quite out in the open, but very definitely between Phyllo and the gate, her rumbling purr of a growl rattling Phyllo's teeth.

Phyllo squeaked and his eyes stretched as wide as saucers. Then a clattering drew his attention away from the dragon to the mezzanine walkway on the other side of the cabin. Panya had dropped her bucket to the metallic floor and was staring down at him. She was up on the mezzanine, not in the dragon den at all. She broke eye contact and ran, the wrong way, and disappeared from view.

Phyllo's eyes swivelled in his frozen body back to the dragon.

Thamineh lowered her head to glare at Phyllo on his own eye level. Smoke huffed from her nostrils.

The dragon didn't move, but at the same time he saw it lunge toward him, flames flying from its mouth. Phyllo's mind swam and he staggered backward. Sweat broke on his neck and he reeled to move around behind the barrow.

He looked again at the dragon and saw that it still crouched in the same position, staring intently. Phyllo blinked and the dragon opened its terrible jaws and roared. Hot breath and ash blew Phyllo's hair back. Its amber eyes burned into Phyllo's and he felt a question hanging there.

You dared to enter my lair?

Phyllo's jaw flapped as he tried to find the words to excuse himself. "I, er—" His mouth dried to dust.

Crack! The snap of Tamer Venor's whip split the air and Phyllo's eyes shot back to the gate to find her there – the most welcome sight he'd ever seen.

"*Waqef!*" Venor yelled, cracking her whip again and the dragon lumbered around to face her.

"Get out of there, Phyllo, while she looks at me."

Phyllo's legs had turned to stone. His eyes flicked back and forth between the dragon and Venor. It was all very well to say that, but he had to get past.

"Phyllo, now. Thamineh, *Wada!*" She cracked her whip again and Phyllo willed his legs into action. He pushed at the barrow, out of habit as much as anything else, and lunged for the gate. As he drew level with Thamineh he felt the familiar pins and needles brush over him. She was still, but she was moving and Phyllo saw her lunge, fire belching from her mouth to ignite Phyllo's retreating behind. He rushed out of the gate, held open by Venor and dropped the barrow handles to swat at the seat of his pants.

Tamer Venor stood and watched until he'd calmed down and stopped. His trousers were not on fire.

"What's going on? I don't understand?" He craned around to look, checking for smoke.

Tamer Venor smirked. "I think Thamineh likes you," she said inexplicably.

Phyllo shook his head and blinked, "What? She attacked me!"

"She did not like you in her den, but still you are alive."

Phyllo shook his head and puffed.

Tamer Venor wagged a finger at him. "She got you with a vision, didn't she? It's been a while since any of us have been fooled by that. A dragon is a wholly wonderful magical beast." She turned to look at Thamineh, quite misty-eyed.

Adrenaline in Phyllo's system was making him shake.

"This ability to repel aggressors before any contact has even been made has contributed to their mystery over the centuries. They can project directly into a subject's mind. You saw what Thamineh wanted you to see. A true dragon Whisperer is one who can manage that in the other direction, to break into the dragon's thoughts.

"Judging by all this," she patted at her own behind and mimicked Phyllo rushing from the pen, "I assume she had you thinking your rear was on fire?"

"Well, yes," said Phyllo, and Venor chuckled. She had a most disconcerting habit of finding terrifying things funny.

"Scared for your life, but still pushing the dung barrow. We could put that on your gravestone, no?" She slapped Phyllo on the back and laughed.

"Ha, ha, yeah." Phyllo grimaced; wouldn't that just top it all?

12

Grim Discovery

It had been a few days since Phyllo'd laid eyes on Roly, so when he'd spotted him out amongst the cabins, he made a beeline to collide in a shoulder-bump that was the closest they were ever likely to get to a hug.

"How's dragon wrangling?" asked Roly, peering back over Phyllo's shoulder to the Menagerie, a glint of mischief in his eye.

"Piece of cake," replied Phyllo, deadpan.

Roly raised an eyebrow and laughed. "Oh yeah?"

"What are that lot up to?" said Phyllo, changing the subject and nodding toward a chatty handful of adults that were gathered beside Schlepper's cabin. They seemed to be having a picnic.

"Skinner's telling everyone that the Ringmaster's got a new family of exotics in mind if the dragon thing doesn't work out. Apparently, they're very cheap or something. I don't know, it didn't really make any sense, but Bain reckons that the Ringmaster's got it in for the Menagerie, so this might be the shortest apprenticeship in the history of the circuit," he grimaced at Phyllo, "He reckons that the animals cost too much to look after."

"The female dragon's days are numbered if we can't find a male, I know that much. It's doesn't sound like he's got much faith in us, then. Not if he's already got a plan B." It sounded almost as if the Ringmaster were setting him up to fail.

"I don't know about that," said Roly, "Skinner and Bain have been building a cabin extension to house it. I was just on my way to have a nose, while they're busy." He nodded toward a gap in the cabins and they started walking, Roly leading the way. "It's around the back of the Odditorium," he said in a low whisper.

They ducked out of the gap and around the outside edge. A new construction in rough wood stood back from the haphazard circle of cabins. Phyllo and Roly walked all around it, looking it over. Rough and unpainted, it was clearly a work in progress and Phyllo noticed Schlepper had donated the concertina-jack feet to the project as one was attached in each corner.

"Looks like Skinner and Bain have had a bit of help from our newest recruit," said Phyllo, pointing to the feet.

"Yeah. What do you make of him?" Roly replied.

"Schlepper? I haven't quite made up my mind. So far, he's been nice to me, gave me a lift into the Nevershade so I could buy that dragon hide suit, and he bought me a lemonade at the Club."

As for the new cabin, Phyllo wasn't sure what he'd been expecting, but it didn't even look big enough to hold the female dragon and he knew from the photograph that the male would be much larger.

"Do you think it's got an expansion charm on it?" mused Phyllo.

"One way to find out," said Roly. He looked furtively about for onlookers then tried the door handle. It was locked.

"Crackers," said Phyllo. He kicked at a tuft of grass then said, "I see you've got your bandage off."

Instead of the bandages Roly was wearing a single blue glove that made his hand twice its normal size. He tucked it behind his back. "Dad's idea. There are still dressings and stuff, but this way I can do a bit more."

"Yeah, good idea," said Phyllo. He cringed with guilt, even if Roly *was* getting on with it. He kicked at the tuft of grass again and the monkey with the tufty ears came to mind. That and its gift.

"You know," he said, feeling around in a pocket for the key, "I ought to be giving this back to Bain."

Roly stared at it. "Where'd you get that?"

"One of the capuchins stole it out of Bain's pocket first day here."

Both their eyes slid to the door. "What are the chances…?" breathed Roly.

"I'd say they were high." Phyllo was pretty sure they'd been starting working on it at the time. The key slid into the lock and it turned with a click. They dove immediately inside and slammed the door shut before anyone noticed. That was when Phyllo realised there weren't any windows.

"Crackers, it's really dark," said Phyllo.

"Gobstoppers," said Roly, and Phyllo stifled a laugh.

They held still, willing their eyes to adjust, and gradually Phyllo began to make out occasional shapes in the velvety void. The pair of them crept forward, the rough beginnings of the floor creaking with every hollow step. Slivers of light slunk in through gaps in the hastily panelled walls, catching dust motes that hung in the air like fairy dust.

"Can you see anything?" whispered Roly and then banged into something solid.

"What was that?" hissed Phyllo.

"Ow."

Phyllo found Roly's outstretched arm first. "Where? What?"

"Down here. On my other side. Something solid."

Phyllo side stepped around him. "Glass," he said, recognising its cold smoothness. He found the point of a corner and moved around it, tracing the edge. He crouched down to get what he felt certain was a glass box at eye level, between him and the glimmer of light. The horribly ugly profile of the Equatorial Mermaid revealed itself in the dim illumination.

"Round here, Roly," Phyllo said, pulling him to his side, "Say hello to the first member of the Ringmaster's Exotic family."

Roly bent down to kneel beside him. His breath fogged on the glass while he tried to make sense of what he was looking at. Then Phyllo felt him recoil.

"What in Barnum's name is that?"

That night Phyllo sprawled on top of his bed, too hot to even consider getting under the itchy blanket. He dangled the brass cabin key from its ribbon above his face and twiddled it around and around, watching the light glint on its teeth with a sort of glazed detachment. He batted his eyelids lazily. He was tired. So tired that he couldn't even be bothered to lean out of bed to blow out his candle, although he knew he must before falling asleep.

Days at the Magical Menagerie were much longer than he was used to. The whole cabin was awake at first light, the creatures snuffling and stomping impatiently about in their pens while Panya prepared breakfasts. Their trumpeted, brayed and screeched thanks put a definitively noisy end to any stolen lie-in.

Then it was on to an endless round of cleaning and grooming, treatments for ailments, preparation of feeds and stall maintenance. This was not to mention the ongoing programme of training and practice of show elements and tricks that Tamer Venor continued on repeat. Phyllo had come to realise that although the season had finished, the animals of the Menagerie were never really 'off'.

Also, he was used to his evening meal flagging the end of the working day, but it had no such meaning in the Menagerie. Ad hoc clean-ups and the rounding up of any creatures who'd spent the day outside came next, then bedding them down for the night. More straw, water top-ups and yet more dung shovelling was inevitable. By the time any of them managed to get to their beds, they were utterly exhausted and Phyllo himself was only able to help here and there.

He was learning not to step on anyone's toes nor to interfere with the self-sufficiency that Panya was tasked to master. How she would manage on her own, Phyllo could not fathom. Daily activities would have to be pared down to the absolute bone. Phyllo and Tamer Venor's hunting trip could not possibly last more than a couple of days or Panya would be swamped. He couldn't see how they were going to manage it.

He'd have gnawed at a fingernail, if he could have been bothered. Instead, he flapped at his pyjama top to waft unsatisfyingly warm air across clammy skin. So many creatures under one roof. So much breath and smell. It made his senses reel.

Beneath him the rumbling purr of the sleeping dragon rattled at the floorboards. Nothing created more heat than the dragon. Phyllo felt the stifling waves of it radiating from its stall.

He rolled over onto his side and dropped the key to the table.

That key was the first gift he'd ever received from an animal. How convenient would it be if his *familiar* lived right here already? What if he'd paired up with Tufty that first day out on the Horseshoe and not even known it? What if Tufty had known exactly what that key unlocked when he'd stolen it from Bain and then given it to Phyllo on purpose?

Phyllo sighed. He'd have loved to believe it, but even trying to make a case for it in his head, he couldn't believe it was true. He hadn't felt any kind of connection with Tufty at all.

Tufty was an opportunist. The gift of the key had come as part of his growth as a Tamer, yes, but its ability to unlock such an interesting door had been entirely coincidental.

Phyllo's mind's eye slid to the taxidermy mermaid.

Learning that the Ringmaster intended to get more of its grisly relations if they failed to find a male Sand Dragon was chilling. If this was the direction the act roster was heading, the Circus of Wonder was drifting into grim territory. The mermaid was appalling, borderline horrific. It wasn't the magical wonder that Phyllo knew and loved. It wasn't what the Circus of Wonder was about at all. He had to find that male dragon somehow, he and Venor, they just had to.

He leaned forward to huff out the candle and flopped back onto his pillow. In the newly formed shadows, movement twitched in the corner of his eye.

The wall that divided Phyllo and Panya's pens was built from vertical wooden slats and was more thoroughly finished in some places than others. Gaps ranged from a hair's breadth to several inches. Most gaps were snugly closed next to his bed, but just one remained, an inch or so wide, through which light from Panya's stall flickered weakly. It was too pale to shine, but strong enough to pick out the rounded silhouette of a mouse.

It sat on a crossbeam about halfway up and watched Phyllo steadily, occasionally twitching a whisker.

"Oh, hello," said Phyllo, who was starting to think that attempted communication with any creature was worth a try.

It wiggled its whiskers then reversed rather gracelessly off its little platform and clawed down the wooden wall to plop onto the bed. Phyllo lifted his head to peer at it. Without hesitation, the mouse clambered up Phyllo's nightshirt onto his chest and marched straight up to Phyllo's neck where it put a forepaw on his chin, as if keeping him steady. It got up on its back feet and then looked directly into Phyllo's face.

For a moment they stared at each other.

"Help you with something?" said Phyllo, wondering if under ordinary circumstances he might have been more likely to jump up and scream than try to engage it in conversation. A mouse in the Confectionary would have been very unwelcome.

Its beady little eyes glinted in the half-light. It twitched its whiskers and sniffed the air, then climbed up onto Phyllo's chin and leaned over to sniff his right eye.

Phyllo blinked away the little puffs of breath, astonished.

It clambered scratchily over his nose to sniff at the other eye and then slid off his cheek, fell to the pillow and rolled down to the dent at his neck. Its fur tickled at Phyllo's skin as it scrabbled to right itself then it scampered to the edge of the bed, reversed jerkily down a fold in the fabric and disappeared into the stacked palettes beneath. Phyllo could hear its little claws tapping as it ran.

Well, that was odd, thought Phyllo. *Not at all what you'd expect from a mouse.* Its behaviour had been rather too specific. Rather too human.

Then, on the other side of the wooden wall, he heard Panya moving about and a very faint squeaking. He scrambled to his knees to find the gap in the slats and peered through to spy a slim slice of Panya's stall.

Panya sat on her bed with her back to him. The mouse sat on its haunches on her knee. It was washing its face. Panya swept a hand over the top and side of her own head, front to back, in a similar motion to that which the mouse was making, then produced something small – a grape? – and gave it to the mouse. It clutched it to its chest, scampered across to her bedside table and into an open cage.

It was Panya's mouse and, unless he was very much mistaken, it had just been on a mission.

13

THE CLIFFS

Phyllo and Roly sprinted pell-mell. Arms and legs pumping, they plummeted into potholes and scrambled up hillocks.

"Wait!" they both yelled.

"Mr Schlepper, stop!" Phyllo cried out.

Schlepper's van bumped along ahead on the lumpy grass, the hammock swinging wildly about to one side and a loose anchor rope tap-tap-tapping at the back window from the roof. Phyllo stretched out his stride. This morning felt full of possibilities. Tamer Venor had given him the day off chores, provided he spent time on his Whispering skills while they were out, and the cliffs beckoned.

They didn't strictly *need* a ride. They'd walked there plenty of times before, but Phyllo wanted Roly to experience Schlepper's van and spend a little time up close to the man himself. He wanted to see what Roly thought of this curious addition to their troupe.

Schlepper drew the van to a halt and they caught up to pant sweatily at his door. He rolled down the window.

"Hello, boys," he said with a twinkle, "I didn't see you there."

Phyllo puffed and gasped. Roly bent to lean on his thighs.

The driver's door clunked then pushed out to rise and Schlepper drove out on his three-wheeler. "I noticed there was something loose back there," he said and rolled around to the back of the van, where the rope dangled. He engaged a hidden lifting gear in the three-wheeler which bore him upward an extra three feet, still sitting in the leather cushioned chair. He secured the rope and came back down to earth.

"Well, if you'll excuse me." He rolled back around to the driver's door.

"Mr Schlepper, are you going into Honeyholde?" puffed Phyllo, "Can we have a lift?"

Schlepper looked them both over. "I'm afraid I can't take you to the Club today, Phyllo. I have pressing business and I'm not sure how long I'll be, so a lift home—"

"Oh no, no problem. We weren't thinking, I mean to say, it would just save us a walk. We're heading to the cliffs."

"The cliffs?" Schlepper's eyes jumped between them and he thought for a moment. "I could take you as far as Smuggler's Fork?"

"Brilliant," said Roly, at last regaining enough breath to speak.

Smuggler's Fork was on the other side of the Whispering Wood, just before the final approach into town. The lift would save them a good hour of walking.

"Thanks," said Phyllo, and Schlepper opened the passenger door with a whir. "You can both squeeze into the front, I expect."

Phyllo pushed Roly in first so that he could get the best

view of all the gadgets and gizmos, then perched himself on the edge of the seat and leaned against the door.

"Wow. This is excellent," said Roly, "What does that do?"

Before Schlepper had had a chance to answer, Roly had pulled down a lever marked *Emergency Landing*. There was a loud pop, like the cork being pushed out of a gassy bottle, and a judder ran through the floor.

There was a moment's silence before Schlepper said, "Ah," in the resigned voice of a man too late. He craned to look in the van's wing mirror. "I've taken some precautions," he said, "Going over the edge once is enough." He was still watching the mirror's reflection. "A bit slow. More canister pressure needed, I think and, as I will now have to refill it," he looked meaningfully at Roly, "a few extra pounds seem prudent."

Phyllo turned in his seat to look out of the window and saw a construction of metal frame and fabric being sucked back beneath the van as Schlepper flicked the lever in the opposite direction.

"Were they wings?" he said incredulously.

"I've not had the nerve to test them. The curve of the leading edge is giving me pause. That and the drop." The pointed tips of his moustache quivered and he looked over to Roly. "Best not to touch anything else though, sonny. Other results might be more dramatic."

More dramatic than sprouting wings? Phyllo felt that it might be worth risking it just to find out what they did. Roly, however, shrank back into his seat as they set off and they rolled along for a good while in awed silence. Lights winked on the dashboard and the small green screen on Schlepper's side occasionally pinged.

As Smuggler's Fork drew near, the forest began to thin.

"Is that a homing beacon?" asked Phyllo, sensing that their chance to ask questions was almost at an end.

"Experimental," said Schlepper. "What are you two planning to do on the cliffs?"

"Oh, you know, explore," said Phyllo.

"Got your own Pioneers Club?" Schlepper smiled in his slow way.

"There are these brilliant caves in the cliff face, aren't there, Phyllo," said Roly, "I reckon we should try for the high one."

Phyllo had been considering this himself. He and Roly had already reached a good number of the smugglers' caves over the years, but there was a particular one that had always eluded them. With the recent conquering of his height phobia, well at least partially anyway, he felt that now was a good time to try.

Schlepper rolled his van to a halt at the fork in the road and the boys scrambled from the front seat, thanking him for the ride.

"Before you go." Schlepper waved a leather-gloved hand. He opened a compartment in the dash and pulled out a palm-sized metal gizmo. "Some pioneering kit," he said and passed it out to Phyllo, "It's not dangerous as such, but probably best not to point it at each other."

Phyllo weighed it in his hand. The gizmo was extraordinarily heavy for its size, smooth on its casing front and back, but with lots of intricate buttons and levers in a band around the circumference. It looked to Phyllo like an oversized pocket-watch. "What is it?" he asked.

"A survival widget, as used by the Pioneer Club Expedition Force."

"Brilliant," said Roly eyeing it enviously.

Phyllo pocketed it as Schlepper roared away toward town, van-hammock swinging. He and Roly set off down the well-beaten path to the clifftops. Phyllo tried to see the trail with his developing *Beast Whisperer* eye and immediately spotted some interesting imprints in the earth. He pointed them out. "Tracks," he said knowingly.

Roly looked impressed. "Expect you've learned all about them from Venor, have you?" He said, "Do you know what it is?"

"Oh yeah," said Phyllo, who didn't, "I'd say that's a bear."

"A bear!" Roly scanned around anxiously.

"Might even be a grizzly. I hear they migrate here in the autumn." He gave a sort of involuntary jiggle of his head that made Roly squint at him.

"You're having me on," Roly said and gave Phyllo a dig in the arm with his good hand.

Phyllo laughed. "Come on, let's see if we can catch it." He started to run.

The pair of them careered along the woodland paths, jumping logs and calling out occasional pretend cries of fear like 'Aaargh, grizzly!' or 'It's gaining on us, run!' until they galumphed to a halt where the path ran out. The ground fell away in a sheer drop and the twinkling waters of Honeyholde Bay spread out beneath them. Phyllo and Roly leaned on each other panting and looked out at the view. This point marked the start of their usual rocky trail along the cliff face.

"I reckon we should start a bit higher this time," said Roly, looking up at the rising craggy edge. The ground was thick with bramble and low growing ivy, but they couldn't climb the sheer rock-face. This way had to be easier.

"Good idea," Phyllo said, then scouted about for a good

thwacking stick, thinking that if they beat down the barbed creepers it would be easier to get through. Progress was slow and laborious, Phyllo and Roly taking it in turns to clear the path ahead.

"Let's take a break and have a look at the gadget," said Roly, sweating and puffing and pausing to lean heavily on the thwacking stick. Phyllo pulled it from his pocket.

It was like a slightly flattened bronze ball, basically round and about the size of Phyllo's palm. A series of lugs were positioned all around the outside edge, each with a different symbol engraved upon it. Roly tweaked one and a circular section released to slide out. It neatly held a pair of folded scissors which Roly removed and revolved into shape. He made an experimental snip at a leaf.

"Cool," he cooed, put them back and tried another lug. This one revealed a magnifying glass. Roly held it closer and then further away from one eye while pinching the other one closed and turned on the spot, looking for something to examine. He stopped on Phyllo and minutely examined his nose.

"Give me that," said Phyllo, snatching it out of his hand. He snapped away the lens and then poked about for something else. The next lug released in a curious double curl and it was only when Phyllo experimentally poked his finger through the middle that he got any sense at all of what it might be. He held the gadget steady with his other hand and squeezed.

With a *crack* something small and bullet-like shot out of the other side, rocketed past Roly and embedded in a tree fifty feet away. A thick wire trailed from the tree to the gadget.

"Galloping gobstoppers, you almost shot me!" squeaked Roly.

"A miss is as good as a mile," said Phyllo with a nonchalant shrug, but it was a cockier reply than he felt. Roly scowled and Phyllo looked down at the widget with a new kind of respect. They scrambled together over to the tree to examine the impact point.

The *bullet* had split itself into three and was embedded solidly in the bark. They both tugged at it ineffectually and it was only when Phyllo spotted a tiny release button on the *bullet's* base, and then an alternative one on the body of the gadget, that they were able to wiggle it free. After that they spent a happy half-hour taking it in turns to aim at different targets and argue about who was the best shot. Eventually Roly produced a raspberry liquorish and marshmallow man from his pocket and waved it in Phyllo's face.

"That's not going to put me off," said Phyllo, although in truth it had been a good long while since he'd enjoyed a treat from the Confectionary, and marshmallow men were a favourite.

"Best of five wins Eric Mallow," Roly said.

"You're on."

This new challenge filled a fun competitive ten minutes, but Roly stalked off grumbling bitterly about the glove when Phyllo beat him 3:2.

They carried on up the climb, hacking their way, until finally they made it to a clear spot that marked the beginnings of a previously undiscovered ledge. They stopped to assess it.

The ledge itself started off a respectable couple of feet wide, but narrowed to half that after twenty feet or so. About another ten feet on he could see the dark mouth of the cave –

the one they were aiming for. Above and below the cliff face was vertical and offered no other paths to try.

"What do you reckon?" Roly asked and Phyllo looked down. They were already considerably higher here than any other point they'd climbed to before. Their usual escapades took them along the cliff at a reasonable scramble up from the footpaths, but this one was a much loftier kettle of fish.

Boats bobbed in the bay far below, their detail lost in the glimmers from the sea. Seagulls circled above the beach, but beneath their eye level. Phyllo's mouth dried. It was higher even than the trapeze. Higher than anything. His head gave a little swim and he checked his breathing. Tiny beads of sweat popped on his lip.

"You all right?" Roly's round face loomed up close to Phyllo's and his vision swam out of focus.

Phyllo didn't want to be fearful. He didn't want today to be about that. There had to be a way for him to cope with the height. They'd made it this far.

"Just give me a minute," he said and quietly obeyed the sudden wobbly command of his knees to sit down. He sucked in some deep breaths.

How had he managed it before? What had his apprenticeship with the Volantes taught him? He didn't need physical strength as such, more mental. Confidence. Momentum. What else?

"Can I do anything? To help, I mean?" Roly stood by his side and shuffled uncertainly.

Team spirit, he remembered. Phyllo had the best team mate he could hope for right there. He never would have gone into the new cabin to investigate without Roly by his side. He didn't need to be flexible, except perhaps in his approach. Phyllo chewed on his lip.

Then he'd got it. He knew his wobbly knees would never let him walk along the ledge, but if he went along it, just as he'd gone along the ledge outside his cot in the Birdcage, that could work. This ledge was wider, if anything. His fear didn't have to hold him back.

He jammed the gadget into his pocket, shuffled across the ground on his bottom and looked out along the ledge. It was solid rock, he reasoned with himself. There was more than enough space to get his centre of gravity well back from the edge. It was definitely doable.

"And the plan is?" said Roly.

Phyllo manoeuvred himself out onto the ledge and leaned back. Sweat prickled on his palms. "Low centre of gravity," he said and then told himself to reach a little to his left, leaned on his hand and slid his bottom along to catch up with it. Small progress. He did it again and again. He found that actually the ledge was wide enough for him to push away from the edge and press his back to the wall. He flicked a glance to Roly. "Come on. Even you could do this," he said with a wobbly smile.

Roly had got the idea. He shuffled out and together they bumped along on their hands and feet and bottoms to the cave mouth. It wasn't so bad if you got a bit of a rhythm going and remembered not to look down. Phyllo didn't let himself think about anything but the solidity of the ledge beneath them until they'd reached the cave opening and he could reverse inside, heart hammering.

"Gobstoppers," huffed Roly as he slid in next to him, "That was crazy."

The pair of them rolled onto their stomachs and peered over the edge, relieved to have made it.

The cave floor was cold and smooth, its rippling surface

dusted with sand that had ridden up on the wind from the beach below. The cossetted space stretched back a surprising six or seven feet. It was weirdly peaceful and quite the best cave they had ever discovered.

Too inaccessible for casual human visitors, there was enough space for both him and Roly to sit or even lie down, whilst the ledge provided the perfect place for a campfire. Nature had even seen fit to supply the dry remains of a vine which snapped easily into campfire-friendly pieces.

Under Phyllo's examination, the survival widget gave up a flint which sparked a handful of dry, leafy kindling into flames. Together, he and Roly heaped pieces of vine into a crackling tepee and Phyllo impaled Eric Mallow on the thwacking stick for toasting.

"It's what he would have wanted," said Roly, then produced another from his pocket at which Phyllo rolled his eyes. "Well, you didn't think I'd only brought one?" He grinned.

They gazed out at the view, munching on Eric and his delicious friend and Phyllo couldn't remember ever having felt more content.

The twinkling waters opened out to the sea down on their left and to their right the opposing bank drew in the shrinking funnel that led to Steam Star Port. The dark frames of the docking towers speared into the sky, peppered with dirigibles moored at high platforms.

Phyllo twiddled with the survival widget and pressed a lug which opened it exactly in the middle, like a book. Each side had a lens, no, two lenses, one on top of the other, and a thumb wheel which pushed the top lens up and down. He frowned at it, found a hinge on the top edge and folded the lenses out.

"Binoculars," said Roly and Phyllo saw at once he was right.

They were very awkward though, until Phyllo realised he had them upside down and that the case could rest on the top of his head. He fiddled with the thumb wheels and was delighted when the dirigibles across the bay came into focus. "Brilliant," he breathed.

He scanned up and down the towers. A red and white swagged pleasure cruiser was disembarking its passengers. At the next platform up, the black tarred hull of a gundalow displayed its name in golden lettering: *The Nelly Bly*.

"That's Schlepper's old ship on the highest pontoon," Phyllo said and tried to zoom in.

"Let's have a look." Roly reached out for the binoculars, but Phyllo wasn't ready to give them up just yet. "You never said he had a ship." Roly strained to see across the bay.

"He pointed it out to me that first time I came to help him. I think he was a bit of an adventurer in his day, said he needed more space so decided to give it up." Phyllo dropped the binoculars down slightly to look at Roly. "And that's another thing. We still don't know what his talent actually is, do we. He obviously likes his gadgets and when we went to his workshop it was huge, I mean really huge and really empty."

Phyllo looked back out to the airship, his curiosity growing. He could see people on the pontoon beside it, stacking up crates. He rested his elbows on his knees, trying to keep the binoculars steady. Steam Star Port was at a considerable distance and even breathing was making the magnified image jump.

"There are a couple of people in work overalls and then there's another one in black," Phyllo commentated for Roly's benefit, "That one's wearing a long cloak with his back to me and is waving his arms about, telling the others what to do by the look of it. That must be the new owner." Phyllo twiddled with the thumb wheel, trying to get the image a bit clearer. The man in black swished out of sight, then returned to look out over the water.

Phyllo fumbled and almost dropped the widget. "No way," he breathed.

"No way what?" Roly leaned to look back and forth between Phyllo and the view, itching for his turn to look through the widget.

Phyllo snatched the binoculars back up to his eyes, the line of sight swinging wildly about as he tried to find the pontoon again. When he found it, it was empty of both crates and people. A dry dread crept over him as he searched the walkways, but either they'd taken the crates to the lifts in the tower or onto the ship.

"But it can't be, can it?" He dropped the widget into his lap and looked over to Roly. What he'd seen, however fleeting, had been clear. That black cloak. That black beaked mask. He shook his head. "The Crow Man, Roly. What's he doing with Schlepper's ship?"

14

THE GIFT OF SOUND

THE AFTERNOON PASSED in flights of wild speculation and target practice, but all too soon Phyllo and Roly were trudging down through the Whispering Wood, drawn back to the Circus of Wonder encampment by the rumbling of their stomachs.

Spending the day with Roly had been just what Phyllo'd needed and they parted ways at the edge of the wood in high spirits, promising to do it again soon. Roly made for the Confectionary, but Phyllo, who hadn't done any work on his Beast Whispering senses all day, thought it best to devote a few undistracted minutes to it before returning to the Menagerie. If he could make just one new discovery, he felt he'd be able to balance out the fun of the day with some legitimate progress.

He tramped along the path to the dell, trying to remember Tamer Venor's instructions that morning.

"All your senses must be in tune with the natural world," she'd said and he could picture her emphatic finger-pinching to get the point across.

"You have seen. Now you must hear. Again, find a place you can relax and close your eyes. Make your incantation. Interpret the world around you with only your ears. Be as a man lost in the dark. Divert all your powers of deduction to sound. Can you hear the weather? Wind, rain, a rumble of thunder? Does water flow nearby? What animals cry? Do you know what species? When you have heard, then try to see. Put the information together. All senses contribute to experience and understanding. Capture everything."

He was to attempt to see with sound.

He wove his way back into the wood, found his favourite tree in the dell, sat down on the smooth root and tried to relax. The light had dimmed considerably in the last half hour, his carefree afternoon now fading into the imminent responsibilities of evening. Soon darkness would fall and he'd have no choice *but* to use his other senses.

He closed his eyes, spoke the words of the incantation and listened hard.

It took a moment to focus. What he'd previously taken for peace and quiet wasn't actually that at all. The air was filled with hundreds of tiny individual noises. Realising it would take some working out, he imagined the hollow of the dell as a clock face, positioning himself at the bottom at 6, then tried to pinpoint each sound.

At 11 o'clock a bird made a soft two-tone *coo-ee*. Then again. Another made the same sound but was fainter, probably farther away, but still in the same direction.

At 3, a *chip-chipper-chip-chipper* came from the high branches. A different kind of bird. Insistent. Repetitive. Birds were by far the noisiest contributors to the soundscape.

A low hiss of wind wrapped around behind him and then out to his side, at 7, 8, 9. The tone of it changed as it moved.

Phyllo looked to see why and noticed differing types of trees, different leaves, interpreting the wind in their own way.

"Huh." He nodded to himself with this new understanding.

A sound just like the toll of a wooden wind chime clonked close at hand, around 4. He stared up into the canopy to find the source and saw the closely spaced vertical branches of a species of tree unusual for the area. The breeze bounced them against each other to make a hollow call. Bamboo perhaps, but not green. It was dark and gnarled and dead looking.

He closed his eyes again and listened for the sounds he'd already identified, pinpointing locations and visualising what had made them.

Crack! A twig snapped close by at 7. Phyllo jumped.

He twisted around to look between the giant trunks of the trees.

Snap! Another twig cracked close at 5.

He twisted the other way to peer into the gathering gloom. That had made his heart beat faster. "I-Is somebody there?" he stuttered.

Only the wind answered him, rattling the chime of dead wood.

Goosebumps rippled up Phyllo's arms. Perhaps he'd left it a bit late to sit in the Whispering Wood with his eyes closed.

He stood up and glanced up at the tree, searching for the face he'd discovered a day or so earlier, the face that had made him feel like he was making progress, but now he couldn't find it.

Phyllo stepped backward, into the dell to scan a greater area of the trunk. Lumpy bark, flowing lines that travelled vertically and the knobble of a small branch that had long since snapped away. No face.

This *was* the right tree though, wasn't it? He scanned around the circle. Yes, this was the one. His favourite with the smooth root for sitting on.

The wind buzzed around the low bushes and with it came a ripple of laughter, carried on the evening air.

Phyllo whipped around. Where had that come from?

His heart stepped up another gear to beat harder in his chest.

He turned slowly, listening, but now desperately looking too, gawking into the twilight.

A giggle on the breeze. He spun toward it. "H-Hello?"

Talking. Someone was talking, but he couldn't make out the words, just the patterns and the pitch, high and childlike. Goose bumps crept up his neck. Was someone laughing at him? Who? Quietly and with as much stealth as the blood careering through his veins would allow, he crept toward it.

It led him into an unfamiliar patch of the wood, a sweep of holly trees that led down closer to the encampment. It was a route of rough ground that he usually avoided because it slowed him down.

The low babble of a voice.

Closer now.

He crept between two trees, and then another two. A small glade opened up, carpeted in thick mossy grass. A girl sat cross-legged in the middle. She had a froth of strawberry blonde curls and wore a dress in his mother's familiar rose and lime stripe, the stripe of the Circus Confectioner.

Phyllo stopped and blinked. It was Dodo, his little sister.

"Oh, it's you," he said, crumpling with relief, but Dodo didn't smile. "Shh," she hissed.

"Shh yourself," said Phyllo, and Dodo scowled back.

"Be quiet. You'll frighten them."

Phyllo shook his head. "Frighten who?" There wasn't anyone there but the two of them. He looked around again just to make sure and just as he'd concluded that they were definitely alone, he saw it; the ground around Dodo shimmered.

It wobbled as if cloaked in a heat haze and then, as he squinted trying to make it out, tiny little men flickered into focus. Seven or eight of them. Each one no more than three or four inches high, with legs that looked too small for their bodies and vibrant red hair that flourished in mops on the tops of their heads and sprouted from their chins in wild, bushy beards. Scattered around Dodo, they appeared to be making something or at least they had been. Now every last one of them stared up at Phyllo, aghast.

"Don't come any closer," Dodo said in an urgent whisper, but Phyllo was already stumbling forward, blinking stupidly.

"Dodo, what in Barnum's name...?"

She waved her hands at him, shooing him back. "No, Phyllo," she hissed.

The closest of the little men *popped* in a shower of sparking dust and then, after the briefest of pauses, the rest of them followed suit in rapid fire, like a handful of popcorn kernels all exploding at once in a hot pan.

"Oh, oh no—" Phyllo began and Dodo threw up her hands in frustration.

"Well, thank you very much," she sputtered.

"Dodo, I didn't mean to – I mean who—"

"Great, just great. How typical." She banged the ground with a clenched fist. "You scared them off, you marshmallow head. Brownies, Phyllo. They're Brownies, were Brownies, and we hadn't even finished." She looked down at the small items lying in the fabric scoop of her skirt.

Phyllo gawped at her, bewildered. "Marshmallow head?" He let out a little laugh, but that just made Dodo madder.

"It's all right for you," she snapped, "You and Roly, running off together." Dodo's freckled cheeks had turned puce and her eyebrows were in that slant Phyllo recognised as a precursor to a hissy fit. She got to her feet and pumped her fists at the ground. "Never mind me. Just leave me here, why don't you?"

"Dodo, I'm sorry, I didn't mean to—"

She folded her arms in a fury.

Phyllo floundered. He'd hardly seen Roly at all lately. He didn't think he deserved this. "I don't see why *I've* got to apologise, anyway. You left out? What about me? I'm the one being forced out of the family business. Haven't thought about that, have you?"

"Ha!" she fired back at him, "That's right, it's all about you." She put on a whiney voice. "I'm Phyllo and I need all the attention."

"That's not fair—" interrupted Phyllo, but internally he had to admit Dodo's impression of him was strikingly similar to some he'd done of her in the past.

"How unlucky am I?" Dodo continued to whine, "I've set light to the big top, and the Confectionary. Aren't I silly? Never mind anyone else's things that got ruined, what about me? Oh, look I've got to actually learn something. How terrible. Oh, look at me, I'm on the trapeze—"

"Dodo—" Phyllo interrupted, but she carried on.

"Oh, look at me, I managed one stupid trick and now I'm everyone's hero. I can do everything. I can do Dodo's jobs at the Confectionary suddenly, too. What's the point of her?" She flopped her head from side to side, sing-songing out the words.

"Look, Dodo, this isn't fun for me—"

"Me. Me. ME!" Dodo shouted, tears springing from her eyes. "I've had enough of you." She burst into full-on sobs and then lurched out of the glade, breaking into a haphazard run beyond the treeline, blundering back toward the encampment.

Phyllo watched her go. What had gotten into her? That was extraordinarily unfair. He kicked at the grass. Possibly, it was also a little bit true, but mostly it was really unfair. He shuffled his way over to the spot where she'd been sitting, pouting at the ground, and saw there was something poking out of the grass. He bent to pick it up.

There turned out to be two items, actually, things which must have fallen from Dodo's lap when she'd got up to yell at him. The first was a cone made from twisted oak leaves. It was secured in its shape by a feather at the bottom, stitched through the layers like thread. Its peak was held together by the cup of an acorn.

The other item was made from woven blades of grass. Phyllo squinted at it. One part had rough unfinished edges, where the grass stuck out haphazardly, but there were sleeves and a collar of petals and even bright yellow buttons made from the fat centres of daisies. It was a tiny jacket, likely on its way to becoming a perfect fit for one of the little men, for one of the Brownies. So that was what they'd been making. Phyllo marvelled at it and then suddenly saw that the cone was a hat.

His shoulders slumped and he blinked down at these

amazing items in disbelief. Where had the Brownies come from and why had he never seen them before? More importantly, why could he see them now?

15

A CURE FOR LONELINESS

THE MENAGERIE WAS BEDDING down for the evening by the time Phyllo got back. Panya was putting new straw in the butterphant pen and he found Tamer Venor up in their living quarters, standing at the table and poring over a map. A bulbous earthenware pot balanced on their small iron stove in the corner of the room. Its lid jiggled occasionally to release a puff of fragrant steam that smelled spicy and delicious and made Phyllo's stomach growl.

Tamer Venor looked up from the map and bowed a little in her customary manner, pressing her palm to her chest. "I hoped that you were near. Our evening meal will soon be ready." She turned away from him to grasp the handle of a silver teapot. "Tea?"

"Oh, yes, all right," he said and Venor lifted the pot high into the air to pour a measure of amber liquid into a glass, then refilled her own in the same theatrical manner. She passed him his glass and Phyllo found that the bubbles which had frothed right up to the rim, dissipated instantly as he took his first sip. The tea was minty and oddly sweet with liquorice.

"Your expedition was a success?" she asked. Her golden eyes twinkled with enthusiasm. She seemed excited beyond the question and Phyllo wondered what else she was thinking.

"Yes, very much," he said quickly.

"Time with family is rarely wasted," she added sagely and Phyllo felt his conscience prickle. Dodo probably didn't think so right now. He wondered if Tamer Venor guessed quite how little effort he'd put into honing his Whispering skills that day.

"I've just come from the Whispering Wood," he said defensively and then went on to tell her about the sounds he'd heard around the dell and the little men who'd shimmered into existence out of thin air. She listened attentively.

"Your fervour gives great credit to you," she said when he had finished, "Each truth learned will be to you as new as if it had never been written. It is as encouraging as your newfound ability to see indecipherables. Excellent progress, I believe."

"Indecipherables?" said Phyllo, "The Brownies?"

"A genus. The Fae family are various and wondrous, but almost all are cloaked from the eye of the casual observer. The Brownie is oft times friend to a young and lonely child, whose mind remains open to the extraordinary.

"They are a most agreeable subspecies. Ingenious and motivated by delight, they could be of great value to adults too, if only they weren't too disconnected to appreciate them. But not you, oh no!" She thumped Phyllo heartily on the back. "You are growing, Phyllo Cane. Your mind opens. It is most excellent and timely news."

"Friend to a lonely child?" Phyllo frowned to himself. He'd felt angry with Dodo for the insults she'd thrown at him in the Whispering Wood, but now his chest twanged with guilt.

He hadn't sought her out when he'd got free time. Roly was his brother – he'd always go to him first, but he'd taken away her only other sibling and left her behind. It was obvious to him now why she'd gotten upset.

"It is most unusual for them to be seen by more than one person at once," continued Venor.

"They popped, when they saw me, I mean. Just sort of turned to dust. She told me not to come closer—"

"Fascinating, aren't they?" Tamer Venor pulled herself up to full height. "I too have made progress," she said, knocking on the map. "Our quarry is a most difficult beast to locate and an even profounder challenge to capture. I have wracked my brain," she slapped her palm to her head, "for the best road open to us and I think I have uncovered a route.

"A bull Sand Dragon will not be forced. It will be a willing participant in our game or none at all, and I for one have no intention of enforcing servitude upon an animal that does not willingly come." She wagged a finger. "No. It is stronger and more ferocious than any other creature in our blessed Menagerie, yet too, is it more loyal and family oriented, more beautiful in flight and masterful of fire. It is a prize beyond the wildest dreams of our Ringmaster, if only he knew it. So, what will make our venture succeed?"

Phyllo shrugged and took a sip of his tea.

"I have spent today re-reading every Dragon Scroll in my own library, and scoured too through Albertus's. It has confirmed to me the core nature of our quarry."

She began to pace back and forth, along the length of the

table. "They do not live in packs. Such a formidable creature could not share territory with another male. Nor a female with another female. Only close family groups ever cohabit, but more often, in these sparsely populated times, they live alone. This is excellent news." She flung her arms out to clap Phyllo on both shoulders at once, slopping his tea. "Do you know why?"

"Less chance of getting toasted?" Phyllo ventured, brushing at his jacket.

Tamer Venor laughed heartily. "No, no, they don't like it. A bull dragon alone will be far worse tempered than two happily mated, but this fact is our ticket. For every joy there is a price to be paid." She shrugged. "It is as Thoth has willed it."

Phyllo stared at her. "It is?"

"It is. Our Sand Dragon does not like to be alone. He prefers company and if there are no females to canoodle there is but one alternative, and our solution."

Phyllo blinked helplessly and shook his head.

"Parpadillos." She grinned widely.

"Parpadillos?"

"Precisely. The only other creature with which our Sand Dragon is willing to share his lair. Look here." Tamer Venor reached across the table to snatch up a book which she flopped open at its ribbon in front of Phyllo.

Phyllo read the entry.

PARPADILLO
pɑː.pæ.dɪl.əʊ
Also known as Draco Pirum or Pear Dragon
Cousin to the Screaming Hairy Dracodillo, the Parpadillo is

smallest of the FLIGHTLESS MINIATURE suborder of the DRACO (Dragon) family.

Indigenous to the Nubian Desert, populations cluster on the Tropic of Cancer, where they can be found sunbathing on the banks of Lake Nasser during the spring and summer months.

As temperatures drop in late October, they will retreat to their burrows to ride out the sub-30-degree temperatures of winter, where they will super-heat a highly organised collection of gathered rocks to maintain an optimum hibernation body heat of 45 degrees.

They are prolific diggers and will exhume hundreds of feet of tunnels over the course of the summer months to identify new heat spots and protected dens.

Hunted aggressively over the last century, the Parpadillo is highly prized by the Peruvian Paranguista bands who use its tough outer shell to manufacture the body of the 'Parango' – a six-stringed musical instrument renowned for its inability to stay in tune, and forming the backbone of the tuneless orchestral tradition for which the Paranguista are famed.

There was a photograph of a small guitar-like instrument, captured side on, which showed the creature's hairy shell forming the back of the instrument's body. Phyllo grimaced.

Understandably shy of humans, the Parpadillo is instead a natural companion animal to many of the larger dragon species. The plentiful supply of heat radiating from the full-sized adult dragon, combined with the mothering and exceedingly neat habit of the Parpadillo, who will gladly

*tidy, stack and organise lair gold as it would its rocks,
makes for a happily symbiotic relationship.
Between 30 and 60 inches in height, the Parpadillo prefers to
walk on its hind legs unless burrowing, its pear-shaped body
being better suited to vertical locomotion. Usually emerald
green (with occasional sapphire variants), the majority of its
body is covered in scaled reptilian skin, with only the back
portion being protected by articulated bony plates.*

An accomplished watercolour painting on the facing page depicted a pear-shaped lizard, standing on its skinny hind legs with rather a hopeful expression on its comparatively thin face. It clutched a gold coin between the long-clawed paws of its stubby front legs. Phyllo couldn't help but feel a bit sorry for it.

Tamer Venor tapped on the page. "This little fellow may not be so keen on us, but if we can capture him, we might be able to tempt a lonely bull dragon out into the open."

To Phyllo it all seemed a bit hopeful. "So, you think it will just come then, from wherever it is to get it?" said Phyllo, unable to hide his scepticism.

"Not exactly, no. We will have to be relatively close. Close enough to fall within the Sand Dragon's range of hearing, no more than a mile. You see, I have a hunch where a bull Sand Dragon might be. An old site. A difficult site. To get to it, to force our way in, it would be gravely dangerous, almost impossible and most likely deadly. No. Our best chance will be to tempt it to us."

"But if the dragon can hear it, why doesn't it just go and get one for itself?" asked Phyllo, seeing a bit of a problem with this theory.

"Because a Parpadillo is self-sufficient. It is industrious. It doesn't want to be cold so it builds itself a hot-den. It is always on the move, always doing. It will only cry if it's stopped from doing what it wants to do."

"Cry?"

"Yes." Tamer Venor rubbed uncomfortably at her face. "I don't like to make it, but the end will justify the means. It will bring about a better outcome for all."

"Oh." Phyllo was feeling even more sorry for it now.

"And that brings us to our next impediment. Transportation. Lake Nasser is thousands of miles away. Already, we are in October and the Parpadillo prepares to hibernate. Once inside those tunnels, he will prove very difficult to find and our quest will come to a premature and most unsuccessful conclusion. We must make haste if we are to catch him. I can travel through my altar, but your lack there holds us back and I cannot see any other option."

"We should go by airship," suggested Phyllo hopefully, but Tamer Venor just shook her head.

"By airship the journey would take three days at best, even if we could travel directly, which we could not." She tapped at the map again. "It is a highly specific destination. There would be many connections and potential for losing time, if we were able to secure passage at all."

"What about the Machine?" ventured Phyllo.

"The Machine is down for maintenance and cabins of the big top are disassembled, so there is no help to be had there. I can only conclude that we must rely upon our own abilities, on the magic of the Beast Whisperer. My altar glass can take me to where the Parpadillos reside, but, as I have told you, it can transport only one. I see no other way around it, Phyllo, your altar must also be complete. Your familiar, have you identified it? Let me see what you have."

Phyllo felt his stomach hollow. He'd not really managed any outstanding moments of animal communication just yet and there hadn't been much progress on the altar front either. He hesitantly put down his tea and turned to go and fetch his tin, the guilt he'd been feeling for Dodo now spreading to encompass the lack of improvement in his altar. He knew it was still exactly the same as the last time she'd looked and squeezed his brain frantically for things he could add.

Tamer Venor fell in step behind him and followed him back to his stall to studiously watch as he laid out the pieces.

The upturned tin with its polished lid.

The bit of twig.

The feather.

The catkin.

The key.

He balanced the candles rather precariously either side.

He smiled at Tamer Venor sheepishly and she leaned in to move the pieces around contemplatively with her forefinger.

"Oh, and this." Phyllo suddenly remembered the Brownie hat and unfinished jacket. He added it awkwardly to his eclectic selection.

Tamer Venor looked down at it for a good long time then, not speaking, cast her eyes to Phyllo and examined him and his reactions minutely.

"You are closer than you see," she said at last.

Phyllo thought that was lucky, because he couldn't see anything at all.

16

BEETLING ABOUT

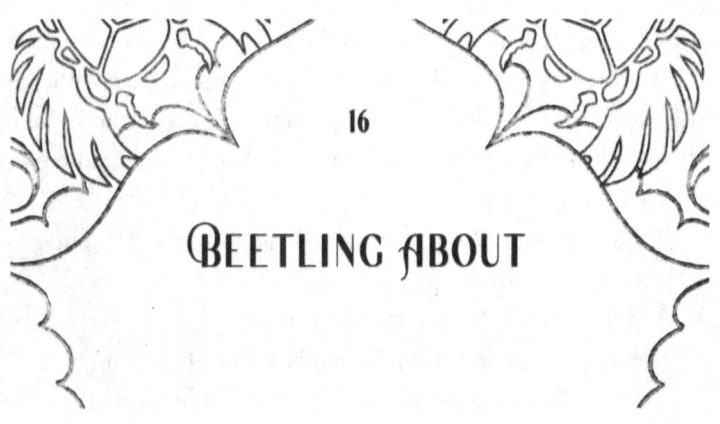

Dinner was an unusual but quite delicious mixture of rice, pasta, chickpeas and spices, that left Phyllo cheerfully flopped out on the floor cushions. Stuffed and drowsy, his body could quite happily have dropped off to sleep right there, but his mind couldn't settle. What he'd seen at the cliffs nagged at him. Had it really been the Crow Man? They had been very far away and a black cloak wasn't that unusual, not amongst the *charmed* community. At such a distance he could have been mistaken.

Phyllo chewed at his lip. That mask though, it was so distinctive. He'd never seen another one quite like it and while it was commonplace to see carnival-goers on the Brampton levels in masks, in other towns it was considerably more unusual.

There were some exceptions. Canal workers wore them. Medics too. Members of the Guard had them as part of their uniform. Then there were the professional assassins and ne'er-do-wells of the In-between. Phyllo fidgeted. The cushions were too lumpy. This Crow Man character was appearing a little too often. The ruckus with the Jester on the banks of the Brampton Levels. His infiltration of the horseshoe with the thieves of the In-between. His presence in the stands while the Jester did his worst. The Crow Man being there had never meant anything good.

It had to be unlikely that his association with Schlepper's old ship meant anything good either.

Phyllo's stomach gurgled and griped.

Schlepper. What did Phyllo really know about him?

He shuffled himself out of the floor pillows and thought that perhaps a walk would shake down his dinner. He grabbed his jacket and headed for the stairs, the Survival Widget bouncing heavily in his pocket. Schlepper's gadget. He ought to give it back and it would make an excellent excuse to visit him and ask some questions. Perhaps he could discover who was the new owner of *The Nelly Bly*.

Phyllo clanged down the staircase and out onto the loosely constructed horseshoe. The night air had lost its afternoon warmth and was lit by strings of jewel-like bulbs that draped between the high canvas walls of the big top and the widely spaced cabins. Phyllo rubbed at his belly as he walked and pulled his jacket tighter.

Schlepper's van was parked beside the Confectionary and next to it sat a smartly clad wooden box about double the van's size. Phyllo could only assume that this was Schlepper's trailer even if, now all polished wood and riveted brass, it bore virtually no resemblance to its former rusty self.

Phyllo pressed his face against the van window, hoping to spot Schlepper, but found it quiet and empty. He eyed the trailer. It offered no windows to peep through and was shut up tight. He leaned an ear against the panelling and could just about detect the sound of someone moving about inside. He rapped his knuckles against the wood.

"Mr Schlepper, are you in there?"

The faint noises stopped and then became a low whir. The wall Phyllo was leaning against popped forward at the bottom, making him jump back, and then slowly continued to rise, opening out the whole front section on a hinge at the roof. As it reached head height purple awnings tumbled from the front and side edges. They unfurled and flapped, they clicked and slotted into place and finally lights rippled through a sign, lodged high over the entrance now revealed. It read 'Schlepper's Contraptionist Carousel'.

Bizarrely, the entire inside of the trailer was given over to a kind of entrance hall. To the left and right sides, the beginnings of two staircases led up out of sight in a curve that would lead outside of the trailer's internal space. Dead centre, steps led down to a thick velvet curtain, with whatever was beyond it also outside of the trailer's physical dimensions. Schlepper's face appeared at the curtain's edge and he beamed up at Phyllo.

"The pioneer returns," he said and then pulled the curtain open, "Come in."

Phyllo stepped forward, trying to peek up the staircases as he drew level with them, but their wooden treads rose in tight spirals that made it impossible see where they led. The ground beneath his feet was still the grass of the field even though he was now inside. He squinted at Schlepper, confused.

"Down here. You find me mid-dilemma," he said and then moved out of sight.

Half a dozen steps took Phyllo down into a dimly lit workshop. Like Schlepper's other workshop in the Nevershade, its walls were filled with shelves jam-packed with bits and bobs: switches and springs, boxes of bolts and trays of light bulbs. Here, however, his careful organisation had fallen into disarray.

Stacks of labelled boxes had tumbled sideways spilling their contents, and the tool wall, a greatly reduced version of the one in the Nevershade, was mismatched and untidy. Tools dangled from single hooks in spots that didn't correspond with their outline. Nowhere near as large as Schlepper's other workshop, it could still have accommodated the trailer in the open space in the middle, which of course was impossible as Phyllo knew he was already inside said trailer with space to spare.

He blinked around.

"I think it might be a faulty carbon pulse booster," said Schlepper, returning to his messy workbench, "The journey over here shook the ride units. Transportation is going to be a problem, I can see that now." He was already wearing a pair of glasses, but added a second to inspect the mess of wires sticking out of the back of – wait – what was that?

Phyllo drew closer.

There were six articulated legs and a long body, constructed from riveted sections of metal, all of it enamelled black. It was a replica of a stag beetle, but not like any Phyllo had ever seen before. A mechanical marvel, it squatted on Schlepper's workbench, huge and surprising – six feet at least from the tip of its giant pincers to the rounded end of its shelled-back. A saddle with stirrups was slung over its middle.

Schlepper pushed the wires inside and then stepped back. "Cross your fingers," he said and felt about for something underneath.

The beetle's legs lifted in turn in a ripple front to back, then it reared up with a jolt and began to bounce violently up and down, sparks flying from its pincered jaws.

"Oh, no, no, stop that." Schlepper jabbed for the switch, trying to reach underneath, but the beetle whacked its underside down on the bench in a mounting frenzy, belching smoke and preventing access. Phyllo backed away. Sizzling electrics stung at his nostrils.

Schlepper dove into the clutter on the bench, shoving scraps of metal and rolls of wire aside. "Where is it? Where is it?" he muttered.

A jet of flame shot from the beetle's mouth and Phyllo's heart jumped into his throat.

"Stanley. Stanley? Where are you, boy? Here, boy." Schlepper lunged to his desk, yanked open a drawer and pulled out a tin which he rattled furiously. Stanley, who'd been nowhere in sight, immediately appeared from behind a pile of boxes and wagged his way over with a springy whir. The beetle was crashing about so energetically now, one leg had worked its way precariously over the edge.

"Good boy," exclaimed Schlepper and tossed Stanley a small something from the tin which he caught in his mouth and golloped down. Schlepper opened the toolbox doors on Stanley's back, snatched out a gadget and furiously stabbed at its buttons. The crazed mechanical insect froze mid slam.

"Good grief and Galileo," Schlepper puffed and tossed the gadget back into Stanley, "Sorry about that." He shoved his beetle contraption backward on the bench. "Not the carbon pulse booster then," he said and waved a hand at Stanley and the gadget. "Thank Barnum for the destabilizing node mallet, eh?"

Phyllo gaped at him. "The what?"

"That gadget has saved me more times than I care to admit. Cuts through any frequency to stop automatons dead." He peered into the opening in the beetle's back. "Hopefully it will have preserved my circuit boards."

The fog around Schlepper and the creature started to lift and at the head of the beetle Phyllo saw movement. He thought, for an unlikely moment, that he could pick out the shadowy outlines of little people. Brownie sized people. Could there be others? Was it possible he had opened some kind of perceptual door that was now allowing him to see the previously un-seeable? The indecipherable, as Tamer Venor had put it. He remembered how the Brownies had popped out of existence when he'd looked at them directly and tried not to stare.

"Mr Schlepper, what even is this?" he said instead, purposefully turning his eyes away, "What are you making?"

Schlepper bounced gently on his springy legs and rattled his lips with a great puff of breath. "One of my contraptions." He arced his hand through the air as if following the curve of a sign. "Schlepper's Contraptionist Carousel. Destined to be as famous as the Circus of Wonder itself one day, perhaps." He allowed himself a modest smile then waved that same hand to direct Phyllo's attention to the ceiling.

"The roundabout is functioning upstairs, but the contraptions are proving to be more delicate." He nodded to himself with a rueful smile. "The molecular warp collector that allows me to use the spatial interverse also acts on the creatures. The spatial interverse?" Schlepper seemed to note the bewilderment in Phyllo's eyes. "The reason all this fits in here. I believe it is spacing out the components—" he leaned thoughtfully against the bench "—unfortunately."

There was very faint laughter coming from the head of

the beetle and Phyllo risked a glance out of the corner of his eye. Oil-smeared, skinny-limbed figures, even smaller than the Brownies, were jumping around in a raucous huddle, waving about springs and screws. Phyllo snapped his eyes back to Schlepper, who was taking another bit of whatever it was out of the tin.

"Good for us that Stanley has a weakness for grease nuggets, isn't it, boy?"

Schlepper bent over so that Stanley could snaffle it from his hand and Schlepper rubbed the residue of grease from his fingertips behind Stanley's ear. Stanley's back leg kicked convulsively.

"Exploiting the spatial interverse allows us to manipulate mass. Size and weight stretched or reduced at our convenience, yes, but it is a hall of mirrors. Everything inside is affected and, unfortunately for my mechanics, everything inside that too. See for yourself."

Schlepper lifted a flap on the beetle's shell and Phyllo edged over to peer in.

There was a metal frame, a good deal of wiring, gears and springs, but beyond that there did also seem to be an awful lot of space that reached on beyond the size of the beetle's body. Something that involved valves was dangling limply. Schlepper closed the flap and patted it affectionately.

"Not furry or cuddly, I know, but they are my preservation of the species and that space within, well I may come up with a use for it yet. I've never been much cop with the living breathing kind. I'll leave that up to you." Schlepper's moustache points quivered and he looked enquiringly at Phyllo. "How are you getting on with that, by the way?"

Phyllo pushed his hands into his pockets and said, "I've learned some useful stuff. Actually, there is something that might be of interest to you, but I just need to check on it first." Those little people had to be some kind of fae, but he didn't want to make the same mistake he had with the Brownies by rushing in.

Schlepper raised his eyebrows. "Indeed?"

"And Tamer Venor has a plan to catch a bait animal," Phyllo continued, "but it means travelling a long way, all the way to Egypt. I suggested going by airship, but she says that we can't. Shame you haven't still got yours." He laughed nervously and gave Schlepper a cheeky grin. "Although it's parked up in Honeyholde, isn't it? Maybe you could ask the new captain if he'd take us. Who is that by the way?"

Phyllo mashed his lips together in anticipation of the answer.

Schlepper rubbed at his nose. "I believe she's being readied for an expedition as we speak, so is busy in any case." He extended a hand. "I'd take you myself, but she belongs to the Club now." He shrugged and then turned his back on Phyllo to return the tin of grease nuggets to his desk drawer. "I do miss the thrill of a journey."

"An expedition? By who?"

"Any one of the top-ranking explorers could be using her."

"Anyone Crow-ish?" pressed Phyllo.

"Mallum Oswald, you mean?"

"Not necessarily—"

"I wouldn't be surprised." Schlepper turned back to the beetle contraption and poked about in the wiring hatch. He pulled out a handful of wires that were melted and black. "I wonder if a microfilament monitor would help."

"Who's the captain? Do you know him?"

"Phyllo, I really can't say. It's not up to me who flies in her now, I'm sorry. I must to get on."

"Right. Right then." Phyllo had hoped for a bit more information, even if he couldn't cadge a lift to Lake Nasser. Schlepper sighed and looked back to him over his glasses.

"I know you want to find the dragon, Phyllo. You want to keep your place in the Circus of Wonder. Who wouldn't? This big top," he pointed toward the curtained doorway, "It's the envy of the circus fraternity, do you know that?"

Phyllo shrugged.

"Even in its slightly dishevelled state. I never imagined I'd get a second chance to join. An outsider looking in all my life and now I'm on the inside." He smiled at Phyllo kindly. "I can scarcely believe it."

"A second chance?" Phyllo wasn't aware that he'd had a first.

"Oh, a long time ago, there was an open audition. A party the Ringmaster at the time put on for his cast. The cast were his guests so they were looking outside for entertainment and word was that if you could impress Verne Barker with your act there was a chance of getting in.

"No-one wanted to pass up an opportunity like that. We came in our droves. Verne was famous for what he'd achieved here. The Circus of Wonder, it was the best, the bravest, the most magical, the most innovative and *The Machine* well, there's not another like it. If he'd seen my automatons, my creature contraptions…" Schlepper tailed off.

"The party. I've heard about it," Phyllo cut in, "The fire that killed the Ringmaster's family." Phyllo had only learned about it from his father quite recently. The whole Circus of Wonder cast had been invited to a surprise party at Winter's

Deep, the Barker family home, by the current Ringmaster's father, Verne. Outsiders from the In-between had set light to the house and Lazarus Barker had taken his distrust of the people of the In-between to extreme levels ever since.

"I was shocked," said Schlepper, "All the performers that I knew were desperate for a chance to join the Wonder cast. I myself was hopeful, but Verne never got to see a single one of my automatons." He shook his head sadly and his eyes seemed to mist over as he drifted away in the memory.

"The fire killed him before he could see them." Phyllo finished the silence.

"Him and the rest of the family. Save for Lazarus, of course." Schlepper pressed his lips together in a thin sort of resigned smile. "But at least Lazarus will get to see them now. If I can get the damn things to work, that is."

"I-I brought back your gadget," stammered Phyllo and pulled it from his pocket, "It might have something that can help." He held it out for Schlepper to take.

He looked at it, but shook his head. "Thank you, Phyllo, but it's of no use here. A survival widget's place is in the field. You keep it for your hunt."

17

DECIPHERING THE INDECIPHERABLE

ELLWAND'S ENCYCLOPAEDIA OF INDECIPHERABLES was a thick tome of tissue-thin pages. Phyllo pulled it from the haphazardly stacked book selection in the Menagerie common room and then set to scouring it for clues.

It meticulously mapped out the relationships between leprechauns, pixies, boggarts and Brownies, to name but a few, the profile for each accompanied by a colourful watercolour sketch for identification purposes. The book outlined fae habits, along with their likely impact upon adopted humans, and this was the part Phyllo read with the greatest interest.

He had found the Gremlin listing about a third of the way in and it jumped out immediately as the most likely cause of Schlepper's troubles. Its entry revealed that, much like the Brownies, Gremlins had originally been considered a helpful species. They held a natural affinity with technicians and engineers and were drawn to relieving the squeakiness of a wheel or the free movement of a cog as a matter of pleasure. Over time, however, the acknowledgement of their existence had waned and as a consequence so had the enthusiasm of the Gremlin to do good work. They grew tired of receiving no credit for the help they provided, so much so that eventually the average Gremlin was more likely to toss a spanner in the works than it was to grease it.

Their profile fitted Schlepper's predicament perfectly and Phyllo was delighted to discover that the book also gave useful tips on how to manage them. He made notes in his scrapbook and resolved to pass them on to Schlepper first chance he got. He hoped that Tamer Venor would be impressed if he'd deduced it correctly, as scoring points in this battle against Panya was proving incredibly difficult.

He closed the book and returned it to the haphazard pile. It was late. Even Panya had finished her duties and was now scuffling about in the neighbouring stall, getting ready for bed. Part of Phyllo really wanted to ask her for advice on the Gremlins. A second opinion would have been invaluable, but at the same time, he really didn't want to lose any of the credit for solving Schlepper's problem, if he'd got it right. She probably wouldn't speak to him anyway.

He stretched and yawned and got up to shuffle back to his stall, passing the gate to Panya's pen deliberately slowly, in a sort of uncertain hope of catching her eye.

She sat cross-legged on the floor with her back to him, wiry hair exploding from two thin plaits that were finally giving up after a full day's arduous restraint. All her attention was focused on a miniature model of a circus ring. Playing there, suddenly she seemed extra young. Fully absorbed in her game, she reminded Phyllo so forcefully of Dodo, when he'd found her sitting with the Brownies, that a pang of guilt stabbed right through him again. Not just for frightening the fae away either, but for leaving her so lonely that she needed them at all.

Panya looked smaller still down on the floor and Phyllo's guts writhed with a confusion of feelings.

He had to be better than her.

He had to win this apprenticeship to protect his family. If he got thrown out, he knew they'd follow him and he just couldn't let that happen.

It was hard to feel sorry for someone who didn't seem to like you, but then, who could blame her? This was her home. Tamer Venor was her family. If she lost, Panya would be homeless again, and it would be his fault.

She was so small, smaller even than Dodo, although he felt sure she must be older. His instincts said he ought to be looking out for her, but instead they'd been forced into this weird competition.

None of it was fair.

He shook his head as if hoping that some sense would rattle down into place and looked beyond her, to the miniature circus.

There were a series of platforms standing in its ring, much like those used by the Agile Arethusa, the Circus of Wonder tumblers. The model even had towers either side with tiny ladders dangling to the ground for imaginary acrobats to climb. Adverts for tankards of cream fudge soda and overflowing cones of caramel corn were propped up at the ringside, and rows of benches, just like those in the real big top, hunkered around the ring waiting to be filled. Phyllo shrank against the lip of the wall, settling in to watch.

She tapped at a pedestal with a red and white striped stick and a mouse, upright on hind legs wearing a pink tutu, flung open the red velvet curtain at the back of the ring and strode out with its pink nose poked high in the air. Three more pranced behind, all similarly dressed and stepping in synchronisation with the first.

Together, they sprang smoothly up onto the pedestals. Panya held the tip of the stick six inches higher, above each of their heads in turn and gave it a little swirl. The mice pirouetted, one after the other, on the spot, their forepaws coming together in a little point above their heads. Panya squeaked delightedly and the mice squeaked back.

She tapped her stick on the perfectly formed mouse-sized trapeze bars, tied off to the poles on either side of the ring. The mice hopped and cartwheeled their way across the platforms, then climbed the ladders to take up positions on the bars. All the while they postured and posed, sweeping their pink-skinned paws in elegant arcs and finishing with little flourishes.

Panya chirruped and they swung away, but not clumsily, nor scrabbling to hold on. They spun elegantly around the bars, one leaping to the other to be caught and then back again. They struck poses worthy of Birdie or even the ballerina she longed to be, fluffy little chests thrust out and forepaws held aloft like flying professionals.

Phyllo gawked at them. The mice had a trapeze act. You had to be kidding.

Panya chirruped and the mice spun around their bars, then released them to turn somersaults in the air and land solidly on all four feet. Panya squeaked, Phyllo assumed appreciatively, and gave each rodent flyer a grape which they accepted flamboyantly then bowed.

Phyllo rolled around the stall end post into his own pen and out of sight.

Could he really be expected to compete with someone

who not only had years more experience in the talent, but also had taught mice to perform just as well, if not better than he had in his last apprenticeship? The one he'd worked at for two months! Phyllo's throat constricted. He didn't know whether to be awestruck or utterly depressed.

He shucked off his clothes and got into bed. Try as he might to fend off the negative whirl of thoughts, he couldn't shake the feeling that failure was utterly inevitable. He fought to get to sleep, but every time he came even close to nodding off the Sand Dragon made that curious purr of hers or buffeted the cabin walls with her long muscular tail. And it was hot, hotter than ever, like the dragon had taken its heat up a notch in panic. It was restless too, Phyllo could feel it, hear it, pacing and prowling as if it knew its fate was in the balance. Anxiety gnawed at Phyllo's gut and he wondered if it clutched at the Sand Dragon too.

By the next morning he felt as tired as if he hadn't gone to bed at all. His covers had been knocked to the floor in all his flailing about and his jaw ached through to the roots of his teeth. He rubbed at his cheek blearily.

Had he been clenching his jaw in his sleep? It felt that way. He stretched out his mouth experimentally. Grinding his teeth wasn't something he normally did, but it occurred to Phyllo that perhaps his subconscious was sending him a message: *grit your teeth, boy, and get on with it.*

He swung his legs out of bed. It was time to stop messing about. He had to complete his familiar altar so that Tamer Venor could work her magic on it and their journey to Lake Nasser could begin. He had to identify what his familiar was.

Tamer Venor gave him an extra-long look as he strode in for breakfast and he wondered if she could see the shift he felt in himself. That day she looked every bit the formidable hunting goddess, prickling with impatience to depart. Her black harem pants were tucked decisively into knee-high boots, and a black tunic embellished with a thick golden collar of embroidery picked out the gold of her eyes like flames. She bore down upon him, the lion's mane of hair radiating from her head in a dark halo.

She sniffed at him and a glimmer of a smile pulled at the corner of her mouth.

"Something special today, hmm, Phyllo? Electricity in the air. Do you feel it?"

"You know what," he said, "I actually think that I do."

He'd only picked up a little bit so far, but his conversation with Schlepper the previous evening had taught him two more things. There was no other way for them to travel apart from the altars, and the Club was readying the Nelly Bly for an expedition. The Club, who liked nothing more than the hunt. The very same people who the Ringmaster had bragged to about hunting a dragon. He didn't know where the Nelly Bly was going, but the tick of the dragon's clock was getting uncomfortably loud.

"Let us take the next steps in your Whispering journey," Tamer Venor said, "Today you must explore the sense of smell. Least valued among humans, yet most important of all among our friends, the beasts. So much information is encrypted within, only the most skilled Whisperer may decipher it entirely. It is a challenge worthy of Thoth to come even close to the instinctive understanding of a pup."

Phyllo had been expecting this. His journey through the senses was bound to come around to smell eventually.

"Breathe everything in. Consume the air." She scooped the air around her in. "What are the smells of the season? Rotting leaves? Fresh snow? Falling rain? A sunny morning?

A foggy night? Could you identify them by smell alone? Can you detect the hand of man? Diesel fumes, cooking meat, burning herbs. Many are the facets of the perfume of home and too the stench of danger. Think. What smells do you already know? What do they mean?"

Phyllo thought hard. Examining taste and smell felt more like home ground. "Recipes in the Confectionary included smells," he said, "I've had to pick them out before."

"Welcome news." Tamer Venor nodded encouragingly.

"Dad's got a bit of a fondness for lavender in all the wrong recipes," Phyllo said, giving way to a smile. Funny how those lavender mint truffles could make him smile now that he didn't have to eat them, "And the Apothecary was burning sage when I visited with Schlepper. It was so strong." Even the memory of it caught in his throat.

"And let us not forget the dragon hide suit," added Tamer Venor.

Who could forget that? The stink of sulphur had been impossible to wash off. The stench had been bad enough for him, but as nothing compared to the effect it had had on the ponies. At least for him the terrible smell had been reassuring, an indicator of its fire-resistance. For the ponies it had said something quite different. It had filled them with the terror of a deadly predator close at hand.

"Remember that lesson well. The meaning of a smell hinges greatly upon who is doing the smelling. Always consider what else shares your space. There will be much to learn. For this purpose, take your time, and be mindful of your familiar, Phyllo. The Parpadillo seeks its winter burrow even now. Sniff out your missing piece before he is lost to us and our dragon too."

Sniff it out. Right.

18

SMELLS LIKE HOME

PHYLLO YOMPED across the grass toward the Whispering Wood, the dragon-warmth of the Menagerie melting away in the chill of autumn. He clutched his bag to his chest. Inside were a flask of mint tea, a soft bundle of honey cake, his scrapbook and Dr Mandrill's Monkey Wormer tin. It rattled its contents to the rhythm of his stride. Candles, twig, feather, catkin, Brownie clothes and key all tumbling together, eager for their missing piece. Or pieces.

Phyllo closed his eyes and recited the incantation in his head to match their beat.

By ray and beam,
By dell and mound,
By sip and stink,
By sight and sound,
Let east meet west,
Let all be seen
Of creatures known and in-between.
Lady of the Elder bow
Reveal to me, thy servant, now.

He sucked in a deep breath and tried to clear his mind. Thin air filled his lungs, no golden sunshine that morning to plump it with perfume from the flowers. Up ahead a bird cawed high in the treetops, but none swooped to catch their insect breakfast. The thick warm days of summer had passed and the birds were reluctant to leave their nests.

The Whispering Wood loomed. Dense and vast as ever, its inhabitants' leaves were turning with the season. Pale apple and lime rolling into ochre, russet and brilliant red. When Phyllo reached the path he found it carpeted with fallen leaves. Quite separate from the shrubs and ground cover to either side, it wound ahead, leading deep into the forest, a thick oil paint sweep of Mother Nature's brush. The leaves squished beneath his feet, not yet dried to the crisps of autumn proper. He kicked them along, hefting their leathery weight on the uppers of his boots.

If the air was thinner, then the light was greyer now too. Leaves lost from the tree canopy had changed the quality of the light, turning the scene it on its head. Now the colour was on the ground, above him only the feeble grey of a cold sky.

Phyllo shivered. Where once he'd felt protected in the wood, now he felt a prickling creep at the back of his neck. He felt exposed and open to attack. The fear of the dragon he was destined to meet escaped from the box in his mind where he'd been trying to keep it locked away. It wouldn't be much longer now. One day soon he'd have to face it. Butterflies of fear fluttered in his throat and Phyllo struggled to quell them. He took in another long slow breath and tried to put that terrifying thought out of his mind. *Focus on the forest.*

But the forest felt strange, like it knew he was looking at it differently, like its hackles were up.

A breeze swept through the shrubbery far ahead, along

the path. Just like the time he'd visited before. The sweep of movement petered out to nothing when he focused upon it. It was not the wind. He knew it, but he didn't know how.

The clonk of the dead wood chimes drifted to him from the dell and he continued along the path toward it, called by its hollow song. The hairs on the back of his neck bristled.

The dell was the place he knew better than any other in the Whispering Wood. It had been the focus of his childhood games during the off-season and the place he'd gravitated to throughout his explorations of the Beast Whispering talent. When the path spat him out at the rim of the hollow, he felt a wave of relief at the familiarity and an expansion of space in his head. More oxygen and light. Less weight.

Cha-chirrup, cha-chirrup at 3 o'clock.

The clonking of the dead wood chimes at 10.

Phyllo closed his eyes and took in the air, determinedly searching for something he could identify.

Faintly there was smoke. Not fumes, not a machine. Somewhere there was a fire burning but it seemed pure, someone back at the encampment preparing to cook outside.

He searched the air some more and took a tentative step forward, keeping his eyes closed. The ground was familiar beneath his feet. A hard mound of a root where he'd known it would be, then soft ground once again.

The aroma of damp earth, rich and tangy. The smell rolled like colours around his mind. It was this place in particular, but what, specifically?

Crack! Behind him a twig snapped and Phyllo's heart leapt to thud in his chest, but he squeezed his eyes shut tighter. *Don't lose the smell*, he told himself. There was more to it, if he could just concentrate. The forest made sounds like that all the time and he'd never seen anything yet.

A familiar pattern of stones pushed up through the soles of his boots. Phyllo reached out his hand and touched the rough bark of his favourite tree, just like he'd known that he would. He leaned against it and took another deep breath. Dust? Moss? Lichen? There was something more. He slid down the trunk to sit on his comfy root.

"What is that smell?" Phyllo said aloud. "Something really stinky. Something rotten even, maybe?"

His question hung in the air.

"UNNECESSARILY RUDE," said a voice, and Phyllo whirled around.

Behind him, the forest was as empty as ever.

"IS THAT THE WAY THE FATHER WOULD HAVE YOU SPEAK?" The voice spoke again.

Vibrations tickled at Phyllo's nose and he sneezed. Ahead the path and the bushes looked as deserted as ever. He frowned, trying to suppress his rising heart rate. "Where are you? Are you hiding?"

Distantly a bird twittered, but that was all the forest had to say.

"The father?" he pressed, then listened extra hard, hoping to pick out the source of the voice.

"IS THAT THE WAY HE WOULD HAVE YOU SPEAK?"

Phyllo couldn't quite believe it. Weirdly, yet undeniably, the voice was coming from inside his own head. Strong and sure, yet soft enough to have carried to him on the wind. He had not *heard* it as such, not in the normal way and he was almost certain that it had not come from his imagination. The voice had got into his ears from the inside.

Phyllo turned back to sit squarely, utterly mystified.

Directly in front of him something like a fox, about two feet tall, sat on its haunches, its tail held jauntily to point at the sky. Fox-like in size and shape that was, but flesh and blood it most certainly was not.

The tree root beside Phyllo, which ordinarily reached down into the ground, had changed its path to reach up into open air. As he watched it moved and grew to better form a creature the like of which Phyllo had never seen before.

Creeping vines slithered over its surface where fur should have been, writhing and curling and gripping soft wads of moss. The red gold leaves of the tree beneath which they sat swept over its back and, growing in number, filled out the tail in a russet brush. The creature gave it a flick and one detached to weave a zig-zag to the ground.

Its head was the most solid thing about it. Bleached as driftwood and smoothed by time, the fox's features were softly hewn in expressive contours. The dark watery pools of its eyes looked straight into Phyllo's own and, gazing back, Phyllo felt as if he was looking into time itself. His head whirled and his jaw flapped.

"Excuse me?" he managed.

"WE ARE DEATH AND CREATION ETERNAL. ALL ENERGY IN THE PHASES OF THE SUN, THROUGH GROWTH AND DECAY TO BE BORN AGAIN." The fox's head dipped and tilted expressively, but it had no mouth to speak with. Phyllo's teeth vibrated in his jaw.

"Born again. Right, I see. What—" he stammered.

"THE MOTHER GUIDES THE ESSENCE IN ALL ITS FORMS. THE PERFUME OF ABSORBTION IS SACRED TO US."

"Oh. Of course, I didn't mean to. A perfume, right, yes," Phyllo said, finally managing to truly engage with what he was seeing. He blinked confusedly. "Erm, sorry but, who are you?"

"OUR NAME IS ALITURA. WE ARE THE ETHER-WEARD. THE GUARDIANS OF THE FOREST. THE PROTECTORS OF NATURE AND YOU ARE PHYLLO CANE."

Phyllo stared blankly back. "How do you—"

"WE EXIST IN THE AEONS OF TIME INDECIPHER-ABLE. REBORN, REFORMED, REABSORBED. WE EVOLVE AND WE SENSE AND WE KNOW WHAT YOU ARE."

Phyllo stared at it, trying hard to understand what he was hearing and seeing. "You know me?"

The fox stood up and then stepped off the root it had been perched upon. Its skin of living creepers swirled and flowed like strands of muscle, propelling it along. Leaves shimmered from its back to the ground to be immediately replaced. Dangling hair-thin roots reached for the earth from its paws as it stepped forward.

"THE WHISPERING WOOD HAS BEEN OUR HOME FOR A MILLENIUM. THROUGH TIME EVERLASTING WE WATCH AND WE EXPERIENCE ALL. WE HAVE SEEN YOU, PHYLLO CANE. WE HAVE ABSORBED THE ESSENCE YOU HAVE LEFT IN THIS PLACE."

"I, I left something?"

"THE THRILL OF ADVENTURE. THE PROTECTION OF AN ELDER. CAMARADERIE BETWEEN SIBLINGS. LOVE LOST. AN OPEN SOUL POURED GRIEF INTO OUR SOIL. THE MOTHER. FIVE ROTATIONS OF THE SUN DO NOT DIMINISH HER PLACE IN YOUR HEART. YOUR TEARS BIND US, PHYLLO CANE. OUR CANOPY IS YOUR SHELTER, OUR ROOT IS YOURS TO REST UPON, OUR TRUNK: YOUR SHIELD AND YOUR SAFEHAVEN."

Phyllo blinked back at the fox. The mention of his mother had dumbfounded him. Since she'd suddenly and unexpectedly left them, Phyllo had floundered. Until very recently he'd obsessed about a recipe in the Confectionary with which he'd been determined to summon up the essence of her. He'd wanted to take himself back to the gloriously sunny days of his early childhood, when she'd still been alive. It had been an ill-fated mission that had led to him setting light to the big top, being ousted from the Confectionary by the Ringmaster and his current precarious predicament on *the circuit*, searching for his true talent.

"You've seen me here?" His voice came out in a whisper.

"WHEREVER THERE ARE TREES SO TOO CAN WE RESIDE, YET ESPECIALLY IN THIS PLACE. WHEN YOU NEED US, WE ARE HERE."

Phyllo stared at the fox, agog. "Alitura," Phyllo tried out the name and the fox nodded.

The hollow wood chimes clonked distantly.

"SHE COMES." Alitura sat, facing down into the dell and as Phyllo turned to look that way too, he noticed other creatures built in a similar way to the fox by his side. At the base of the next tree along there was a coiled snake, more recognisably root-like in its form, yet here and there, airy spaces were bridged by nets of fine creeper, and flowering mosses grew in checkerboard patterns along its back. It held its head off the ground and swayed in rippling curves from side to side.

Phyllo looked from tree to tree and found a creature at every one that stood as guardians around the dell. A stoat, a deer and, directly opposite, a great hook-beaked bird perched on a low branch, its long tail of fern fronds sweeping down to almost brush the ground. It gazed down at Phyllo benevolently, its eyes as dark and deep as Alitura's.

Then every creature bowed.

On any other day Phyllo would have said that the wind whipped around the crest of the dell, but not that day. He saw her.

Limbs as slender as saplings, she was clothed in a flowing ghostly dress of silvered leaves that rippled as if caught by the lightest breeze. She slipped around the edge of the clearing at the very limit of Phyllo's perception. Dark berries scattered the path in her wake and a veil of tiny white flowers floated around her head and upper torso. Phyllo felt the tiniest hairs on his skin lift as if floating on a static charge, and the quality of the air changed. Her presence washed over him in a breathtaking wave of, what was it? Contentment? Joy? Suddenly it felt like all the best days he'd ever experienced rolled into one, as if his chest was filled with fluttering butterflies, his body as light as a feather.

Branches creaked in the canopy above them and a language Phyllo had never recognised before spoke inside his head. *"ALL HAIL THE LADY OF THE ELDER BOW,"* it said, but not in English. The sounds were creaks of wood, moans in the wind and the fluttering of leaves.

She melted ghostlike into the trees.

"Who – who was that?" Phyllo stammered, feeling the weight of himself return. He strained his eyes to look into the last place he'd seen her, willing her to return and bring back the wonderful feeling she'd cast over him.

"THE ELDER IS THE MOST MAGICAL OF ALL TREES. OUR LADY SWEEPS THE WOOD TO STRENGTHEN ALL. SHE IS ESSENCE PURE."

"Will she come back?" Phyllo desperately hoped that she would.

"SHE IS EVER IN OUR HEARTS."

Ever in our hearts. Phyllo really wasn't sure what to make

of that statement, but he'd felt that she was everything good in the world.

"Those noises, was that tree language? You can speak tree?"

"DID YOU UNDERSTAND IT?"

"Yes."

"THEN I AM NOT ALONE." There were no lips on Alitura's face, but Phyllo felt sure he was smiling.

"DOES THIS FEEL FAMILIAR TO YOU, PHYLLO?"

Familiar? Familiar. "Are you my familiar?" Suddenly it seemed so obvious.

Alitura looked back at him serenely and Phyllo reached out a tentative hand. When his skin met the warm twirling wood of its back a stream of memories flooded through Phyllo's mind: the best wigwam he and Roly had ever built; the day the storm had raged all around them, but the dell had stayed dry; the perfect fallen branch for a swing that had not been there the day before. He could remember hearing the sounds that Alitura played in his head, the soundtrack to this place that was as familiar to him as his own hand. Blood rushed through Phyllo's veins, making him giddy. He took a step back, blinking, and his heel turned over on a lump on the ground. He bent to pick it up.

Smooth and bleached, a nugget of wood about the size of a walnut in the same shape as Alitura's head.

"WHEREVER THERE ARE TREES I CAN COME TO YOU, PHYLLO. IT IS A PIECE OF US, OF NATURE, OF THE ESSENCE.

19

LIGHT BRINGS INSIGHT

Phyllo pelted back to the Menagerie, his discovery bursting in his chest. He'd found it. He'd found his familiar and the missing piece. All this time Alitura had been right there. For years he'd been playing right next to them and never even known they existed.

He charged into the Menagerie and took the steps up to the mezzanine two at a time.

"Tamer Venor," he gasped, "I've found it."

He galumphed to a halt beside her at the table where she walked a silver compass across a map, making notes. He presented her with Alitura's token and she took it from him curiously and rubbed the smooth shape of the fox head with inquisitive fingers.

"Let us see," she breathed, "You have your tin?"

Phyllo pulled it from his bag and tore off the lid to dump its contents onto the table.

"Such excitement." She laughed. "Your familiar, Phyllo, you think you have found it?"

"Yes, yes, I really think so. His name is Alitura. Actually, I say he, could be she, I don't know." Phyllo thought hard. "They only ever said 'us' or 'we', now I come to think of it. They said they were a guardian, I think. Yes, that was it. A guardian of nature."

Tamer Venor's golden eyes stretched wider. "The Ethelweard?" A crinkle appeared between her eyebrows.

"Yes. How did you know? Have you met them? What do you know about them?" Phyllo's words continued to fall out in a rush.

Tamer Venor's hands lodged on her hips and she leaned back. "No, no, no," she said shaking back her mane of hair and laughing, "The Ethelweard are creatures of legend. Was it not a squirrel, protective of its den? Or a rabbit guarding its burrow perhaps?" She nodded to Phyllo encouragingly.

"No, I don't think so. I mean they did *look* like animals, in a way, but they were made of tree."

"Tree." Tamer Venor stared at him. She opened her mouth to speak, but closed it again without having managed it. Eventually she said, "You are sure?"

"Yes, yes. They spoke, in my head, which was weird, but kind of easy."

Tamer Venor looked down to pick through the items from Phyllo's tin. "When I saw the fragments you had collected, I wondered where it was heading, but this." She took a deep breath and frowned in contemplation, "Do you see a connection between them?"

Phyllo stared down at his things on the table.

A fork-shaped twig.

A fluffy feather.

A perfect catkin.

The Brownie hat and unfinished jacket.

The key.

And now the fox head token.

He tried to see what they were supposed to mean as a whole, but could only remember the individual circumstances by which he'd found them.

"You are drawn to the indecipherable, Phyllo, and to the flora."

She stepped back from the table and rolled back the rug to reveal a white pentagram painted on the wooden floor. She grasped a handful of finger-width candles from a box on the table, gave them to Phyllo and directed him to the oil lamp.

"Light the candles and position them as I instruct you. Let the wax drip to form a puddle, then set them into it. That will keep them steady enough. We will ask the gods for their help."

Phyllo eyed the pentagram warily. For the first time they were really getting down to some magic. His mouth went dry.

"If you are correct and you have found your familiar the altar will activate. Your Whispering skills may be about to go up a notch. Are you ready?" The twinkle of adventure flashed in her eye.

Phyllo nodded mutely, his heart beating harder now even than when he'd been running.

"A Whisperer's altar is personal. Their familiar; particular. Every action is accountable and by their own hand, so it is in nature and so shall it be here. Ready your altar, Phyllo, with a candle either side."

Phyllo stumbled forward on numb legs. This had to be it. He'd never felt a connection with another creature like he'd felt with Alitura in the Whispering Wood. He fumbled the tin and its contents into position, as Panya had shown him. The wicks of the candles caught to burn in tall steady flames. Their light bounced from the uneven polished surface of his makeshift mirror and danced over the collection.

"The head of our pentagram points to your familiar," said

Tamer Venor, "We ask for light so that we may see from all points. A candle at 2 o'clock to begin."

Phyllo lit one and placed it on the tip of the first point moving clockwise around the 'clock face' of the pentagram.

Tamer Venor lifted her arms to address the heavens. "*Amun-Ra*, supreme ruler of air and sun, creator of the wind's invisible force and the visible majesty of the life-giving sun. Share your light." Tamer Venor nodded to Phyllo to proceed to the next point around.

He lit a candle and placed it there.

"All praise to *Nun*," she boomed, "God of the abyss and source of all divine existence. Rise from your watery depths and share your light."

The flames reached flickering tongues into the air and Phyllo's lungs struggled for oxygen. He stooped to place a third. The air hummed.

"*Nut*. Child of air and rain, bring the wisdom of the stars and share your light."

Then Tamer Venor stepped onto the final point herself and held out her hand. "Namesake and daughter of Ra, Bastet, protector and guardian of life, share your light."

Hand shaking, Phyllo passed a lit candle to her and as he did so, all the other flames stretched higher around him, burning more fiercely. The rest of the cabin fell away into darkness.

Tamer Venor turned to face the altar and Phyllo felt himself drawn toward it too, breath catching in his chest. The light from the candles danced and bounced off the dimpled mirror, hitting his collection from every angle and spot-lighting details Phyllo had not noticed before.

What could he make of it? Every piece looked more defined and three-dimensional. In this new light he could feel their texture and weight without even touching them. Something told him to pick up the coned hat and as he did so he realised that it would fit snuggly onto the end of the stick. He pushed them together. Then he noticed that there was a tiny hole at the cone's tip which turned out to be just the right size to securely hold the shaft of the feather. He smiled at the convenient precision of it and he poked the feather into place. It held firm.

Assembled, the pieces happily stood on the stick's forked end. Phyllo chuckled, shaking his head. It was crazy that he'd never seen it before. It was quite obviously the shape of a sitting fox, the fork of the stick representing its legs, the coned hat its upper body, and the feather, the handsome ruff of its chest. The catkin, when he held it close by, happily wound itself around the base, transforming into the perfect brush-like tail. Of course it did.

Now it was obvious where the Brownie jacket ought to go, and instinctively Phyllo wrapped it around the form to see how it might fit. The unfinished strands took on a life of their own, growing and stretching. They curled and wove themselves around the miniature fox-shaped body.

Whether it was Brownie magic or the effect of the altar, Phyllo didn't know, but the little jacket all but melted to fit, the golden yellow daisy-head buttons gently rotating and skimming over the surface to slide satisfyingly into place. Finally, he placed the head-shaped token given to him by Alitura on the tip of the cone. It clicked home.

Light from the candles flared and the polished tin lid began to vibrate on its plinth, the hum in the air growing into something physical. Cups rattled on their hooks and the silver compass jiggled on the map where it had been discarded.

"Alitura," Phyllo breathed. A rush of energy swept up from his toes, charged through his legs and torso and then shot out of the top of his head, making him shudder. It bounced off the ceiling, rocketed back down and slammed him to the floor. All the candles blew out.

For a long moment, shocked silence lay over Phyllo like a heavy blanket, keeping him in place. Slowly he lifted his head to find Tamer Venor's face, frozen but grinning, eyes alive with excitement.

"Ha!" she exclaimed, "Ha!" She pulled Phyllo unceremoniously to his feet, squeezed him in a bear hug and then held him out at arm's length to look at him.

"Did I do it? Was that it?" said Phyllo, finding his voice.

"Was that it, he says!" She gripped his shoulders firmly and shook him back and forth.

"But the altar, I didn't get it working." Phyllo looked across to where the tin lid had now fallen over to lie flat on its face.

"But look." The miniature figure of Alitura still sat proudly on its plinth, "And the power was most definitely there, you just need the means to direct it. You need a wand."

The animals of the Menagerie shuffled and screeched in their pens, at last reacting to the shockwave which had shaken the cabin. From the depths of its pen, the dragon roared.

Phyllo blinked at her. He had power?

20

WHAT ABOUT A WAND?

"A WAND?"

Tamer Venor released him. "An artefact through which you direct your intentions, such as this." She pulled her whip from the holster behind her back and passed it to him.

Phyllo found that the whip was much heavier than it appeared. The handle was about the same length as his forearm and the perfect size for his hand to grip securely. Its thick leather fed into a long, tapered plait, at the end of which dangled red tongues of fabric. He turned it over in his hands and found that the base of the handle was decorated with a jewelled scarab beetle.

"My whip is a part of me, an extension of my arm. It is my sting, my voice in any language. It demonstrates my intention and directs my power."

"Where can I get one?" Phyllo asked.

Tamer Venor sighed. "I regret that it is not so easy. This was the property of my mother. She too was a Whisperer. It was old and awaiting the inclination for repair, hung from a hook in our barn. I snatched it down to protect myself when the leopard escaped from its cage and my mother's back was turned. I was half your age and my strength was as nothing compared to the suffocating power of those terrible jaws. I learned that day to sting without pain. My mother added the scarab as a reminder of our eternal connection to the life force, the key to our powers. She taught me how to repair the whip and it has been a part of me ever since."

She took the whip from him and returned it to its holster. "Thoth wills that a Tamer's artefact cannot be bought. It is a found object, Phyllo. Natural at its heart and discovered through necessity. Do you possess such a thing?"

"A whip?" He really didn't think so.

"Not a whip. Something from your experiences. Think of the things you have done and what you have used in times of need."

Phyllo frowned. Before coming to the Menagerie, he had served an apprenticeship with *The Fabulous Volante*. He'd swung from their trapezes and climbed their ladders, but he couldn't ever remember grabbing for anything to save himself. The focus of the flyers' magic was in their sash, but that wasn't something he could use to point.

He chewed on his lip. "They don't really have anything like that in the flyers and when I was in the Confectionary the only thing I ever really wielded was a spoon."

Tamer Venor looked encouraged. "There is potential. It is the focus of the Confectioners' magic, yes?"

"Um, not really. It's just a spoon. I mean it's the apron that's important. Every Confectioner has their own apron. You know, it's the stains and the burns. The spills. They all add up. Well, they do if you're me."

Tamer Venor frowned at that and turned away to pace the room. "In time of need, is there something you would always go for? In a difficult circumstance, has just the thing presented itself to you? Think, Phyllo. Think."

Phyllo thought as hard as he could. When had he been in need? He rubbed at his scalp.

"I've got it," he cried out, "When Roly and I went to the cliffs, we decided on a different path because we wanted to get higher, but the ground was rough. It was overgrown with brambles and I found the perfect stick to beat it down to make a path. The perfect stick!"

"Yes, yes, this is promising." She strode back toward him, waving her hands about with her words. "And a stick, of course. More flora, you are drawn to it. Where is this stick? Did you keep it?"

Phyllo scrunched up his face, trying to remember what he'd done with it.

"We climbed to the higher cave. We shuffled out along the ledge. I still had it then. Oh." Phyllo's face fell. "We built a fire to toast our marshmallow men. I speared mine on the end of it."

Tamer Venor grimaced at him.

"And then I burned it. The stick's gone."

Venor threw her hands into the air and turned away from him again. She stomped her way across the room, but returned wearing a new expression of determination. "There is nothing else for it. You must dive in at the deep end. It is time to swim with the sharks." Her eyes were wide and bright.

"Sharks?" Phyllo did not like the sound of that.

"Experience brings circumstance. Circumstance brings need, the mother of invention. Come, come." She strode out of the room and clanged down the stairs.

"Sharks?" Phyllo said again, following, but a good deal behind.

"Don't worry. We don't actually have any sharks." She swept his concerns away without really looking at him.

When they reached the Menagerie floor, Panya had the capuchins out of their pen and was corralling them on the small stage they used for show practice. The butterphants stretched their trunks to sniff at Phyllo as he neared. The larger beast of the two puffed air into his ear and down his neck. Phyllo patted its furry trunk.

"I've no chocolate mice today, Manana," he said softly. Manana, however, was not so easily put off and continued to snort and sniff hopefully around Phyllo's pockets.

On the stage Panya directed the capuchins with little flicks of the striped stick he'd seen her use when conducting the mice. They scrambled over each other to stand on shoulders and formed a gangly pyramid, which wobbled dangerously. Phyllo was surprised to see them out.

"How come the monkeys are practising?" he asked, "I thought that Panya was just doing pen maintenance at the moment."

Tamer Venor came to a stop by the gate of the dragon pen and frowned at the stage. "That had been my intention, it is true, but I think we must accept there can never really be a period of rest for the capuchins. Without practice they forget the routines and worse, get rowdy."

A purple-waistcoat-wearing monkey with tufty ears refused to climb to the place Panya was indicating. Instead it yanked at the tail of another, who squealed shrilly and leapt at it. Phyllo recognised this as the monkey who'd given him the key. The key that had not been incorporated into his altar familiar, he now realised. It was just a key after all.

The pyramid collapsed in a tangle of scrambling limbs and screeching.

"I can see we have already left it too long," sighed Tamer Venor as the monkeys rolled about the stage, "But this presents us with an opportunity, I think. While Panya continues to remind our simian friends of their manners, the deep end is clear for you to throw yourself in." She gave Phyllo a wide smile then turned her head to look into the darkness of the dragon pen.

Phyllo gulped. His last encounter with the dragon had not been fun. Truth be told, he was secretly glad that, for the most part, it could not be persuaded to leave the depths of its lair.

Yet, there was no forgetting its alarming presence. Thumps of its great tail and growls punctuated Phyllo's days and the dragon's self-soothing guttural purr rattled the night. The heat radiating from its pen had become so intense now that even in the falling temperatures of late autumn, the whole Menagerie was swelteringly hot. Phyllo wondered if the dragon burned with loneliness so badly that one day she might actually burst into flames.

He followed Tamer Venor's eyes into the depths of the pen and a low snarl rumbled out from the darkness. It was difficult to interpret it as anything other than a threat.

"I will find you a mate, Thamineh," said Tamer Venor softly, "and when I do your love will be all the sweeter for this time of solitude." She turned to Phyllo. "She suffers, Phyllo. We must help her. It's up to us now. You understand the significance of it, yes?"

Phyllo blinked at her. Making the leap from utter terror to sympathy wasn't easy.

"Without a bull dragon, Thamineh cannot stay at the Circus

of Wonder. She will pine and consume herself more with every passing day and the Ringmaster will not allow an animal who cannot work lodgings in his cabins. Numbers in the wild are now so low that our task is great, but imagine if we could bring together a breeding pair. We could save Thamineh, return her to being the star act of the Menagerie and in doing so, help to save the species. Imagine a calf. We must be more than showmen, Phyllo. We must be conservationists too."

Phyllo swallowed hard. It was so much responsibility. "I'll do my best," he croaked.

"You must push yourself forward. I know it is much to ask, but to suffer for truth is to give it true meaning."

Phyllo pulled himself up to his full height, pushing down the knot of fear in his throat. He reached for the latch on the gate. He was terrified of the dragon, but if this was the only way.

"OK, I'm ready," he said in a wavering voice.

Tamer Venor goggled at him and snorted.

Phyllo stared at her. "No, really. I can do it."

"You're not going in *there*. As fortuitous as your previous visit was, let us not tempt fate. We'll not kill you today." She laughed uproariously.

Phyllo stared at her, utterly confused.

"Peril, yes. Possible death, I think not. Let us find another creature less… lethal." She looped an arm around his shoulders and guided him away.

The adrenaline racing around Phyllo's veins stuttered and his head spun. He let out a slightly maniacal laugh. "OK, good, ha, ha, ha."

"Bears then." She steered him toward the metal spiral of steps to the second mezzanine.

Bears. That didn't sound especially safe either.

"What about butterphants?" Phyllo spluttered as they passed the reaching trunk of Manana.

"Our butterphants are much too fond of you already. No, we must find the balance between being the provider of snacks whilst stopping short of actually becoming one." She bounded up the second spiral staircase to the other mezzanine and strode to the pen at the end.

"Kin schersa!" she barked to the occupants out of sight and there was a sudden shuffling about inside.

All Phyllo had seen of the bears since his arrival in the Menagerie had been on the day of the great escape. Panya had dealt with their day-to-day care and being up on the second mezzanine, he'd not had reason to go near them.

Up here it was hotter than ever and Phyllo's feet tingled with the heat radiating up through the floor from the dragon below. Sweat popped on his upper lip.

"The Astral bears like their sleep and don't take kindly to being disturbed," Tamer Venor said in a loud voice, seemingly quite unconcerned about disturbing them, "But their quarters must be cleaned so *wakey-wakey-wakey*. Just move them into next door."

She snatched open the gate of their pen and banged it, quite unnecessarily, back on its hinges, then stepped into the small neighbouring pen to drag out equipment. One thigh-high bin which held a variety of implements including a twiggy broom and a shovel, and a second bin which was equal in size, but empty.

"Dirty bedding into this one," she said and scraped them into the bear pen where she hammered her hand on the wall several times. *"WAKEY-WAKEY.* Time to be ferocious." She grinned at Phyllo then grabbed him by the shoulders and pushed him in.

Phyllo squeaked involuntarily.

The bears lay in nests of hay, their bodies settled into curls for sleep, but their eyes were now wide open, beady and black. They glared at the noisy intruder. The nose of the closest wrinkled with a rumble.

"Kin schersa!" Tamer Venor cried again from behind him and the bears lumbered to their feet.

Their heads were now as high as Phyllo's own. They glared at him, sniffing at the air. The closest raised both front paws and then slammed them down onto the ground.

"What do I do? What should I do?" Phyllo squeaked.

"Charge," said Tamer Venor, "Show him who is the boss."

"What? Are you nuts?"

"All right, circle behind, then. Get the advantage, let him know you mean business."

"But there are more over there." Phyllo threw an alarmed hand at the back of the enclosure, where three more pairs of eyes blazed.

"Are you man or are you mouse?" Tamer Venor stamped her foot.

Phyllo squeaked out a laugh.

The bears at the back shook out their shaggy fur and stretched long-clawed paws, limbering up. Phyllo threw his hands out in an involuntary shield and scurried to the wall, heart in his throat.

"That's it, circle behind. Stalk. Keep moving."

Phyllo inched deeper into the pen while every cell in his body screamed for retreat. The bears glanced between each other and back to him, eyes narrowing. The largest, who'd been at the front, gave a gruff bark.

"Kin schersa!" cried Tamer Venor again and all four bears rose up onto their hind legs to let out a ragged roar. Phyllo reeled, his hair on end with fright. Then the largest bear lunged, massive teeth bared, and the bottom seemed to fall from Phyllo's stomach. He squealed and dove for the centre of the pen, only to find the other bears waiting, swiping viciously at the air. He skidded on his heel and scrambled to change direction.

"Come on, time to clean," called Tamer Venor from the gate, "Get your tools."

Phyllo spun incredulously to face her, but found that she wasn't even looking at him. She was shoe-horning a few more items into the bins. They sank from sight before he'd been able to make them out.

She looked up to catch his eye and winked. "Roar back. Don't let him get away with that."

"Roar?" said Phyllo feebly.

Tamer Venor nodded encouragingly. "Roar!"

"Roar," he repeated, louder this time, but voice cracking.

One after the other the bears crashed down to all fours and slunk menacingly forward.

Phyllo scrambled for the bins, straining to keep the bears in his sights.

Again, they looked between each other and back, and somewhere at the back of Phyllo's mind it struck him as odd, like they were co-ordinating in an un-bear-like way. Then together they sprang. Phyllo scrabbled backward, made a wobbly turn, tripped over his own feet and sprawled into the bins, knocking them flying. Their contents spilled and slid away, beneath the gate.

The only thing left within reach was the empty bin itself which he dove beneath, sucking in a panicked breath as it rolled leisurely around its rim, gaining in speed until finally it settled over him.

Inside this cocoon the silence was thick. It was utterly dark and it stank. Well of course it did. What had he expected from a container used for clearing bear poo? But there was no helping that now – beyond its protective walls, dagger-sharp claws tapped on the floorboards as the Astral bears circled.

In no time at all he was hyperventilating. Wide-eyed but still seeing nothing, scouring every sound for clues, he felt sweat dripping from every pore in the airless, stifling heat inside his protective prison.

The bin tipped suddenly to one side and Phyllo pushed out his hands and feet to cling on. Together they slid along the floor. The great weight of one of his pursuers knocked against the outside of the bin, sliding it back the other way. Phyllo scrabbled to stay beneath it, pushing at the inside of the walls to keep it down.

A gruff bark issued from behind his head and he cringed away. Claws scrabbled at the floor. Jagged bursts of light flashed beneath the rim as it jumped and skipped. Phyllo clung to the bin with his fingertips for as long as he could, but then it was yanked from him and skittering away before he could do a thing to stop it.

The bears barked in unison and Phyllo scrunched down into a protective ball, his eyes squeezed shut.

This was it.

They'd got him.

He waited for the blow, for the slash of a claw, for the sharp sting of a bite.

The suspense was terrible.

He listened for the scrabble of claws on wood.

But there was no scrabble. Just a crackle. The crackle of a

needle on a gramophone record, then the plinky-plonk of a banjo and the soft wail of a muted trumpet. Panya had put on the music for the next section of the capuchin act. An off-key piano chimed in and a zany tune belted out from the stage downstairs.

Phyllo could hear her shouting orders, and the bolshie monkeys screeching in defiance. He opened one eye. The largest of the bears was standing up on its hind legs within touching distance. It was tapping its foot.

Phyllo goggled at it.

It nodded its shaggy head to the beat. Its eyes were closed and it was smiling. Smiling.

Phyllo slowly turned his head to look for the others. One leaned on the top bar of the gate, bobbing its head to the music and watching the monkey mayhem. The other two were both up on their hind legs and holding each other's forepaws. The beat dropped and they broke into a jive.

Phyllo snapped his head around to find Tamer Venor. She rolled her eyes and huffed out a sigh. "That is *not* ferocious. I said *ferocious*. *Kin schersa!*" she said exasperatedly, but the bears completely ignored her.

And then Phyllo remembered: these were the Astral Dancing Bears, one of the Menagerie acts. Phyllo allowed himself a small smile, but any relief he might now have enjoyed was entirely short-lived as the bear close at hand had suddenly decided it was in need of a dance partner.

It snatched Phyllo up from the ground, squeezed him unceremoniously to its chest and then flung him away sideways in a spin. It hauled him staggering back and then set off around the pen in a polka, dragging Phyllo along and dipping him at the corner before careering back, whirling them both in dizzying circles.

"Aaaarrrrgh," Phyllo wailed as the bear threw him up into a lift.

"Oh, for the love of Thoth," Tamer Venor cried from the gate, "You're dancing with him now?"

Phyllo caught sight of her rubbing at her forehead and looking annoyed. "It's not me, it's him! I can't stop him," Phyllo wailed.

"I wasn't talking to you; I was talking to twinkle toes here." She gestured derisively to the bear who had segued into a tap routine. The music coming from below was getting more and more energetic and with it the bear's dance moves. It completed a particularly complex section of tap steps and threw out a paw to Phyllo.

It was irresistible.

Phyllo laughed, took the paw and the two of them polkaed off around the pen again. This time the other two, who'd been doing their own thing, joined in, keeping in step.

They swept past the last single bear, who finally realised what was going on and, now minus their usual partner, joined in to skip happily behind.

"Open the gates," Phyllo yelled as they raced toward Tamer Venor and she swung them wide to let them pass. Phyllo and his dancing companions whirled into the second pen to make a circuit, the trumpets of the capuchin music parped to their conclusion and the bears flourished paws in the air, spinning Phyllo away to one side.

He wobbled, grinning and ungraceful, then collapsed into the hay.

Tamer Venor stared down at him, hands on her hips, her expression incredulous. Eventually she said, "Clearly the bears are too easy," and turned to walk away. "Come."

21

PHYLLO'S CANE

PHYLLO STRUGGLED to his feet and followed behind as she strode along the balcony to a third enclosure with a gate of glass. Phyllo peered inside. There was sand and seaweed and rocky pools and hundreds of brightly coloured crabs.

"Pinchy, evil little beggars." Tamer Venor scowled bitterly into the crab enclosure. Vast numbers squatted in clusters around the pools, motionless and beautiful.

"The bears are better trained. Pretending to be ferocious is the beginning of their act so they ought to have been good at it, but I suppose they are bored. I hadn't bargained on the capuchin music and I should have known better than to rely on an Ursu's attention span. Too easily distracted. Music or food and you've lost them." She rubbed at her chin. "Fake danger is no danger at all. I was a fool to try it. The crabs, however, are not yet trained."

Phyllo looked down at them. They looked rather small and sedate to him.

Tamer Venor followed his gaze. "Don't confuse size with danger. The bears put on a good show, but perhaps it's not size and strength that will achieve our goal. Attitude may be the key and there's no shortage of that in here. I would not normally venture in at feeding time, but perhaps it suits our purpose."

She passed Phyllo a large silver bucket filled to the brim with shrimp, unlatched the gate and bowed him in.

The heat from the dragon seemed quite appropriate in this pen. The azure blue of the ceiling and walls combined to feel like the sea and sky of a tropical island. The rockpools reflected sunlight that Phyllo couldn't quite see the source of and the inhabitants crowded contentedly at the water's edge.

"Jewel crabs," Tamer Venor called from the other side of the gate. "A most handsome display. Notice the shell variety."

The crabs were quite beautiful, there was no denying it. The shells on their backs were sparkling and translucent. Colours spanned from the deepest sapphire blue right through to palest golden citrine. A ripple of movement went through them as Phyllo approached.

"Are they valuable?" asked Phyllo, "I mean are these really jewels on their backs?"

"An interesting question and one that brings me consternation. It depends where they hail from and upon the natural deposits close at hand. Shells are manufactured within the creatures' own internal systems, much like hair or nails, and depend entirely upon what is ingested. Like the flamingo, who gain their colour from the copious amount of shrimp in their diet, the jewel crab will likewise take on its environment. I hope for more pinks, hence the shrimp." She gestured to the bucket.

"Regrettably, the natural mineral deposits of a circus cabin, however brilliantly constructed, "she gave a little bow, "does not provide the constituents for the real thing or, trust me, my financial worries would be at an end." She gave the crabs a little sneer.

Phyllo couldn't see what her problem was. The crabs were quite stunning.

Tamer Venor mimed grabbing a handful of shrimps from the bucket and throwing it. Phyllo did just this and immediately fat claws appeared as if from nowhere to wave above the jewelled carpet. A lucky few snatched food from the air while the others snapped, disappointed.

"Oh," said Phyllo, "They were so still, I thought they were asleep."

Tamer Venor shook her head and looked pointedly down to the ground. In the few short seconds he'd had his eyes on her, a circle had formed around his feet. She waved him forward but Phyllo hesitated. He took another handful of shrimps and threw them as far as he could into the enclosure. Crabs on the other side of the rock pool thrust their claws into the air to catch them. The crabs at his feet stretched up to follow the arc of the food, but when it landed at the claws of their peers, too far away to reach, they didn't run to fight for it. Phyllo had a bucketful after all.

The blanket of jewels rippled along the ground and hundreds of crustaceans got to their feet. They scuttled toward him, pincers held high.

Phyllo's eyes popped and he shot a look at Venor.

"Feed, feed, feed," she punctuated with nods.

Phyllo grabbed great handfuls of shrimps and threw them in every direction. This had the combined effect of annoying the crabs at his feet, who weren't able to reach it, and alerting others in the furthest corners of the enclosure to the fact he had food.

Crabs climbed onto his shoes and began to scale his trouser legs. Reminiscent of that time with the capuchins when Tufty had climbed his leg to search his pockets, the crabs were much less dextrous, climbing jerkily and clumsily, hoisting themselves up with those vicious claws and pinching Phyllo's flesh.

"Ow! Ow! Get off!" He shook his leg out, but no sooner had he dislodged them from one leg than newcomers were climbing the other. He threw a handful on shrimp to the ground a few feet away and the crabs closest to him switched their attention to the mound of easily attainable food and sidled toward it.

Phyllo backed away, tossing more handfuls down around him. This had the terrifying consequence of making yet more of the creatures run at him, but those who were closest scuttled away to beat their companions to it. He dumped the final scraps from the bucket onto the ground and dove for the gate.

One particularly determined crustacean still dangled from the back of his thigh. He levered its claws open and tossed it unceremoniously back into the melee.

"Pinchy, evil little beggars," Phyllo grumbled under his breath. Tamer Venor laid a hand on his shoulder and they sighed together.

"That was quick thinking, throwing food to the ground so close. I'll remember that."

Phyllo gave her a half-hearted smile.

"Yet still we are no closer to our goal and the means to get there eludes me. Perhaps some honest work will bring inspiration." She turned away from Phyllo to head back to the vacated bear pen, stooped to pick up a fallen broom and swept her way into the stall.

Phyllo craned to look over the mezzanine rail to the stage, rubbing at the welt on the back of his thigh. The capuchins had gone. The gate to their enclosure was closed. Panya had completed yet another task while he had continued to struggle with the basics. He puffed out another sigh.

Behind him a gate unlatched.

As light on her feet as ever, Panya had come up to their mezzanine unheard. While he'd been getting pinched by the crabs, she'd completed her task and moved on to the next job, caring for the magical creatures of the Menagerie. How was he ever going to win this apprenticeship? Panya was so far ahead it was laughable.

The gate she had unlatched was tall and narrow and made from a complex fretwork of scrolling vines and flowers. In truth, Phyllo had not realised it was the entrance to a pen at all. She disappeared inside without paying him any mind.

A tiny butterfly flapped out through the gap. Brilliant blue, it bobbed lazily out into the open. Then another came behind it and another and another, a ribbon of blue widened as more bobbed out into the central space, falling and climbing with easy sweeps of their delicate wings. Blue became turquoise, vivid green and lemon yellow, woody brown and gunmetal grey. Numbers growing, they swept up in a curve and as they got closer, Phyllo could see the intricate detail of their wings: patterns that shone in golden threads and fat little bodies, furry and soft.

Chameleon-like, they mirrored their environment. A shimmering transformation from deep grey to bright silver swept through the group which stretched in a curling ribbon six feet wide and fifty long from the gate to the very roof of the Menagerie.

They wound around Phyllo in a broad curve, the soft

flutter of their wings silencing every other sound and bringing with it something indefinable and distant, like birdsong. Phyllo's eyes slid from one to the next. A soft breeze kissed his face and swept a wonderful calming cool across his skin.

The kaleidoscope of changing colour coiled around him and up to the roof then rippled down through the central space in a wave, twisting and turning as one.

"*Papilio Aves Pacis*," said the voice of Tamer Venor from inside the bear pen, "Birds of Peace. Of course, they are not birds but the way they move in murmuration is typical of swallows. A fascinating creature. The *Aves Pacis* is one of the few hive minds."

She went back to her sweeping and Phyllo's attention was sucked back to the butterflies or the *Aves Pacis*, as he now knew them to be called. They had grouped together to hang in the air in the shape of an enormous fish. After a moment's awe and then of wondering why it looked so familiar, Phyllo realised it was modelling itself on one of the pictures displayed in the common room. Every wing represented a scale, every movement was fishlike and flowing from the next. It swam through the air, an articulated and iridescent floating carp, pearly white and vibrant orange. Its mouth popped open and closed with such astounding reality that Phyllo found himself mouthing back.

Panya backed out through the enclosure gate dragging a jumble of dried branches, faded flowers drooping at their tips. She heaped them up to one side and returned to the pen. At the top of the stairs Phyllo saw that she'd brought up fresh bales of the same plant, the fresh vegetation sporting plump green leaves and stiff purple cone-shaped flowers.

He realised at once that this was the new enrichment for

the butterfly enclosure and while Panya worked at gathering a second dry bundle to drag out, he decided to prove himself not totally useless and set about cutting the bales open. He scooped up the largest armful of foliage he could, and made to take it in.

Once they were loose and waving in the air, the flowers' fragrance was intoxicating, a smell as sweet as honey. It became clear very quickly that they were an absolute favourite of the *Aves Pacis*.

They swooped down to settle on the pendulous flowers and drink their nectar. Phyllo grinned happily up at them. More came and more until Phyllo was surprised to find that the branches had become really quite heavy, so heavy in the end that their smooth bark slipped through his fingers and out of his grip. Branch after branch banged to the ground.

A great cloud of butterflies was shocked from the branches and fluttered around him so feverishly that, for a moment, it was difficult to see. He awkwardly grappled the branches up from the floor and noticed, to his horror, that two creatures had been crushed in the fall. Their beautiful wings were scrunched unnaturally, damaged beyond repair. Their soft little bodies, too flat.

"Oh no." Phyllo felt devastated. Moments ago, he'd been marvelling at how incredible they were and now two had been squashed.

The soft flutter in the air stuttered. The rhythm of the group faltered and became jagged. The wonderful sensation of peace Phyllo'd been feeling evaporated and in its place a buzz of hostility prickled.

Phyllo looked about at the thousands of butterflies surrounding him and saw that their beautiful colours had changed to acid yellow and black. One flew at his face, all scrabbling scratchy legs, then others were in his hair and he felt a sharp sting on his ear.

"Ow! Ow! I'm sorry. It was an accident. I didn't mean to," Phyllo yelped. The insects swarmed around him. He dropped the branches and backed away, trying to distance himself from the squished bugs on the floor. They flew at him regardless, stinging and biting. Phyllo flailed his arms to bat them away, whilst at the same time trying not to hurt them, an approach as confused as it was hopeless. Then his feet left the floor.

Determined legs hooked at his clothes and thousands of wings beat the air to lift him from the balcony, up and up and over the edge, up to the ceiling, as high as it was possible to go.

Phyllo flailed and struggled and then he was free, but now he was falling, rushing toward the ground with nothing to break his fall.

Then he saw it.

Jutting out from the balcony – a stick, a broom handle perhaps. One of the items that had spilled from the tool bin. It had slid almost off the edge, but was jammed in the railing. He grabbed for it and momentarily it held, slowing him down just enough to swing back and forth. Then it broke free.

They were falling again, but not so far now. The tip of the stick met the ground first and Phyllo pushed against it, reducing the force that met his feet as he allowed his legs to fold with the force of the drop. He came to rest in a crouch.

BOOM!

A shockwave rippled out from the place he had landed, sending the clawing insects that pursued him whirling away.

Phyllo looked confusedly at the broom handle and found

that it was not that at all, but a wooden walking cane with carvings all around. It was elaborately fashioned from dark wood, and its maker had wound a fatly sculpted snake around the shaft, a wide head forming the handle. Its jaws were wide, exposing long fangs. Its eyes sparkled, deep and green.

A vision from that first day filled Phyllo's mind's eye: Tamer Venor commanding the animals to stop.

"*Waqef!*" Phyllo yelled – remembering the word and the crack of the whip. He slammed the tip of the cane down to the ground.

Above him the advancing insects stopped in their descent, as if caught in a spiderweb. Phyllo gaped at them, not quite able to believe that had actually worked.

The next command came to him in a flash of inspiration. He lifted the cane and pointed to the haze of black and yellow.

"*Monzel!*" It was the word Tamer Venor had used to send the animals back to their homes.

The insects bobbed and struggled, then they seemed to calm. The black and yellow melted from them and the blue of the butterflies returned. They fluttered uncoordinatedly for a moment, then seemed to pull themselves together to peel away, up to the mezzanine.

In a string the butterflies pulled from the cluster above his head like an unravelling ball of yarn and when the last of it had flicked from sight the wide-eyed faces of Panya and Tamer Venor were revealed, staring down.

"Ha, ha!" Tamer Venor threw out her hands in exultation. "We leave tonight."

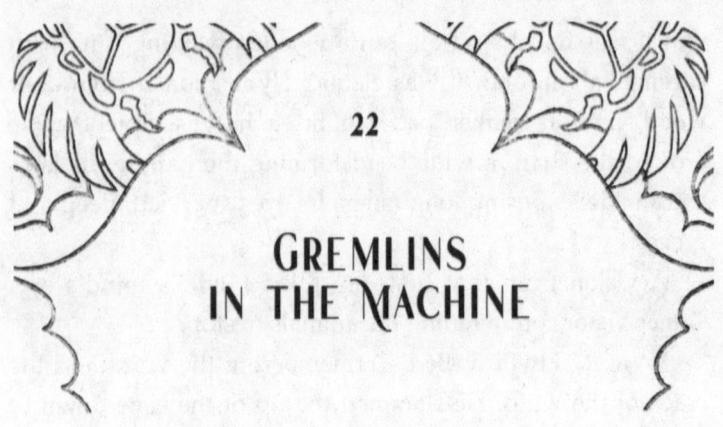

GREMLINS IN THE MACHINE

THE MENAGERIE BECAME a whirl of activity. Abandoning the cleaning of the bear pen, Tamer Venor struck out immediately for her own stall, where she crashed about locating essentials for their mission.

Phyllo was encouraged to do the same but after an initial flurry of activity, gathering up his altar tin and stuffing spare clothes and a toothbrush into his bag, he quickly ran out of things to pack.

He dropped to his bed and gazed at the walking stick, rotating it slowly in his hands. It was quite a work of art. As far as he could tell it had been carved from a single piece of rosewood. Scales overlapped uniformly from the snake's broad head which formed the handle, right down to the rattle at the end of its tail. He shook it experimentally and found that it did indeed make a rattling noise.

The woodgrain was rich and deep, the surface so smoothly polished that when Phyllo ran his fingers over it, he expected to feel the cool surface of glass. Instead, he found that it was warm. His fingertips fitted satisfyingly into the scoops of the scales in places and ran over their mounds in others. Their pattern was precise and featherlike. He marvelled at it.

It must have been one of the items Venor had dropped into the bin when he'd been distracted by the bears, one of the potential Beast-Whispering wands waiting to be claimed. He wondered what else had been in there. Had he chosen the right thing?

It had definitely helped him in that terrifying moment when he'd crashed to the ground. He'd known what to do. He'd known what to say and the creature had obeyed, but now that he sat here holding it, studying it, it was remarkable, yes, but did it feel magical? No.

Had it been a fluke? What if the creature had just recognised Tamer Venor's commands and really done *her* bidding?

He'd fallen a long way, he reasoned, and spotted the cane in time of need. It *had* broken his fall. Or was that just the skills he'd learned from *The Fabulous Volante* coming back to save him? He chewed on his lip and tugged at his collar. It was hotter than ever.

He stood up to flap at his tunic, and the need to escape overwhelmed him. Too many conflicting thoughts were whirling in his head and he needed space. He needed air. He stomped from his cell to search for Tamer Venor and found her in the common room, rolling maps.

"Ah the Whisperer approaches," she teased when she saw him, "Such excitement you must be feeling. Our adventure begins." Already she looked the part of an explorer, a leather waistcoat of straps and buckles, pockets and zippers thrown over her usual tunic. She slid a folding knife into one of its compartments and clicked a popper closed.

Phyllo thrust his hands into his trouser pockets and shuffled distractedly, searching for the right words. "I can see you're busy so I won't keep you and, well, I've done my packing and I really just need to get out of here."

Her expression hardened and Phyllo's stomach clenched. His tone hadn't hit the right mark and he didn't want her to think that he wasn't keen, not when he needed this apprenticeship so much.

"I mean to say," he floundered, "I was wondering if you wouldn't mind if I just popped out." He scoured his brain desperately for a better way to put it and an idea struck him. "There's something I wanted to try." He attempted a hopeful smile. "It's Mr Schlepper, he was having trouble with something in his workshop the other day and I thought that I saw something, something indecipherable. I thought perhaps I could help him so I looked them up. Thought I might pass on a tip or two, before we go, if that's OK?" He bowed slightly and the gesture allowed him to cast his eyes away. It wasn't a lie, but he *had* forgotten about it until that moment.

She wagged her finger and the smile returned. "A tip. Most excellent. Such progress you have made." She pressed her hand to her chest and returned his bow, "May Thoth bring you success."

Phyllo turned to go, feeling relieved, but found Panya standing in the gateway, feet apart and fists jabbed to the ground. She was swamped as usual in her baggy boiler suit, plaited hair wildly unravelling and chestnut skin, dirty from the labours of the day. She was just the same as always, yet different somehow. She was looking at *him* differently.

So far he'd found her dismissive, pitying even and unwilling to engage. Now her narrowed eyes bore into him. He knew she'd seen what he'd done. She'd seen him send the Aves Pacis home. She'd seen he was learning. Now she'd heard that he was going out to give tips, even if the truth of it wasn't quite so confident. She couldn't see the doubts and insecurities that plagued him on the inside, only the threat he was beginning to pose. Phyllo pulled himself up to his tallest and stalked past. One thing he was certain of, he wasn't going to show her.

~

If Schlepper's workshop had been in a mess last time he'd seen it, now it was a wreck.

Heaps of gadgets littered the workbenches and cluttered the space, so much that Schlepper had been forced to relocate to his desk. He hunched in the dull glow of a single bulb.

The over-sized stag beetle had been completely disassembled. Its legs and carapace were scattered all over the place, a single piece of it now on Schlepper's desk, submitting to scrutiny. Schlepper looked up as Phyllo entered and a smile of welcome distraction spread across his face. He pinched away the second and third pairs of glasses that were perched on his nose.

"Phyllo, good to see you," he said, then stretched out his back in an arch. Something clicked.

"Mr Schlepper, what's happened in here?" Phyllo gawked at the mess.

Schlepper rolled his chair back and stood up, his concertina-spring legs creaking as he made his way over to a cupboard to extract a bottle and two glasses. "Dandelion and burdock? I'm due a break."

He poured them both a drink and passed one over. "Every adjustment brings a new problem. Every investigation, another question." He rubbed at his shadow-rimmed eyes.

Phyllo scanned the worktop. It was too dark to see anything clearly, but he could just pick up the soft hiss of whispering. Should he tell Schlepper that he believed there were tiny fae ruining his automatons? He took a sip from his drink and as nonchalantly as he could said, "Mr Schlepper, have you ever heard of Gremlins?"

Schlepper smiled faintly. "A gremlin in the machine? It is a common expression. The projection of a problem into a physical being."

"What if I were to tell you that it wasn't just an expression?"

Schlepper eyed Phyllo over the top of his last remaining pair of glasses. "Which would make it what?"

Phyllo steeled himself. "Fae."

Schlepper snorted. "Much as I would like to blame my automaton's failure on the fairies, I have to take responsibility."

"That's also true," said Phyllo, and Schlepper's moustache twitched.

"I've been learning about fae, about indecipherables. I think I can help you, Mr Schlepper. We can do things to help. Things that the Gremlins don't like, to get rid of them, and things that they do, so we can get them on our side."

"I see." He nodded in his slow way, but the expression on his face was one of pure indulgence.

Phyllo pressed on. "The first thing is light. It's so dark in here."

Schlepper blinked around. "It has become very gloomy. I confess, concentration had blinded me to it." He flicked a couple of switches on the wall and long banks of bulbs in the ceiling winked to life. The new barrage of light revealed the incredible mess that the workshop had gotten into.

"Good grief and Galileo," he said and made for the workbench, legs squeaking, and Phyllo thought he caught sight of the tail of a Gremlin-sized coat disappearing into the jumble.

"The second thing is tidiness."

"I won't argue with that," said Schlepper, already scooping a handful of spilled screws back into their box. Phyllo came to his side and together they set to work, returning spares to their boxes and tools to the tool wall, slotting them neatly into their outlines. Phyllo sorted different sized nuts and bolts into trays under Schlepper's instruction and slid them onto shelves, while Schlepper himself gathered up some of the larger gadgets he'd left lying around.

"Bulky items, like the Teflon bubble sander here, have spots at the base of the wall," he indicated the empty compartments beneath his mapped-out wall of tools. "Smaller gizmos are looked after by Stanley. Like the isotopic dorsal stabilizer, here." He waggled a fat screwdriver in the air, the handle of which was filled with a sparkling blue liquid. "Why don't you call him?" Schlepper said and nodded to the tin of grease nuggets on his desk. Phyllo picked up the tin and shook it.

Stanley immediately appeared, trotting out from under a bench, and Phyllo tossed him a nugget. He golloped it down and Phyllo replaced the fancy screwdriver in the toolbox that made up his body. It left a slippery residue on his fingertips.

"The next thing is maintenance," said Phyllo, "Cleaning tools and greasing hinges, that sort of thing. May I?" He pointed to the squeaking joint on the Perambulator Mark IV's and when Schlepper nodded, he rubbed the grease from his fingers into the offending spot. Schlepper flexed and found the squeak silenced.

"Huh." He raised his eyebrows to Phyllo and a small smile crept across his face, "I should have been on top of that," he murmured. "What else?"

"After maintenance comes cleanliness," said Phyllo, feeling slightly abashed by Schlepper's reaction to stopping his squeak.

"Maintenance and cleanliness it is," said Schlepper. He produced clean rags and a pot of grease and together they polished up the tools, wiped down the surfaces and swept the floor. By the time they'd finished the workshop sparkled.

"Clarity returns," said Schlepper in his slow way, "I can't thank you enough, Phyllo."

Phyllo smiled and out of the corner of his eye noticed the tiny movements of a pair of Gremlins. Determined not to make eye contact, he monitored them in his peripheral vision. They were no longer cackling wildly nor wrenching springs from Schlepper's contraption. Instead, they looked down at the parts and scratched at their heads. One reached down to twiddle with wires.

"It occurs to me that I have been too haphazard. A scientific approach is all that's required," said Schlepper, "I don't know why I didn't see it before." He pulled a schematic drawing from below the workbench and unrolled it. "If I start here and work my way through..." He tailed off, already peering at beetle parts and sorting them into order along the bench. "Still, I think a little more light."

Phyllo tapped at the workbench and a collection of coiled filament lightbulbs pinged to life. "Over here, you lot," he said. The lightbulbs sprang up on wiry feet, the bulbs like the abdomens of fat metallic spiders. They scuttled at Phyllo's command over to the spot where Schlepper was working and into position, shifting a little left and right as Schlepper leant to look around them.

"That's better," said Schlepper. He continued with his work, but then paused to look at Phyllo, as if finally noticing what had just happened. He scanned his face and just for a moment everything was still. "The lux-a-pods, you've seen them before?"

"The lightbulbs on legs? No, never."

Phyllo stared at the mechanical creatures which had done his bidding without him even really knowing they were there.

"Interesting," said Schlepper. He tapped a screwdriver into the palm of his hand and nodded. "Would you like to take a look?"

Phyllo leaned in to examine the internal workings of the beetle. He didn't really know anything about automatons, but felt somehow that what he was looking at was unbalanced. He pointed to a cluster of valves on one side. "Is it a bit wonky, maybe? All that weight on one side, when there's nothing over here." He pointed to an empty space.

Schlepper twiddled with his moustache. "The weight itself shouldn't be a problem. The spatial interverse would cancel that out, but proximity, well now, that's a different matter. Interference, Phyllo, that *is* a possibility." He set to unscrewing fixings and moving them about. "There's a lot to be said for a fresh eye."

Schlepper continued to work, Phyllo passing him sections and gadgets to test theories as he was asked, and before too long the stag beetle had been entirely reassembled. They stepped back to admire it.

"Our patience is rewarded," said Schlepper, "Do the honours, Phyllo. Switch him on."

Phyllo reached for the switch.

The antennae twitched, then the hooked feet tapped, each one in turn. It lifted its great jawed head and then dipped it, pinching in and out the claws.

"The start-up procedure. Promising. Very promising."

It lifted each leg then reared up onto its back four and lowered down again. Each movement was smooth and controlled.

"Let's get him down," said Schlepper and together they lifted the beetle from the workbench. It was surprisingly light.

"Why isn't it heavier? There's so much metal."

"The spatial interverse again. The air to mass ratio negates weight. It is the key to this entire construct. I believe he's ready to be attached."

Schlepper took a new device from Stanley. It was smooth and black with a single button on one end and fitted snuggly inside his fist.

"Automata homing widget," he said by way of explanation, "Anywhere this goes, he'll follow." Schlepper waggled the device and depressed the button in an obvious fashion for Phyllo's benefit. The beetle snapped to attention and as Schlepper made for the steps out of his workshop, the stag beetle trotted nimbly behind. It followed him up the steps to the entrance way and then up one of the curving staircases that led out of sight.

Phyllo'd gotten used to Schlepper's space-bending abilities by now and imagined that the space upstairs was likely to be a repeat of the workshop footprint below, but rounding that final bend, it was as if he'd climbed out into the night sky itself.

The space was immeasurably vast – its edges cloaked in a thick darkness that sparkled deeply with stars and it wasn't just the lack of boundaries that made this place remarkable. It was the thing that stood spot-lit and centre stage: Schlepper's Contraptionist Carousel.

Phyllo had never ever seen anything quite like it before.

The creatures of this carousel were not the usual ribboned horses that rose and fell on poles. Here every beast was different and fantastic, a giant mechanical recreation, beautifully enamelled and detailed with articulated limbs or fins or wings.

Phyllo followed the stag beetle, its angular legs drumming forward to climb the gilded steps, up onto the platform.

Above him a mechanical albatross, its formidable wings spread wide, was frozen mid-flight suspended from the roof. It had a saddle across its back, and steps wound up to reach it on the broad central pillar.

Ahead was a fat orange and green enamelled caterpillar, at least ten feet long, curled in a tall arch, supported at either end by wheeled feet. It ran on a rail like a bizarre single-person train with just one seat.

Farther around, a fat puffer fish dangled from the ceiling. A net had been slung over it and, like a hot air balloon, a basket for two passengers hung beneath.

Phyllo looked from one creature to the next, delighted.

"Mr Schlepper, this is awesome," he breathed, "Your creatures, they're amazing. Do they move?"

"Do they move." Schlepper chuckled under his breath, "Just one test remains. Would you mind? I'm not wearing the right legs." He threw a saddle over the beetle's back, slipped on a harness then led it over to an empty space on the carousel floor. He snapped a carabiner into place on its underside. "Hop on," he said and Phyllo clambered into the saddle. He couldn't quite get his legs down to the floor, but there were stirrups to wedge his feet in. He took up the harness and gripped it uncertainly.

"Excellent," said Schlepper then bounced away around the curve of the carousel, disappearing from view. Very slowly at first, the carousel began to turn.

Music, sweet and clear like the tinkle of a music box, pinged overhead. The xylophone chimes were joined by the rasp of harmonica, and a smile of delight spread over Phyllo's face as the albatross flexed its wings. Their considerable length swept up and down, the body of the bird dipping and rising in response. The carousel picked up speed and air rushed through Phyllo's hair.

A trombone parped its way into the tune and Phyllo found himself overtaken by the caterpillar. It stretched and contracted its body to slide along the rail that Phyllo now saw snaked between the other creatures. Enormously oversized, its empty saddle rose with the arch of its back and Phyllo imagined what fun it would be to ride. He'd have a go on that next.

Schlepper came bounding back around the curve to cling to the leg of a giraffe. Its neck was stretching longer and longer until a trap-door opened in the carousel ceiling for it to pop straight through, taking any would-be rider out into the starry sky.

Phyllo sat astride his stag beetle grinning, but still motionless.

"Did I forget to mention," said Schlepper, "You'll need to knock him into gear. Pull the antennae back."

Phyllo did it. The beetle's legs flexed and together they sprang forward. It darted left and then right to scamper around the caterpillar while Phyllo clung on, eyes popping.

"I assure you it's perfectly safe," called Schlepper as Phyllo galloped past, completing a full circuit in a matter of seconds. The stag beetle paused to rear onto its back four legs, then dropped back to the ground to career off along a different groove in the floor.

There was the rattle of a drum, the crash of a cymbal and a pipe organ added to the jolly riot of sound with its breathy notes and Phyllo could just imagine Schlepper running up and down a line of bottles, blowing across their rims, breathing life into it all.

All Schlepper's creatures moved in one way or another. They gave the impression of dancing along, whether by the stretch of a neck or the ripple of fins. On Schlepper's Contraptionist Carousel every creature co-existed happily beside its neighbour, moving in wonderful co-ordinated harmony.

Phyllo whooped as he galloped past for a second time, but all too soon the carousel began to slow and when it had come entirely to a stop, Phyllo clambered off to wobble over to Schlepper, who was bent over the caterpillar, adjusting its saddle.

"So, how was it?" Schlepper said.

Blood was still pumping wildly in Phyllo's veins. "Brilliant," he said, "Just incredible. Can I have another go?"

Schlepper laughed and he patted the caterpillar affectionately. "All are modelled on the real thing. It is my small attempt to preserve the wonders of nature and present them for all to enjoy. I need to make a few adjustments though before it runs again."

It looked like Phyllo would have to wait for his ride on the caterpillar. He gazed around. "In a funny sort of way, we're on the same page, aren't we? You preserving animals like this, and me off with Tamer Venor tonight to try to save our dragon."

"Tonight?" A little furrow appeared between Schlepper's eyebrows and he straightened up to look Phyllo in the eye. "There have been developments?"

Phyllo shook his head. "In all honesty, it's been a mad day. *I* can't even believe it," he said. "Earlier today in the Whispering Wood, I found my familiar and then later, a cane to help with the Beast Whispering. Tamer Venor thinks I'll be able to use it with my altar to travel, somehow." He rubbed at his chest, thinking about it. A familiar knot of anxiety was forming there. "No idea how it works. Tamer Venor said she and Panya would help.

"And you wouldn't believe the animals in the Menagerie, Mr Schlepper. You should come and see. I think you'd like it. It's not just the ones in the show. There are others she's working on, creating acts. There's the Aves Pacis, the kaleidoscope of butterflies with a hive mind. That's really amazing. They all sort of move together and turn into different creatures. Then there are crabs that look like jewels, only they aren't really, but Tamer Venor says that if they live in the right place then they can be really valuable."

Schlepper nodded. "That does sound good."

Phyllo thought so too, but found himself rubbing at the pinched flesh on the back of his thigh.

"I must say, I'm impressed," said Schlepper, "You've learned a great deal in such a short space of time. The Gremlins, your familiar, and now you're getting ready to hunt the dragon." He looked down to wipe oil from his fingers with a rag, "Just be careful, won't you, Phyllo. Keep your wits about you. Hunting a dragon is perilous, but I wonder if you understand all the dangers involved."

Phyllo wasn't quite sure what he meant.

"A dragon is a rare beast. For you and Tamer Venor the value is in the creature itself, but for others, the place it is found will be of the most interest. Our Ringmaster strives for a profitable circus, there's no doubt, but his Tamer is learned and conscientious. She seeks to conserve the species. Others will seek the dragon with quite different motivation, not for the creature, but for its hoard."

"Treasure?" Phyllo breathed.

Schlepper's moustache tips quivered. "And a significant amount."

23

'ALTAR'ED REALITY

CANDLELIGHT FLICKERED in the multiple eyes of the Menagerie. Their owners watched from the darkness, the air thick with their breath, with the heat of the lonesome dragon and anticipation's thrill.

Tamer Venor held out her whip, and Phyllo, the cobra cane. They stood in the central hall facing their altars – Tamer Venor's, a graceful curve of intricate wooden drawers with the elaborately engraved animal mirror at its heart, and Phyllo's, the Dr Mandril Monkey Wormer tin, its bent lid oiled to the best shine he could muster.

Phyllo sucked in a steadying breath and together they began to turn on the spot.

Tamer Venor spoke, her voice a low purr. "Mighty dragon, beast of wisdom, loyal friend. Find me in the darkness. Protect this circle." She caught Phyllo's eye and he stuttered into speech.

"N-noble Ethelweard, Guardian of the Forest and friend as old as time, find me in the darkness. P-protect this circle." They were the words that he and Tamer Venor had agreed would be his version of the spell. He gripped the cane so tightly that it shook. Together they turned, whip and cane outstretched.

Everything they'd need for the trip was packed into the two rucksacks they wore, one apiece. Phyllo's was so heavy its thick straps dug painfully into his shoulders.

"Breathe fire and smoke to build our path. All matter universal shared," Tamer Venor said. Incense burned on her altar and tendrils of it snaked toward her to follow the path of her whip through the air. Phyllo watched it, eyes stretching wider by the moment. It wound around her, motes of red-gold shining with the fire of the candles.

Phyllo flexed his shoulders, trying to relieve the pinch of the straps. "Vines and, er leaves, um," he floundered for the phrase and the words danced tantalisingly out of reach in his memory. He snatched a look to Tamer Venor. She looked back at him then closed her eyes to take in a long deep breath, as if encouraging him to relax.

Stay calm, Phyllo told himself, and sucked in a lungful of the sickly incense-filled air. It made him cough, but the phrase did come to him.

"Um, vines entwine, yes, vines entwine to weave a vessel. All matter universal shared." He'd remembered it, thank Barnum. He looked at his own tin altar and incense. It looked pretty ordinary still, the incense rising in a pathetic thin ribbon.

Tamer Venor's eyes were still closed and she revolved on the spot, wrapping the smoky tendrils from her altar around herself.

Phyllo slid his eyes to Panya, who glared at him. She stirred the air with a single finger.

Turning! He'd stopped turning! He began again immediately.

"Parpadillo, dragon's friend and quiet soul. Find me. Show me. Reach me now," said Tamer Venor, her voice a breathy chant. The items set out on her altar hummed with vibration: a small dish of rock salt, a goblet of water, a golden ankh and a sand-coloured rock. Tamer Venor's book of beasts lay open on the page about Parpadillos, and the corners of its pages flicked and jumped.

"Vines entwine to weave a vessel," said Phyllo again, still stuck on getting his incense to behave. It belched into a smog.

"Reveal to me. Connect to me. Parpadillo, hear my call," said Tamer Venor continuing to turn, but now her eyes stuck with her altar mirror, her head snapping back to it like a dancer pirouetting. The surface of her mirror cleared, its mist resolving to show a fat green little dragon-like creature, curled up asleep on a bed of sand.

"Vines entwine to weave a vessel," said Phyllo again, the pitch of his voice rising. Tamer Venor was getting too far ahead of him in the ritual and still there was no sign of incense vines for him. "Vines entwine. *Vines entwine!*" He looked desperately to Panya, who had her lips clenched hard together. She darted looks back and forth between Tamer Venor's mirror with its shining image, and Phyllo's grubby, blank one.

"Mighty dragon, familiar and friend." Tamer Venor released the coil of her whip and cracked it once in the air above them. "Seal this circle." Air rushed to join the incense and it swirled around her.

Phyllo gawked at her. Hadn't she noticed that he was stuck? She was going to leave without him. Tamer Venor had said she'd crack her whip three times and on the third would be consumed by the altar mirror. Phyllo hadn't much liked the sound of that and had liked it even less when she'd assured him he would be sucked in right after – if he'd got his familiar ready, that was. Right now, that looked like a very big *if*.

Phyllo spun to find Panya, the free wisps of her hair whipping with the air sucked toward Tamer Venor's whirl of smoke.

"Panya! What am I doing wrong?" he trilled, "I can't get past this bit. I can't remember the words."

Panya rubbed at her forehead and wrinkled her nose.

"Panya, please!" Phyllo begged. She had to help him.

Panya screwed her eyes closed then seemed to collapse against the battle waging in her mind. She pulled the striped conducting baton from her pocket and jabbed it at Phyllo's travesty of an altar.

"Vines entwine to weave a vessel. All matter universal shared," she said in almost a snarl. Phyllo looked desperately back and forth between her and the altar. Still nothing was happening. "Turn, Phyllo," she snapped, "And it's you that has to say the words."

He jumped to obey and, at once tendrils of smoke snaked toward him from the incense burning on his altar.

"Call your familiar, Phyllo. Tell it what you need," Panya spat.

"Alitura, Guardian of the Trees, help me to, er, follow Tamer Venor, and quick." His voice wobbled with the fear of being left behind. The model Alitura rattled about on the upturned tin, sounding a metallic drumroll.

"The *right* words," Panya yelled at him, "Alitura—"

Phyllo cut her off, remembering, "Alitura, Guardian of the Trees, do my bidding, come to me."

Phyllo had hardly heard Panya utter a word in his time in the Menagerie and now she was shouting at him. He goggled at her and then at the indistinct shapes forming in the smoke. Vines of incense coiled and stretched to wind around him.

Tamer Venor cracked her whip for a second time and the surface of her mirror became a whirlpool, spinning the image of the Parpadillo away into a pool of liquid light.

Phyllo squeaked at her progress and the next words came to him in a rush, "Reveal to me. Connect to me. Alitura, hear my call."

Phyllo's makeshift mirror sloshed about beneath the oily tin surface. He lifted the cobra cane and pointed determinedly at it. "Alitura, please!"

"Again," Panya growled from beside him, still pointing her own stick at Phyllo's altar, he hoped lending her own Whispering power.

"Alitura—"

"From the beginning," Panya snapped.

Phyllo said it again and again, until a misty image formed on the surface of his mirror and resolved to show the vine woven fox that was Phyllo's familiar.

-CRACK-

The third whip crack. Phyllo stared, panicked, at Tamer Venor. The sparkling smoke stretched above her in a whirling cone.

"Seal the circle, Phyllo. Do it now."

Phyllo flummoxed about in his brain for the words.

Panya growled. "Guardian of the Trees, familiar and friend," she prompted and Phyllo echoed her words, "Seal this circle." He banged the end of his cane to the ground.

The tip of the cone of incense surrounding Tamer Venor leaned over to touch the centre of her whirlpool mirror. He could not see her anymore, just the shrinking cone of smoke, lifting from the ground. The outermost column of drawers on either side of her altar folded in.

Phyllo banged the tip of his cane to the ground for a second time. The image of Alitura in his mirror was lost to ripples. Scummy foam formed at the edges. The next column of drawers in Tamer Venor's altar folded in on itself and Phyllo let out a cry of desperation. Her cone of smoke had almost entirely disappeared into the mirror and her altar was closing itself.

He looked desperately to Panya. She glared back at him, defiance blazing in her eyes.

"She's leaving me behind," Phyllo wailed, "What have I missed out? What should I say?" He was going to blow it. He'd never manage it in time.

Panya took the deepest of breaths and her eyes fell to the ground. "You have to tell your familiar what to do," she grumbled.

"Yes. Yes. What should I say?" said Phyllo, desperation becoming unbearable.

Panya's voice cracked. "Alitura, follow my master," she said, and her face fell into a mask of misery.

"Alitura, follow my master," Phyllo yelled then slammed down his cane for the third time. The smoky vines around him whirled taller and denser and he looked up to the inside of the tip of the forming cone to see the oily mirror of his altar. A lazy bubble bobbed to the surface, shining with the rainbow glaze of an opal, then popped and the smoke above him seemed to suck into the space it had left behind.

At once Phyllo felt himself become nothing. Like the smoke, he was neither touching the earth nor levitating above it. Weightless and body-less, yet at the same time as vast as the universe and as miniscule as an atom. For a wonderful moment he did not exist, yet was connected with everything. He was water and air, fire and earth.

Then he was hot, the air around him hotter even than the Menagerie. Heat seeped into his chest, into the side of his face and stinging dryness gripped his throat. He gasped a great breath to try to relieve it and with it sucked up a mouthful of sand. Choking and shocked, he scrambled up from the ground to his hands and knees. Spitting and coughing he found himself kneeling in hot, sandy dirt.

Heat radiated from the ground into the palms of his hands and the bony knobble of his knees. A warm breeze ruffled his hair. Disoriented, he looked up and found Tamer Venor picked out in a halo of moonlight just a few feet away. Her booted feet were spread wide and her hands were planted jauntily upon her hips.

"Ha, ha!" she boomed, "You did it. We did it." She snatched at Phyllo's hands and hauled him to his feet.

Phyllo clutched at himself, checking for solidity. "We did?" He squinted into the night, "Where even are we?" He couldn't see a thing he recognised.

"Our intended destination. See here."

She gripped Phyllo's shoulders and turned him around. Fifty feet away dark scrubby bushes gave way to the smooth reflective surface of a vast body of water that reflected a cloudless sky. On the far bank, which Phyllo thought at least a mile away, a smattering of golden lights indicated people. Where they stood, however, all was quiet, with no light aside from that provided by the full moon.

"Khonsu favours us," said Tamer Venor, "The moon will guide our labours."

The moon was so large and bright that it lit the landscape with an odd monochrome clarity.

"Should be easier for us to set up camp anyway," said Phyllo, relieved to be able to shuck his huge backpack, but Tamer Venor held up a hand.

"No camp, not yet. Retrieve your altar." She pointed to the tin, which lay in the sand at his feet. He scooped it up and checked inside. All his items were there. It appeared that *his* altar had packed itself up as they'd left too.

"The Parpadillo are here on this bank, somewhere," said Tamer Venor, "The altar brought us to them. They will have dug their dens far from the people across the water and will not be wandering about at night. Already the temperature is too low."

Phyllo raised his eyebrows at that. Too low? It was hot as an oven.

She strode away, the tails of her tunic flapping. "Our timing is serendipitous. We can search while the Parpadillo sleep. Be mindful of their fear of humans, Phyllo. We must not alert them to our presence."

Phyllo hurried to catch her up, the backpack jiggling painfully on his shoulders – he'd been looking forward to putting it down. "What are we looking out for?" he whispered.

"Burrow entrances with signs of foot traffic. The Parpadillo are a good deal smaller than a dragon, but not so small as to be hard to spot. About the size of a cat. Most are green and easily seen. Their burrows, less so." She dropped suddenly down to one knee.

"See here." She pointed to a sloping rocky area, partially hidden by twiggy brush. "Already this one sleeps in its hot den."

Phyllo knelt at her side, and for a moment couldn't see what she was looking at. Then he found its edges. A roughly circular patch, about the size of an average fruit cake, differed from the sandy ground around it. A mosaic of small rocks and pebbles had been slotted perfectly together to make a solid wall which blocked the entrance completely.

"Couldn't we break it down?" said Phyllo, "It's only a few rocks, after all." He poked at it experimentally, but found it quite solid.

Tamer Venor shook her head. "The architect of this could be twenty feet below the surface, away in any direction. Even if we could dig our way to it, there would most certainly be other exits and the ruckus would alert it to our interest. It would escape and then be wary to boot. No. The animal we must catch is not yet in hibernation." She brushed herself down. "But see in essence, the entrance to a den. It is what we seek."

Phyllo was encouraged by how quickly they'd found a burrow, albeit a sealed one. He scoured the ground for signs of another, feeling hopeful. But an hour of searching later, his shoulders were complaining bitterly under their straps and his conviction was waning.

They stooped to peer at yet another sealed burrow hole. "That makes thirteen," Tamer Venor uttered, "The Parpadillo population is not so vast. Odds rise against us. We most hope that one yet remains."

She stood tall to look out over the lake and spread her arms, seeming to draw in the environment. Phyllo had to try to put what he'd learned in the Whispering Wood into action too. He concentrated as hard as he could to get his mind into the right place and rolled the verse he'd learned over in his mind.

By ray and beam, By dell and mound...

He filled his lungs with the alien air of the desert and willed himself to hear and see, to smell and feel.

He'd heard the background hum of a thousand chirruping insects already, of course he had, but now, focussing that much harder, the blanket of sound crystallised to the creak of individuals in the thrum. The hoot of a bird calling to its mate travelled thinly across the water at 3 o'clock. Wind sighed through a narrow pass in the rocky landscape that Phyllo could not see at 5. Its moan spoke of a storm that was building far away.

Little feet scuffled in the sand close at hand. Phyllo turned to track the sound, his heart jumping with excitement. A twiggy shrub jiggled encouragingly five feet away and Tamer Venor raised a finger to her lips. They edged toward it.

An irregular pitter-pat of paws scampered toward the water's edge. Phyllo strained fruitlessly to see the source, but Tamer Venor had it in her sights and led them forward around mounds of rock and low wiry trees. Phyllo crept, bent low and holding his breath.

Then he saw it. Not the Parpadillo he'd been hoping for, but a twitchy little rodent.

A moment's concentration lost, he stepped on a twig and *crack!* The creature jumped to stand on its hind legs and stare in their direction. Phyllo held as still as he could. The animal jerked down with a stamp, squeaked and shot down a burrow hole.

Phyllo flicked his eyes to Tamer Venor. "Sorry," he said with a grimace.

"No matter. *Psammomys obesus*. The fat sand rat. Its presence is encouraging. They share nutritional needs with our quarry and build their burrows beneath mutual food sources." She moved forward to examine the bush it had disappeared under. "Yes. Look here about for an open burrow hole. Quietly now." She picked her way nimbly through the brush toward the water and Phyllo peeled off the other way, feeling for some reason that the Parpadillo would rather its burrow entrance not be visible from the lake.

A shadow, no, a hole in the ground revealed itself beside a wiry thicket. If he hadn't been focussing so hard upon finding it, Phyllo felt sure that he could have walked right by, but an opening was there, about eight inches across at the base of a gentle slope in the rock. The ground at its entrance was scraped into grooves, but the sand a little farther away was peppered with three-toed footprints.

"Tamer Venor," Phyllo hissed. He waved her over.

She fell to one knee and sniffed at the ground. "Musk," she said, "This is not the dwelling of a sand rat." She got up and walked smartly away, leading them behind a sand dune a good fifty yards away.

"Not it then?" said Phyllo, confused.

"Most certainly it," Venor replied, "We retire downwind to unpack. Quietly now." She lowered her voluminous pack to the ground and loosed the buckles holding it closed.

She pulled from its depths wooden rods, rope, chicken wire, a clinking drawstring bag and a surprising number of planks of wood. Phyllo wasn't sure how she'd got it all in there. He turned his attention to emptying his own bag, assuming that he must have their camping gear. He did not.

Phyllo's bag contained more chicken wire and planks, a bag of pony feed, twenty or so jewel crab shells and a very heavy knobbly sack.

"Er, where's our camping gear?"

"Our method is temptation," said Tamer Venor, ignoring

the question and keeping her voice low, "Our tardy Parpadillo will be keen to join its fellows below ground. Being last has great disadvantages. Supplies for hibernation are depleted. The best hot rocks are already taken and if it has not yet built a larder, pickings are slim. Continued time above ground is likely filled with fruitless searching. We will provide."

She plucked specific planks and rods from the ground. There were metallic loops on one side of the boards that the rod slid through.

"Such is our trap," said Tamer Venor, "Pass others to me with fixings like this." She indicated the loops and Phyllo did as he was asked. "Quietly now. The shorter ones combine to make our gate. Lay those separately."

They carefully sorted the puzzle of pieces and slotted them together to make a pen, and when Phyllo looked impressed Tamer Venor chuckled. "This is not my first capture. Did you think we would come without a trap?"

"I wasn't really sure how we would do it," admitted Phyllo.

"With magical skill, you thought, perhaps? Whispering intuition guides us, certainly, to work with nature. To work with our creature and handle it in the way that suits it best. Free will remains paramount. Our Parpadillo will choose to come inside, just as our dragon will choose to rescue it. Regrettably, we must deceive it a little."

She unrolled the chicken wire and scrunched it haphazardly around the wooden crate. "A coat of local flora," she said passing Phyllo a knife and he understood at once that they were going to dress the trap to blend it in.

As he worked, Tamer Venor lay on the ground to assess their progress from Parpadillo eye level and when they pushed it into an existing thicket even Phyllo had to admit that they'd done a sterling job.

"Now bring me the drawstring sack from your backpack," she instructed and when they tipped it out Phyllo understood why his rucksack had been so very heavy.

"You had me carrying rocks?" he hissed, looking pointedly at the stony ground all around them. His shoulders were still smarting from the straps of his pack.

"Not just any rocks. Excellent rocks. Rocks with great hot den potential." She grinned broadly. "Do not whine. You did not have to carry them for long."

"Actually, I carried them for 4,000 miles," said Phyllo sulkily, but Tamer Venor gave the subject a dismissive swipe. "And so, it is done. Help me to organise them. Some we will stack neatly at the very back. Most we will scatter about to give the appearance of a hoard abandoned. Bring the pony kibble too. Our little friend will be hungry."

"What about the crab shells?" asked Phyllo, "and what's in this other bag?"

"Activities to keep it busy once captured. Our Parpadillo will not appreciate confinement but if it has riches to discover and sort, we can hope to keep it distracted."

"A busy Parpadillo is a happy Parpadillo."

Tamer Venor gave him a bow.

Once the breadcrumb trail of pony kibble was laid from burrow to trap, there was nothing left to do but wait.

Their backpacks, now empty, unzipped pleasingly into thick individual groundsheets which cushioned the ground well enough if you avoided the buckles and dangling water bottles. Tamer Venor produced a thin but opaque sheet, which they strung between two trees to create both shelter and camouflage from the spot where their trap squatted in the bushes, anticipating its captive.

Phyllo accepted a falafel from Tamer Venor and a small cup of liquorice tea that she poured from a flask, this time without the theatre.

"Dawn is not far away, even then we will have to wait for the heat of the day to build. We should sleep."

Phyllo lay back and rested his head on his altar tin. After their increasingly desperate search and the frantic quiet build of the trap, it was peculiar to just be lying there, doing nothing at all. He felt as if he ought to be dashing about, getting things done. Quite what though, he didn't know.

One thing he could say was that he ached from head to toe.

"Crackers, I'm tired," he said aloud, "Exhausting, this Parpadillo catching lark, isn't it?"

Tamer Venor huffed and rolled to lean on one elbow to look at him. "You have had an exceptional day. To progress so far as to be able to travel by altar. It is extraordinary."

That part of the evening seemed so long ago he couldn't quite believe he'd done it.

"How did you find the journey?" she asked.

Phyllo rolled his mind back. "Travelling by altar is a weird feeling," he said, "Like everything's been wiped away, kind of neutral, but really happy. No, not happy. Peaceful." It was very difficult to pin down. "It felt like I was part of everything, like we all share the same space. Animals, plants, water, earth. Just for a moment I felt connected to everything. Like I *was* everything, but at the same time was nobody and nothing." He tried to remember the sensation.

"Actually, in a small way, it was similar to how the Aves Pacis made me feel." He remembered the kaleidoscope of butterflies that had swirled around him, "Until they tried to kill me."

"Nature reveals itself in wondrous ways."

Phyllo snorted at that. "Is it going to appear in the show, the Aves Pacis?" asked Phyllo. It seemed such a waste to keep it out of sight in the Menagerie.

"It is a little *unpredictable* at present," smiled Tamer Venor, and Phyllo had to agree. "It could sway audiences to be at one with nature, to understand their part in it and appreciate it. What a great feat that would be for our world. With more practised handling and, perhaps, a more intimate setting than the big top, it would be an experience of immeasurable worth."

Phyllo thought that really would be an act worthy of the Circus of Wonder.

"And the spell? I lost sight of you. Were there any complications?"

The spell. Phyllo wasn't sure he wanted to admit how badly he'd done. It had been difficult, almost impossible. Without Panya's assistance Phyllo didn't think he would have made it at all. In this game of one-upmanship, he was reticent to confess.

"It wasn't easy," he conceded.

She looked into his eyes and nodded. "Not easy, no."

Silence settled over them and Phyllo thought about Panya's stricken face when she'd given him the final line *'Follow my master'*. Tamer Venor was everything to her. The Menagerie was the only home she'd known. Giving Phyllo the power to stand in her shoes had been painful.

"Do you think Panya's getting on OK in the Menagerie?" he ventured, clearing his throat.

"Panya will throw herself into the challenge. Such is the mark of a true Whisperer. I have every faith. The Ringmaster knows she is alone tonight and will no doubt come to her aid, should she need it. If things get really out of hand it is possible for her to alert me."

"It is? How?"

"This mission is important, but the needs of one cannot outweigh the many." She tugged a necklace out from behind the fabric of her tunic. From it hung a bronze ankh, into the head of which was set a tiny bowl. "It is a means to communicate. If Panya really needs me she can send vibrations and I will feel it. Going home is always an option."

Phyllo felt both relieved and slightly unsettled by this, by the potential tug of loyalties that Panya could exert if she chose. The faster they captured this Parpadillo the better.

24

SNAP!

Up on his toes Phyllo crept forward, arms held away from his body, tense and ready. His heart thundered in his chest. The dragon was close. He could feel its blazing heat getting stronger all the time.

It had the advantage in the dark. Phyllo was blind, but he knew it could sense him.

Another step. Wobbling on the uneven ground. A little farther forward.

Great wings beat the air down upon him and he ducked low to avoid the attacker he could not see. His throat dry. His hair on end. Beyond the dust and heat he felt its presence, something indefinable he'd also felt at the Menagerie, something more than the vibrations of a rumbling purr.

Down again, the force of the beat blew hot breath across his face.

"No!" he cried out and threw up his arms in protection.

Hot grit tumbled into his face. He shook his head to be rid of it.

Snap!

The sound was so close it was almost on top of him.

"Phyllo."

That voice. He was not alone.

"Phyllo, come quickly. The trap."

He peeled open his eyes. Above him the tarpaulin that had been their disguise and shelter flapped in a wind that had risen while he'd slept. He got up to lean on his elbows and crane in the direction of the voice. He was just in time to witness Tamer Venor vault the prickly shrubbery and disappear from view.

"Phyllo! The time for rest has passed."

"OK." Phyllo's voice came in a dry gasp as he pieced together what was real and what was a dream. He wasn't under attack. The tarpaulin flipped and cracked above his head. Just the tarpaulin. No dragon wings. "I'm up." He wobbled to his feet.

If it had been hot when they'd arrived, it was nothing to the temperature now. Sweat slicked hair to his neck and his shirt to his back. One side of his face felt dry and tight. The side that had been in the sun. He rubbed at his eyes adjusting to the dazzling desert sun.

Then he heard it. Long and low. *Hooooonk.*

Phyllo's eyes grew wide. He lunged from beneath their makeshift shelter and made for the trap.

Hooooonk.

Tamer Venor was down on one knee, peering through the mesh ceiling of their snare.

"All is well, little one," she soothed.

The Parpadillo on the other side of the mesh didn't seem to think so. Up on its skinny hind legs, it scuttled around the circumference of the trap, honking. Standing like this, it was about two feet tall, one third its thin legs and the rest a dark green pear-shaped body and lizard-like head.

Large brown mournful eyes rolled from Tamer Venor to

Phyllo. *Ho-ho-hoooonk*, it bellowed. It was the most pitiful sound Phyllo had ever heard.

"Already he pines for his freedom," said Tamer Venor as she pushed a date experimentally through the chicken wire.

The Parpadillo eyed it suspiciously then trotted over to give it a sniff. Its fat little body bobbed up and down as it moved, small front paws grasped together as if nervously pleading. It pulled the date through the wire and nibbled at it.

"Such riches you will find, little Parpadillo. Our meeting will be most serendipitous for you." She looked up to Phyllo and her eyes were quite alive with appreciation for their captive. "Is he not everything you expected?"

Hooooonk.

"And more," said Phyllo, who was already feeling quite fond of it.

"Now that we have him, our task is to transport him. Our destination is thirty miles or so south west. We can walk him—"

"Thirty miles?"

"—with the aid of a camel."

"Can't we use the altars?"

"In a way we will, but no more than I could take you through mine are we able to transport a Parpadillo. This journey was always going to have to be in the physical world, as will our journey with the dragon itself. You see now why it is essential to have the willing participation of these creatures."

Phyllo stared at her, the implications of that statement settling in. "How exactly would one travel with a dragon?" he asked, suspecting that he already knew the terrifying answer.

Tamer Venor, however, looked delighted. "A dragon is the most accomplished traveller there is. Magical in the extreme, it can cover great distances without rest and in timescales incomparable to any other means. Except perhaps our altars, but I have already explained the shortcoming there. To ride a dragon is to sail in Madjet with Ra himself."

Phyllo chewed at his lip.

"But for now, let us concern ourselves only with the ship of the desert." She patted him heartily on the shoulder. "Travelling by night would be more comfortable, but it will not help us to delay. Our captive will soon tire of what little entertainment we can muster and we do not want the attention of a dragon before we are prepared."

Phyllo turned back to the Parpadillo. It had finished the date and was sniffing at the chicken wire.

"I will consult my altar to locate our desert transportation. You must too – it will be instructive. With any luck we will have hailed our ride before the sun is risen to the full."

Hooooonk. The diversion of the date was over.

"Fetch the pony kibble, Phyllo. Food salves most ills. Distract him with morsels for your part and I will add treasures to discover for mine. With luck he will come to appreciate his new surroundings and when time comes to move, we may have earned a little trust."

Phyllo fetched the kibble although it looked quite unappealing. Those dry, uniform pellets might be a staple back at the Menagerie, but he couldn't see a creature used to natural food going for them at all. He offered one up dubiously and found that once again, he was quite wrong. The Parpadillo snatched it from him, then another and another, his long-clawed dexterous paws stuffing them into surprisingly capacious cheeks.

He must be used to eating dry stuff, Phyllo reasoned to himself. As habitats went, this one was harsh and unforgiving. Any colour in the landscape seemed already to be bleached by the unrelenting glare of the sun, all plant life stiff and prickly. By comparison he supposed that the kibble was smooth and convenient. In actual fact, just the thing to stash away in a hibernation larder. Tamer Venor knew what she was doing. Of course she did.

The Parpadillo stuffed its cheeks to knobbly capacity then shuffled off to deposit its stash in a dark corner of the crate and when it returned, sat down to wait patiently on the other side of the wire. Phyllo himself was starting to succumb to the pangs of hunger and produced the small bag of dates he'd been given as breakfast. He offered one to their prisoner who whistled softly as it took it. They ate side by side in companionable silence, the Parpadillo now comfortable enough to peel its gaze from Phyllo and look around.

"Don't worry, buddy," said Phyllo in a soft voice, "Life's about to get really interesting for you. No more struggling on your own. Everybody needs friends. You'll see." He passed the creature another date.

"Phyllo, come," the voice of Tamer Venor called from their shelter.

He scrunched up the bag and got to his feet, seeing now that the Parpadillo's crate was sunk just low enough to be protected. Since he'd kneeled beside it the wind had got up even more. Sheets of sand were now being transported in its grip and whipped through the air to sting at Phyllo's exposed skin. He dipped to protect his face and made for their shelter.

Tamer Venor had been busy. The tarp was secured once more, now angular like the prow of a ship pointing into the wind, the loose edges cracked like a kite. She squatted in the protected corner, her altar open before her, rifling through its drawers for materials. She waved him over. Squalls of sand waltzed around them and pelted the tarp, pushing in the centres like sails.

"The basics are always required. Earth and sea, fire and air." She produced the corresponding materials – a jar of rock salt, a vial of water, a candle and an incense cone – then motioned to Phyllo's tin, which she'd brought over to sit by her own.

He prised off the lid and got to setting it up. He had his own containers of essentials now, curated with the help of Tamer Venor before they'd left. He set them out on the upturned base of his tin and together they went about lighting the candles and setting the incense to smoulder.

"And so, to our purpose," said Tamer Venor, "A location spell. It is simple enough when proximity is on your side. Locating the Parpadillo over such great distance was challenging, but our subject now will prove easier to find, I am sure." She smiled at Phyllo reassuringly and wind curled around them, lifting their clothes away from their skin, plumping Tamer Venor's mane of black hair to ripple like waves in the sea.

A sound like humming came in and out of focus to Phyllo's ears and he stilled to listen for it. The sound pulsed and grew in strength, becoming melodic and sweet. What was that? He flicked his eyes to Tamer Venor, but before he could phrase the question, she had pulled the bronze ankh from inside her tunic. It sang with vibration, like a glass trilling to the stroke of a damp fingertip.

They both stared at it.

"Panya," Phyllo breathed.

"We must return."

Phyllo shuffled back a step. "But why? What's happened?"

Tamer Venor's face had fallen from the excitement of their capture to a mask of concern. "The signal does not explain, only indicates a state of great calamity. There is no time to delay."

Phyllo blinked at her, adjusting to this new turn. "What—"

"Home is the easiest, the swiftest of all. Our route is already marked. Our familiars already deployed. I will ensure that you travel first. When I tell you, you must say 'Alitura, take me home' and strike the ground with the tip of your cane. Until then, repeat what I do and say." Her words flowed in an urgent stream.

Phyllo nodded, his mouth drying. The travelling spell had not gone well before and now she would see.

She took out her whip. "The cobra cane, Phyllo. Pass it hand to hand around your body like this." She exchanged hands with the whip behind her back and then in front and continued to do so as she spoke the next words. Phyllo snatched up his cane and did the same.

"Familiar and friend, nature's guide and magic's vessel." She nodded to Phyllo.

Phyllo rushed out the words before he had a chance to forget them. Sand whirled around his feet. The melodic hum of the ankh grew louder.

"Reopen the path we travelled together. Prepare the road. Secure this circle."

Phyllo watched the incense plume forcefully from Venor's altar. It rushed toward her, following the whip. "Reopen the path we travelled together," Phyllo said, his voice cracking,

"Prepare the road…" he struggled for the next words then remembered. "Secure this circle."

Incense from his own altar rushed to consume him. Wind roared in his ears, sand blasted at the tarpaulin and the pitch of the ankh escalated to a wail.

"Now, Phyllo," Tamer Venor shouted above the din.

With as much conviction as he could muster, he yelled the words that he'd been given and, gripping the cobra cane with both his hands, thrust it down into the earth.

25

Duplicity and Disaster

Phyllo stumbled and dropped to one knee. His tin clattered to the floor.

"Panya, what has happened? Panya, where are you?" Tamer Venor bounded up the spiral staircase that led to their quarters.

The butterphants bumped around in their pen beside Phyllo, scuffling and harrumphing. To the other side, capuchins tore up and down their bamboo frame, an assault of screeching. A barrel rocked on its side beside the main door. The rush of the altar abated and a sick feeling formed in Phyllo's stomach.

"Panya?" Venor dipped in and out of every stall on the mezzanine and returned to the balcony to look down at Phyllo quizzically.

He shrugged and got to his feet, squinting into the darkness of the stalls, trying to see past the animals. "Panya?"

"Here." A small voice came from the mezzanine above.

Phyllo looked up but could not see her. Tamer Venor

sprinted down one stairway and pushed past Phyllo to climb the other. Phyllo ran behind.

"Panya? Where are you?"

"Here." Her voice was faint.

Together Phyllo and Tamer Venor charged from stall to stall searching. The mezzanine was a mess. Scattered animal bedding littered the floor. Purple flowered branches were trampled underfoot.

Then Phyllo saw the shine of her frightened eyes from the back of a dark, unoccupied stall. Legs curled up to her body, she was as far into the corner as it was possible to go. "Here, she's here," said Phyllo, and Tamer Venor rushed in.

"What has happened? Panya, are you injured?"

She shook her head, eyes wide and mouth clamped tight shut.

"Panya, tell me."

"I could not stop them," she said, her voice barely louder than a whisper. She gasped in a huge breath, as if she hadn't dared to breathe all this time, waiting for them to return. "The Ringmaster, Skinner and Bain," she said, answering the unasked question, then clamped her mouth shut again and her eyes brimmed full.

"I don't understand. Did they hurt you? What has happened?" Venor gripped Panya's shoulders and squatted down to be at her eye level.

Again, she shook her head. "I was sleeping. After you left the animals were agitated. The magic upset them. It took hours to calm everyone down. I was sleeping," she said again and looked imploringly to Tamer Venor. "I didn't hear until they were already on the mezzanine with the crate, then I couldn't get past. They took it. They knew how to do it."

Venor sat back on her heels, turning her head away,

turning toward the neighbouring pen and the purple-headed branches that were flattened on the ground. Phyllo stepped backward, out of Panya's stall toward the filigreed gate in the wall. Immediately he saw that it was not shut, that leaves jutted out between the gate and its frame. He reached for the gate and the sick feeling in his stomach intensified.

Panya's carefully constructed butterfly house had been destroyed. Branches that had been strung in the semblance of a tree hung limp and wonky, leaves crumpled and flowers smashed. The air inside was completely still. Phyllo scanned the branches for life but could not find a single baby blue wing hidden amongst the leaves. Where was the Aves Pacis? Phyllo stepped forward scanning high and low then spotted a handful of creatures on the ground, their wings bent and their bodies still. He stooped to examine them.

Heavy breathing came from behind him and Phyllo looked over his shoulder to see Tamer Venor framed in the doorway. She too scanned the branches for life and found none.

"I don't understand. Where is it?" said Phyllo, struggling to make sense of what was happening.

"Taken." Fury ignited behind Tamer Venor's eyes.

"But how? I mean it's so hard to control. How?" Skinner and Bain were the Ringmaster's lackeys, but skilled Whisperers? He didn't think so.

"They were prepared." She hissed out the words and spun on her heel to charge away. Phyllo leapt from the floor to chase her.

"Prepared? Why?"

"A good question. An excellent question." She pulled at her chin and spat to the ground. She rocketed down the stairs and across the Menagerie to throw open the door. Phyllo ran after her.

"He goes too far." She touched at her face and swiped through the air, sweeping out into the cold air. The tails of her tunic billowed behind.

The ground was slick with new rain and leaves and Phyllo slipped about behind her trying to keep up. His skin prickled at the dramatic change in temperature. Chilly autumn had made itself at home for October on the Plains. The encampment was overcast and quiet, the only sign of activity at Schlepper's trailer, where Phyllo noticed him closing the door.

Tamer Venor peeled away to the left, making straight for the Ringmaster's cabin. She flung both doors open wide and stormed in.

"Lazarus Barker!" she roared and Phyllo stumbled into the Ringmaster's cabin behind her, skidding around the wall of machine.

The Ringmaster looked up coolly from the papers on his desk and snapped the top back onto his pen. He stood and strolled around to meet her in the centre of his cabin, looking down his nose at her, imperious and cool even though she was terrifying beyond anything Phyllo had seen of her so far. Shorter and slighter than Lazarus Barker, but certainly no less formidable and radiating fury. They squared up to each other, Tamer Venor an unexploded bomb of energy, the Ringmaster dispassionate and superior.

"Where is it?" she spat, "Where is my Aves Pacis?"

The Ringmaster raised one eyebrow. "*Your* Aves Pacis, Venor? Whatever do you mean?"

"Where is it?" she repeated.

"Quite safe and secure. It's a valuable thing."

"I know what it is."

"Quite." A flicker of a smile.

They stared at each other and Phyllo half expected Tamer Venor to leap at him like a cat, claws out and hissing.

Lazarus Barker sucked at his teeth for a moment and then said, "Keeping dragons is an expensive business—"

"We have been through—" Tamer Venor cut him off but the Ringmaster cut back.

"Destructive too. Damage that must be repaired. More damage." He flicked his eyes to Phyllo who understood that the Ringmaster had not forgotten his debt either. "The Aves Pacis makes no return."

"It costs nothing to keep," Tamer Venor countered, "A few flowered branches. A dish of water."

"Yet is highly lucrative to sell. A gross of wings will fetch 500 Coin."

Tamer Venor recoiled from him. "You would sell it for parts?"

"Do not pretend to be so conservative. Animal is consumed by animal. What do you feed to your bears? Or even that dragon you are so determined to protect? Be glad I did not take its hoard."

"You would not dare."

The Ringmaster's eyes hardened and Tamer Venor took a step back from him and lifted her chin. "Thamineh may be weakened, but it would be a foolish man who tried to steal from her."

The Ringmaster bristled. "Do you think you make its continued presence in my circus more appealing?" He took a step forward. "Tread carefully, Venor, or your precious pet will go the way of the Aves Pacis. I need no more reason. You think I could not do it? You think I *would* not do it?

"My associates at the Club are more than able to handle beasts ferocious as that. What am I saying? As *weak* as that. A little advice and sufficient motivation and you'd be amazed by the possibilities. Schlepper assures me of an interested buyer for the Aves Pacis. I don't doubt there will be one for the dragon."

Schlepper? Phyllo couldn't believe what he was hearing.

Tamer Venor too seemed temporarily shocked into silence, turning on the spot to track the Ringmaster's movements as he strolled to the window, the tap of his cane on the floor marking his progress.

She floundered for a moment, but then mastered herself to speak in a more measured tone. "Forgive me, Ringmaster, but trapping a dragon is not like netting butterflies."

"But whoever said anything about trapping? Do not be mistaken, Venor, I am many things. Head of this proud family business, for instance." He waved a demonstrative hand about the cabin. "Responsible for the welfare of a troupe of exceptional performers, yourself included in that number. I am guardian and guide of the most ingenious and splendid big top on the circuit. Devilishly handsome, some may say—" he twirled at his beard, absurdly entertained by himself "—but one thing I am not is a fool. Trapping a dragon would be dangerous in the extreme, even one as feeble as mine."

Mine. Phyllo felt the word sting Tamer Venor and when she spoke again her tone had taken another step down.

"As Thamineh is, her value is greatly depreciated, Ringmaster." She bowed her head a little then looked up to continue, "Unable to perform while she pines. I continue to assure you that completing her with a mate will bring her back to magnificence, will bring glory to the Circus of Wonder like never before."

The Ringmaster climbed the step to his viewing platform and looked down at her pityingly. "Trapping a dragon is ill-advised, Venor. You know that. Fortunately, much like the Aves Pacis, dragons have value beyond their performances. Dragon blood, claws, teeth and hide, it is all of enormous interest to the traders in the Nevershade. Think on it, Venor. Clear the Menagerie's debt and stop this foolishness."

"No!" The word escaped from Phyllo before he'd had the chance to censor it. Both Tamer Venor and the Ringmaster turned to stare at him.

"Phyllo." The Ringmaster smiled serenely "I'd almost forgotten about you, standing there." He looked him up and down. "How's the apprenticeship coming along?"

Phyllo could have been quite wrong-footed by this change of tack, but the horror of what the Ringmaster had just suggested still hung in the air.

"Excellent, it's excellent," he fired back, "Learned loads. On the brink of capturing the dragon, actually. Might even do it by myself." Phyllo rocked slightly, side to side, clenching and unclenching his fists.

"Is that so?" The Ringmaster's grin spread into a twinkling slash. "Well, that is good news." He turned his gaze back to Tamer Venor. "Then it seems we have nothing to worry about."

~

"Lock every gate. All field exercise must be struck from the rota. I regret it, Panya. It will mean more work for you, but there is nothing to be done. The Ringmaster's fixation upon

Coin demands it. There will be no more contributions from us."

Tamer Venor heaved a bulky harness down from the wall and caught Phyllo staring. The harness would have fitted one of the butterphants easily, and would undoubtedly accommodate a creature larger still. Phyllo's imagination conjured the terrifying beast of his nightmare and the fear returned to his chest.

"Tungsten and iron mesh will endure dragon fire," she said not looking at him, "and is light enough to wear permanently, if you have the build of a fully grown Sand Dragon." She grappled to get a better hold "It was a grave mistake to remove it from my Mohareb. A dragon that was *truly* mine." Momentarily her eyebrows furrowed. Phyllo could see that the Ringmaster's assertion of Thamineh's ownership still stung.

She dragged the harness to the centre of the Menagerie floor. "It will be a burden initially," she said, recovering herself, "but I think it will prove its worth. At best a dragon girdle bonds it to its master. At worst, well, at least there'll be something to hold on to." She gave Phyllo a wink.

He laughed uncertainly, but his throat was too dry to make a convincing job of it.

Panya scurried from pen to pen, checking food and water and then throwing bolts to secure the occupants. She skirted around Phyllo, keeping her head down and making it impossible for him to catch her eye. He wanted to tell her that she wasn't to blame, that once the Ringmaster had set his sights on the Aves Pacis, there was nothing she could have done to stop him. Lazarus Barker always got what he wanted.

But she smarted from the failure she perceived. The

balance of power between them rocked perilously back and forth.

"Here. Fill these." Tamer Venor thrust an armful of water bottles into Phyllo's chest, strung together on a line. "As we have the opportunity we may as well take fresh supplies. Take this too—" she gave him a bundle of fabric "—A ghutrah, to protect your head. A storm is rising."

Phyllo took the bottles to the water butt, glad of a task. "Tamer Venor," he called across the cabin, "Do you think that the Ringmaster is telling the truth? Could he really take Thamineh? How do you think they managed to wrangle the Aves Pacis into that crate?"

Tamer Venor stuffed dates and nuts into her pockets. She shook her head derisively. "Forcing a creature into subservience does not require the skills of a Whisperer. Pain and brutishness are persuasive in their own right. Whispering is a bond that finds the best between man and creature and, if we are lucky, will allow us to reveal the magic of that to an audience who shares our wonder. Greed and selfishness have no need of such childish things. The reward of a handful of Coin requires no empathy. The Aves Pacis would not perform in return for fear and, as much as I would like it to, that small justice will not reverse its fate." She rubbed at her forehead. "We must not be distracted."

Phyllo filled the bottles and, when Tamer Venor was satisfied that security was the best it could be, the pair of them took up position by their altars once more. Phyllo was relieved to discover that travelling the same cosmic road again presented fewer difficulties than the initial outbound trip and soon he was shaking off the giddy glow that altar travel left in its wake.

The sun now was at its highest, but its relentless beat was

muddied by the fog of sand that rode in the air. He squinted to Tamer Venor to see her wrapping a scarf around her head and pulled his own from his pocket to do the same. It dulled the sting of the sand, but only left him with the barest of slits to see through.

The landscape had changed.

The well-trodden path through scrubby bushes had been smoothed to a fresh rippling surface. Where previously there had been a dune rising between their camp and the trap, now it had gone. Plant life close by was half buried in the shifting sand.

Phyllo turned on the spot, trying to get his bearings. Their tarpaulin flapped wildly in the wind, having broken loose of its anchor to one side. Phyllo stood as close to it as he could, without getting whipped, and looked toward the lake. The Parpadillo trap should have been directly in front of him, but he could not see it. Tamer Venor strode out to the spot and he followed, feet sinking and sliding as he struggled through the storm.

"Is it buried?" he said. It was the only explanation he could think of.

They scoured about, pulling at shrubs to see how far the sand had crept up them, and dug experimentally. There was no sign of the crate. No sign of their chicken wire enclosure. No sign of the Parpadillo.

Phyllo made his way back to the camp spot, utterly confused. Tamer Venor hustled in behind him. She pulled at the tarp and secured it best she could in the storm.

"The carrying bars are gone too," she said, "They, most certainly, would not have been taken by the wind."

They looked at each other confused and then around themselves, searching for an explanation. Then Tamer Venor stooped to pluck something from the ground that pinned the other corner of the tarp in place. It flapped around her forearm like a fish struggling out of water and she grabbed at it with her other hand to hold it out flat. It was a flag on a short stick on which was printed an emblem: a man in fur-trimmed exploration gear planting a flag of his own. The motto 'Discovery by ocean, land and sky' ran boldly in a circle around the outside edge. The initials 'B. A. V. G.' were written by hand in one corner.

Tamers Venor screwed it into her fist and looked up to meet Phyllo's gaze.

He knew that emblem. "The Pioneer Club," he said.

26

HUNKER IN THE BUNKER

THE MENAGERIE common room felt like a war bunker, locked down and dark, save for the flicker of lanterns. One hung from the wall and a second stood at the centre of their circle of floor cushions, where an open tagine sighed steam in its glow. Phyllo liked the lanterns. In a day where there had been little to appreciate, the flames lent an air of comfort and security. With the dragon below kicking out so much heat there was no need for a fire, the gentle flicker of light felt right for the cold days of autumn. They ate in silence and the food filled a void.

Phyllo's initial outrage had been replaced by dull acceptance. A blanket of shock seemed to have quelled them all into an odd sort of calm. To his right Panya sat with her back against the wall, legs folded toward her so she could balance her bowl on her knees. She ate with quick jerky movements, but didn't seem scared anymore. Even though she kept her eyes on her food, Phyllo didn't feel like she was shutting him out. Her small brow was wrinkled beyond her years and her eyes were full of worry. She seemed to have moved on from their rivalry to more important things.

Tamer Venor sat to his left. Perched on the edge of her cushion with her feet planted wide, the bowl cradled in one hand between her knees while she spooned her food thoughtfully from it with the other. Her eyes were glazed, mind far away.

"It's Schlepper that bothers me the most, I think," said Phyllo suddenly. "He talked about conservation when he showed me that carousel. I should have realised he wasn't interested in the real thing when I saw the machines. The automatons," he corrected himself, "Whatever they are."

"You will know a man by his deeds and not his words. Trust unwisely and you trust water to a sieve." Tamer Venor's eyes continued to look into nothing.

Phyllo didn't know Schlepper, not really, but he had trusted him. Schlepper had seemed kind and helpful, but now Phyllo thought he could finally see him as he truly was; the Ringmaster's man with dubious connections. Phyllo didn't like to admit it, but he'd got him wrong.

The Club's quirky allure had faded. All those stuffed animal trophies had been repulsive, but he'd come away feeling that underneath it all, the explorers did have good intentions, that they were seeking knowledge and building a repository of information. It had felt important, even if he hadn't liked it. Now it felt sick. Taking the Aves Pacis for the value of its wings wasn't right. He remembered the crate in Pepperwort's Apothecary in the Nevershade with their emblem burned into the wood. What had been inside? He shuddered.

Tamer Venor put down her unfinished bowl and pushed

the heel of her palm into her chest. She bowed her head, the mane of dark hair hiding her face from view.

Phyllo shuffled uncomfortably then quietly said, "We'll get past this. I know we will. You're amazing with the animals. It's like nothing I've ever seen. You have to believe in yourself—" his eyes flicked to Panya "-in us."

Tamer Venor swiped the back of her hand across her eyes, then got up and left the room.

Phyllo bit at his lip and wished he'd kept quiet, but then she was back, holding a tattered old envelope. She squatted down beside him.

"Magic is in my blood," she said, "My mother was a Dabtara. Ethiopian ancestors passed the tradition from mother to daughter. She was unusually skilled. I learned at her knee. My father moved animals for richer men. Often, we had them lodge in our barn before they travelled on. I was young, too young to work, too young even for school, but old enough to fill water troughs through bars when my parents were busy. They were humble golden days." She opened the envelope and pulled out an old photograph. A child of three or four with sparse braids grinned broadly up at them. She was tickling the stomach of a big cat. A really big cat.

"Is that a leopard? Is that you?"

"Cats have always been a particular favourite. The leopards were my first conquest. My whip was snatched to defend me from their fear. We became friends, until they moved on."

Phyllo could see that. It was incredible that a child so young was already so advanced in the Whispering talent. He felt a stab of ineptitude.

"My mother was exceptionally talented and my father became renowned. It has long been the injustice of Nubian women that their husbands shine in their stead. When I was ten my father decided that my mounting skill should be employed so I joined them. My first outing was to be an undertaking of great importance. We travelled by camel, my father unable to travel by altar and my mother too devoted to travel without him. When we arrived in El Kharga my father went about drumming up interest and raised a workforce. He even managed to get us into the local paper."

She pulled a second item from the envelope. It was a newspaper cutting, folded to the edges of another photograph. To one edge stood a woman wrapped in multiple layers of patterned fabric, her head covered, her expression severe. In front stood an older child this time. Her hair now taking on the shape that was familiar to Phyllo. It was clearly Tamer Venor. She too looked serious.

"I was excited to join them. The job was unusual, prestigious. My father had employed a team of *fellah*, his own man this time. We set off again, into the desert. A camel train of many now and we came eventually to a welcome expanse of water and then a day later to an ancient building, almost lost to the desert. A tomb."

Tamer Venor's expression fell into a scowl. "Such things should be respected, but my father had no respect. These were not his ancestors, not his people. My mother was too tolerant." She threw her hands up and then laid her palm over her heart, "They were *her* people. I considered them my people too. She said that we might find our salvation there, that there would be riches enough to guard us from hunger for the rest of our lives. What good are riches to the dead? she asked and it seemed a sound argument.'"

Tamer Venor sighed.

"The *fellah* worked, digging and breaking through stony

gates to the chambers within, to what seemed to me to be the underworld. The work was terrible. Men collapsed in the heat, and the trials to gain access were many. Some deserted the dig, declaring it cursed. My mother had told them the way, but would not participate. She stayed with me until it was time. When they finally broke through to the burial chamber, we were called down to join them. What do you know of the Pharaohs of Egypt, Phyllo?"

"I know about the pyramids. They built great big tombs to show how powerful they were. How powerful they'd *been*, I suppose, by then."

"Power, yes, but more than that, there was a great desire to travel smoothly to the afterlife. That is the key to it. The rulers of Egypt were rich beyond measure and did all they could to take it with them. This Pharaoh's riches, however, remained in this world. Treasures heaped around the walls in such quantity as I had never seen, nor my father I think, for the light of greed burned brightly in him. Immediately he ordered his men to seize everything they could carry."

A wry smile formed on Tamer Venor's lips. "But great riches do not remain in lonely places for long unguarded. A reckoning was inevitable. I felt it before I heard it – the rumbling purr of a dragon's displeasure. You know it already, I think."

The rumblings that came from Thamineh had become so familiar to Phyllo that he was almost unaware of them these days. He nodded.

"Dragons have long been associated with treasure and while it might hold little loyalty to the Pharaoh who imprisoned it there, it would defend its hoard ferociously. It was my mother's purpose in this undertaking to quell the dragon's wrath.

"When it came it was fearsome, incredible and wild. The walls folded back to clear its path – some ancient mechanism triggered by the intrusion of thieves. It crashed about the burial chamber, talons, teeth and fire. I thought that we would surely die." She swept her hand through the air. "Fellah perished in its flames; others fled. My mother stood her ground and faced it down. She was magnificent, in tune with the beast. The dragon was a female and, as soon became apparent, a mother with a single calf. It too found its way to the burial chamber from the hidden depths of the tomb."

Tamer Venor's eyes took on a glaze and crinkled lightly at the edges, remembering.

"There is no fiercer creature than a mother defending her young. My own mother held me at her side and penetrated the dragon's consciousness to show her we meant the calf no harm. The meld was strong, like a wave that rolled out through the tomb, picking up all consciousness in its path. I saw inside the dragon's mind. Strange and beautiful. Powerful and loyal. Such loyalty. I came to understand the dragon way that day. For any that are able, a bargain struck with a dragon is unbreakable. Mighty and eternal. From that day on my familiar was found. My mother had the female subdued. There was no need—"

Tamer Venor cut off to swallow awkwardly, the edges of her mouth pulled down. "The Sand Dragon is a mighty beast, stronger and more majestic and more magical than any other I have encountered, but is no match for a hundred rifles in such close proximity and a hunter that wears the protection of a Dabtara. My father's men killed the female dragon while she lay docile and I felt every moment through her calf's eyes. It was pain beyond enduring."

Phyllo's gut twisted at the thought. "Why would he do that? That's awful."

"He was greedy and cruel, but mostly afraid." Tamer Venor's nostrils flared. "He did not believe that the dragon could be kept at bay long enough to steal all the riches that were there. He gave orders for the calf to be slaughtered too, but I dove before it, protecting it with my own life. My father was foul with rage. Declared that I was only delaying the inevitable; that it would be slain one day by the hand of man for gold, one way or another; that without its mother it could not survive. My mother came to my aid and a confusion of spells ensued. I took the calf and ran. Melded to me, it came willingly to escape the riot of destruction. I saved it from the tomb and it took me on its back to save me from my father, our pact of protection sealed. My Mohareb."

So that was how she had come by him. At last Phyllo understood.

"From that moment I vowed I would not follow in my father's footsteps and dedicated my life instead to understanding animals, to conservation, to be a force for good and not greed. I left him and his mercenary ways behind. That was many years ago."

Phyllo looked down to the photograph again. It seemed incredible that a child so young could have melded with a dragon. He unfolded the cutting, hoping to read the story that accompanied the photo, but found it was printed in Arabic. He also discovered that the photograph itself was larger than it first appeared and continued around the fold to reveal a third person. A man, presumably Tamer Venor's father. He was not at all how Phyllo had pictured him. Not Egyptian and not dressed in local clothes like her mother. He was a military man, dressed in an army uniform. Definitely a westerner. He squinted down into the face. It looked familiar.

Tamer Venor flopped the flag she had plucked from their tarpaulin over the photograph and pointed to the handwritten initials.

"B. A. V. G.," mused Phyllo, feeling like he was on the edge of something.

"Brigadier Alfred Valentine Grosvenor," said Tamer Venor, "My father."

27

RESCUE MISSION

EVEN AFTER HIS meal had been consumed, Phyllo could not shake the uncomfortable hollow in his guts. He felt manipulated and deceived. For the Brigadier to have discovered their camp, to have known where to find them and their newly captured Parpadillo, he must have been acting on information from within the Circus of Wonder itself.

Phyllo clenched and released his fists. The most likely the source was Schlepper. Schlepper the fixer, the Brigadier's friend. Why hadn't Phyllo seen that before when it was so blindingly obvious? Had he sold the Aves Pacis already? Could it be still alive? It was only a matter of hours since its abduction – it could even still be there, at the Circus of Wonder encampment.

Phyllo got to his feet, thinking hard. How many places were there to keep such a creature? It had to be somewhere fairly large, yet contained. Schlepper's workshop was certainly big enough, but in there it could easily scatter about. No, that was far from ideal. Where else would work? Phyllo scoured his knowledge of the cabins and a possibility occurred to him. The new cabin that Skinner and Bain had been building would be ideal. Last time he'd looked, it had been empty, aside from that appalling mermaid. If the Ringmaster had laid claim to it for that, it wasn't much of a leap for it to be used as a temporary hiding place for the Aves Pacis.

What a coup it would be if Phyllo could steal it back. He hurried to his stall to find the key Tufty had lifted from Bain, a fluttering building in his chest at the thought of scoring a point for the Magical Menagerie. A point for the Menagerie and a point for him. It was definitely worth a look.

He pulled his coat in tight against the cold night air and surveyed the horseshoe. When he'd chased Tamer Venor across it earlier there'd been no other soul in sight, but now many of the cast were out in the open, buzzing between cabins and talking in low voices. They trickled into the big top in two and threes. Signor and Signora Volante, arm in arm; Harrick and Garrick shoving each other from side to side, fighting as usual to be first. Something was happening in there and no-one had seen fit to tell the Menagerie.

The temptation to investigate tugged at Phyllo's resolve, but a diversion in the ring was just what he needed. Something else to draw eyes would make it less likely that he'd be seen. He fell into the shadows and skirted behind the Ringmaster's quarters, ducking low to pass beneath his great circular window, slipping and sliding on the wet ground.

Wedges of light spilled out between cabins – three exposed tranches to cross before he'd reach his target. Phyllo lurched across each, absorbing the waves of excited chatter that rode the cold air. The final shadow took him right up to the new cabin door, breathing heavy and heart pounding in his ears.

It looked considerably more polished than the last time he'd seen it. The exterior panels were now trimmed with scrolling mouldings that matched in with the rest of the horseshoe. Only the doorway itself remained rough and unfinished. The style, it seemed, was undecided, much like its final purpose. It was an unhappy reminder of their situation, but the same door also meant the same lock and the key slid easily home.

"Hey, what's the story?" A voice boomed from the darkness behind him and Phyllo felt the hair on the back of his neck stand on end. He jumped and spun around.

Bain advanced into the light, closing the gap between them in two easy strides. One of his meaty hands clamped down on Phyllo's shoulder and the other reached around to pluck the key from the lock.

"Thieving these days, are you? Found your talent in the end." Bain's potato-head split into a nasty grin.

"I'm not thieving," said Phyllo.

"Where'd you get this?" Bain held the key uncomfortably close to Phyllo's face.

Phyllo tried to lean away, but Bain had him pinned against the cabin wall.

"A capuchin gave it to me."

Bain snorted. "Do you take me for an eejit?"

Phyllo stared back, thinking it best not to answer.

"You'll not find anything in there, besides." Bain backed up a little, "If you're wanting to see her, she's in plain view. Come on now, why don't you." He pulled Phyllo forward and then pushed him along in front, down the narrow alleyway between the Odditorium and Schlepper's van, across the horseshoe path and through the grand entrance of the big top.

By this time quite a crowd had gathered in the ring, surrounding something that they were taking it in turns to examine. It didn't take much imagination to guess what it might be.

Bain released Phyllo's shoulder. "Things are changing. Never mind your lovesick beastie, it's the macabre that's pulling the crowds in now. Know how much you and that dragon'll be missed when the Ringmaster sends you both on your way? It'll be like pulling your hand from a bucket of water and looking for the hole."

Phyllo glared at Bain who shoved him aside to muscle into the crowd. Phyllo eyed the wall of backs anxiously – every eye was drawn to the creature entombed in glass on a high plinth. What would they make of it? He stepped in a little closer to make out what they were saying.

"A family of exotics, you say? A *family*?" Albertus Crinkle spoke from the other side of the group, his woolly cardigans layered three deep.

"You could describe them as a family," said Schlepper slowly, "I believe the Ringmaster intends to. Other specimens similarly presented is the truth of it." Schlepper dropped a hand to wave over the Equatorial Mermaid. Phyllo caught sight of its ugly stretched face and frozen, grasping claw-like hands. It still made his skin scrawl.

"I see. I see," Albertus said in a small voice, nodding and letting his eyes drop away from the creature. "Well, it certainly wouldn't take much to keep it fed and I've read about such exhibits in *The Ballyhoo*. Draws the crowds and the Coin and there's no doubt we could do with a bit more of that.

Phyllo moved around the circle and spied Birdie Volante through a gap. She stood in front of her father, his hands on her shoulders and, by the expression on her face, feeling utterly revolted. Signor Volante's face was more considered. "It is a side-show. A distraction. Not an act. Lazarus can no be considering replacing anyone with this."

"The Magical Menagerie is a heavy stone on his chest." Schlepper's voice. Phyllo ducked and wove around the group to find him. He looked tired, older. Purple hollows sank around his eyes.

Signor Volante let out a hissing sigh. "We do not want to be known for this."

"The Ringmaster feels that exotics could be deployed at any location, even those which are *ordinary*. I have heard him say that the Magical Menagerie is a drain on resources and a liability. We cannot show a dragon to an *ordinary* crowd. Imagine the mayhem."

"The Magical Menagerie sells tickets to the *charmed*, which is far more of our route." Signor Volante rounded on Schlepper. "We are the Circus of Wonder, Schlepper. What do you know? You have been here five minutes and already you are a chameleon, huh? The Ringmaster's mouthpiece. What do you bring?"

Schlepper turned away, smoothing his jacket down with the palms of his hands. "I have yet to prove myself, I know."

"What's in that wreck of a trailer? Not more horrors like this, I hope."

"You'll be welcome to see, just as soon as the final adjustments are made—"

"Pah!" Signor Volante pulled his mouth down in a grimace, "When it is ready, when it is ready. You run after butterflies, Schlepper. And what of the Menagerie? What of Tamer Venor and Panya and Phyllo? They are no concern of yours, huh? They can swim or drown."

Schlepper's jaw flapped. "Now wait a minute. I'm in the middle of all this by circumstance, my links with Lazarus are through the Club and that just happens to be where he met the Brigadier is all."

Signor Volante waved a derisory hand at him. "Save it, Schlepper. Lazarus is his own man. I know him better than most. I just prefer my exotic animals alive."

All eyes returned to the taxidermy and a silence settled over them. Even Schlepper sighed before speaking again.

"Taxidermy is in vogue. The Pioneer Club has many specimens, although their purpose is in the realms of discovery and scientific research. They can be a fascinating record of the natural world. A preservation, if you will. This creature, however, is something else entirely." Schlepper turned and caught Phyllo's eye by chance. "Men like the Brigadier have a different goal in mind. The Equatorial Mermaid is a fabrication."

Phyllo stared at him. A fabrication?

"If I had to hazard a guess, I would say that the head, arms and torso are capuchin monkey, perhaps a subspecies with less fur or possibly shaved. The other part would be some kind of exotic fish. Those fins have a touch of the Lionfish about them."

Phyllo's gaze slid back to the glass case. He hadn't thought it possible to hate this thing any more than he already did, but now he found that it was not just one creature, killed and stuffed to be ogled at, but two. The Equatorial Mermaid was a sick figment of someone's imagination, designed to trick coin from the gullible.

28

THE HEART OF A DRAGON

Phyllo awoke to the juddering of furniture dragged across floorboards. The barest glimmer of apricot light crept in through the window high in his stall. He yawned and stretched and rolled out of bed, pulled on his dressing gown and padded sleepily to the common room. Tamer Venor was pinning a map of the world to the wall. She stepped back to assess it, spied Phyllo out of the corner of her eye and gave him her customary bow, palm to chest. He returned it automatically.

"Up with the lark, Phyllo. This is good. We have much to accomplish."

Phyllo blinked about the room. Books and scrolls had been lined up on the rear table. Another map was unrolled there and weighted down with candles. Tamer Venor poured Phyllo a glass of liquorice tea which he accepted blearily.

"With regret I must accept Thoth did not approve of my plan to lure the dragon to our side and, with our Parpadillo lost to my father, our troubles are doubled. We have missed our chance. Our captive was likely the last left above ground and the creature's theft has revealed to us a determined adversary. We have no choice now but to go into the dragon's den. It will not be for the faint of heart."

Phyllo swallowed down his tea and nodded mutely. So, this was it.

"But not all is lost," she said with a tremor of excitement in her voice, "We have much to work with: maps, star charts, ancient texts. I still possess artefacts from the time my Mohareb was discovered. Things entrusted to my backpack that were never returned. My mother's treasures, preserved by me in wistful reminiscence, now made important by our quest."

She gestured with a snap of her wrist to the map pinned on the wall. Phyllo rubbed at his eyes and drew closer.

"Dragons are surprisingly far flung in their habitats for a creature so rarely seen. Canada and the Americas have several indigenous species and in themselves demonstrate the variety of temperature and geography these creatures can embrace." She tapped at the map. "Imagine the differences to be found in the icebound rocky caves of Alaska to that of the sun-stripped dunes of Argentia. Temperature, sustenance, water, all are greatly affected.

"The dragon is adaptable, enormously resilient and strong. I tell you this because through our studies I hope you will come to feel you know them, that you will understand the dragon way. It is my intention to enable you to align with their consciousness, but it is essential that you never underestimate them, Phyllo, that you never, ever relax."

Phyllo tried not to choke on his mouthful of tea.

She pointed to the north of Africa, bouncing on the balls of her feet. "Our Sand Dragon prefers the heat of Egypt. The Pharaonic tradition of sealing vast amounts of treasure in protected vaults has suited it well over the years, but now, as little remains undiscovered, so too do fitting dens. The Sand Dragon wanes with the inquisitive greed of men."

She moved to the star charts and leaned against the table, looking down. "There is meaning here, but I know little of astrology. I don't suppose you have any experience in divining the stars?" She squinted at Phyllo rather hopefully.

He shook his head. "Albertus might have something that will help in the archive," he suggested. Albertus Crinkle did have an awful lot of books.

Venor nodded with a tilt to her head and returned to the items on the table. "A road for you to travel, perhaps." She picked up a fat scroll of papyrus and brought it to the front edge of the table. "We also have this. Our last source. The Book of Gates, a section of it at least." Phyllo drew in closer to look at the scroll she now unravelled with great care.

Stiff and unwilling to lie flat, the papyrus rippled in broken curves and stretched six feet along the surface of their table. The edges were ragged, the fibres of the papyrus fraying at their tips. Phyllo held his end down to keep it from rolling back.

"The ancient Egyptians believed the deceased travelled through the night to reach the afterlife. They mapped the route hour by hour, through a series of gates and trials. The construction of tombs has taken cues from this manuscript in many forms. There is information here vital enough for my mother to have taken note. We too should understand it if we are to break through to the dragon's lair."

Phyllo looked down at the series of brightly painted scenes. He knew enough to recognise the figures as Egyptian gods and see that they were surrounded by a solid mesh of hieroglyphs, but it meant little else to him. "I might have to leave this one to you," he said in a small voice and Tamer Venor patted him on the back.

"You are right. There is enough for you to learn. A road for us each to travel then."

She reclaimed the scroll and rolled it loosely.

"And so, to the beast itself." She pulled forward a book Phyllo recognised as that in which he'd read about the Parpadillo. She opened it at the ribbon and Phyllo saw that an entire chapter was dedicated to dragons. It began with layered diagrams of the skeleton, muscles and skin.

"The bone structure you will find largely unsurprising, I think. Quite similar to any other creature with a backbone. The vertebrae extend into the tail. See here." She pointed to the appropriate point on the diagram. "It is much like a lizard in that respect. You may wonder how wings affect the skeletal structure, but when you look to the muscles—" she took Phyllo's attention to a second diagram showing their form "—You can see the support for the wings is greatly increased from that of any other part of the body.

The drawing looked like something that would have been at home in a butcher's shop. Sinewed flesh wrapped the dragon's form with unnerving realism.

"Immensely heavy, the strength required for flight is considerable. Even so, without its magic, I do not believe it would be possible." She turned the page. "This image shows the Hebridean Green, but the essentials remain similar in all breeds. Horns, fangs and claws are common to all."

Phyllo remembered the jagged rows of long spiked teeth that filled Thamineh's broad jaw and claws, not just on her feet, but at the elbows of her huge wings too. He took another slurp of his tea.

A close and detailed drawing of scaled skin filled the next page.

"You are familiar with the properties of dragon hide already, I know. Interlocking hard scales produce an almost impenetrable shield, protecting the creature itself from almost all reasonable forms of attack. The underbelly and joints are the weakest areas, where scales are at their thinnest to allow for movement. Fire proof by necessity and immensely durable, you have already worn the dragon's skin. Do you think that you emulated it well?"

Phyllo remembered waddling about in the stiff, smelly suit. "It certainly made the ponies afraid of me."

A faint smile crossed Tamer Venor's face.

"But I was more of a lumbering idiot than anything else."

"Impersonation of such a magnificent beast is beyond even my capabilities. You'll not fool it with a costume. The way to a dragon's heart is through the meld." She clutched both hands to her head, fingertips digging into her skin, then moved one hand to Phyllo's head to grip him in the same way. "You must find the magical link. The road travelled by Whisperers alone. No pretence will fool a dragon into being your friend, only purity of heart. Nature, as always, is at our core."

Phyllo nodded as best he could under the circumstances and she released him.

"I think that a little hands-on experience will serve you well. After all, we have a specimen close at hand." Tamer Venor looked over Phyllo's shoulder into the central space of the Menagerie. "Thamineh will make for good practice." She clapped an enthusiastic hand upon his shoulder.

So far, Phyllo had found Thamineh rather reluctant to engage.

She was always a looming spectre of the Menagerie, and he had felt her presence much more than he'd seen it. The increasingly oppressive heat she produced had become the norm and the vibration of her listless purr was now so familiar that its tremor soothed him in bed at night, far more than it rattled. Even so, he wasn't sure how he felt about getting too close.

Tamer Venor swept past him, out onto the mezzanine balcony. "To be a dragon Whisperer means more than just learning commands," she called back to him. "You must learn to connect. To find your inner dragon." She thumped at her chest as she walked and, upon reaching the store cupboard, unlocked the padlock and disappeared inside. "What is the essential element of a dragon, Phyllo?" she called from its depths.

Phyllo followed along the balcony and caught up just in time for her to emerge clutching a pair of batons and a metal container of sloshing liquid.

"Consider your altar," she prompted, "All elements are represented: earth, water, air and fire."

"Fire then."

"Fire." She waggled the batons at him and grinned. "Come. We need a little space." She descended the spiral staircase, two steps at a time.

Phyllo had noticed that Tamer Venor's level of enthusiasm usually seemed to tally with the associated level of danger. This skip to her step made his stomach clench.

He forced down the last of his tea and followed. By the time he'd got to the bottom of the stairs she'd already rolled an empty barrel to the centre of the floor and placed her acquired things upon it, adding a jug of water, cups and a wet cloth.

"Today, you breathe fire," she said with a grin.

"I see," whimpered Phyllo, comprehending at last. Suddenly he could guess at the contents of that metal flask.

Venor opened a wall lantern and lit one of the baton tips. "Fire. It is a living, breathing thing with its own soul." She twirled the baton, leaving the imprint of a circle on Phyllo's retina. "Loose and uncontrolled, it will consume all before it, no matter how small its beginnings.

"But not for the servants of Ra." She gave him a wink. "We are masters of fire, Phyllo, you and I." Petals of red and gold shone in the whites of her eyes. "To control it you must respect it; understand how it moves. Flames that reach nothing but air are at their journey's end."

She took a swig from the metal container and spat a jet of liquid across the lit baton. A tongue of flame stretched out into the air and died.

"And flames without oxygen are nothing at all." She laid the burning tip of the baton in the palm of her hand and Phyllo fought the urge to knock it from her grip, but she curled her fingers surely around it and when she released it the flame had been snuffed out.

Phyllo goggled at her and she squinted back at him, examining his face.

"You think this too dangerous for a boy your age? Years make no difference, only acceptance of the truth. The flames will not harm us when we understand." She waved a hand toward the stairs. "Panya passed through flames to the meld and so shall you."

Phyllo turned to see that Panya had descended the stairs to sit on the bottom step. He'd neither seen nor heard her approach. "Panya's done this?" The little girl with wild pigtails returned Phyllo's gaze, deadpan.

"Panya is able to communicate with all the creatures of the Menagerie to a degree. This is why it is essential she be the one to stay here and look after them. Only one is needed for you."

"Right. Just a fire-breathing dragon." Phyllo turned back to Tamer Venor.

"If Thoth wills it," she said with a smile. "We begin with water. Half a sip. Try. Try."

She pushed a cup into Phyllo's chest and he took a sip. Her eyes bored into him as he found even working out how to hold it in his mouth oddly challenging. Spitting it out was even more unnatural and awkward. He tried to propel it ahead of him, but it slopped down his chin as if spilt from a bowl and plopped to the ground. Panya snorted.

"No matter. You must learn to shape your mouth. Force the water past your lips with the air from your lungs. With your *life breath*. It is the depths of your lungs that will find the meld." She waved the cup back up to his mouth and Phyllo took a bigger sip this time, then a deep breath and managed to suck some of the water down into his lungs.

He choked and retched to get it out and cringed with embarrassment, determinedly keeping his back to Panya.

"It is as well to learn that with water. The lamp oil is pure but no replacement for air." She patted him heartily on the back until he stopped coughing and straightened up. "Again."

A deep breath. Half a sip of water. This time the water sprayed away from him more convincingly. Tamer Venor clapped her hands. "That's it. Again."

Phyllo took another sip, larger this time, but ran out of air before all the water had been blown out.

"You have it, I think. Let us try with the lamp oil before you tire." She passed Phyllo the metal canister. "An amount that is equal to the capacity of your lungs, spat away with the ferocity of a dragon." Her golden eyes bore into Phyllo's. "Do not swallow. Do not breathe in. Search the fire for consciousness."

"Right."

She stepped back by his side and Phyllo took a tentative sip. The oil was sweet – not at all what he'd expected. He half-filled his mouth and Tamer Venor passed him the flaming baton. He filled his lungs with air through his nose.

"With your life breath," she whispered and Phyllo sprayed the oil with all the force he could muster. It ignited on the flame and roared ahead of him, filling his vision with gold and heat. His eyes dried instantly and he squeezed them closed to turn away.

Unendurable cold ran goosebumps up his back.

Phyllo's head spun, his knees crumpled and the feeling disappeared. He looked up to Tamer Venor to see expectation burning in her wide eyes. "Did you see?"

Phyllo searched his mind. See? Had he *seen* anything? Not really. "I felt something. Just a feeling. I felt cold."

"Yes." She reached down and pulled him to his feet. "We try again. You will watch me first. Find the meld with the last oxygen in your lungs. Find it here." She pressed the palm of her hand to the centre of her chest.

Phyllo nodded mutely.

Tamer Venor took in a deep breath through her nose, released it and then took another. She sipped from the canister, tipped her head back and then almost seemed to leap forward, though her feet stayed planted firmly on the ground. She spat a jet of flame out into the Menagerie, back arching like a hissing cat. Phyllo stumbled backward, away from her ferocity.

She turned to him, the fire still burning in her eyes. "Intent is essential. Embodiment. Think of your familiar. How did you communicate?"

Phyllo's jaw flapped. In that moment Tamer Venor was so fierce and intense, she could have been part dragon. The focus of her attention so fully upon him made his guts squirm. She smiled faintly and softened to become his mentor again and Phyllo flummoxed around in his head, trying to switch from awed observer to focused student.

His familiar, Alitura. Phyllo thought hard about their connection. "They were just there, in my head. It was effortless. Could they help me, do you think?"

Tamer Venor twitched an eyebrow at him and Phyllo instantly saw that of course they could. Communication with his familiar had been so easy, as if they already lived inside him. This had to be what he was trying to achieve with the dragon.

He scrambled upstairs to his stall to find the token of Alitura and as soon as he touched it, knew he was right. He came back down the stairs much slower, starting to believe that he might actually be able to do this.

"Can we go outside? It's just that I think I need to be near trees. I know we will be farther from Thamineh but..."

Tamer Venor waved him toward the door. "If instinct seeks your highest ability, then no action can be wrong."

I am a Whisperer, Phyllo told himself, *I can do this*. He squeezed at his brain to find the connection with nature and recited the memorised incantation inside his mind as together the three of them walked out onto the horseshoe.

The encampment was quiet, and cold morning air stung

at the tight skin on Phyllo's face where only minutes earlier flames had licked. He smelled the singed hair in his nostrils and observed how rain had softened the ground beneath his feet. Birds chirruped from deep in the Whispering Wood and drew him forward to greet the huddle of spindly saplings nearest to their clearing.

The first he reached was especially thin and tall, its gangly branches extending leafless to the sky, but when Phyllo touched its trunk, he felt the strength of the ancient oaks that stood in the Guardian circle. The clonk of dead wood chimes sounded in his ears.

"Alitura," he whispered to the tree and at once felt the ground beneath his feet shift. Vibrations ran in lines through the earth, tree roots squirmed beneath the surface, pushing upward, stretching and changing. Then the tip of a root found air. It sprang from the ground like shoots from a bulb in springtime, sweeping up in an arch that spread and multiplied. Vines and leaves exploded in a network across its surface, curling and moving with the growth of the Ethelweard beneath.

Then Alitura was before him: the strange and otherworldly fox, formed from roots and vines and leaves. It sat on its haunches, front legs straight and shoulders back, the smoothly hewn head held at an inquisitive tilt.

"PHYLLO."

The name echoed inside his head and Phyllo laughed out loud, delighted to have been able to find Alitura again so easily. Visions of the Guardian circle pulled in and out of focus in his mind's eye. He squeezed his eyes closed and gripped the tree, fighting off a ripple of motion sickness. "Alitura, can you help me keep this awareness inside my head? I'm learning to meld with the dragon."

"WE KNOW AND FEEL THE DRAGON. THE ETHEL-WEARD ARE AT ONE WITH EVERY BEING. WE FEEL THE LIFE FORCE OF ALL FLORA AND FAUNA AND CAN AID YOU, PHYLLO."

"Great, I thought perhaps you could. Thanks, Alitura." Phyllo turned his head to look over to Tamer Venor and Panya. Panya stood furthest away, clutching the flaming baton and flask of oil. Her eyes were wide and she stared unashamedly at Alitura. Tamer Venor, on the other hand, was down on one knee, her head bowed. When she looked up, she said, "It is an honour," in a misty sort of voice that Phyllo hadn't expected. Alitura nodded simply and then said inside Phyllo's mind, *"WE ARE READY."*

Phyllo took the baton and flask from Panya. The nerves he'd felt in the Menagerie muted now, faded almost completely with the knowledge that Alitura was by his side.

"Show me," he said, took a sip from the flask and then, with every last scrap of lung capacity he had, sprayed the fuel from his mouth across the flame. It roared in a jet toward the Menagerie and Phyllo felt his consciousness fly with it, over the damp ground, impossibly fast and through the cabin wall as if it were nothing at all.

White cold. So cold. Winds of ice crept under her scales and she hunched against it. The pain was unrelenting.

Phyllo shuddered and tried to understand. The consciousness around him stirred and then he saw it: the Sand Dragon's eye, wide and wary, scouring him from the inside out.

Another? A human.

Phyllo felt her disappointment cave in the depths of his chest and the eye closed.

I will endure until Mohareb returns. Until the end.

And then she was flying, high above the Circus of Wonder on a summer pitch far from here. It was a memory. The heat of the sun warmed her back and there, ahead, was Mohareb, majestic and glimmering like fire, the air around him golden and glowing. His vast and muscular form soared on the air currents like an eagle. She felt his presence in the hollows of her bones. He was the core of her, the life breath. She felt their union in the binding of fire that would keep them together always, that would keep them with the human saviour who had become one of their own. She imagined the young she knew would come. The huddle of eggs they would keep warm together.

And then the air was empty and dark and panic rose inside her. No! It was not possible. He would never leave them. She scoured the horizon, turning and rising to see yet farther, to search the barren sky, but the golden glow had been lost to steely grey. Loyalty and love pulled at her heart. Had her Mohareb not felt it too? To defend each other until the end was the dragon way. He could not have gone.

And yet the heat had gone from the world and she was alone.

The wave of grief rose in Phyllo's throat and stung his eyes. He choked on the terror of loss and snapped out of the vision.

He was down on his knees. Tamer Venor had one hand on his shoulder and he looked up into her face. Her eyes were clear and knowing.

"You saw," she said.

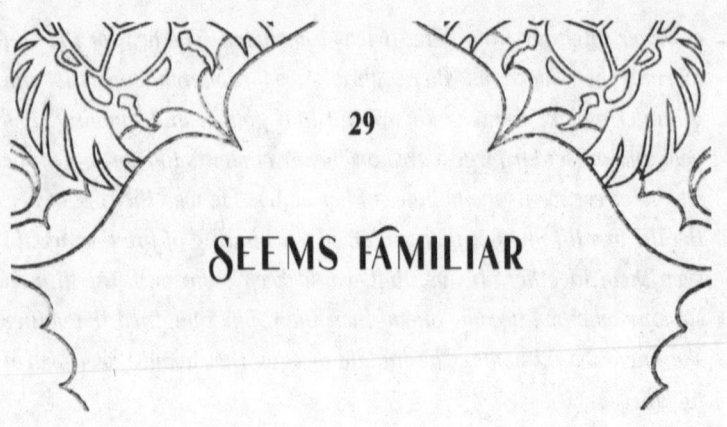

29

SEEMS FAMILIAR

PHYLLO WALKED A LITTLE TALLER, striding across the horseshoe toward the Archive. The task he'd been set had escalated in danger, yes, but somehow he was finding what he needed to be equal to it. He'd learned more than he'd imagined possible in the few short weeks he'd spent in the Menagerie.

Finding Alitura had made everything click into place. With his familiar by his side, he felt as though almost anything was possible. Even he'd noticed the jaunty bounce developing in his gait.

Breathing fire. Wow, just wait until he told Roly about that. Even without the meld, the rush of it had been incredible. Adrenalin and fear replaced by heat and flame and a sense of achievement that had startled him. He lengthened his stride and the tin in his pocket rattled.

The tin was a pre-emptive thank you for the help Albertus Crinkle might be about to provide. It was filled with *jelabi*, a kind of sugar-syrup-soaked pretzel, popular in Tamer Venor's home village. She'd cooked up a batch on their small iron stove that morning. A confectioner at heart, Phyllo'd been delighted to see her producing something that might have been at home in his world, and rather liked their unusual tangled shape and extreme sweetness. He imagined Albertus trying to dip one in a cup of tea and smiled, and didn't notice that Stanley had fallen into step beside him until he tripped him up.

"Stanley," he gasped, just saving himself, "Hello, boy. What are you doing out here?" Phyllo looked about for Schlepper, but couldn't see him. "Should you be out on your own?"

Stanley sprang from foot to foot and wagged his articulated metal tail. He nudged at Phyllo's pockets with his nose and Phyllo withdrew the tin to show it to him. "Oh, I see. Not grease nuggets, I'm afraid." He patted Stanley on the top of his shiny head. One of his toolbox-body doors had flopped open so Phyllo could see Schlepper's tools crowded inside. The destabilising node mallet lay on top.

He remembered the night Schlepper had used it to stop the carousel beetle from blowing itself up. Now he felt sick to his stomach that he'd actually tried to help him. All that effort he'd put into researching the Gremlins and improving his workshop. Now all he could think about was how Schlepper had let him down.

He snapped the toolbox door closed. "Go home, Stanley, before you get lost."

Stanley drooped then turned to whir and click away. Phyllo watched him go, then turned himself to discover he'd been snuck up upon for a second time. Frú Hafiz stood serenely behind him, arms folded and hands tucked into the cuffs of her coat. She gave him a nod of greeting.

Her skin was as pale as moonlight, silver-blonde hair tamed loosely into a long plait. She sported a pair of round dark glasses, even though the day was cold and overcast. Her long black coat draped elegantly over a full, floor-length dress of deep red wool and she wore, as always, the silver chain that hung about her waist and ended in an ornate shining dagger. The scarlet tassel on her cap fluttered slightly in the breeze. She smiled, ethereal and unnerving.

Phyllo's heart jumped. "Frú Hafiz," he said, "I didn't see you there."

"And I have seen little of you over the past weeks. Your new apprenticeship suits you?"

"Yes, I think so. Got its challenges, you know."

"No-one becomes an unbeaten bishop," she smiled as if to reassure him.

Phyllo frowned at her. "Anyway, must get on." He rattled the tin of jelabi. "On my way to Albertus. Hoping for a bit of help deciphering these star charts." He nodded to the rolled-up charts tucked under his arm. "Thought he might have a book in the archive."

She inclined her head to the charts and then back, "You seek assistance divining the stars and the librarian was your first instinct?" Frú Hafiz peered at him over the top of her sunglasses and ice-blue eyes questioned Phyllo's reasoning. "You can think of no other person with knowledge of the astral realm? No other person who forges their living gleaning meaning from the stars?"

Phyllo stared at her.

"I mean myself, of course."

"Well, yes, of course." Phyllo smiled limply. It was obvious really, but he often found her rather difficult to understand and thought that Albertus might have explained things more plainly. "Silly of me," he added awkwardly, "I don't suppose you have a minute?"

"We can lay our heads in the water together." She nodded slightly, which led Phyllo to believe that this meant yes. He was going to have to focus.

He placed his hand over his heart and bowed in return. "In that case, here." He presented the tin to her. "With the compliments of Tamer Venor. Homemade jelabi, it's a kind of pretzel—"

"Sugary sweet," Frú Hafiz interrupted, "Yes, I am familiar. Jida would bring them." She took the tin from Phyllo and immediately popped open the lid. "The best things in life are free," she said softly, inhaling the sweet aroma, "Or really, really expensive. Come, my cabin is warm."

They made a right turn, instead of the left Phyllo had been intending, and peeled off into Frú Hafiz's cabin before they could reach the newly clad lodge that was Schlepper's, or farther still, to reach the Confectionary. Phyllo hadn't been through those doors in quite some time. He realised with a pang that he'd quite like to have his own little wave of nostalgia sometime soon.

Frú Hafiz led them through the circular booth she used for giving readings and into her personal space. Externally the cabin was wooden and similar in style to all the others, but inside its opulence was in great contrast to the straw-strewn Menagerie. Here jewel-coloured rugs swathed the floor and a sweeping chaise longue, upholstered in vibrant blue and gold, dominated the central space. Two overstuffed armchairs completed the amiable circle around a large low table and incense ribbons dipped and curled as they rose from a filigree burner. Gaslight flickered in an overhead lantern.

"Spread your charts here, Phyllo. Let us see what the stars hold."

Phyllo unfurled them to lie one beside the other, and then settled himself onto one of the chairs. Frú Hafiz perched, straight-backed, on the edge of the chaise longue and removed her glasses to peer down.

After a moment she said, "These charts map the realm between the divine and human planes." She swept a hand over one corner, "Astrology is for all men at every level of society, from marketplace to court, but the ability to discern the meaning was the privilege of kings. At least when these charts were conceived." She nodded meaningfully.

"Some believe that the stars exert influence through the rays they emit, did you know that? Some seek to know the future in their arrangement and others still wish to understand the astrological influences of a moment in time to play to its strengths. It is a complex and varied art. Yet, I believe that these are none of those."

She rose from the couch to retrieve an ornate brass and silver disk from a display. "An astrolabe," she said, answering Phyllo's unasked question. She laid it on the table and twirled at the disks that turned within each other. "What information do you seek?"

Phyllo shrugged. "Anything you can tell me really."

She nodded and returned to the charts, switching between them and talking to herself in a low whisper. Phyllo looked about the room while she worked. The astrolabe had been one of many mysterious objects of shining brass and intricate silver kept in display cabinets against the walls. Between them, dark panelling cossetted the space and in one gap a life-size statue of a man stood on a plinth in front of a heavy curtain. Wrapped in a cloak, his shoulders were thrust back, a roguish grin dawning on his face. It was carved from a rich amber wood that bore the patina of years of polish and the touch of passing hands. It gave Phyllo the distinct impression that it was holding its breath.

"Between them these charts describe a location on the Tropic of Cancer. Does that seem relevant to you, Phyllo?" Frú Hafiz said at last.

The Tropic of Cancer was where the Parpadillo lived beside the lake. He remembered that from Tamer Venor's book. "Yes, absolutely."

"These charts are the work of an architect. A person positioning a building to please the gods, to please Osiris." She ran her finger under some text that Phyllo could not read. He didn't know who Osiris was. "It is a building floorplan overlaid with star trajectories. The main chamber is the architectural focus, but a second smaller series of rooms are positioned to follow the path of the sun.

"See here, the Tropic of Cancer intersects its trajectory at the same angle twice in a year. The architect has made a point of it."

Phyllo leaned forward to see the geometric outline set amongst the sweeping paths of the stars. It could quite feasibly have been the footprint of a building. "Does it say when?"

Frú Hafiz returned to the astrolabe, making adjustments. "The last was in February, the next October 22nd." She looked up to meet Phyllo's eyes. "Which I believe is tomorrow."

Phyllo got to his feet. "I need to tell Tamer Venor."

His mentor paced back and forth.

"And then she started talking about how the truth lay within my reach and calling me the *King of Wands* again, like she did when she read my cards, saying how I was drawing closer to my destiny. Sometimes I think she's completely crackers."

Tamer Venor did not react to this suspicion. "I should have guessed the charts were focused on the path of the sun with the arc of scarab beetles drawn at the top." She drew their path in the air with one hand. "The ancient Egyptians believed the scarab god, Khepri, pushed the sun across the sky and eased the journey to the afterlife. Using the sun's path in the architecture makes perfect sense. We must witness its effect."

She returned to the table to gaze down at the stiff papyrus of the Book of Gates with its vivid paintings.

"There is a message clear to me now. A second burial chamber is to be found in that tomb and with it, I believe, a second dragon. The main chamber has already been penetrated so there must remain a path undiscovered. This fragment of the Book of Gates – my mother suspected the trials that lay ahead to gain access. She understood the star charts and now we know there are two days in every year where it is possible to gain entry, two days when the scarab races across the sky to enter the tomb. We cannot miss a moment of the day. We must leave tonight to be there at sunrise."

30

THE TOMB OF MENTUHOTEP

Top to toe now, he had to be a Whisperer. Phyllo checked himself over.

Sturdy lace-up boots, made supple by wear.

Stiff cotton trousers, the necessity of which had been made plain by his experiences with Panya and Tufty in the capuchin enclosure. He hadn't forgotten about the pinching claws of the crabs either.

He also wore the loose tunic of the flyers, held tight by Nonna Volante's embroidered sash that depicted Glumberry defying the odds to soar after a sweet. He'd earned that sash with lessons learned. Signor Volante had taught him how to fly. Confidence, momentum, timing, flexibility and strength, but more than anything else you had to believe, believe in yourself. Phyllo needed to remember that now.

He pulled at the lapels of his Confectioner's jacket, squaring its shoulders. It wasn't the garb of the Whisperer, but it was part of who he was. His family were the good people of *'Cane's Exotic Sweets and Treats'*. It was the love of his family that drove him on to succeed and now he knew he'd do all he could to bring the love of a family to Thamineh.

He clutched the cobra cane by its shaft and tried to release the clench in his stomach. This was as ready as he was ever going to get.

Tamer Venor's altar and his own sat side by side on the Menagerie floor and when she disappeared into the cone of smoke, this time he didn't need prompting from Panya. "Follow my master," he stated plainly, looking briefly into Panya's eyes before his own altar sucked him into the path of energy that ran through everything and everywhere.

When he came back to himself, Phyllo was down on one knee, leaning hard on the cane. His head swam as the cells of his body fought to reassemble and the peace of being at one with the universe subsided. They were back beside the lake, but not the spot they'd visited before. No settlement was visible on the far bank, winking out into the night. The landscape around them now was rugged hillsides.

Distantly, the dark outline of a building cut the stars from the night sky.

"The tomb of Mentuhotep," said Tamer Venor at his side and, despite the balmy desert night, the hair on Phyllo's arms lifted as he followed after her. Moonlight glinted on the metal dragon harness she had managed to double wrap around herself. This was, she maintained, the easiest way to carry it, but Phyllo was sure it was weighing her down. Regardless, the two of them made their way around the edge of the lake toward the dark shape of the tomb.

Bird calls echoed across the water, but Phyllo noticed something else disturbing the night, something rhythmic and manmade. He scoured for sounds in the darkness and, as they walked on, saw that the base of the building they were approaching was illuminated, spills of light revealing themselves as they rounded it from afar. Then, in the sky, the vast form of an airship revealed itself in the halo of the moon. Docked beside the building was a flat-bottomed craft with fins to keep it stable. A gundalow. It was *The Nelly Bly*.

Phyllo gawked at it. "Crackers. That's a Pioneer Club vessel. Someone from the Club is already here."

Tamer Venor let out a low growl. "My father has arrived ahead of us. We must stay out of sight, but it would be as well for us to see what we are up against." She spread her arms to take in a deep breath. "We have an advantage in the dark, Phyllo. Employ every skill you have learned. Listen for the wind, for the birds, for the echoes. See like the hawk and tread the ground light as the hyrax. Let us see how close we can get." She turned and walked surely on.

Phyllo concentrated as hard as he could to tune into the night and found negotiating the ridge in the dark much easier as a result. Even so, he was convinced that Panya would have been much more at home there, scurrying through the loose rocks that still turned his ankle no matter how hard he concentrated. They wove their way closer until to go any farther would put them at risk of being seen.

It was the Club all right and they'd brought quite an expedition party. People and tents and equipment that knocked their own meagre backpacks into a cocked hat. A pair of tents emblazoned with the Pioneer Club emblem had been erected close to the façade and a heavy pounding rippled out from the tomb to vibrate the earth at their feet. Floodlights illuminated the tomb's grand entrance, where giant statues of the Pharaoh at rest there sat in silent vigil while the modern-day grave robbers of the Club tried to force their way in.

Local men in long white kaftans hefted rubble and Phyllo thought, just for a moment, that he caught sight of the black-cloaked man in a mask he'd seen at the tower of Steam Star Port. The Crow Man. It was fleeting and dark and replaced almost immediately by a man he definitely did recognise. Brigadier Alfred Valentine Grosvenor.

Venor let out a derisory puff. "Always the brute," she muttered, "He smashes his way in because he does not have the wit for understanding." She turned to Phyllo and gave him a wink. "This was the way we came before. It is already open to a degree and the obvious choice, but it faces west and the rising sun will not touch it. Our way in lies to the east."

They fell back into the cover of the hillside and rounded the tomb at a distance. The Brigadier and his team were focusing everything on the only visible entrance and as they reached the east side the lack of men and lighting gave Phyllo and Venor the confidence they needed to draw considerably closer.

The only nod to security that Phyllo could see was a low metal wire, strung between posts driven into the sandy ground. It stretched in both directions, marking a wide perimeter all the way around to the front of the tomb. It was so low that he could simply have stepped over it and seemed so easy to breach that he couldn't see the point of putting it there at all. They stood at its boundary and looked across 100 yards of empty ground to the east façade. In the darkness it was impossible to see anything that resembled an entrance.

"What do you think?" Phyllo whispered.

Tamer Venor scoured the ground with her eyes. "We must cross, but the apparent ease is troubling indeed. Why would the hunters of the Club erect such a fence? What deterrent is it?"

Phyllo stared at the wire, trying to make sense of it too. Then a ripple ran through the sand that made it look like water, the tip of something just below the surface and moving fast. As quickly as he could point it out, it had disappeared.

Tamer Venor followed the direction of Phyllo's point to watch the ground. A few feet farther on something snakelike displaced the sand then dove away.

"Did you see that?" asked Phyllo in a whisper, "What do you think it is?"

"What do I think *they are*," Venor corrected, "Now the low fence makes sense. There will be ten feet or more beneath the ground, I suspect. Its purpose not to keep intruders out, but to keep those creatures in. The hunters of the Club have laid a moat around our temple and as good as filled it with piranha. I believe they have released into it bobbits."

Phyllo had never heard of bobbits and told her as much.

"Sand worms, the nasty kind." Tamer Venor scanned the ground beneath their feet. "I think the fence keeps them over there. Be glad of that. I'm in no hurry to make their acquaintance."

"Worms? Really? Surely worms can't be that bad." Phyllo couldn't see what the fuss was about.

Venor dug in the pocket of her vest for a date. "Let us see." She tossed it out into the middle of the flat expanse and for a moment the faint baseline rippling that had been washing across the surface stopped. Then, quite unexpectedly, a sand rat popped its head out from a nearby bush, stood on its hind legs to sniff the air and then dashed out in pursuit of the date.

At once the ground began to seethe, as snakelike forms beneath the surface pushed sand aside to race toward the rat.

The rat itself changed course, suddenly sensing danger, and skittered from side to side, twitching and jumping as if something were stinging its feet.

Then a creature broke the surface that Phyllo had never seen the like of before. Its head, if you could call it that, was a mass of tentacles, the tips of which were outstretched in a wide star two feet across, revealing in the centre a pair of terrible jaws that extended out of the creature itself to snatch at the rat.

There was no time for it to squeal. The jaws closed around the unfortunate beast and snatched it down into the sand in less time than it took Phyllo to blink, leaving nothing behind but a puff of grit.

"Bobbits," confirmed Tamer Venor.

Phyllo turned to look at her, initially lost for words. "Crackers," he gasped, "They *are* nasty."

"And quite problematic. Being specimen hunters for the Club seems to have its advantages. Such a creature is not easy to find."

"What are we going to do?"

Venor stroked at her cheek to think. "The bobbit is blind. It sees only with vibrations, but it is ruthless and indiscriminate in its attack. To touch the ground invites death, but the distance we must cover is too far to jump and neither of us can fly. It is a most effective barrier."

"Can we use our altars?"

"They have brought us to this place, but cannot deliver us to the other side of stone."

As far as Phyllo could see, the tomb from this side was nothing but a solid stone wall. "A distraction then. How about if we chuck something big over there and while they all rush to it, we run from a different spot?" He cast about for something suitable and spotted a small fallen palm tree. "Give me a hand, would you?"

Together they dragged it to the boundary line, swung it awkwardly back and forth a couple of times for momentum and then hefted it as far as they could, out into the bobbit territory. It landed just a few feet away. Once again, the movement that ran beneath the surface stopped.

Phyllo held his breath, waiting in fascinated horror to see if the bobbits would be able to drag a tree down with the same ease as the unfortunate rat. The palm fronds settled against the ground but didn't move after that and the watchful expectation Phyllo felt coming from deep in the sand seemed to wane. Gradually the sand began to shift again, the gentle rippling of the surface just about discernible.

"It seems that without the vibrations of life, the bobbits have no interest in the attack," said Tamer Venor, "A distraction will require greater movement and one of us cannot dash about on the sand to be sacrificed for the other. We both need to escape this alive."

Phyllo chewed on his lip. A creature that sees with vibrations and lives underground. It felt familiar somehow. There was something in that snakelike arch that broke the surface.

"Alitura," he said, suddenly realising what it reminded him of.

Tamer Venor looked to him thoughtfully and Phyllo felt a rush of confidence. If he was going to prove himself as a Beast Whisperer and win this apprenticeship, surely this was the moment to do it.

"My familiar came up from the ground and they stay connected with tiny roots. They can see into other creatures' minds. Tamer Venor, if it could help me meld with a dragon, why not help me communicate with a bobbit?"

If he could manage some kind of mind-meld with Alitura to speak to them, he really would be earning his place in the Menagerie. Phyllo scanned about for a tree where he could find a connection, but saw only gnarled trunks, contorted by the relentless desert heat. He touched one experimentally but, dry and dead as it was, couldn't feel any kind of link. A little farther away stood a stubby palm tree. It wasn't a patch on the mighty oaks of the Guardian circle but it did, at least, look alive.

Phyllo laid his hand upon it "Alitura," he said, "Can you hear me? I need your help."

The ground shifted and Tamer Venor spun around defensively, staring wildly at the ground as if fearing an attack from the bobbits. Unlike in the Whispering Wood, where a single root had burst from the ground to form his familiar, here the full circle of ground that surround the palm tree jiggled and pulsed. Fibrous roots, long and thin, rose from the ground in clumps, bulging and shrinking, extending and curving until the familiar form of Alitura stood before them.

Tiny spikey leaves studded his back and palm fronds plaited themselves into a semblance of a tail. He was the same but entirely different. It was the fox Phyllo had met on the other side of the world, but now constructed from the local vegetation.

"PHYLLO, YOUR TRAVELS HAVE BROUGHT US TO A MOST INHOSPITABLE PLACE." Even the voice inside Phyllo's head sounded dry.

"Sand Dragons like it hot, what can I say."

Alitura stepped forward, creaking and clicking. *"SAND DRAGONS ARE PECULIAR IN THAT WAY."* The tiny leaves and roots rippled across the surface of Alitura's body where skin should have been, whirling and realigning like muscle flexing.

Phyllo grinned. "We think that there might be one, over there in the tomb. The thing is, we need help getting across to it. The Club have laid a moat of bobbits. We need to persuade them not to attack us."

Alitura turned his head away from Phyllo to the tomb and stepped jerkily toward the boundary. *"BOBBITS?"*

Phyllo was certain that an Ethelweard would be familiar with every kind of creature, even if Phyllo had never heard of them before. Alitura looked back and forth along the strip of apparently empty sand.

"WE SEE NO WAY TO HELP YOU HERE."

Phyllo was taken aback. "Really? But I thought you could communicate with every animal there is."

"THE ETHELWEARD ARE OLD AS TIME AND HAVE EXPERIENCED LIFE FORMS MOST HAVE NEVER ENCOUNTERED."

"Yes."

"THIS PLACE IS AS DRY AND LOW ON LIFEFORCE AS ANY WE CAN VISIT. IF BOBBITS ARE HERE THEIR PRESENCE IS INDISCERNIBLE." He swept his gaze back and forth along the blank stretch of sand. Phyllo shot a look to Tamer Venor. She shrugged very slightly in a gesture that batted the responsibility for the conversation squarely back to him. He'd forgotten for a moment that Alitura spoke inside his head alone.

"But you can see them." Phyllo waved a hand to the shifting sand. Alitura turned their back on it to face him.

Phyllo floundered. "Is it because it's so dry here? Does that make it harder?"

Alitura tilted their head, but it was a frustrating non-answer. Tamer Venor stood back on one hip and watched the two of them, quite obviously fascinated by their odd conversation. *Always the Whisperer,* Phyllo thought to himself, *always observing, absorbing and learning.*

And it came to him. He would have to embody the Whisperer too. If they joined forces, he and Alitura could do it.

"OK, Alitura," he said, "I think we can do it if we do it together. I can hear you inside my head and you took me to the dragon meld. If I can tune to this place like I have the forest, you'll be able to see the bobbits too."

"PHYLLO, WE SEE BEYOND THE MINDS OF—"

But Phyllo interrupted. "Just be quiet for a second and you'll see." He closed his eyes and retrieved the focusing spell from his memory.

By ray and beam,
By dell and mound,
By sip and stink,
By sight and sound,
Let east meet west,
Let all be seen
Of creatures known and in-between.
Lady of the Elder bow
Reveal to me, thy servant, now.

Concentrating as hard as he possibly could, Phyllo tried to feel the meaning of the words with every fibre of his being. There were no rays from the sun in the middle of the night, but still he was aware of the impact they'd had upon this dry and barren place. The sun's heat still radiated up through the soles of his feet. He opened his eyes and found the darkness lifted with the help of the moon; a silver glow that changed the colours they touched to a spectrum of blue-grey. The hillsides, the palms, the low growing vegetation and the ground itself were all painted in the contours etched by the moon's glow.

A faint breeze moved the palm leaves and ruffled at his hair. The sand shifted and Phyllo could hear each thing distinctly. He moved a little closer to the boundary, examining the ground and how it changed beyond the wire. The wire. The moonlight caught it brightly and Phyllo stepped over it easily. *How sharp the Whisperer's eyes were,* he mused to himself.

"Can you see what I see?" Phyllo asked Alitura.

"THE WHISPERER'S MIND IS SUPERIOR TO THE MUNDANE, BUT STILL THE CREATURES YOU SEEK ARE BEYOND OUR RECKONING."

"Phyllo—" Tamer Venor's voice rang with warning, but Phyllo could see everything that he needed. He took another step forward. The sand beneath his feet gave as the grains compressed and the cloying dry smell of long dead vegetation swept up from the ground. Phyllo paused to examine the smell and almost laughed out loud. There was something more. He could smell the bobbits.

"Alitura, come out here with me. They're here."

Alitura too stepped out over the wire and Phyllo felt the curiosity in their mind.

"Phyllo, this is ill-advised. Come back to the other side." Tamer Venor's voice now was hard and serious.

"Do you smell it? It's familiar to me somehow." Phyllo wracked his brain for a reference, stepping farther out into the open expanse. The ground beneath his feet had stopped breathing, but the smell was getting stronger. Earthier? No. Somehow the smell reminded him of Schlepper's workshop. The hairs in Phyllo's nostrils twitched with static. Electricity.

Alitura came to Phyllo's side.

The ground around them erupted into a whirlpool of motion.

"Phyllo," Tamer Venor yelled, "Get back here now."

Phyllo looked aghast at the writhing sand. He'd known they were there, of course. What he couldn't understand was why Alitura was so determined not to see them. "Alitura, surely now. Tell them to leave us alone."

A bobbit burst from the ground and flew at Phyllo. Tentacles spread wide, its silver jaws shot out to snap at Phyllo's face. He lurched backward, just out of reach and into Alitura, knocking them both to the ground.

A second creature erupted from the ground behind them and, almost as if it were playing out in slow motion, Phyllo watched the tentacles flex outward as it flew toward them. He saw the tiny joints that ran along the lengths of the tentacles and how they flexed in turn. Then watched as the fabric of the mouth opened to release the jaws, metal jaws that shone in the moonlight. They opened terrifyingly wide and grasped Alitura around the torso. The brittle wood from which Alitura was made splintered and buckled.

Phyllo screamed in horror.

A third bobbit burst up from the sand, knocking Phyllo aside. It snapped at the snake-like body of the second, seemingly confused by all the motion. The terrible teeth broke through its comrade's armoured skin and tore away a strip, revealing the skeleton beneath. The moon reflected on its metallic surface and a wire sprang out – split and frayed where the attacker had torn it from its connection.

Phyllo's arms windmilled backward and his feet kicked up sand as he scrabbled for purchase. He flipped over to his fingertips and toes and pelted for the boundary. The ground boiled with creatures bursting through. He stamped down one before it had a chance to open its tentacles and snatched his hand away from another as razor-sharp teeth scraped away skin.

Tamer Venor jumped up and down at the boundary. She grasped at the air as far over the line as she could manage, desperate to snatch Phyllo from his feet at the first possible opportunity. She hauled him over the wire and they staggered backward together to collapse on the ground.

"Alitura!" Phyllo craned his head around just in time to see the fox-like body snap in two as it was dragged beneath the surface. No reply came in his head.

"No! Alitura!" Phyllo flexed to launch himself back to the spot where his familiar had disappeared, but Venor held him firm. "They can't... He hasn't..." He snapped his eyes to her. "Alitura couldn't see the bobbits because they aren't alive." He gasped at the appalling knowledge that was rising in his throat to choke him. "Automatons. Alitura couldn't see them because they are machines."

Alitura was gone and it was all his fault.

How could he have been so stupid?

The will to fight abandoned him and his throat dried, all the excitement and confidence of the Whisperer bleeding away into the desolate earth. He'd thought he'd been so clever. He'd thought he'd known it all.

When One Door Closes

Phyllo stared mournfully into the middle distance. His hands stung where the bobbits had torn at his skin and he prickled with cold. It was all he could do to plonk one foot in front of the other, to travel a slow and endless circuit around the Circus of Wonder encampment. How could he have been so foolish?

Without Alitura he couldn't meld with the dragon.

He scrubbed one hand over his face. Why had he imagined that he'd known what he was doing? What had made him think that he, Phyllo Cane, failed flyer and exiled fire-hazard of a Confectioner, was capable of *teaching* an Ethelweard? He shook his head. *It was ridiculous. He* was ridiculous.

He pulled air into his lungs to expel it with a dejected sigh. At some point he'd have to face Panya. He didn't want to admit what he'd done and he didn't want to face his dad to bear that loving disappointment, not again. His chest ached at the thought of it.

He was an idiot.

Phyllo felt the air temperature rise and looked up to see that he was beside the Menagerie. Even a few weeks ago he wouldn't have noticed that. He *had* made *some* progress. He had *found* a familiar, even if he'd messed that up now. He'd activated his altar and selected the cane. Why hadn't he used the cane? Phyllo rubbed at his forehead.

Like he knew how. It was all *ridiculous*. So far, this apprenticeship had been a mish-mash of lucky discoveries and other people's skill. He kicked at a stone and noted the thumps and scrapes coming from inside the Menagerie cabin – the sounds of Thamineh moving about. A sick wave of remorse rolled over him. How was he going to help her now?

Tamer Venor probably hadn't realised that he'd fled yet, still blissfully unaware of just what a pathetic loser he was. He dismissed what felt like dishonour. She'd be better off without him. Phyllo was a liability, everyone knew that.

The huge round window of the Ringmaster's quarters loomed, impenetrable and black. It gave nothing away of the cabin's interior, but reflected Phyllo's mournful progress as he passed, altar tin clutched to his chest and cobra cane held limply by his side. He'd told Lazarus Barker he was going to capture the dragon *by himself*. He shook his head at the wild optimism of it. Would the Ringmaster be angry that he'd failed or pleased to be proved right about the impossibility of it all? Neither option appealed.

He clumped to a stop beside the Confectionary and laid a hand on the wood-clad wall. He pressed his nose against the porthole window to peer inside. Every part of him yearned to return to how things used to be. He didn't want to be the problem child nor the thorn in everyone's side. He just wanted to be one of the family, imperfections and all.

He looked down at the small form of his little sister,

Dodo, curled up under blankets in what used to be his bed. Roly's leg dangled contentedly out of the top bunk. He couldn't hear it, but he knew he was snoring.

Phyllo wanted to hammer on the glass and tell them to let him in. He wanted to shake them all from their easy slumber and gather them around him to make him feel better. He didn't want to feel this alone. A single tear escaped to roll down his cheek and he swiped it away. The sudden movement brought his eyes to focus upon his own reflection, rather than the cosy scene within.

Pathetic. Crackers, he was selfish.

Giving up would put that happy sleeping bundle of Dodo in such danger. Abandoning the apprenticeship circuit would mean a life of uncertainty for them all, not just him. He took a deep breath and straightened his back. He needed to stop thinking about himself all the time. The thing he craved, the companionship of his family, he should be trying to give that to Thamineh. That was his job now. He sniffed in a breath. *Come on, Phyllo.* There had to be something he could do.

He cast about, looking left and right in the darkness, searching for the snippet of inspiration that could show him the way. Something to help him shake off this self-loathing. The new cladding of Schlepper's trailer stood out against the weathered boards of the Confectionary. Schlepper. Phyllo couldn't help but wonder if those mechanical bobbits had been anything to do with him. Schlepper and his automatons. Schlepper and his tools.

And it was as if a golden coin had fallen from the VIP seats to roll to a stop at his feet. Schlepper's tools.

-

Schlepper's van was parked to the side of the trailer, blinds pulled across its windows against the night. Phyllo had to assume that the man himself was in there asleep, but what remained uncertain was how much of a pet Stanley was. Phyllo had to hope that he 'slept' in the workshop and not in the van with his maker.

He crept around the trailer, looking for a way in. There were no obvious doors and Schlepper had opened it from the inside when he'd visited so had not revealed any controls. He examined the sides and then ran his fingers along the underside of the front flat panel. It seemed to him that it would be a very satisfying place to hide a release switch and was not at all surprised to find a button, which when pressed set the entire front side into rising motion. He pressed it again to stop it when the gap was large enough for him to squeeze through.

Inside, pin lights illuminated the treads of the curving stairs to either side and threw just enough light out for Phyllo to make out the space. He felt his way down the central steps and pulled at the curtain. The workshop was pitch black. He knew where the light switches were, but floodlighting the place didn't seem sensible. The last thing he wanted was for Schlepper to realise that someone was in there.

"Stanley," he hissed into the dark, "Here, boy."

He listened for sounds of movement. None came.

"Stanley."

He waited and listened, but if Stanley was there, he wasn't coming out. Phyllo drummed his fingers on the altar tin he still held. The tin. He smiled, then shook it experimentally. The things inside rattled about.

"Stanley," Phyllo hissed again, "Are you here, boy?" He rattled the contents of the tin some more and the unmistakable springy whir of Stanley's legs came from somewhere deep in the workshop, getting louder until his shiny head and wagging tail bobbed up to the curtain.

"Good boy." Phyllo patted his head and encouraged him out, up the steps.

Phyllo opened the tool box doors on Stanley's back and took the two items he needed, while Stanley sniffed at the tin.

"Sorry, boy," Phyllo said with a shrug, "I'm going to have to owe you."

32

THE WAY OF THE WIDGET

THE MENAGERIE HAD BECOME hotter inside even than the desert by day. Phyllo dug about in the trunk at the bottom of his bed, pulling at his collar and sweating with the effort. He yanked out the dragon hide suit, hefted it into a heap on the floor and then returned to the trunk to dig some more.

"There you are," he breathed at last. The Survival Widget lay heavy in his hand. The size of a fat pocket watch; he thumbed the smooth casing then slid it into his pocket.

Down on the main floor, the once shadowy depths of the dragon pen now smouldered with the red-gold glow of embers. Heat radiated from it so fiercely now that it dried Phyllo's throat and made his eyes sting. Even so, it appeared that Panya had recently braved it. The visible front section of the pen was swept clean and a sturdy wheelbarrow stood on the outside of the gate, piled high with blackened straw and dung.

He heard a rustling behind him and looked up to see Panya's small frame descending the mezzanine steps. She looked rumpled and exhausted, like she'd been asleep in her clothes. She rubbed at her eyes with the backs of her hands and scanned around the cabin, her dark face pinched with confusion.

"Tamer Venor's not here," said Phyllo, guessing at what she was wondering, "I've come back alone."

Panya's eyebrows came together in a frown.

Phyllo steeled himself. He'd have to tell her sooner or later. "Truth is, Panya, I've messed everything up, just like everyone was waiting for me to. My familiar, it's been destroyed—" he cleared the croak from his throat "—It was me, my fault, and I can't meld with the dragon without them. So, there we are." He scrubbed at his hair. "Truth is, Panya, we need *you*."

Panya goggled back at him like he was nuts, then let her eyes slip from stall to stall, automatically checking the animals she was tasked with looking after. She didn't look like she wanted to go anywhere.

Phyllo followed her eyes then came back to her. "After tomorrow it might not matter one way or the other. If we can't capture this dragon, the Menagerie is in big trouble anyway. One day locked in their pens, Panya, that's all. You'd only be away for a matter of hours, but we have to be at the tomb before sunrise. That means we have to go now."

Panya circled him, squinting into his face to sniff out the lie.

"You don't trust me. I don't blame you. We're in competition after all, but I promise it's not a trick. Tamer Venor is still there in the desert, trying to work out a way in. I – I left her there. I gave up, I admit it. I ran away, but now I've had an idea and I think it will work."

The longer he thought about it, the more hopeful he was

and stooping to set out his altar on the Menagerie floor, Phyllo felt the buzz of optimism spreading in his chest.

"I've got to do what I can, even if you don't want to come. Thing is, getting here was easy, but going back, well that's a bit harder, isn't it? I don't think I can do it without you." He turned and gave her a weak smile.

Panya folded her arms across her chest. Her expression shifted from mistrust to exasperation.

"Oh, and as I can't meld—" Phyllo's eyes snapped to the barrow of dragon dung "—I read in the Dragonology Manual that masking your scent with the dung of a female dragon is as good a protection as any." He went over to the barrow and scooped up a handful. It was soft and smelled of old roasted meat. "Crackers," he wrinkled his nose at it, "but in for a pinch, eh?" He gingerly rubbed it onto his jacket sleeves, under his armpits and then smeared what remained onto his cheeks.

Panya stared at him with utter incredulity. Then she started to laugh, a snorty squeak that he'd never heard before.

Phyllo grinned broadly, then spat out the stray piece of straw that fell into his mouth.

Panya managed to compose herself, but the smile still lingered when she said in her small voice, "Don't you care what anyone thinks?"

Phyllo shrugged. "Guess I'm a bit past that now."

She sighed, but her demeanour had changed. Covering himself in poo seemed to have got her to trust him. If only he'd known that earlier.

She scuttled up the stairs and returned a minute later with a small bag slung across her body and an old biscuit tin, battered and painted with Egyptian motifs; her altar. She put it down next to Phyllo's and went about setting up, lighting her own incense and then his. She nodded to him and they took up position, striped stick and cane outstretched.

Synchronised, they began to turn. Panya, who rarely spoke at all, now did so in a voice so small it was barely a whisper. "Cunning hyrax, protector and friend, find me in the darkness. Protect this circle."

Phyllo knew that there were more Ethelweard and was pinning his hopes on there still being some kind of connection he could rely on. He spoke the words Tamer Venor had taught him. "Noble Ethelweard, Guardians of the Forest and friends as old as time, find me in the darkness. Protect this circle." The stick and cane traced circles in the air around them.

Panya took a deep breath and said, "Kick sand and dust to reveal our path. All matter universal shared."

The incense from Panya's altar curled toward her in jerky hops and skips, then followed the tip of her stick to wrap around her.

"Vines entwine to weave a vessel. All matter universal shared," said Phyllo. He knew this part well enough now. The incense from his own altar seemed to sprout and grow. Like shooting vines, it stretched to envelop him.

Panya tugged a leather cord out from inside her boiler suit. From it hung a bronze ankh, into the head of which was set a tiny bowl, an exact replica of the ankh Tamer Venor wore; their means of emergency communication. "Bast Venor, master, mentor, family. Find me. Show me. Reach me now." She flicked her striped stick at her altar and the items on it began to vibrate.

Phyllo didn't know what to say now. He'd gone as far as he could. He continued to turn, snapping his head to Panya's altar instead of his own. He banged the tip of the cobra cane to the ground, hoping to be able to join in. Panya did not look at him and he felt a wave of panic rising. Would she take him with her? It would be so easy to leave him behind.

"Reveal to me. Connect to me. Bast Venor, hear my call." She flicked her wand again. The misty surface of the oiled lid serving as a mirror swirled and then cleared. It revealed Venor herself, pacing up and down in the desert night.

Phyllo banged the tip of his cane to the ground again, hoping against hope that this could work. He looked to his own altar. It was inert and blank.

"Hyrax, protector and link to nature, take my equal by my side." She extended her hand and Phyllo took it. She'd called him her equal. Gratitude welled inside him for her leap of faith.

"Seal this circle," they said together, flourishing cane and stick. The incense tendrils wound around them both, faster and faster until it blocked the Menagerie from view. Then Phyllo was aware of lifting from the ground and losing himself in the path.

When he opened his eyes, Panya was brushing dragon dung from her boiler suit. They had rematerialized to the east of the tomb. Phyllo didn't know how much of a commotion they had made, but Tamer Venor was already standing over them. She put out a hand and pulled Phyllo to his feet, then pulled him in for a back-slapping hug. She peeled away, looking down at the front of her tunic. "You seem to have picked up something on your travels." She looked him up and down.

"Panya, yes," said Phyllo, "I'm pretty sure we're going to need her."

Panya wrinkled her nose and shook her head very

slightly. Tamer Venor flicked at the dragon dung now sticking to her own clothes and looked back and forth between them. "But, Phyllo, the bobbits—"

Phyllo looked to the east. Already the sky was changing to a bright sapphire blue. "I've got a plan for that. Come on, it looks like we don't have much time."

"But, Phyllo—"

Phyllo gathered up his altar tin and stuffed it into the backpack he'd left behind. "Let's go."

He jogged to the boundary line, the other two in his wake. From here the ripples in the sand were now even more evident. The light of approaching dawn drew contours on the ground that described the paths the bobbits travelled. Some moved slowly, while others tore along, each as deadly as the next.

"Schlepper's going to give us a little help for a change," said Phyllo and he pulled a flat brass box with buttons on the top from his pocket. "I don't know if these bobbits are his creation, but I don't think it matters to this." He flourished the box.

Tamer Venor peered at it uncomprehendingly.

"This," said Phyllo with a smile, "is a Destabilising Node Mallet. It will stop any automaton dead." He stabbed randomly at the buttons, sure that one of them would do the trick and sure enough, the movement beneath the sand halted.

Phyllo looked at Tamer Venor and grinned. "I might not be much cop at Whispering, but I press a mean button."

Venor laughed and slapped him on the back. "That you do." She looked back over her shoulder to the lightening sky. "We should hurry, dawn is almost upon us."

They stepped out over the boundary line, hearts in their

mouths. With every step Phyllo fought off thoughts of the deadly metallic jaws only inches away and what might happen if the Node Mallet suddenly stopped working. Panya, oblivious, scampered ahead annoyingly unfazed, but Phyllo had to admit he was glad of the lead she gave and even happier when they all reached the other side and the tomb's east façade. Making it unscathed it was a relief beyond words.

Up close and in the growing light, it was possible to see that a scene had been carved into the tomb's stone wall. Tamer Venor ran her fingers over the lines. "It is a scene from the Book of Gates," she said in a low whisper, "In Egyptian mythology the newly dead must pass through seven gates to reach the afterlife. A journey that takes the entire night.

"During the first hour, the sun god approaches the underworld and is greeted by the Gods of the West." She pointed to an arc of beetles that Phyllo recognised from the star charts. "The sun god, Khepri, takes the form of a scarab beetle and metaphorically rolls the sun across the sky." She traced the path with her fingertips and at that moment the first rays of the sun burst over the horizon. The scene carved on the wall fell into sharp relief and revealed a strangeness to the final scarab beetle in the arc. Venor explored it with her fingertips and sand tumbled from what turned out to be a beetle-shaped indentation. She looked at it thoughtfully, then pulled her whip from its harness to examine the handle.

"This too was given to me by my mother," she said, removing the scarab jewel from its hilt. "A reminder of our eternal connection to the life force, the key to our powers. Could it be?" She held it up to the hole in the wall, its golden case glinting in the sun. The pale blue stones that made up its body seemed to glow from within, the shape and size an exact match to the mysterious indentation. Excitement rushed in Phyllo's veins. It was as if it belonged there.

"The key to our powers," said Venor and she pressed it into the wall where it sank away, far deeper than the hole should have allowed.

Somewhere cogs engaged and vibration rumbled through their feet. The section of wall where they stood juddered then slid slowly backward with a grinding of stone and away to one side to reveal a corridor into the tomb.

"Ra has opened the first gate," said Tamer Venor in an awed whisper. She stepped over the threshold. Phyllo followed, heart hammering, then Panya too. Inside the air was stale and cold and lifted the hairs on the back of his neck. Carvings continued around the walls, the angle of the sun hitting them perfectly to pick out every detail.

Tamer Venor ran her fingers over it, absorbing the minutiae. Then, as abruptly as it had opened, the section of wall they had entered through began to close. Venor rushed to examine the carving and soon the rectangle of light being thrown by the dawn had reduced to a triangle, then to a shrinking line and then to nothing at all.

Phyllo's head swam in a wave of claustrophobia and Tamer Venor spoke, but her voice brought little comfort in the darkness. "None shuts the door against you, and the damned do not enter in after you."

Phyllo squeaked in panic. "What?"

"It says that on the wall. The carvings tell us that this is our journey now, and ours alone. Draw a fire baton from your pack, Phyllo. It will have its uses yet."

Phyllo squatted down and brought his pack around to the ground in front of him. No light at all came into their chamber now. He searched in the bag, trying to steady his breathing. He found the batons and matches and fumbled with the strike. Something plopped to the ground behind him and then something else. A skittering sound pierced the chamber's still air. Plop. Plop.

"The baton, Phyllo, can you manage it alone?"

He struck another match, this time keeping it alive long enough to light the baton. Golden light bloomed to create a globe of visibility. Venor stood before him, her black mane of hair wild, her eyes flashing more gold than ever. The skittering sound rose to a buzz and Phyllo turned.

Hundreds of beetles poured through a head-height opening in the stone wall. A mass of black shining bodies and wiggling legs formed a spreading pile on the ground that heaved and writhed. Horrified, Phyllo scrabbled backward.

"Venomous ground beetles," said Tamer Venor, "The unjust will pass no farther. We should find our way out quickly. Bring that here." Venor beckoned Phyllo and his torch to her side. The light from the flame stretched up the wall where three Egyptian figures were depicted, standing uniformly on a raft. Painted flames licked round them. Venor pointed at a pair of figures to one side, taller than the people on the raft and with the heads of lizards. She muttered to herself.

Something scrabbled on Phyllo's boot and weighed on the cuff of his trousers. He swiped at it and shuddered at the gloom of insects building around them. Panya was busy tucking her boiler suit into the tops of her boots which struck Phyllo as an excellent idea. He stooped to do the same and Venor took the torch from his hand. She walked the length of the wall taking the light with her and reading aloud.

"There is darkness on the road of the Duat, therefore let

the doors which are closed be unfolded, let the earth open, so that the gods may draw along him that hath created them," she said, "The path continues here."

She turned toward the back wall, lifting the torch ahead of her. Two lizard-headed men, ten feet tall at least, loomed three-dimensionally out of the stone.

"This is a test of knowledge. We must identify the Guardians of the Gate."

Phyllo gazed wide-eyed at the reptilian features carved into the rock. In the flickering torchlight he could almost have believed that their eyes moved to watch him. "So, who are they?"

Venor peered up into their faces. "Atum is a sun god, often represented by a lizard. Potentially it could be him. For the path of the sun to continue would make great sense, and yet I see no way to use this knowledge." She felt around the edges of the cartouche they were framed by, searching.

Something tickled at Phyllo's neck and he flapped at it. "This tomb is meant to be a secret, right? Maybe the usual rules don't apply."

"There was magic in the scarab beetle, of that I am sure." Venor looked thoughtfully back at him. "This is not just a place of mythology. Creatures are of great importance."

"Who could be better to fathom it then, than you?" said Phyllo, "Beast Whisperer and all." He swatted beetles from his jacket. Beside him, Panya had started doing a kind of stompy dance which shooed the beetles temporarily backward. It also had the bonus effect of her only having one foot on the ground at a time. Phyllo joined in.

"Could it be that every traveller has their own path?" Venor transferred her gaze to the lizard men and Phyllo couldn't help but notice that the beetles were not paying her any attention whatsoever. He itched all over. "Yes, absolutely, definitely," he said without really knowing what that entailed, "Go for that."

Venor pulled her whip from its holster and twirled it around her head before cracking it, sharp and shocking, at the lizard men. She uttered a series of hisses and spits, twirled the whip around her head and cracked it again. The torchlight jumped and flickered and Phyllo could have sworn that one of the figures turned its head.

"I choose my path and I give you identity. Knowledge is the key we hold. Duku Dagenda is the being we choose." She cracked her whip a third time and both lizard men thrust their chests outward, drawing in the first breath in centuries. Their bodies flexed with a thunderous grinding of stone against stone and they stepped down out of the cartouche to the ground, great feet thudding to the earth.

Rock-solid and enormous, even down on the ground they towered over them. Phyllo stopped hopping about and wobbled into the wall. Tamer Venor stood firm.

"You shall not pass," the lizard men boomed together.

"Crackers," gasped Phyllo, "What have you done?"

33
THE DUKU DAGENDA

Venor clapped her hands with excitement. "Already we are on our way. They have accepted their identity. This is exactly what I would expect from the Duku Dagenda."

Phyllo shook his head in exasperation. "Then why did you tell them to become that?" Surely it was madness?

"Knowing what we are dealing with is half the battle." She grabbed Phyllo's shoulders and jiggled him about excitedly. "The Dagenda believe themselves to be all-knowledgeable. We must prove ourselves to be their superior." She smiled broadly.

"Excellent," said Phyllo, who didn't see how this was good news. The clicking and ticking of the beetles seemed to be getting inside his head. He blinked up at her, trying to clear it.

"We seek safe passage through this gate," said Tamer Venor to the Duku Dagenda, so confidently Phyllo almost believed they'd just let her.

"None who asks shall have this granted," replied one and Phyllo couldn't help but goggle at how gigantic they were.

Standing side by side with their feet set wide apart, they formed an impenetrable guard to the opening they'd left by climbing down out of the wall.

"The Duku Dagenda cannot be persuaded," said the other, "Our knowledge is unparalleled, our determination unrelenting."

Venor bounced on her toes and looked between Phyllo and Panya. "Let us pool our resources. What might you know that the Dagenda would not? Think."

Phyllo blinked back at her. The rustling and clicking of the growing horde of beetles that pressed in upon them wrenched at his attention. He screwed up his face in an effort to concentrate.

Panya met Venor's eyes. "What about the voice of the hyrax?" she said in a whisper.

"Yes." Venor pulled her to her side. "We challenge your knowledge, Duku Dagenda. What can you make of this?"

Both stony reptilian heads swivelled to focus their gaze upon Panya. She shrank under their stare and just when Phyllo felt certain that the pressure was going to be too much, she started to make a noise. It was a sort of chuckle. Phyllo listened more closely. No, perhaps it was more of a bark. She moved her body low to the ground and perhaps that was what gave it away.

"The Cape Hyrax calls to its mate," one of the Duku Dagenda said, "We have waited for a thousand years in the desert for a challenge and you imagine this to be a new language for us?" The other Dagenda laughed. The sound was hollow and mirthless and set Phyllo's teeth on edge.

Panya backed away from them to get behind Tamer Venor, who patted her on the shoulder in consolation.

Beetles pooled at their feet, a constant stream of them

now marching up Phyllo's legs. He batted them away, again and again, and thanked Barnum for the experience with the capuchins that had caused him to switch his silky flyer's blues for thick utility trousers.

Tamer Venor narrowed her eyes at the Dagenda and then, without preamble, started to make a most peculiar sound. It sounded to him like the coo of a pigeon crossed with the bray of a donkey.

Phyllo held his hands over his ears, the combination of sounds really starting to overwhelm him. Tamer Venor's peculiar call built upon the canvas of creaks and clicks in his head that were already making his teeth hurt. He pushed his palms hard against his head trying to block some of it out.

The Duku Dagenda didn't look happy either. Their already terrifying faces pinched into a scowl. They rumbled incoherently to each other until suddenly both of their expressions cleared and their heads turned back to face Venor.

"You speak as a penguin," said one triumphantly, "We may be prisoners of the desert, but still, we are masters of the animal kingdom."

Tamer Venor's confident stance melted. "I was sure they would not recognise that," she said, turning to meet Phyllo's eye, "If animal calls pose no difficulty, then truly we are in a jam."

Phyllo managed a grimace and rubbed wildly at his head. "How can you stand it?" he blurted. Tamer Venor didn't seem bothered by the sound at all. "The beetles are driving me mad."

She looked at him quizzically.

"The noise!" Phyllo rubbed at his head some more, "Doesn't it set your teeth on edge?"

Venor shook her head. "I hear nothing beyond the quiet tapping of their feet."

Phyllo stared back at her, confused. There was so much more than that. Creaking and clicking. Vibrations that made his head hurt. Inside his head, almost like—

"Alitura." Phyllo breathed out the name in a whisper, his eyes widening with realisation. The Duku Dagenda might be all knowledgeable when it came to the animal kingdom, but what about trees?

"Let me try," he said and stepped forward.

All this time it had been the voice of the Ethelweard chattering away inside his head. Why hadn't he recognised the vibrations rattling his teeth and bouncing around inside his skull? It seemed so obvious now that he'd realised.

The Ethelweard were attempting to communicate through him. His affinity with the Guardians of the Forest had been enough to allow him a piggyback ride with Panya back to the desert. Could they be enough to get them through this gate?

The Duku Dagenda glared down at him with their carved, unblinking eyes and Phyllo felt his mouth dry. He did not have the voice of a tree. How on earth was he going to creak like a branch or rustle like leaves in the wind?

He tried to find the muscles to flex to release the sounds inside his head. He dropped his backpack to the ground and clutched the cobra cane with both hands, its open hissing mouth pointed toward the Dagenda.

He didn't know a spell, but knew what he heard in his head was praise of the Elder Lady, the phrase he'd heard the trees in the Guardian circle utter as she passed. He remembered the feeling of peace she'd brought, remembered the feelings of happy days gone by and knew he wanted to feel that way again.

He closed his eyes and said, "All hail the lady of the elder bow," the words the Ethelweard had said, and meant them with all his heart. The cane vibrated in his hands and the anxious pressure that had been weighing him down lifted from his shoulders, like leaves blowing away in the breeze. He said the words again, aware this time of the sounds that left his mouth.

He wasn't speaking English. He wasn't even speaking a language he could recognise as human. The creaks and clicks that had been inside his head were, somehow, being translated into sounds that others could hear.

The Duku Dagenda shuffled on the spot. Their heads twitched side to side, as if changing the angle of their ears would allow them to make more sense of what they were hearing. "Again," said one, its eyes narrowed.

Phyllo repeated the phrase and dared to sneak a glance at Tamer Venor. Her eyes sparkled with hope. The Dagenda turned to each other, muttering theories. Each dismissed the other as wrong, taking it in turns to shake their head fervently or beat their chest with frustration.

Venor sidled up to Phyllo and whispered into his ear. "They are at a loss, let us take our chance." She picked up his bag and handed it to him, then side-stepped past the Dagenda who were too preoccupied by their arguments to pay her any mind.

She gestured urgently for them to follow then clambered through the hole in the wall. Panya scuttled immediately after her and Phyllo backed away from the lizard men, not taking his eyes from them until he too was safely on the other side of the wall. He let the cane drop to his side and puffed out a breath.

"I spoke tree," he said, almost unable to believe it himself. The creaks and clicks had cleared from his head and clarity had returned. He didn't know if he'd ever be able to do it again.

Tamer Venor was a few steps ahead of him. "Fortune smiles upon us, Phyllo. Make haste. Let us get out of sight before the Duku Dagenda miss us."

They hurried forward, the corridor turning sharply left and right until a golden glow of light crept around the walls. They turned one final time and arrived in a sizeable chamber.

They found themselves on a stone embankment, beyond which a lake of dark water stretched away to a far bank. On the other side a vast double wooden door, three times Phyllo's height at least, stood closed against them. Golden metallic bands ran horizontally across it at intervals, their smooth surface glimmering with the firelight of torches spaced along the water's edge.

Tamer Venor made her way to a spot where a raft was tied by a thick looping rope. Hieroglyphics ran along the stone verge and she walked slowly along it, reading aloud the parts she could interpret.

"Come you unto us, oh you who sails in your boat, whose eye is of blazing fire which consumes, and has a pupil which sends forth light. The beings of the Duat shout with joy when you approach; send forth your light upon us, O great god who has fire in your eye."

She looked up to Phyllo and Panya, eyes shining even brighter than usual against her dark complexion.

"We must cross on the raft."

Panya hurried to where the raft was tied and attempted to haul it in, but something un-seeable held it back from the bank, keeping it a dangerous leap away. Venor went to her side, taking in the problem, then lifted her chin and spoke out across the water.

"I am your goddess with fire in my eye." Her voice boomed around the chamber. "I am Bast, nurturing mother and terrifying avenger. I seek use of the boat as protector of the Pharaoh and of the sun god Ra. You will give it to me."

Again, it was that voice of supreme confidence. Phyllo goggled at her. She gave every impression of being exactly what she said. Feet solidly apart, arms by her side and chest thrust out, she stood as if facing down an army. The black mane of hair plaited away from her face made her appear more lion-like than ever, but the most remarkable thing of all was her eyes. Phyllo did not know if they reflected the torchlight from across the water or if they themselves now radiated the golden glow of fire.

Panya hauled at the raft again, and this time it bobbed obediently in to the bank. Venor strode on board and Panya scuttled on after her, turning to untie the rope. Phyllo watched them, rooted to the spot, his mouth dry. His mentor had never been more impressive nor more terrifying. Here in the tomb, she radiated power like he'd never seen.

"Cast us off," she commanded and just in time Phyllo came to his senses to also leap aboard. The momentum from his jump bobbed them out into the lake, but when this faded to little more than a slow drift, the other bank was still a long way off. There were no oars or any other means that Phyllo could see to bring them any closer.

"Paddle with your hands," said Tamer Venor, dropping to one knee. Phyllo and Panya followed suit to also plunge their hands into the water. The surface of the lake rippled away from them, glossy rainbow patterns swirling unexpectedly from their touch, then there was a dazzling flare of light and a sound like all the air being sucked from the room. Torches at the far bank dropped down into the water, but far from being extinguished, whatever it was that made patterns on the surface of the lake ignited with a *whump*.

A tidal wave of flame hurtled toward them, a rolling fireball that would engulf anything in its path.

Tamer Venor gasped. "Get away from the water," she cried, but Phyllo and Panya were already moving and the three of them collided in the centre of their craft, sending the raft rocking dangerously to and fro. Flames flooded around them, greedily licking at its wooden edges and obscuring their view of the far bank.

"Fuel on the water," Venor panted, "I should have seen it."

Phyllo fought to organise his thoughts. They'd been tricked. It was a trap. They had to get to off this raft before it was consumed by the flames. He cast wildly about the deck for something to help them, but still found no means of propulsion, and to dive overboard would be madness.

Phyllo scoured his brain. What could they use? Did he have anything that could help? Inching to the side he jabbed his cane down into the water, hoping against hope that the bottom might not be too far away and he could get some purchase against it, but the cane swished hopelessly about. What were they going to do?

His eyes stung from the heat and the fumes. He fell back toward the centre of the raft and pulled at his bag to dig around inside. His hand dropped upon the survival widget. "Yes!" He yanked it out and fumbled at the buttons around its circumference. The widget flopped open in his palm to reveal a magnifying glass. No, not that. Phyllo snapped it shut and tried again. This time the double-looping curl he'd been hoping for slid out. He put his finger through the middle and took aim at the door.

"Look out, everyone, and hold on," he yelled, "And for Barnum's sake, don't let me fall in." Phyllo clenched his teeth and squeezed the trigger.

CRACK!

The tiny silver bullet shot out, trailing wire. It rocketed through the flames and thudded into the wood of the door. Phyllo braced himself and pressed the button on the widget to wind in the line. The wire tautened and the widget jerked, almost escaping from his hands, but he snatched it back and held on as tight as he possibly could, leaning back to dig in his heels. The raft began to move. It slid across the water and, cutting a path through the flames, crept toward the far bank.

Panya wrapped her arms around his legs from her crouch on the deck and Venor gripped at Phyllo's shoulders, levering him backward into her. "Well done, Phyllo. Well done. Together, truly we are a formidable team."

Smoke filled the air and the fire-kissed wire coiled in the widget, heating the brass case against his skin. They picked up speed and flames scooped into them over the raft's blackening leading edge. Phyllo felt his eyebrows singe.

"Crackers, get back," he yelled and together the three of them shuffled awkwardly backward, enough to lift the prow a couple of inches, enough to give them just a little protection. Flaming liquid sloshed onto the deck behind.

Hotter and hotter, the widget wound on and Phyllo tried to change his grip, getting as much of his hands away from its scalding surface as he possibly could. The bank was getting closer: fifteen feet, ten, five. The nose of the raft slid up onto the stone and as one they lurched onto the embankment, and not a moment too soon. Fire tore at where they'd been standing only seconds before, the wooden raft finally overwhelmed by the flames.

Phyllo stumbled on, finding himself dragged right up to the door before he'd remembered to release the widget button. He retched and coughed to clear his lungs. Tamer Venor lurched to his side, the scarf around her throat now tugged up over her nose and mouth, Panya at her heel. She lunged for the doors and shoved them wide for the entire party to fall through. Phyllo detached the widget and together they heaved the doors closed again, blocking out the furious scene of the lake.

Backs to the door, they sank to the floor, gasping. The air on this side was blissfully cool and clear by comparison and they gulped grateful breaths in the darkness.

After a moment's recovery Tamer Venor spoke. "A happy acquisition from Schlepper's collection, I presume?"

"That's right," gasped Phyllo, "Only this one, I'm actually supposed to have." He couldn't see Venor's face, but he suspected she was smiling.

"He is a more useful addition to our number than I could have imagined." She paused for a breath. "Tell me you still have your pack, Phyllo? We will need to light the other torch. I regret, the first has been lost to the lake."

Phyllo dug in his bag. They had to be more careful with this one. As it was, they were trapped in the tomb, but to be locked in in the dark would be another experience entirely. He lit the baton and light flared to reveal a narrow corridor sloping down. The ground ahead rippled with movement, dark bodies slithering one over the other. Snakes. Phyllo swallowed hard. Perhaps it would have been better without light after all.

"What should we do?" he said in a whisper.

Venor craned to assess them. "The snakes are numerous, but individually our inferior. We are Whisperers, Phyllo, after all. This is not a hive mind. Each will cower from the fire. Not to mention you have a most ferocious member of their number in your grip." She nodded to the cobra cane. "Bluster and noise are our friends."

She got to her feet and hissed. The snakes nearest tumbled over each other to move away. Phyllo swept the flaming torch low to the ground with one hand and brandished the cobra cane in the other. Panya hissed by his side. The three of them moved forward in their capsule of light, descending the ramp. The carpet of snakes parted before them, making just enough space on the ground to let them through before closing again behind.

Down they went, the air cooling, the oxygen seeming in shorter and shorter supply. Phyllo's chest ached with the effort of breathing and his head swam with the unknown depth and dimensions of the corridor they were negotiating. The tunnel seemed to close in around them the farther they went until suddenly they were at its end, the ceiling and walls now all within touching distance. A doorway, carved inside a second doorway and then a third, filled the final end wall. At its centre there was a narrow gap, just wide enough to pass through if they turned sideways and took off their packs. Venor didn't hesitate, but Phyllo paused.

This gate felt as if it was designed to disarm intruders. It certainly would not allow any would-be thieves to bring booty back through it. It felt like entering a trap, but he could see no other way. He took off his pack, sucking a breath and, torch first, squeezed through.

Once out on the other side Tamer Venor took his hand,

not to bring him forward, but to direct the flaming baton to a gully in the wall. Immediately he understood why. Flames caught on the liquid held in its trough and then raced off around the walls, drawing lines around the edges of the chamber to reveal its shape and contents.

They had found the secret burial chamber at last.

34

THAT WHICH IS LOST

CATHEDRAL-LIKE IN ITS PROPORTIONS, the chamber stretched up above them, the roof held high on solid stone columns. Vibrant paintings in warm ochre, dark red, white and black of Egyptian figures paraded around the walls, scenes of the Pharaoh navigating the final gates to the afterlife. They were as sharp and fresh as the day they were painted, likely more than a thousand years ago.

The Pharaoh's riches mounded up around the walls, treasure such as Phyllo had never seen: golden tables heaped with platters; a golden chariot, the bones of long dead horses crumpled in their harnesses before it; chests, scrolls, huge model ships, their bows and sterns curling with cobra heads. The quantity was astounding.

A great stone sarcophagus, five times the size of any man, sat centrally, but more incredible and affecting than any of that was the dragon.

It lay in a curl more suited to a cat on a hearth rug and was colossal, fifty feet at least from spiny nose to tail tip. Unlike Thamineh, the Sand Dragon back in the Menagerie, its scales were a bluish-grey, muted by the grit which had settled on it over time. It looked to Phyllo as if its insides had rotted away leaving nothing behind but a dry husk.

Tamer Venor cried out at the sight of it, but there was no time to discover what had caused its demise. Rhythmic booms that Phyllo had almost mistaken for the beating of his own heart rose to a crescendo and the chamber rocked with an ear-splitting *boom!*

The far corner exploded in a shower of rubble; treasures blasted from their ancient resting places. Phyllo threw his hands up to protect himself from the hail of rock and grit, while Venor snatched both him and Panya close, stooping to shield them. They staggered together into a wall and slid to the ground.

Phyllo's ears rang and his eyes blurred. Then there were voices speaking in a language he did not understand, shouted exultations, jubilant and excited. He struggled up to one elbow to see figures emerge. Men in long tunics and turbans came first, yellow with dust. They chattered animatedly and punched the air.

Then someone quite different came into view. Even masked by the dust cloud, Phyllo could see they were of another stock, broader, taller, shoulders back, posture straight and stiff, golden embroidery sparkling on his shoulders. The man's gaze ran around the chamber, past the dragon and on to the mounds of treasure.

"Oh ho! Look at this."

He clapped his hands together and descended the rubble, rounding the sarcophagus and banging on its top with an irreverent fist.

"Looks like we found you, Mentuhotep, and your treasures too. Although now they're *my* treasures, of course. Do you hear me, Mentuhotep? Never mind your bally secrets. Dynamite, that's my secret!" He barked out a laugh.

Where every instinct told Phyllo to stay low and out of sight, it was as if Tamer Venor could not help herself. She rose to her feet, transfixed. Phyllo pawed at her, hoping she'd see sense, but it was the grubby locals who reacted first. On sight of her they yelled and drew guns from holsters to wave them inexpertly about. Panya squeaked and tried to sink back into the wall, pulling at Phyllo.

"*Alastaila aliha!*" the Brigadier roared, seeing Venor at last. His men rushed forward and engulfed them, descending to pin Phyllo and Panya down. They brandished their revolvers at Venor, but didn't seem to dare to touch her.

Between the legs of the huddle of men, Phyllo could see that a single figure remained on the rubble mound. A woman.

She was swathed in layer upon layer of emerald green flowing fabric that almost entirely covered her form. A golden headdress, in the shape of a pair of eagle's wings, pinned the scarves to her head like a crown, leaving only her dark and heavily lined eyes visible through the fluttering folds around her face. A wide belt of woven golden mesh weighted the fabric to her hips, from which hung an ornately decorated whip. She stood surely on her vantage point and surveyed the scene.

The Brigadier leaned ostentatiously against the sarcophagus, smoothing at his considerable grey moustache. "Bring her here," he growled and the huddle of men got behind Venor to prod her forward.

Phyllo was surprised to see Venor touch one hand to her chest before making her customary bow. "Father," she said.

The Brigadier barked out another laugh. "All grown up

and still as arrogant. Think you've got more right to be here, don't you? Well, look around you, child. After all your efforts to capture that damn annoying Parpadillo thing – thank you for that by the way—" he gave her a saccharine smile "—It looks like there's nothing to tempt anyway. No wonder the bally thing didn't come out, look at the state of it." He wafted a derisory hand at the husk of a dragon.

"Never could resist a beast in distress, could you? That one's past even you. Silly girl. Told you before, dragons always die in the end."

Venor continued to stand her ground, but Phyllo could see her careful neutrality starting to slip.

"Still, I can't deny, it's been very convenient. When Lazarus told me you were determined to find another dragon, how could I resist? Couldn't. Another hoard, just when I thought they'd all been found. What luck. And all we had to do was follow you." He thrust out his chest and laughed.

"It's not possible." Tamer Venor scowled at the Brigadier, but he brushed it off.

"Physical proximity is irrelevant when everything's connected by the cosmic forces, or whatever guff it is that you lot go on about." He waved a condescending hand at the woman on the rubble hillock and Phyllo understood that she too must be a Whisperer.

The Brigadier's expression shifted into amusement. "Don't know everything after all, eh, girlie?"

Venor's mouth opened and closed, but she didn't speak.

"Been a blast catching up, but if you could just get out of the way." The Brigadier's eyes shifted to the man at Venor's side and he wafted one hand to dismiss them both. The man rounded on Venor to begin shouting incomprehensibly and waving his gun. Phyllo couldn't understand a word, but his meaning was plain. They were at the Brigadier's mercy now. Venor backed up to the wall, eyes still fixed on her father, back to the place where Phyllo and Panya waited.

"You there, where are the crates?" Already the Brigadier's attention had shifted to a member of his workforce. "Thought someone else'd get 'em did you? Chop, chop." The Brigadier shoved him impatiently and he stumbled to fall into the dragon. A large section of tail cracked and collapsed in on itself. With a sound like tinkling glass, the scales crumbled apart to heap on the floor.

Venor flinched and her eyes welled. There was no dragon to rescue. It had all been for nothing. Phyllo's throat clenched in shared misery. Venor turned her face to the ground and a silent tear dripped to the dust.

A handful of the Brigadier's men scrabbled back out the blast hole, presumably in search of those crates, and the Brigadier's Whisperer shifted from her vantage point to allow them to pass. She slipped toward Phyllo through the bustle and noise, passing seemingly unnoticed through the growing mob to come to stand by their side. She whispered something to their last remaining guard who shrugged and walked away to join his fellows.

Phyllo had never seen another Beast Whisperer before. She was almost identical in height and build to Venor, the most striking difference between them being the image they projected to the world.

Tamer Venor in her knee-high boots, jodhpurs and utility vest, wore the garb of the practical Circus Tamer, only her lion's mane of hair and bright golden eyes giving away the magic in her heritage.

The Brigadier's Whisperer wore her magic like a cloak.

The flighty layers of scarf that enveloped her rippled of their own accord around the person hidden within. She lifted her chin to shake back the fabric and revealed a little more of herself. Deeply lined, she was either extremely old or had lived the hardest of lives. Her voice, however, was as smooth as the silk she wore.

"Why do you cry?" she said to Tamer Venor.

Venor ran tense fingers over her scalp but did not lift her head. "All hope is lost. The dragon is dead and with it dies the dream of saving my Thamineh."

The Brigadier's Whisperer did not ask who Thamineh was. She tipped her own head a little farther back and flexed her shoulders. "Dead?"

Venor snapped her head up to gesture desperately at the crumbling husk.

"The dragon of this tomb is not dead," the other Whisperer said. She spoke so softly only those in their huddle would hear. "It has shed its skin."

Venor's eyes snapped up to look directly into those of the other woman. "I've never seen such a thing."

"It is rare, perhaps once in a thousand years should it live long enough. Well beyond the life span of any man. The dragon continues to serve its master. Like my husband, it lives for the hoard. What good are riches to the dead?"

Venor glowered into the other woman's face, her brow wrinkling with confusion and ultimately recognition.

"Mother?"

The Brigadier's Whisperer smiled, the furrows around her eyes deepening. She touched her chest and very slightly bowed her head. Venor lifted a hand to draw back the fabric. The puckered scar of a burn disfigured one side of her face. Phyllo winced.

"The only people who really live are harder than life itself," Venor's mother said.

"Did he—"

"Do not pity me, Bast. I have made my own choices just as you have made yours. I have lived a life beyond the dreams of a girl from Marzouk. I have travelled and seen sights no peasant girl would ever see."

"But with him."

"It has brought me opportunity to meld with dragons and chimeras. To save creatures that would otherwise have been destroyed by greed." She smiled faintly. "My only regret is that it has meant our separation all these years, but I've kept a wary eye upon you. Have you felt it, I wonder?"

Tamer Venor frowned and shook her head, "I don't know what—"

"The Whispering gift connects all things. To watch your progress in my altar has been a privilege."

Behind them a gang of the Brigadier's men levered at the lid of the sarcophagus with their shovels. Venor's mother shook her head and raised one eyebrow. "They never learn. Always the step too far."

The gigantic stone lid tipped to the point where gravity took over and it slid with an all-mighty crash to the ground.

"Ordinarily, I would warn them against it. They summon the very thing they fear the most, but often silence is the best answer to the stupid. Bad for them—" she laid one hand on Venor's shoulder "—Good for you."

"Summon?" Phyllo couldn't help but overhear. The journey through this tomb had been full of unexpected and unpleasant surprises and he didn't like the sound of something being summoned at all.

"The dragon will have been awoken by the blast, I'm

sure, but desecrating the Pharaoh's final resting place should hasten its arrival."

"The dragon's coming? Should we tell them?" said Phyllo, who couldn't help thinking that the more people who knew about this, the better.

Venor's mother chuckled. "They'll find out soon enough." She closed her eyes and seemed to be tasting the air.

Phyllo squinted at her. What was she feeling? Could *he* feel it too? There was a vibration that made his fingernails buzz, an addition to the atmosphere inside the tomb that had not been there before. If it hadn't been for its familiarity, he was sure he would have been more afraid. If it hadn't been for so many nights where the dragon's purr had lulled him to sleep, panic might have been taking him over. The dragon was coming and he didn't know if he wanted to see it or wanted to run.

"Escape may yet be possible." Venor's mother looked about the chamber, not at the men now fighting to heave the next layer from the sarcophagus, but at the walls. She pointed to a square flat section in a frame, thirty feet high and wide. "The beast will come from there. The wall will open and when it does you must get through to the other side before it closes."

"You'll come with us?" Venor looked hopefully to her mother, but the woman only smiled.

Venor sighed. "We came here for a male, to take it with us. I don't want to leave without it."

Venor's mother sucked in a breath. "A beast so old will be beyond taming, Bast. Escape with your life. Live to fight another day."

Phyllo felt the rumbling purr getting stronger, now accompanied by the thuds and crashes of something immense moving about outside their chamber. His heart thudded in his chest.

"Just how big do Sand Dragons get, exactly?" he said, really starting to feel a bit worried now, "Reptiles shed their skins because they're growing, right? They need space to expand?"

Tamer Venor nodded, only now tearing her eyes away from her mother. "Size is proportionate to age and, of course, as a male it will be larger still."

"And how long ago do you think it shed that skin?"

The thing Phyllo had mistaken for a dead dragon was decayed and crumbling, especially now that it had been disturbed. Clearly it had lain there a good long while, decades even, maybe more. The dragon *was* what they'd come for, but it sounded like Tamer Venor might have bitten off more than she could chew.

Something ground behind the wall, stone upon stone. Cogs turned and thunked into place.

"Prepare yourselves," said Venor's mother. She stepped away from them, out into open floor space to stand, feet shoulder-width apart, whip in hand. The Brigadier's men paid no attention, the Brigadier himself totally immersed in barking orders at the next poor unfortunate who'd got in his way.

On the opposite side of the burial chamber, raiders heaped golden platters into crates, making them so heavy that even with two, they struggled to shift them. They dragged treasures along the floor, noisy and arguing, all of them oblivious to what was coming.

Phyllo got to his feet, Panya too. Tamer Venor released her own whip from its holster. Phyllo gripped the cobra cane tightly in one hand and the still flaming torch in the other.

His throat was so dry that no matter what happened next, he was sure he wouldn't be able to scream.

Suddenly, the section of stone wall inside the frame jumped backward by a foot and then, with a scraping wail, began to slide to one side. This, at last, caught the attention of the Brigadier's men, who turned to watch.

A reptilian scaly foot, as long as Phyllo was tall, clawed at the ground through the growing gap and an impatient growl tore through the babble of voices. Dust rained down from the ceiling. The dragon scratched and pounded at the door and, as soon as the gap was large enough, thrust its head out of the opening. Phyllo wobbled into the wall at the sight of it.

The dragon's blazing amber eyes fell upon the raiders stealing its hoard and their vertical pupils contracted with fury. Head low to the ground, it bellowed out a roar that rattled plunder in the thieves' crates. The beast dragged itself through the doorway and lumbered into the chamber.

It was utterly enormous, four times the size of Thamineh at least and, quite unlike the old shed skin, its scales were pale and golden. It rose up onto its hind legs to reveal the iridescent shimmer of fire surging across its massive muscled chest and spat a jet of flame high over their heads.

"Now. Go now!" Tamer Venor pushed Panya and Phyllo ahead of her, "Circle behind. There is no time to delay."

Phyllo wanted to run in the opposite direction, but he knew the only way to escape was forward. He edged along the wall; torch thrust out in front of him like a protective amulet. Then the shooting started, the Brigadier's men emptying their revolvers at the great magical beast in a wave of panic.

Bullets bounced off its impenetrable hide and ricocheted about the chamber. The dragon swept its tail around, smashing tables and spilling scrolls across the floor. Men scrabbled for the blast hole, but the dragon spat a jet of flame directly into it and their exit collapsed. Screams of horror rent the air.

Away to his left, Panya scurried from column to column, pausing to peer around their protective curves with eyes as wide as saucers. She was closer to the beast, it was true, but what she did have was cover. Phyllo sprinted over to her in a crouch and together they lurched from one column to the next, reaching the opening in the wall as the tomb dragon moved forward into the chamber, wildly angry and belching fire.

Ancient mechanisms clunked into life and the section of wall began to move again, in the opposite direction now. Phyllo and Panya had made it to its threshold and stood staring into the dark tunnel that led who knew where. Behind them the dragon roared and swept shooting men from their feet with gigantic claws.

Venor was still two columns away, waiting for the right moment to run. Her mother faced the dragon, circling her whip around her head. It was ridiculously inadequate to overpower such a beast yet somehow an orb of power surrounded her, a protective glow that magically seemed to be shining from Venor too.

Tamer Venor caught Phyllo's eye and she waved him frantically into the tunnel. "Get in, get in, now!"

They were wasting time, the wall had already closed halfway. Whatever was in there couldn't be more dangerous than the furious dragon in the chamber. They stumbled inside.

Phyllo's heart pounded painfully in his chest, even and strong, so strong that he could feel his clothes jumping on his skin with the beat. It was weird. Too much. He looked down at himself and could see his clothes ripple with what he suddenly realised were impact vibrations. He looked up to Panya's face and saw her turn, as if in slow motion, to look down the tunnel.

A blur of golden scales and light, a second dragon hurtled out of the darkness toward them, no, toward the doorway. Phyllo pressed himself against the wall, pulling Panya with him. It charged to race through the closing gap and, once through, Phyllo could see it was much smaller than the first but still massive, twice the size of Thamineh at least.

Phyllo goggled after it. The wall slid closer, only a matter of a few feet now before it shut completely. The second dragon skidded to a halt behind its larger peer and Tamer Venor stood open-mouthed, gazing up at it, her whip slack in her hand.

"Tamer Venor," Phyllo yelled, "The door, hurry!"

Panya bobbed up and down next him, not knowing whether to stay put or run back to Venor.

"Stay here," said Phyllo, "The last thing we need is to split up." He waved desperately at Venor. "Tamer Venor, please. The door is closing!"

It slid inexorably toward them. Three feet. Two.

"Tamer Venor!"

The wall thudded against its frame and ancient systems out of sight pushed it backward into the hole. The screams of the burial chamber died.

"No!" Phyllo yelled and pounded against the stone. "Open up. She didn't make it. Tamer Venor!" Panya hammered against the wall too, the two of them shouting themselves hoarse.

It didn't make any difference.

35

Destiny Calls

The torch flame flickered on Panya's terrified face, now wide-eyed and twitching. The springy tufts around her hairline stood out on end as if she'd suffered an electric shock. Phyllo suspected he might look rather similar.

It was eerily quiet after the mayhem of the adjacent chamber. He struggled to swallow, his throat now sore from all the shouting. Beyond the circle of light in which they stood he could discern no information about the place in which they were trapped. They could have been standing on the edge of a precipice or at the start of tunnel a mile long. The edges of the light closed solidly around them like walls. He noticed his breathing, shallow and fast.

"Don't panic," he said mostly to himself, "We're still OK. Hardly anything has changed, just on the other side of a wall, that's all." A very thick wall. "Tamer Venor's mother told us to come in here. She wouldn't try to trick us, would she?"

That was ridiculous. He actually let out a laugh. Of course, she would. She was the Brigadier's wife. "Do you think it's really the way out?" he said, trying to keep hopelessness out of his voice.

Panya's expression looked for all the world like she was going to say something, her features almost seeming to inflate, before she snapped her head away to look down the tunnel. She stalked off, into the darkness. Phyllo jumped to life and ran after her.

"I don't think we should split up," he said again. His head was feeling fuzzy and he didn't want to have to worry about where she'd got to. She marched purposefully along, silent as ever. "Where are you going?"

She didn't answer.

"Just checking things out, eh? Good idea. See what we're dealing with." He tried to arrange himself into a purposeful stride beside her. The tunnel climbed and banked around to one side. A good sign, Phyllo thought, that they were heading back toward the surface. Good until they were greeted by a dead end. Phyllo held up the torch the better to examine it. It was flat with a frame around the edge, similar to the one at the other end of the tunnel.

"Looks like another door, don't you think?" he said, trying to be chatty, "But how does it open? Look around for a mechanism."

Phyllo searched around its edges, throwing himself into the activity, looking for a lever or a button, something that might operate it. "I just can't see anything, can you?"

"Dragons don't use door handles," said Panya behind him and it made Phyllo jump, he'd gotten so used to doing all the talking.

"Right," said Phyllo, "something that burns, then? No, I can't see anything like that."

"Or something that's triggered by great weight."

Phyllo turned to see that Panya was tracing around a large rectangle in the floor with her foot.

"A pressure pad? Yes, that would work."

Panya beckoned him to her side and Phyllo went immediately to stand in the rectangle, utterly convinced that the wall was about to open. Nothing happened. Phyllo jumped up and down and Panya joined in, increasingly desperate for it to make the difference. It did not.

"Let's see if there's one by the other door," he said and the pair of them dashed back along the tunnel, back to where they'd started. Sure enough there was a similar panel in the floor there, which also failed to react to their ever more frantic jumping up and down.

It felt like progress but really, they were no further forward.

"We need the weight of a dragon to open the door," said Phyllo despondently, "Awesome."

He scrubbed at his hair. It was all so frustrating. They'd been doing so well navigating the gates. Now this – trapped in a corridor in the middle of the desert with a dragon beyond taming, not to mention the shocking appearance of another one that was sure to make capture even harder. Then there was the Brigadier and his treasure hunters. Crackers, they were up against it.

Tamer Venor was, quite frankly, the only person who really knew what they were doing, and she was currently on the other side of a foot-thick stone wall. How could they tell her about the pressure pads? They couldn't even use their altars – Venor had told Phyllo already that they would not work through rock.

The inside of his head rattled with barely controlled

panic. He tried to reason it out, pacing back and forth, fear swooping around him. He dragged in a deep breath. He could not allow himself to panic. What about Panya? What about Tamer Venor and Thamineh and all the other creatures of the Menagerie? He could not fall to pieces. *Get a grip, Phyllo.* Why couldn't he think?

Then it was obvious – it was the Ethelweard in his head again, disrupting his thoughts with their creaks and clicks. In his time of great need they were there for him, just like Alitura had said. In good times and bad, the Guardians of the Forest had witnessed Phyllo's journey.

It had been his link with Alitura that had allowed him to meld with the dragon at the Menagerie. His continuing connection with the Ethelweard meant they were able to whisper to him; he wasn't sure it was strong enough to allow him to do it again, but if he called the dragon and it resulted in their freedom, that was the kind of thing that might cinch the apprenticeship.

It would have been fair to say that this apprenticeship had been on the back foot right from the start, the result of his overwhelming need to prove himself, but what had he actually proved? Pretending to Skinner and Bain that he wasn't afraid to enter the Magical Menagerie had triggered the mayhem that landed them all in this mess.

He'd made a lot of mistakes, but there was something he'd learned: the thing that was best wasn't always what was best *for him*.

Out of the two of them it was Panya who deserved this apprenticeship most. Panya with her quiet knowledge. Panya, who was often hard to pick her out of the shadows, unassuming and getting on with it.

Phyllo rubbed at his head and tried to clear it. He needed this apprenticeship, but so did she.

"Panya, do you think we could meld with a dragon through the wall? Do you think we could call it, to get it to open the door?"

Panya looked thoughtful. "It might be possible, but what would we do with it once it was in here?"

Being enclosed in such a small space with a fire-breathing dragon was a terrifying prospect.

"Tamer Venor," Phyllo said simply. They had to get her out of there.

Panya nodded and Phyllo thrust the torch into her hand. "Hold this," he said and pulled his bag around to dig inside. He extracted the flask of fire-breather's oil and Panya made to give him back the torch.

"No, Panya," he put out a hand and pushed it gently back, "It has to be you."

Panya goggled at him, but Phyllo knew it was better this way, knew that she could do it. Reliably do it. He could have a bash, sure. It might work, but there wasn't time to make mistakes.

Phyllo sighed and shook his head. "We both know you're the one. You're the best Whisperer, Panya. It's always been you. This is too important for me to just *have a go*."

She blinked up into his face, the angry crinkle he was used to seeing between her eyes smoothing away. "Really? But—"

"You think I'm mad not to try," he interrupted. Shrugging, he allowed himself a tight-lipped frown. "Why stop being an idiot now?"

She puffed out a laugh. "You have been a bit of an idiot,"

she said with a grin and gestured to the smears of dragon dung over Phyllo's clothes and face, some of it still shining in the torchlight.

"Yeah," he huffed out a laugh of his own.

Then Panya did something quite unexpected. She stepped forward and threw her arms around him, burying her face in his chest. He patted her on the shoulder, "Yeah, I know."

She pulled back.

"It's all a bit overwhelming."

"Oh no, I just wanted to get some of that on me." She rubbed her hand over the dung on Phyllo's coat then smeared it across her face. "Going to be bloody great dragon in here in a minute."

He gave her the flask and she fought off a smirk.

"Let's go this way a bit," he said. It was a good excuse to walk off.

He led them to the bend in the tunnel from which they could see both doors, while putting a bit of distance between themselves and the door where the dragon would appear. They stood back to back, Panya facing the burial chamber, Phyllo facing the door he hoped led outside.

There had been other things he'd picked up along the way these past few weeks, not just things he'd learned from the Menagerie, but from Schlepper too. Before he'd turned against them, he'd become a valuable new source of information, and of tools.

Phyllo held the automata homing widget in his left hand. It was smooth and black with a single button on one end and fitted snuggly inside his fist. Schlepper had told him that anywhere it went his automaton beetle would follow. Phyllo was betting everything he had on it working for the bobbits too. He'd immobilised them on the way in, now he wanted to wake them up and bring them to him. He needed their powerful metallic jaws to cut through the stone of the tomb to set them free.

He pressed the button with his thumb and held it there. There was no way of knowing if the bobbits could hear it and, even then, if they would heed its call. The widget made no sound that Phyllo could hear, but he thought he could feel it warming in his hand since the button had been pressed.

"Now you," he said to Panya in a wobbly voice.

She was breathing heavily, and he could feel her little body heaving with it against his back. It was natural to be afraid, he thought to himself, but when she took an immediate swig from the flask, he knew it hadn't been that at all; she'd been preparing her lungs for the meld.

The jet of flame that Panya spat into the darkness lit up the tunnel like a flare and Phyllo felt the air around him flex against it.

She spluttered out the last of the oil and folded at the waist.

"What? What happened? Did you do it?"

She shook her head. "No, but I can feel them." Panya straightened up, steadying her breathing, "It is possible, I think. The big old one is closed off, like a fortress, but the smaller, the smaller..." She tailed off, as if lost in thought.

The smaller one was still gigantic as far as Phyllo was concerned. "Try again. You can do it, Panya, I know you can."

Panya lengthened her breaths, deeper and slower, then took another pull from the flask. At the other end of the tunnel Phyllo could hear scraping and grinding – the bobbits were coming, gnawing at the stone. A thrill of fear ran up his back and he gripped the homing widget a little tighter.

Panya blew a second jet of flame out into the darkness and again Phyllo felt the pressure wave wash over him. She leaned into the air, her arms outstretched toward the burial chamber. Phyllo held his breath.

"I feel him," said Panya in a small voice and Phyllo remembered his meld with Thamineh. He remembered how emotional the dragon had been, how he'd seen its memories of losing its mate and how desperately sad it had been. "What's it thinking?" he said in a whisper.

Panya shook her head as if trying to dislodge something misplaced. "Wait, what? That can't be, can it?" She flexed her neck in an odd, uncomfortable way. "There is someone stronger here already."

"Tamer Venor," said Phyllo, "It has to be."

Panya seemed to blink out of her trance and looked up to Phyllo. "I tried to summon the dragon, but I don't know if it —" She stopped short and shook her head, "It's calling someone else master."

Phyllo's face fell into a frown and noise filled the tunnel, coming from both ends at once. Crunching and scraping ground from the door at the top of the slope while at the bottom the door thumped backward out of position, activated from the other side. A wave of sickness crashed through Phyllo's guts. The dragon was coming.

Sounds of the burial chamber flooded over them and Phyllo's attention was drawn unavoidably to the slow slide of the door.

Beyond it men cried out in terror, while the furious dragon crashed about. Thumps and cracks were punctuated by the splintering of wood and tumbling of treasure. The dragon roared with rage, the crackle and hiss of its fiery breath clear above the din.

It was obvious conditions in the burial chamber had not improved and Phyllo found himself wondering if opening the door had really been such a good idea. Whatever the case, it was unstoppable now.

36

SLIDING DOORS

THE DRAGON FILLED every inch of the expanding gap, heaving and snorting, biding its time for a space wide enough to squeeze through. At any moment Phyllo knew there would be enough. He desperately craned to see around it, hoping to spot Venor in the melee.

The door crept ever wider, revealing the creature's gigantic claws and the huffs of smoke that escaped its wide nostrils. Muscular and golden, it dug at the ground as the door moved wider still until eventually it bowed its head and Phyllo saw something that made his heart leap. He recognised it now to be the second dragon to enter the chamber, the smaller of the two and Tamer Venor sat astride its neck, her expression exultant. She gripped the harness it now wore with one hand, the other loose by her side, as if she were riding a bucking bull.

The dragon sprang forward into what suddenly felt like the tiniest of spaces. Phyllo recoiled and Panya grabbed at his arm to pull him close. "It is Mohareb," she breathed, her voice full of awe, "I thought I felt him in the meld, but could not believe it. It is Tamer Venor's childhood dragon."

Iridescent fire swelled in the dragon's chest and the very same light sparkled in Venor's wide eyes. Her mane of black hair rippled with magic. Whisperer and familiar, bonded and fantastic, they took up every spare inch of space, their magnificence sucking the air from Phyllo's lungs.

The vast stone door ground back into motion and slid back to close and sink away and throw them back into semi darkness. Light came from the glowing fire pouch in the dragon's chest, its long, spiked fangs and flaring nostrils lit eerily from below. Phyllo staggered backward, gasping.

Crunching and grinding came from the top of the slope behind him and he turned to see air misted with dust rolling toward them. Shards of light stabbed into the foggy gloom from the base of the wall and he squinted into it. Something flashed, reflective and metallic; steel jaws breaking the surface. Phyllo counted four, six, no eight at least that tore their way through the rock, stone crumbling as they cut their path. The bobbits were tearing holes in the rock through which Phyllo and the others could escape.

They munched through the stone wall and then into the slope of the corridor, kicking up grit and slicing into the floor. Phyllo was at once both relieved to see that they were finally going to be able to get out of the tomb and horrified when he realised the speed at which those terrible jaws were racing toward them.

The automata homing widget was still in his rigid hand, the single button on its top squeezed hard by his thumb. He released it at once. The button, however, had other ideas and remained jammed stubbornly down.

Mohareb the dragon reared at the rippling ground and his

considerable wings unfurled as much as the narrow corridor would allow. Panya squealed, threw her hands over her head and scurried to get behind Mohareb, who snapped at the ground.

Phyllo stabbed at the button feverishly, struggling to make it pop up.

"Turn it off. Turn it off!" Panya squealed.

"I'm trying, it won't!" Phyllo jabbed at the button and hopped from foot to foot as the ground boiled beneath him. Then he remembered the other gadget and rifled madly through his pockets for it. He snatched it out and squashed all the buttons at once.

Immediately the mechanical mayhem stopped, one bobbit in particular frozen mid snap, only inches from Phyllo's backside. He gaped at it for a moment then snatched a look at the equally shocked faces of his companions. Tamer Venor, up on Mohareb's neck, flexed to keep her seat on the bucking dragon and goggled at him, blinking away the dust.

Then behind them the door to the burial chamber whumped out of position and began another slow crawl to one side. This could mean only one thing; the other dragon had opened the door.

"We must go," said Tamer Venor, "Phyllo, Panya, get up here." She reached down her free hand.

"Up there?" Phyllo swallowed hard.

"Quickly, the ancient dragon comes."

The door was already open by a couple of feet.

Panya, already familiar with Mohareb, did not have Phyllo's reservations. She jumped up onto the leg he now noticed was bent and slung herself behind Venor. Tamer Venor reached for Phyllo again and her eyes locked with his.

Then a jet of flame blasted through the open door that hit

Mohareb squarely on his outstretched wings. He reared and roared then lumbered to turn and face the door. Phyllo leaped to get out of its way. The ancient dragon of the tomb stooped to glare down the tunnel from the burial chamber, its eyes red as the fire rolling through its chest. Men from the Brigadier's team continued to fire their hand guns at it. Bullets bounced from the dragon's thick skin and pinged holes in the rock of the walls.

The ancient dragon roared its displeasure and, with a sweep of its tail, knocked men from their feet. Mohareb squared up to face it, but the old dragon's attention was snapped back to the burial chamber with a jolt. Finally, one of the weapons being used against it had managed to penetrate its skin. It roared with fury and spun to face its attacker.

The Brigadier strode into sight wielding a shot gun so huge, Phyllo marvelled that he had the strength to hold it up.

"Ha-ha! I've got you!" he crowed. He bent the barrel down to reload then snapped it straight to bring the gun back up to his chest. He cracked out another shot that tore at the dragons back. "No match for my bally 4-bore are you? I'll say not!" He strode closer, wild madness gleaming in his eyes.

Phyllo couldn't deny that the Brigadier's gun was effective, but this was a ferocious creature he was dealing with here and he was getting insanely close. Closer and closer still, until the Brigadier had the dragon's underbelly in his sights. It was the area Phyllo knew from his studies to be the weakest and he understood what he intended to do. The Brigadier raised his gun and Phyllo, shouted out instinctively with all the air in his lungs, "No!"

The Brigadier's eyes whipped around and, in that instant, took in both Phyllo on the ground and his daughter riding

Mohareb. They narrowed with malice and Phyllo knew he had every intention of turning that gun on Mohareb next.

That was when the ancient dragon of the tomb took its chance. With the Brigadier distracted, it stretched its terrible jaws wide and lunged. Its mouth was so huge that it enveloped the Brigadier whole, gun and all. Then it lifted its head high to the ceiling and with a single great gulp, swallowed him down.

"Phyllo!" Tamer Venor reached a hand down toward him from her place high on Mohareb's neck and Phyllo needed no more encouragement. Mohareb crouched to give him somewhere to climb and he leaped once, twice and a third time before Venor's hand came into reach. She clasped it firmly and pulled him around to sit in front of her.

Mohareb reared and then lurched for the light at the end of the tunnel, leaving Phyllo gasping and grappling with the harness to hang on for dear life.

The wall was crumbling, the dazzling day now striking through from other side. Mohareb galloped toward it and Phyllo squinted into the light, his heart in his mouth. The gaps in the walls looked big enough for people to escape through, but not on the back of a dragon. The bobbits could only reach so far after all. Panic took hold, that they would be scraped unceremoniously from the dragon's neck as it tried to squeeze through, just as what was left of the wall began to move, triggered by their thunderous approach.

Damaged and broken, some wall slid away while other fragments crashed to the ground. Mohareb leapt over them and out into the blazing desert sun. Phyllo clung on for all he was worth, while Tamer Venor behind him whooped and called in a high-pitched trill that Panya echoed, joyous and wild.

The relief of fresh air was wonderful. Phyllo had never been so pleased to see the open sky or the sparkling water of a lake, but behind him the roar of flame tore at this all too brief respite from terror. The second gigantic dragon emerged from the tunnel, triumphant in its emergence into the light.

"Our cue to leave," shouted Tamer Venor over the din, and without prompting Phyllo knew what to do.

"Mohareb, *monzel!*" he commanded and Mohareb lengthened his stride. The great wings, previously tucked up on his back, stretched out to the side and Phyllo felt them catch the air. Another bound and a deep sweep of the wings and they were airborne.

Wind pushed at Phyllo's eyeballs, but he didn't want to close them. He didn't want to miss a thing.

Up. The dragon beat against the air, heat radiating from the baked landscape that urged them higher.

Up. The distance to the ground growing so much that Phyllo's fear of heights kicked in – immeasurably higher than he'd ever been on a trapeze, so much higher than the clifftop ledge he'd crawled along with Roly what seemed like an eternity ago. His hands prickled with sweat and his head swam. *Breathe*, he told himself, *remember to breathe*. He clenched Mohareb's neck as hard as he could with his knees.

The dragon dipped one wing and they turned, rounding out to a view of the tomb they had so recently left behind.

Men streamed out behind the dragon and scurried like ants in every direction. The ancient dragon on the ground blasted jets of flame that sent them running even faster, clutching at their backsides and shrieking.

Only one figure stood perfectly still, swathed in emerald green silk that billowed around her, a crown of golden wings upon her head. Tamer Venor's mother held one hand to the sky in silent salute and Phyllo felt Venor remove one hand from the grip she had on his waist to raise her own in return.

"*Monzel*," said Tamer Venor, but more quietly now, "Take us home."

37
THE DRAGON'S TALE

Soaring above the clouds was like being in a dream. The terror of their escape slowly fading to wonder as Phyllo accepted that he wasn't about to fall to his death.

It was actually all rather beautiful, with the soft, marshmallow-like mounds of cloud beneath them and the sunlight sparkling on Mohareb's scales. It sent glimmers into the air that felt like riding on a comet's tail. Up so high, where it should have been freezing, the heat of the dragon kept them warm. The meld between Venor and Mohareb was so strong, that it radiated out to encase them all in a protective cocoon. Inside it they existed in a space out of time and place. It was the space between atoms, everywhere and nowhere and within the dragon's mind. Mohareb flew on, but as they travelled, the three humans at its neck shared in his internal world.

"My beloved," Tamer Venor cooed and Phyllo heard the words inside the meld, "After all these years."

Happiness hummed in the air around them, the like of which Phyllo had never experienced. Golden and dense, it was thrust upon him and at such odds with how he'd felt only minutes before, that it made his head spin. Fear, anticipation and the desperate hope that, somehow, they would all escape alive, had been replaced by so much joy he thought his heart would burst.

The dragon shared its thoughts, not just in words, but in sensations and visions too and Phyllo knew it owed Venor its life breath. The warmth of sunshine on his back would be as nothing without her: the human girl who'd chosen him above her family, would be revered always.

Protective bonds of invisible fire sprang from the dragon's bones to wind around her, tendrils of devotion that no distance would weaken.

"I feel it too, my Mohareb." She patted the dragon's shoulder, "But where have you been? Why did you leave us?"

Mohareb's words sounded within the meld. *"You found me there. I have been fulfilling my duty and awaiting my destiny."*

"I don't understand," said Tamer Venor, "Your place was with us, with me and Thamineh. Was that not your home?"

The glow of golden happiness enveloped them again and Phyllo felt the dragon sigh. *"It is and so shall it be again."*

Venor shook her head, unsatisfied by this answer, and Mohareb continued.

"This tomb is where my life began. When the Pharaoh Mentuhotep sought to protect his treasures thousands of years ago, he turned them over to the laws of the dragon hoard. The treasure became the property of the dragons, so long as they kept it in the temple and protected it with their lives and magical power.

"In the beginning a male and female were bonded there so that offspring might take their parents' place in time to come. A dragon may live a thousand years or more, but still, eventually, all things

must die. Three generations have lived and died guarding the tomb, its treasures all the while protected. My ancestors honoured the bond and all was as it should have been, until the hunters came.

"Their attack coincided with my father's own hunt for fresh meat and he returned to devastation: his mate slain and only calf gone, the treasures of the main chamber plundered. All that was left for him was to retreat into the secret chamber, as yet undiscovered.

"With my mother lost and me gone, he guarded it alone, but he felt the years passing and knew that soon his time would be over. He called to me in the ancient tongue, hoping that I might still be alive, hoping I would return."

Phyllo heard a remembered keening cry, projected into his ears through the meld; the dragon call that Mohareb had heard. It thrummed with importance, impossible to refuse.

"I did not know how long the call had taken to reach me. The language of ages drew me back. I could not refuse. Dragon law demanded my return."

"The ancient one was your father," Phyllo said, "But he spat fire at us."

"At the humans," Mohareb corrected, *"He did not want to lose his calf again."*

"Oh." Phyllo saw the scene quite differently then. Not the Tamer and her familiar, but a kidnapper taking a child.

"I flew to his side and once there joined him in the depths of the tomb," Mohareb continued, *"He was ancient yet still formidable. He was tired and longed to be free of his obligation, but life can be cruel. He lived on and, rebound by the magic of the tomb, I lost my will to leave."*

"So that was where you stayed, until we arrived and the hunters breached the secret chamber," said Phyllo starting to understand.

"At last, the spell has been broken and with the return of my

harness, I have remembered who I am. Remembered my home. The hoard has been attacked and the tomb damaged beyond repair. To honour the bond the only choice left is to take what can be carried and protect it somewhere new.

"The magic of the tomb is at an end and the dragons can leave. My father is released from the place that has restrained him all his life. With their greed the hunters set us free."

38
A Beautiful Thing

Phyllo stood in the sawdust strewn arena, gazing up. Both hands in his pockets, he nodded appreciatively at the marvel flying overhead. Roly stood at Phyllo's side, the very mirror of his brother.

"It's bloody amazing," said Roly, "And Venor's had this thing tucked away in the Menagerie all this time?"

"Pretty much," said Phyllo, "Apart from the time when we thought it had been stolen, of course." He leaned back to catch Schlepper's eye, who huffed, though the points of his moustache gave a jovial twitch.

"A necessary deception, I think we've agreed," he said in his slow way, "While the Ringmaster believed a solution was coming to his financial problems, the fate of the rest of the Menagerie was secure. Time. I knew that was all you would need." He raised his eyebrows to affect an expression of such openness that Phyllo allowed himself a deep breath of satisfaction. He'd been right about Schlepper after all.

The Aves Pacis swooped down to almost touch the ground before pulling away in a curve that skimmed the walls. Its imitation of a Sand Dragon was remarkably convincing and, as the hottest topic of conversation on the horseshoe, a fitting choice for this demonstration of skill in the new dragon arena.

Phyllo, Panya and Tamer Venor's return to the Circus of Wonder with Mohareb had triggered a wave of building activity. It saw the additional cabin built by Skinner and Bain attached to the side of the Menagerie and not the Odditorium, as had been erstwhile planned. Utilising the space-bending abilities of Schlepper, it had been transformed into a spacious second ring in which the Menagerie would display its wondrous beasts. It had become the dragon arena in which they now stood.

"And you reckon it can be anything? Look like anything?" Roly asked, still open-mouthed.

Phyllo shrugged. "Far as I know."

Roly looked back to the kaleidoscope of butterflies as it transformed one wing at a time into a jewel crab.

"Wow. It's a shame they can't turn into something solid and give Skinner a good pinch though, isn't it?" said Roly, eyeing the engineers on the other side of the ring. Skinner scowled at the vast, still empty space they would have to fill with seats to complete the build.

"A beautiful thing is never perfect," said Phyllo, and Roly raised an eyebrow. Both boys turned back to watch the Aves Pacis sweep through more transformations: a fox; a bear and finally taking on their own brilliant blue before settling together, high on the wall.

"You'd never have believed all this could fit inside that pokey little cabin Skinner and Bain made, would you?" said Roly, looking around, and Schlepper huffed again.

"And I'd never have believed that something which was

causing me so much trouble could turn out to be so useful. The molecular warp collector?" he replied to their questioning expressions.

Phyllo nodded knowledgably, but Roly just looked confused.

"Exploiting the spatial interverse allows us to manipulate mass. Size and weight stretched or reduced—" He tailed off, seeing Roly's continuing befuddlement. "Well, never mind. The important thing is that all the extra space inside the carousel beetle made a perfect place for the Aves Pacis to hide while Phyllo went off in search of the dragon. And now that it's here, the newly built cabin can be put to much better use than it ever would have been as home to the Equatorial Mermaid and its ugly friends. It will be quite something when it's finished."

Indeed, the arena was totally unrecognisable from the cabin Phyllo and Roly had snuck into all that time ago. Now it was like being on the inside of a gigantic drum. Seating, destined to climb the walls to hold the audience vertically, currently only extended a row or two, but those that existed were crammed with chattering, laughing cast. Their excitement to see the Menagerie's new offerings electrified the arena, which was lit with winter sunshine through its open roof.

But not quite everyone looked happy to be there. Bain paused in his work to curl his lip in the boys' direction. It seemed Phyllo's success meant they'd got rather a lot of extra work to do installing all those new seats. Phyllo gave Roly a sidelong smirk and Roly coughed out a word which sounded a lot like '*unlucky*'. They allowed themselves a brief spell of enjoying the moment, but then Roly said, "Still, we'll all be working pretty hard from now on, won't we."

The pair of them rocked on their heels contemplatively.

"Now the arena's usable and everything, have you seen? Barker's put up a new rehearsal schedule with double the ring time." Roly looked around the walls that would soon be lined with seats. "And with all this extra capacity, Dad says we're going to have to build a stock of sweets or we'll never keep up with demand. Really could do with you in the Confectionary, mate. Do you think Barker will let you come home?"

Phyllo puffed out a derisory snort.

"Yeah, I don't think so either."

The vast barn doors that connected the arena to the Menagerie opened behind them and the brothers turned to see Panya pushing them wide. The oversized overalls that had previously swamped her small frame had been replaced with a close-fitting tunic, sturdy jodhpurs and knee-high boots.

She brandished a show whip in a whirl about head and snapped out a crack as she strode forward. Mohareb and Thamineh prowled behind her, their massive legs taking leisurely strides to keep slow pace with Panya's quick march. She led them out into the centre of the arena and an awed hush fell.

Thamineh had changed immeasurably with the return of her mate. Her lacklustre scales now shone bright and golden and her demeanour had switched from fearful aggression to majestic ease. Panya swished her whip and the dragons lolloped into a trot to run the circumference of the arena ring, the impact of their footfalls making the sawdust jump. Then with a graceful bound they were flying.

One behind the other, they spiralled upward, sunlight glinting on their vast outstretched wings. Their golden scales, once airborne, seemed to glisten with fire which rippled backward to leave a trail of gilded light in their wake. They swept out of the roof and into the sky, looping and spinning, breathing balls of flame and rings of fire through which they wound and spun with breathtaking agility.

Out in the open air they were graceful and free, but once they had descended back into the arena drum, they were massive, powerful and quite terrifying to behold with their scales aflame. The arena audience held its breath as they circled, aware that if the dragons chose, they could burn their theatre to the ground as easily as breathing out.

Instead, they glowed with magical power, speckles of golden joy cast about them like diamond shimmers from a glitter ball.

Phyllo let his eyes fall away from the spectacle to Panya. She stood solidly in the centre of the ring, feet splayed and whip whirling, her modest striped stick, Phyllo knew, secured at its core. She was the Beast Whisperer's apprentice, not him, and Phyllo knew in his heart that was right.

He brought his hands together in a clap and let out a whoop. She deserved it. The Menagerie was her destiny, not his. He clapped harder and Roly clapped too, then the cast joined in until the applause echoed from the walls.

It was Tamer Venor's hand on his shoulder that broke the spell.

"She looks taller in those boots, wouldn't you say?" Her golden eyes smiled kindly down on him.

"She does," Phyllo replied.

"A fine Tamer, don't you agree, Ringmaster?" Venor proclaimed and Phyllo turned to see that the Ringmaster had accompanied Tamer Venor into the arena.

Lazarus Barker stood tall in his black stovepipe hat and

brocade jacket. The tip of his cane dug into the sawdust as he arced the polished head back and forth with one hand. The other stroked at his magnificent beard.

It was impossible not to be impressed and yet a hint of reservation seemed, momentarily, to stop the Ringmaster from speaking.

"She's done well," he said eventually, "I never thought I'd lay eyes on that dragon again."

"We could not have done it without Phyllo. Truly, a pupil shows you by his own efforts how much he deserves to learn from you, and Phyllo has proved his worth at every lesson." Venor was being kind for the Ringmaster's benefit and Phyllo appreciated it.

"Always the trier," said the Ringmaster with a smile that was difficult to place between snide and affection. "And yet still no permanent apprenticeship, I note."

"The best Whisperer won," said Phyllo, straightening his shoulders, "When it came down to it, getting out alive was more important than the competition. We all had a part to play in the end." Phyllo hadn't risen to the Ringmaster's contest, but that in itself had been a personal challenge. He looked him squarely in the eye.

The Ringmaster blinked languidly. "Very commendable, I'm sure," he said. A tiny muscle twitched under his eye and the Ringmaster took in a long slow breath. "And so, it seems that the circuit will continue. One can't help but think that opportunities for a failed Confectioner, Flyer and now Whisperer within our own canvas walls are somewhat depleted, however." He smiled his toothy grin. "Whatever will you turn your hand to next?"

"The seed includes all the possibilities of the tree," said Tamer Venor with a jovial slap to the Ringmaster's back. He stiffened and glared at her in surprise, but already she'd switched her focus to Phyllo.

"You have grown in our time together, Phyllo, and in ways I could never have expected. In another Menagerie perhaps this progress would have been enough." She shook her head at the shame of it. "You put our conservation first and for that I am both grateful and awed. Destiny will find you, may Thoth will it so," she concluded, and put her palm to her chest before sweeping it to the ground with a bow of her head. "Meantime, the dragon pen needs cleaning while they exercise." She looked up and winked.

He hoped she was right, he really needed to find his destiny, and that magical talent. Phyllo bowed in returned. "Come on, Roly," he said, "There's something I want to show you."

After the thick atmosphere of the arena, the Menagerie felt cool and calm. The butterphants shuffled straw in their pen and extended a friendly trunk to sniff at Phyllo as he and Roly passed. Phyllo produced a chocolate mouse, which Manana sucked greedily from his fingertips.

They found Phyllo's cleaning tools leaning against the dragons' pen along with the dung barrow. Claiming them took both his hands.

"Get the gate, would you, Roly," he said and Roly moved ahead to help.

These days, strolling into the dragons' den had become an everyday occurrence, but for Roly it was an experience well out of the norm. It might have been a daunting prospect, but it wasn't that which held him back.

Roly tried his best to unfasten it, but the gate latch was heavy and stiff and his damaged hand was stiffer still. The injury still bothered him, his pained expression told Phyllo that, and the protective glove he wore made the task harder still. He fumbled at the pin.

"Not an easy one, that," said Phyllo. It had a knack that had taken him a while to work out. It would be faster if he took over, but Roly was delighting in this foray into Phyllo's world, his freckled cheeks pink with the effort and his eyes bright.

"I'll get it," he said, aware Phyllo was watching.

"It's all right," Phyllo sniffed, "I'm in no hurry to pick up poo."

Roly laughed and struggled on against the spring mechanism for another minute or so, but eventually beat it into submission. He pushed the gate wide and bowed Phyllo in with a theatrical wave. "After you, sir," he said.

"I thank you." Phyllo nodded comically and wheeled the barrow in. Roly closed the gate behind them.

"I'll just do this," he said, indicating the messy outer pen and Roly leaned back against the wall to watch. Phyllo pulled down the sleeves of his jumper against the chill.

"You'd never believe how hot it was in here before," he said, busying himself with the shovel, "You'd think that two dragons in this space would make it worse, but actually it's the coolest I've ever known it. I suppose they must be content." He took a moment to muse over the contradiction. "It actually feels like winter now."

"That's November for you," said Roly, and Phyllo nodded, but Roly pulled at the collar of his jacket and looked rather red in the face. "Can't say it feels cold to me. Hotter than when Dad's been baking all day, I'd say."

Phyllo wrinkled his nose in thought and supposed to himself that these things were all relative. For a while he worked in silence, shovelling up dung and laying new straw while Roly watched until Phyllo became aware that he was shuffling about, getting bored. Being allowed to maintain the dragon den might have felt like an honour to Phyllo these days, but he couldn't expect Roly to share his enthusiasm.

"I thought you had something to show me," Roly said.

"That I do," Phyllo said. He put down the shovel and beckoned Roly to follow him into the depths of the den.

A smaller chamber was built at the back, ringed by a solid stone wall. They made their way into it, and once inside felt more heat radiating from the walls, stored there since the dragons had left. It was much darker in the chamber with only the faintest glow from the Menagerie reaching its depths. The boys crept in, feeling their way. Something else was moving about in the darkness.

Hooonnk.

Phyllo almost jumped out of his skin. "Crackers," he breathed, "I wish he wouldn't do that." His eyes were still taking their time to adjust.

"What in Barnum's name was it?" said Roly, clutching at his chest. He spun on the spot trying to see and only stopped when Phyllo reached out to touch him.

"Stand still."

The shuffle of little feet drew closer.

H-H-Hooonnk.

A pear-shaped creature no more than two feet tall came out of the gloom to stand in front of them. Its mournful eyes looked up to Roly and then Phyllo, who patted it affectionately on the top of the head.

"It's a Parpadillo," said Phyllo, "When we got back here

Mohareb had him in his pouch. Dragons don't live well with other dragons, apart from their family," he added knowledgeably, "but they do love a Parpadillo."

"Funny little thing, isn't he," said Roly, his voice still a little higher than usual.

The Parpadillo waddled away and Phyllo followed it into the very darkest part of the den, trailing Roly behind.

"That's probably far enough," Phyllo guessed, though in truth he really couldn't see anything much anymore. He pulled a box from his pocket and struck a match which flared to cast a ball of golden light around them.

It took a moment to take it in.

"Bloody hell," said Roly.

Everywhere the match light touched glittered. Treasures from the tomb of Mentuhotep were neatly stacked, one upon the other, in a broad circle. Golden platters, statues of Egyptian gods, goblets and coins heaped all around.

"Blimey, does the Ringmaster know this lot is in here? It must be worth a fortune," said Roly, in whispered awe.

"I reckon so," said Phyllo, "Tamer Venor's already handed some of it over to pay for the fitting out of the arena, but the rest the dragons will keep. Their hoards are kind of like their security blankets, just having it with them makes them happy. Something else Mohareb had stashed in his pouch."

Roly whistled through his teeth.

"But that's not even what I wanted to show you." He directed Roly's gaze to the centre of the circle. The ground was thick with golden coins that heaped into a mound in the middle.

"There's something here that hasn't been seen by anyone

in more than a decade. It's what Tamer Venor wanted more than anything else."

They drew closer to the central heap and saw that the Parpadillo sat huddled close to an item not dissimilar in shape to its own fat pear-shaped body. Dark as obsidian and facetted like a cut gem, it seemed to absorb the light from the match, taking it into its depths where it swirled like liquid fire.

Phyllo smiled to himself. His life in the Menagerie was almost at an end, but for the dragons it was only just beginning. The real treasure in the den was an egg.

THE ADVENTURE CONTINUES...

Phyllo Cane and the Clockwork Cabaret

Magical puppets, ruthless bandits, and dark secrets. Phyllo's third apprenticeship is his biggest test yet.

When the Circus of Wonder can offer no more apprenticeships, Phyllo Cane is forced to leave the only world he's ever known. A

There's a FREE EBOOK for every subscriber.

'Phyllo Cane and the Magician's Secret'

is a prequel novella featuring *The Great Rufio*, the Circus of Wonder's light-fingered stage magician.

It's lots of fun, I think you'll enjoy it.

Once I've sent you your book, I'll stay in touch in monthly emails with character art, writing inspiration, discount deals and new book news.

GOT A MINUTE TO LEAVE A REVIEW?

If you've enjoyed this second adventure with Phyllo Cane,

PLEASE DO LEAVE A REVIEW.

It makes all the difference to an independent author like me. Telling others about your positive experience really helps me to find new readers. Thank you, and thanks for choosing to read this book. Your continuing support spurs me on to write more stories in Phyllo's fantastical world.

I'm so pleased that you came along for the ride.

AND FINALLY...

Enormous thanks to Julia Gibbs for once again sorting out my grammar and polishing up my punctuation. One day I will learn where it's all meant to go!

Lastly, my thanks go to the indie publishing community, individuals too numerous to mention, whose support through the process makes anything seem possible – you guys rock.

family connection leads him to the Clockwork Cabaret – a travelling show powered by enchanted meals, mechanical marvels, and the spellbinding puppetry of Gian McDonald Singh.

Phyllo joins the magical kitchens, clinging to the hope of learning from Gian himself. But the road is no place for dreamers.

Hunted by the Crows – a ruthless magical mafia, and stalked by the In-Between – a gang of lawless bandits, the Cabaret hides more than its share of secrets. As danger closes in, Phyllo uncovers truths buried deep in the show's shadowy past, truths that tie his fate to the Cabaret's in ways he never imagined.

With enemies on every side, Phyllo must summon all his courage to protect his new friends and unlock the mysteries that are sure to change everything.

SIGN UP FOR NEWS

I'd love to keep in touch so please do sign up for my monthly newsletter at

http://books.sharnhutton.com/news-2

Sharn W. Hutton lives in Hertfordshire, England.

www.ingramcontent.com/pod-product-compliance
Lightning Source LLC
LaVergne TN
LVHW031933070526
838200LV00075B/4477